THE ENFORCER

BY
ANNA PERRIN

AND

THE BRIDE'S BODYGUARD

BY
BETH CORNELISON

MILLS & BOON

All the characters in this book have no existence outside the imagination of
the author, and have no relation whatsoever to anyone bearing the same name
or names. They are not even distantly inspired by any individual known or
unknown to the author, and all the incidents are pure invention.

First published in Great Britain 2011
Harlequin Mills & Boon Limited,
Eton House, 18-24 Paradise Road, Richmond, Surrey TW9 1SR

THE ENFORCER © Anna Perrin 2010

ISBN: 978 0 263 88507 1

46-0211

Harlequin Mills & Boon policy is to use papers that are natural, renewable
and recyclable products and made from wood grown in sustainable forests.
The logging and manufacturing processes conform to the legal environmental
regulations of the country of origin.

Printed and bound in Spain
by Litografía Rosés S.A., Barcelona

THE ENFORCER

BY
ANNA PERRIN

Anna Perrin grew up reading romance novels and thrillers so it's no surprise that she loves writing romantic suspense. A two-time finalist in the RWA Golden Heart contest, she is delighted by the publication of her first Intrigue. She avoids housework as much as possible and enjoys hanging out with her supportive husband, two terrific daughters and pets including a temperamental calico, a blue-eyed husky and a mixed-breed horse.

To Patience Smith, who made my dream of
publication happen. Thank you.

To Brenda Harlen, who brainstorms with me during
dinners and road trips. What an extraordinary CP and
friend. And to my wonderful family.
You mean everything to me.

Chapter One

"What do you mean, he's escaped?"

Dr. Claire Lamont gripped her cell phone tighter and stared out her kitchen window at the slashing rain. Two days ago, she had sent FBI agent Andy Forrester to Ridsdale Psychiatric Hospital for evaluation. *Now he was out?*

Gene Welland, her contact at the Bureau's Cincinnati office, said, "At eight o'clock Forrester was in his room, an hour later he was gone."

The explanation didn't make sense to her. Not with the state-of-the-art security measures at the facility. "How could that happen?"

"We think he had inside help."

"You suspect Ridsdale staff?" she asked, pacing between the wall oven and the granite-topped island. "Or someone within the Bureau?"

"Too soon to point a finger," Gene said, clearly in no mood to speculate. "I'm calling because a nurse at the hospital reported he threatened to kill you."

Dread twisted in her stomach. Her gaze darted to the

patio door. One forceful blow would smash the glass, then Forrester could slip a hand inside, twist the lock and—

She stopped pacing. Exhaled a deep breath. A long day of interviews and flight delays had set her on edge. "Forrester probably lashed out at me without meaning it."

Or maybe he did mean it. Maybe he was in such a rage about her confining him to Ridsdale that he'd try to harm her.

She resumed pacing, her mouth dry, her palms sweating. Thunder rumbled in the distance and a streak of lightning sliced through the sky.

"I'm not taking any chances," Gene said. "In fact, I've already sent an agent to pick you up, so get ready to leave."

"I'm just back from Minneapolis. My luggage is still in my front hall."

"Then you'll be set to go when our guy gets there."

What if her enraged patient showed up first?

"I have a better idea," she said. "You know the coffee shop where we met last month?"

"Java Heaven?"

"That's it. I'll meet him there."

After a short silence, Gene relented. "Okay, Lisa is calling Brent to redirect him to that location."

Brent? As in Brent don't-waste-my-time Young?

Please let there be another agent in the Cincinnati office with the same first name.

"Who are we talking about?" she asked.

"Brent Young."

Damn. That was the field agent she'd met several weeks earlier when Gene had asked her to talk to his

team after the shooting death of a colleague, Pete Sanderson. No degree in psychology was necessary to interpret Young's slouched posture, guarded expression or
impatient tapping of his foot. Obviously, he viewed her
presentation about counseling options as useless and
had only shown up because he'd been ordered to.

Young's disdain for counseling hadn't surprised her.
What *had* surprised her was the surge of attraction she'd
felt for him. With his linebacker shoulders, coal-black
hair and cheekbones that hinted at a Native American
ancestor, he looked like a hard-core renegade. But there
had been something appealing about his smile—which
he'd let loose a few times in response to his colleagues'
wisecracks. Against all logic, she wished *her* remarks
had elicited the same response.

The wind rattled the panes of glass. The storm was
getting worse.

"You can count on Brent to protect you," Gene said,
correctly interpreting her silence as a lack of enthusiasm for her escort.

The overhead light went out, plunging the room into
darkness. "Oh no," she muttered.

"What's wrong?"

"The storm just killed the power." She lifted her free
hand, but she couldn't see it—or anything else.

"Check outside," Gene said, his tone urgent. "See if
the streetlights are on."

Hadn't he been listening to her? No power meant no
streetlights. Unless—

Understanding dawned on her, followed by a stab of
fear. *Unless somebody had cut the power to her house.*

Still holding her cell phone, she rushed to the window. After what seemed like an eternity, her shaking fingers forced apart two slats of the horizontal blinds.

"The whole neighborhood's dark," she said, relief making her voice thin and breathless.

"Go to Java Heaven. Call me when you get there."

Pocketing her phone, she stared into the surrounding darkness. Collecting her luggage and shoes would be a lot easier if she had even a glimmer of light. She headed into the hall, where she kept a flashlight in a maple cabinet. As her outstretched hands made contact with the wood, the basement stairs creaked. She froze, listening for more creaks. The only sounds were the ones made by the storm driving rain against the windows and the pounding of her heart.

She retrieved the flashlight, walked two steps. Stopped and listened again. Nothing.

The knotted muscles in her shoulders relaxed, and she nearly laughed. Gene's call had made her jumpy. She was alone in her home. Of course, she was alone.

No creak this time. A soft rustle. The shifting of clothes. *Someone was in the hall.*

Fear shot through her. She bolted for the front door.

When a deep baritone ordered, "Stop," she whirled around and smashed the flashlight into the source of that voice.

His surprised yelp was extremely satisfying. She swung the flashlight again but didn't connect this time. Instead, a muscled forearm shoved her backward. She fell hard against the wall, crying out as her right shoulder absorbed the brunt of the impact.

The flashlight bumped against the door frame.

Oh God, let the batteries work.

She depressed the switch. A brilliant beam erupted from the cylinder, and she directed it at his face, hoping to blind him. But the circle of light revealed he had his head tipped back and his hand over his nose. Blood streamed down his clean-shaven face.

Forrester had a beard.

"Nice work, doc. You damn near broke my nose."

Anxiety must have dulled her senses earlier because this time she recognized his voice. The man dripping blood all over her front hall was Brent Young, not the mentally unstable agent who'd threatened her.

She sagged against the wall in relief.

"Don't you dare faint on me," he said. "If anybody deserves to pass out, it's me. I got knifed by a junkie last year, and it didn't bleed this much."

If Young expected an apology, he'd be disappointed. She had nearly suffered a heart attack because of him. "You were supposed to meet me at Java Heaven. Didn't Gene's assistant call you?"

He looked at her, his eyes narrowed against the glare of the flashlight. "My cell vibrated, but I was too busy to answer it—"

"—because you were breaking into my house, right?"

He gripped her wrist, redirecting the beam of light toward the floor. "I arrived just before you did and wanted to make sure Forrester wasn't hiding inside. By the way, you should have bars installed on your basement windows."

"I'll add it to my chore list," she muttered.

His next words were barely more than a whisper. "Aren't you glad it's me, not Forrester, here with you now?"

In the semidarkness, his voice sounded intimate, seductive. Warmth from his hand seeped through her skin and traveled up her arm. Her heart beat faster, but this time fear wasn't the cause. It was attraction, raw and potent. An attraction that roared through her blood, demanding release. An attraction she had to suppress.

She jerked her wrist out of his grasp.

He gave a low, knowing chuckle.

Gene respected Young's ability to keep her safe. She shouldn't let him unsettle her.

"Let's head out," he said.

"I need my shoes."

He nodded, then cursed softly. The movement must have started his nose bleeding again. She thought of offering him ice, but it seemed prudent to leave immediately. They could stop and buy ice when they were well away from here.

She shone the flashlight around the hall. The beam illuminated her sneakers in the corner, and she shoved her feet into them. Then she aimed the flashlight toward the spot where she'd left her luggage.

A noise like a car backfiring sounded outside. In the same instant, the pane of glass beside the front door shattered, and a tiny round hole appeared on the side of her carry-on case.

Her blood turned cold.

The bullet had missed her by inches.

BRENT CURSED as a second bullet plowed into the case. The flashlight was a beacon for the bastard outside.

He knocked the traitorous item out of Claire's hand, dragged her to the floor and covered her with his body. Her full breasts rose and fell in agitation. Under other circumstances, he would have enjoyed the softness of those curves, but tonight wasn't about pleasure. It was about staying alive.

The shooting stopped—probably because the flashlight had gone out after hitting the floor. But the threat wasn't over. Whoever was out there couldn't know if he'd hit his target unless he ventured inside.

Brent placed his lips against her ear and murmured, "Let's go."

"Which way?" she whispered back.

"Back door. Stay low. No noise."

"You need to move if you expect me to."

She shifted, her pelvis bumped against his, reminding him that it had been months since he'd been this close to a woman. Maybe after the danger was over, he'd think about remedying that situation—but not with her.

She wasn't unattractive. Far from it. He didn't remember a word of her info session, but he sure remembered *her.* Dark blond hair, full lips, flawless skin and a dynamite figure that even a tailored navy suit couldn't conceal. Claire Lamont had definite assets, but she was also a shrink. In his experience, shrinks were trouble, and he'd be a fool to forget it now just because this one came with a husky voice and a curvy body.

Cool, damp air flooded in through the broken glass

pane. He climbed to his feet and crept along the hall. The back door was situated off the laundry room. When he reached it, Claire was right behind him.

"Now what?" she asked.

"Wait here."

He felt his way through the dark to the connecting door to the garage. Because of the power failure, he couldn't hit the switch to open the garage door. The automatic opener had to be disconnected from the overhead framework so he could lift the door manually.

He descended the wooden steps into the garage. A moment later, his leg nudged the bumper of Claire's car. He skirted around the driver's side and went to stand behind the vehicle. Should be a rope dangling with a handle attached. Reaching up, he moved his hand back and forth, trying to locate it.

Nothing.

Growing impatient, he climbed onto the trunk. The added height made it possible for him to touch the mechanism directly. He reached out, then inhaled as a sharp metal edge nicked his thumb. Damn. This fumbling around in the dark was crazy, but he couldn't risk using the penlight in his pocket. The garage had windows facing onto the front walkway.

Several tries later, he released the hook from the frame. He slid off the car and reached for the garage door. Twisting the handle, he tugged hard. The garage door rolled upward with a loud screech. Hopefully, the shooter would think Claire was attempting to drive away and try to stop her.

He ran back to the connecting door, knowing that it

wouldn't take the shooter long to search the garage. He'd likely shoot the lock off the inner door and head inside.

Brent crossed the laundry room to the back door, stretched out both hands, but encountered only empty space.

"Claire?" he whispered.

No response. *Damn this darkness.*

Retrieving the penlight from his pocket, he shone it around him. The sliver of light flickered over the confined space, revealing a washer, dryer, sink and three-foot-long counter for folding clothes. And nothing else. His frustration surged to a new level. Where the hell had she gone?

Turning on his heel, he aimed the penlight toward the hall. The narrow beam illuminated her suitcase with its two ugly bullet holes. An equally ugly thought crossed his mind. What if Claire hadn't left the laundry room voluntarily? The possibility choked off his annoyance like a tourniquet, and alarm took its place. He'd only spent two or three minutes in the garage, but that could have been enough time for Claire to be dragged out the back door and forced into a waiting vehicle.

A quiet click sounded. The back of his neck prickled.

He removed his semiautomatic pistol from its holster and headed into the hall. As he drew near the kitchen, the pantry door swung open. He aimed his weapon. Despite the cold air seeping in through the broken window, sweat broke out on his brow.

When Claire emerged alone, his relief quickly gave way to anger. "Why didn't you wait for me in the laundry room?"

"Nowhere to hide if the guy broke in before you came back."

A reasonable explanation, but he wasn't about to admit it. "You just took ten years off my life."

"Then I guess we're even."

He knew he'd terrified her earlier. Not his intention, but before he could explain his presence, she'd walloped him in the face with the flashlight. After that, he'd lost all interest in apologizing.

"Come on," he said, turning away.

When he reached the back door, he stopped. "I'll go out first. If it's safe, I'll whistle. Run to the hedge on the right, wait for my next signal, then cross into your neighbor's yard. This time, stick to the plan."

"I will," she promised.

Something settled on the floor beside her. "What's that?"

"My carry-on."

"Leave it. It'll slow you down."

"No, it won't."

He decided to try a different tack. "Look, we'll stop at a store later, and you can pick up whatever you need."

"Thanks, but what I need is in this bag."

He couldn't believe they were arguing over toiletries. "Claire—"

"Save your breath," she told him. "I'm not going anywhere without it."

FORTUNATELY, YOUNG seemed to accept that arguing with her further would be a waste of time. Time they didn't have.

He headed out the back door, and she waited for his all-clear signal. He must think she was absurdly possessive. But if she divulged her reason for hanging on to her case—because it contained cassette tapes of her sessions with Forrester—Young might demand to listen to them later. And although Forrester had forfeited his right to patient confidentiality the instant he'd revealed his violent intentions, it was up to her to decide what information to share and what to withhold.

Young's signal came. She set off.

Freezing cold rain pelted her as she sprinted across the lawn to the hedge. In seconds, her jeans were plastered to her body like a wet second skin. She crouched low, her muscles tense with fear, knowing at any moment a bullet could slam into her. In the darkness, another of Young's low whistles sounded. Remembering his instructions, she followed him into her neighbors' yard. Unfortunately, their dog was outside, and his barking and snarling pinpointed their location with the same intensity as a siren.

"Run!" Young hollered.

She stretched out her legs and raced after him. The wet grass was slippery, but she managed to stay on her feet, pumping her arms to propel herself faster. Across the yard, down the street and around the corner. The speedy pace soon had her gasping for breath, but Young, running beside her, wasn't even winded, damn him. When she stumbled over a curb, he grabbed her arm.

"Keep going," he urged. "My car isn't far off."

A few minutes later, they reached a black Mustang.

"W-where are we going?" she asked, as they rocketed out of her neighborhood.

He didn't answer. He was too busy checking the rearview mirror. When he seemed satisfied that no one was following them, she repeated her question.

"I have a cabin on Camel Lake," he said. "Gene thought you'd be safest there."

She had heard of Camel Lake, but never been there. About a ninety-minute drive from Cincinnati, the lake was known for its clean water and excellent fishing. Gene must really be concerned about a breach of security if he didn't want her staying at one of the Bureau's safe houses in the city.

Rain dripped off the ends of her hair and trickled inside the scoop neck of her tank top. She was cold and uncomfortable. But her soaked clothes were only partly responsible for her discomfort. Young's presence accounted for the rest of it.

She glanced sideways at him. The glow from the dashboard lit up his rugged profile and broad shoulders. All that maleness was unnerving, distracting. How long would she have to stay at the cabin with him?

Another rivulet of water streaked between her breasts. She shivered.

He cranked the heat up to its maximum setting. "There's a sweatshirt inside my gym bag," he said, motioning with his thumb toward the back of the car. "Help yourself."

She glanced over her shoulder at the bag. No way could she reach it without leaning over and sticking her backside up in the air.

"I'm okay," she said, even though her fingers were so chilled, she had to rub them to restore circulation.

"I promise it's clean."

His voice was low and persuasive, the same seductive tone she imagined he would use in bed. She rubbed her hands harder, berating herself for the wayward thought.

"I'll warn you," he said. "This heater takes forever to get hot."

He wasn't shivering at all. Maybe he was too hot-blooded to feel the cold. It certainly wasn't because he carried excess body fat. The sinewy arms and chest pressed against her body earlier were solid muscle.

"Claire?"

She was supposed to be considering his sweatshirt offer, not his physical attributes. And although she was tempted, she'd have to pass—on both. Donning clothes he had worn seemed so personal. She cleared her throat. "No, thanks."

He gave her a long, silent look, then returned his attention to the road.

Claire settled back and tried to assimilate what had happened to her…and what had nearly happened.

Damn, that job offer in Minneapolis was looking good. No more one-on-one therapy sessions with traumatized patients. No more decisions about who was fit to return to work and who should go on disability. And, of course, no more heart-stopping incidents like tonight. Just twenty hours a week of teaching stress management techniques to executives.

"Gene said you had Forrester committed to Ridsdale for seventy-two-hour lockdown."

Abandoning her thoughts, she replied, "That's right."

"Why?"

Young's question surprised her. But maybe Gene had been too rushed for explanations. "During our last session, I uncovered his intention to kill someone."

"Who?"

"I don't know. The fire alarm went off, and we had to evacuate the building. Afterward, he wouldn't come back and continue our session. Sending him to Ridsdale was the only way I could ensure he wouldn't hurt anyone."

"Forrester definitely needs his head examined if he thinks shooting you is a smart move."

Shooting you.

The image of her own bleeding, bullet-riddled body made her shudder.

Had Forrester intended to kill her?

She wished she could believe he'd only wanted to scare her, but the shots had hit too close. A few inches to the right, and she would have died without ever seeing her executioner.

Without ever seeing…

She turned toward Young. "Did you see him tonight?"

"What?"

"When you left me, did you see Forrester?"

"No," he admitted.

"Then how can you be sure he shot at us?"

"You're the one who fingered him as a potential threat," Young said, irritation plain in his voice.

"What if it wasn't him?" Forrester might be the obvious candidate, but they lacked proof of his guilt.

"You lock up anybody else recently?"

She stiffened. "Of course not." Did he think she enjoyed confining patients to Ridsdale? That she got a kick out of exerting her power? Obviously, he didn't know her. An important point to remember the next time she felt the slightest twinge of attraction for him.

"Make somebody angry enough to want to see you dead?" he asked.

Her own anger made it hard to respond in a calm tone. "Not that I know of."

Young stabbed the dashboard with his forefinger. "Forrester had motive and opportunity. That makes him the prime suspect."

When she drew breath to respond, Young interjected, "Don't make this complicated, Dr. Lamont."

Folding her arms over her chest, she stared out the window. Young had made up his mind about Forrester. And although his arguments had merit, so did hers. He was just too stubborn to consider them.

The swishing sounds of tires on wet road and the clacking of the windshield wipers made the trip seem endless. After a while the rain stopped, and Young shut off the wipers. But the tension inside the Mustang didn't diminish.

Thirty minutes later, she spied a sign indicating Camel Lake on the right.

Young made the turn. "Almost there."

Several miles farther, the road became a narrow laneway.

Finally, he stopped the Mustang in a small clearing. Flicking on the overhead light, he dug through the glove compartment. She heard the jingle of keys, then the murmur of his deep voice. "I'm not sure what you're expecting, but the cabin's pretty rustic."

Rustic. A term used to make primitive dwellings sound charming.

She peered through the window at the surrounding darkness but couldn't detect anything that looked remotely man-made. With a sense of misgiving, she turned to him. "How rustic?"

He shrugged. "Basic amenities only."

"'Basic' includes indoor plumbing, right?" She wasn't expecting a complimentary robe, but the possibility of a dilapidated shack and outhouse had her wishing she'd asked for details earlier. Then again, it wasn't as if she'd had a lot of options.

He hesitated long enough to make her nervous before the corner of his mouth kicked up. "Yeah, there's plumbing."

That smile was the one she remembered from their first meeting, the one she had found so appealing, the one she had wanted to make happen. Now that she'd succeeded, she grew wary. Young's smile made him far too sexy.

Careful what you wish for.

Grabbing her carry-on, she exited the car. Young hustled around to the trunk, retrieved his gear and set off along a narrow, winding path through the woods.

A pale sliver of moon glowed in the sky, lending just enough light for them to walk without tripping over rocks and tree roots. Their footfalls made rustling noises in the grass. Other sounds carried on the night air. Water lapped against the shore. Crickets chirped noisily. An owl hooted in the distance. Normally, being surrounded by nature calmed her nerves, but tonight she was on edge. Of course, adrenaline could still be coursing through her blood from being shot at. That explanation was certainly less perturbing than the other possibility: sexual awareness of her companion.

She walked faster, telling herself she wasn't running away, she was merely anxious to reach her temporary accommodations.

A wooden structure appeared at the end of the path, nestled among the trees. Built entirely from rough-hewn logs, the cabin was larger than she had envisioned.

"How many bedrooms are there?" she asked, as Young climbed the porch steps.

"Two."

The right answer, since it meant neither of them would be stuck sleeping on the couch. He unlocked the front door and stood aside so she could enter. She stepped over the threshold, more than a little curious to see the cabin's interior. With Young's guidance, she located the light switches. On the left side was a country-style kitchen. To the right, the main room contained a leather couch and several oversize chairs grouped in front of a granite fireplace. Floor-to-ceiling windows stretched the full length of one wall.

A flash of metal caught her eye. A silver trophy stood on the coffee table. She moved closer. What did Young excel at—besides making her uncomfortable?

The nameplate read 2007 Weir Marina Bass Derby Winners—Brent Young and Pete Sanderson.

Sanderson?

That was the name of the FBI colleague who had been shot—and evidently had been a close friend of

Young. No wonder he had fidgeted throughout her presentation.

She edged away from the trophy, then shot him a glance. How was he taking it? Had the reality of his loss sunk in yet? Did he forget sometimes that his friend was dead? She didn't know him well enough to hazard a guess.

"The cabin hasn't been used since the fall," Young said.

She looked at the living room again, this time noting signs of neglect. Cobwebs clung to the central light fixture and a layer of dust coated every visible surface. Her nose registered the staleness of a place that hadn't been aired out in months.

"I guess you can't fish here in the winter," she commented.

His gaze fell on the trophy. "Sanderson convinced me to go ice-fishing in Alaska once. We just about froze solid…." For a brief, unguarded moment, Young's lips trembled and he squeezed his eyes shut.

Her heart twisted as she witnessed his struggle for composure. One thing she'd learned early in life: healing from grief was a painful process that often unfolded over years. This place had to hold so many memories. Would Young have come here now, if not for her need for a safe haven? His action displayed an inner strength that she couldn't help but admire.

"I'm sorry," she whispered, her throat so tight she could barely speak. "I'm sorry that your friend died."

Opening his eyes, Young pinned her with a furious glare. "Pete Sanderson didn't die. He was murdered. And when his killer is apprehended, he's the one who will be sorry."

His glare discouraged conversation, but she had to ask. "Do you know who killed him?"

He shook his head. "Fifteen agents are assigned to the case. They've interviewed everyone known to have come in contact with him in the past two months. His recent assignments are also being reviewed for possible suspects."

So clinical. So emotionless. As if he were speaking about a stranger.

Everybody had different coping mechanisms. Apparently, Young's was to distance himself.

"With that many men assigned to the case, there'll be a break soon," she said.

A muscle in his jaw flexed. "No matter how long it takes, the bastard responsible for ending Sanderson's life *will* be brought to justice. I'm going to make sure of that."

Chapter Two

Brent grabbed the can of Folgers fine grind from the freezer, tossed half a dozen scoops into the coffeemaker and punched the on switch.

Why had he talked to Claire about Sanderson last night? That wasn't his way. In fact, he was known around the Bureau for being tight-lipped. Nobody knew anything about him outside of work. And even though his reticence had fueled wild speculation at times—especially regarding his choice of female companionship—he valued his privacy too much to divulge details of his personal life to anybody.

The only exception had been Pete. That man had known him inside out. His strengths, weaknesses, accomplishments and failures. And now his mentor—and best friend—was gone. Blown away in an abandoned warehouse two weeks ago.

The lack of progress in the investigation was gnawing at him. A prime suspect should have been identified by now. All those agents on the team and what had they come up with? Squat.

But it was more than frustration he'd felt last night. Returning to the cabin had hurt like hell. He'd never been here without Sanderson. For years, the two of them had deserted the city as often as they could. To fish and swim, drink beer and unwind from the pressures of work. Now the place was his. But everything about it— every stick of furniture, every fishing magazine, every boating knickknack—was a cruel reminder that those good times were gone forever.

Claire had picked up on that as soon as she'd seen the inscription on the trophy. The sympathy in her eyes had drawn him in, dulled the memories, eased his pain a little….

He'd quickly reminded himself that she'd been trained to show concern in these types of situations. Just as she'd been trained to dig around inside people's psyches, ferret out their innermost secrets and then slap labels on them.

Oh, yeah. He knew from bitter experience more than he wanted to about psychologists and their modus operandi.

Safeguarding an FBI shrink was the last assignment he'd have ever chosen. But it wasn't up to him to choose. Guys like Gene Welland made those calls. His role was to fulfill the requirements of the job with kick-ass proficiency. Protecting Claire would be no exception. Even though he couldn't respect her profession, he would watch over her as though she were the most important person in the world.

He'd just have to take care he didn't let his feelings about Sanderson surface again.

CLAIRE REACHED for her carry-on as soon as she awoke the next morning, eager to listen to the tapes of her sessions with Forrester. Fortunately, it was her standard practice, with the consent of her patients, to tape all her appointments. It saved her breaking eye contact to make notes. It also resulted in a more accurate record of the topics she and her patients discussed.

She had packed the tapes for her trip to Minneapolis, hoping to review them there, but there had been no time. The CEO of Balanced Life Consulting Group had kept her occupied with meetings, then made her a very generous offer which she had not yet accepted. There was so much to consider. Such as, was she ready to admit defeat and quit the Bureau? More than pride was at stake. She'd also be betraying the promise she'd made to herself at her father's graveside.

She couldn't dwell on that now.

Last night she'd been too strung out to tackle the tapes. But with Forrester no longer confined to Ridsdale, she needed to gain a better understanding of the man and his intentions. To do that, she would search her recordings for subtle nuances, crucial words she'd missed before, anything that would identify his intended victim.

She retrieved the tape recorder from the center section of the carry-on, then turned the bag over. A bullet had pierced the outside pocket. She dug inside, her heart pounding. Only one of the three tapes had survived undamaged. She peered at the label, breathing a sigh of relief when she saw the tape was of their latest session, the one she considered to be the most critical.

Sitting cross-legged on the bed, she inserted the tape, then put on the headphones and hit the play button.

She heard herself say, "You seem very agitated today, Andy. Do you want to tell me why?"

There was a noticeable pause on the tape.

"Did something happen?" she prodded.

After a while, he muttered, "Should have been a perfect MIOG op. Instead, megascrewup."

"What are you talking about?"

He mumbled, "Research is the key. Most of the time."

Even though she had had no idea what he meant, she'd said, "Go on. Tell me what went wrong."

"IPO was a bad choice. Who knew?"

"I don't understand. Can you talk more plainly?"

A long silence followed her request. "You might be sorry you asked."

"I won't be."

She recalled uttering those words with complete confidence, unaware that he would soon shock her.

"Nobody stops me from getting what's mine."

"Is that what somebody did?"

"Oh, yeah."

She remembered his fists clenching and had the first inkling that rage was fueling his agitation. "So what will your response be?"

"I like that blouse you're wearing. The color suits you."

"Thanks, but you're trying to change the subject."

He let out a low chuckle. "Is that what I'm doing?"

"Tell me what you intend to do about this problem person of yours."

"Why do you assume I'm going to do anything?"

"Because turning the other cheek isn't your style."

"You think?"

"I think I'm not in the mood for games. If you don't want to be open with me, then it's time for you to leave."

"But I've only been here for ten minutes," he objected.

"I see no point in wasting more of my time. The choice is yours."

He had looked disconcerted by her ultimatum, but she'd grown sick of sessions that went nowhere. Andy Forrester wasn't the only agent who gave her the runaround.

"What's your decision?" she asked. "Are you willing to discuss the situation with me?"

"No reason to. I've already figured out a permanent fix to the problem."

Even now, the memory of his sly smile sent a shiver up her spine.

"What do you mean?"

He had stared at her, his eyes as devoid of humanity as those of a snake.

Suddenly, she had known Andy Forrester posed an imminent threat to an unknown party.

"Who's on the receiving end of your 'permanent fix'?" she demanded.

"You don't need to worry about that."

"Tell me who it is."

The tape reproduced his theatrical sigh. "I'm just making an observation, doc. No need to get all worked up."

"I think we need to consider why you're so angry and find a way to—"

A piercing wail had made further conversation impossible. The fire alarm.

Later, she'd learned there was no fire, that some prankster had pulled the alarm. But by then the damage had been done. Forrester had refused to continue the session. However, his "permanent fix" remark coupled with his cold eyes and sly smile had her believing him capable of violence, possibly murder. So she'd arranged for him to be taken to Ridsdale for a full assessment.

She rewound the tape and played it again, this time cranking up the volume and stopping at intervals throughout their conversation. Forrester's references to "MIOG op" and "IPO" remained unfathomable, but her anxiety deepened. A would-be killer wouldn't take kindly to her interference.

Had Forrester been the shooter last night? Gene believed the man wanted to harm her, and Brent clearly thought Forrester was responsible for the bullets that had smashed through her window, but she still wasn't convinced.

During their first session, Forrester had openly admitted that after growing up in foster care, he had joined the FBI because he wanted respect. Then he'd asked her what she thought was fair compensation for risking his life. She hadn't known how to answer him, but the question had prompted her to delve deeper into his priorities since it was apparent the financial aspect of the job had not lived up to his expectations.

Money was a recurring issue with him. One bitter childhood memory was of his third foster mother stealing his paper route money. He had contemplated pouring drain opener in her drink, but fear of her boyfriend's rock-hard fists had stopped him from doing it. Forrester might kill if he felt cheated out of money, but not because she'd sent him to Ridsdale for a few days. The outburst to the nurse had been angry venting, not proof of deadly intent toward her.

Of course, her opinion would have to change if physical evidence linked him to the crime scene that encompassed her house.

A tantalizing smell redirected her thoughts to her immediate surroundings. Was that coffee? Brent must be awake. She could use a cup. Or three. But to get to the coffee, she'd have to see Brent, and she wasn't sure she wanted to do that just yet. Following his revelations the night before, he'd clammed up, then stalked off to his room.

She'd made her way to the other bedroom, the one that had been Sanderson's. Even though she was exhausted, she'd had trouble falling asleep, her mind filled with unanswered questions and images, many of them involving her cabinmate.

The unwelcome attraction she felt continued to baffle her. And her late-night sensual fantasies starring Brent had to be a manifestation of stress. She certainly wasn't going to have hot, grinding sex with him to relieve it. If the symptoms persisted, she would try a different solution. Like a career change.

She checked her watch. 9:04 a.m. She'd been awake and without caffeine for over an hour. Time for a break. Maybe even time to admit she needed assistance deciphering Forrester's tapes.

The obvious person to do that was Brent Young. He and Forrester worked in the same office, shared the same FBI training and job classification. If Forrester was using work-related jargon—which she suspected was the case—Brent would be familiar with it. That might lead to the person Forrester blamed for wronging him.

Last night, she'd been too rattled to ask Brent what he knew about Forrester. And even if she had, he hadn't been in a communicative frame of mind after their conversation about Sanderson.

Hopefully, this morning they could start off fresh.

Because if he couldn't help her decode Forrester's cryptic words, someone would die.

"GOOD MORNING."

Brent finished pouring coffee into a mug before turning from the counter.

Claire stood in the doorway, her dark blond hair falling in soft waves to her shoulders. Her green eyes looked clear and alert as if she'd been up for a while, and he wondered why it had taken her so long to emerge from the other bedroom. Was the prospect of his company so distasteful?

The thought bothered him more than it should have, which irked him further.

"That smells good," she said, gesturing to the coffee.

"Help yourself." He stalked over to the oak table on the far side of the kitchen. His job was to protect her, not fetch and carry for her. He might as well make that clear.

If she noticed his brusque tone, she gave no sign of it as she wandered over to the cupboards and checked through them.

"There's sugar next to the stove," he said, relenting. "But if you want cream, you'll have to wait until we pick up groceries later."

"That's okay. I take mine black."

After she'd filled a mug with coffee, she turned and leaned against the counter. "How well do you know Andy Forrester?"

After their disagreement over Forrester's involvement in last night's events, her question surprised him. "We've attended the same staff meetings, but I've never worked an assignment with him, if that's what you're asking."

"Have you ever talked to him outside of work? Maybe gone out for a beer with him?"

"Nope, can't say that I have." He tipped his chair back against the wall. "In retrospect, I'm glad. If I'm going to be shot at, I'd rather it's done by a stranger than a friend."

Claire frowned, apparently disappointed with his answer.

"You think that's a bad attitude?"

She shook her head. "I didn't say that." Her tone implied that he was getting his back up over nothing.

Maybe so, but it was hard for him not to feel defensive in the presence of a psychologist. "You're the one he shared his deep, dark secrets with."

She stared at her coffee. "He said only enough to alarm me. But he didn't stay at Ridsdale long enough for a full psychological evaluation—"

"Psychological evaluations are a load of crap."

She lifted an eyebrow. "And you know this because…?"

He smiled tightly. "We're not here for you to question me."

"Look, I'm sorry if you had a negative experience—"

The "negative experience" she alluded to had almost wrecked his life. But he had no intention of unloading his personal history to an FBI shrink.

"Nobody can know what Forrester is capable of just because of some boxes ticked *yes* on a questionnaire."

"Is that how you think I evaluate patients?" she sputtered.

No doubt about it. This time, she was the one feeling defensive. That was a whole lot better than her believing they were buddies just because they'd escaped from her house together.

A muscle twitched in Claire's jaw, but when she spoke her voice was calm. "I don't use questionnaires. I ask whatever questions I think will give me an understanding of the patient."

Nice recovery. He caught himself wondering if she ever lost control—and not just of her temper. Because something about her suggested she kept a lot more than anger bottled up inside her.

What would it take for her to let loose? He wanted to witness that explosion. Hell, he wanted to trigger it.

"I even tape our conversations," she said, "so I can listen to them again later."

"Is that legal?" he asked, goading her just because he felt like it.

"With my patient's consent." Her tone was still mild,

but she set her mug on the counter with a solid thunk. "Wow, you really don't like psychologists, do you?"

He folded his arms across his chest. "I'd have to tick the yes box on that one."

She considered him for a long moment. Then her lips curved in a smile. "Well, at least you're honest about it. Which is more than I can say for some people."

Her words defused a little bit of his resentment, and he found himself wanting to smile back at her. He frowned instead.

She shifted uneasily. "If this assignment is a problem for you, maybe Gene could find somebody else—"

"How I feel about your profession won't affect my ability to protect you. As I proved last night."

"You saved my life," she agreed. "Now I'm hoping you can do the same for Forrester's other target."

"How am I supposed to do that? You said you don't know who it is."

"The case I brought with me last night contains tapes of my sessions with Forrester."

Brent gave a low whistle. "No wonder he came to your house. He wanted to get rid of you *and* your tapes."

She flinched.

For a moment, he was sorry he'd been so blunt. He pushed the regret aside. He always called a spade a spade. Claire should get used to that about him. "I want to listen to them."

She smiled faintly.

He racked his brain but couldn't come up with anything amusing about her situation. "What am I missing?"

She shrugged. "After the way you dismissed psychologists and their methods, I wasn't sure you'd be
willing to help me."

"Just what kind of help are you talking about?"

"I don't understand certain terms Forrester used," she
admitted. "I'm hoping you will."

Even though he knew it was a cheap shot, he couldn't
resist. "And I thought shrinks had all the answers."

She turned and walked down the hall. "Not this one."

He caught himself admiring her honesty and
humility—and the way her jeans hugged her backside.
Dangerous thinking. Especially since the two of them
were stuck alone together in a remote cabin. A few
minutes later, she returned to the kitchen table with the
tapes and player. While she fiddled with the equipment,
he tried not to notice the long curve of her neck or the
shadowed cleavage revealed by her tank top—and failed
miserably. She wasn't trying to entice him. But the effect
was every bit as powerful. He cursed under his breath
as his trousers became uncomfortably tight.

She handed him the headphones, but he needed a
moment to refocus before listening to the tape. "Why
would Forrester admit to anything incriminating?"

"I think his ego got in the way, and he let slip more
than he intended to."

"Or maybe he was yanking your chain."

"That was my first reaction, too, but I changed my
mind. Listen for yourself."

When he had the headphones in place, she started
the tape.

After he'd listened to it twice, she asked, "What do you think?"

"The tape's ambiguous, but after last night, I agree that he's dangerous."

"Can you explain 'MIOG op' to me?"

He scratched the back of his neck. "MIOG refers to the FBI Manual of Investigative Operations and Guidelines. So a perfect MIOG op would be an operation that goes like clockwork."

"Any idea which operation he's referring to?"

"Maybe it's one he worked on recently. I'll ask Gene to review Forrester's timesheets."

"Could he have been involved in a financial investigation?" she asked. "That might explain his reference to an IPO."

He shook his head. "The Cincinnati office doesn't handle them."

"If IPO isn't an initial public offering, then what is it?"

"I don't know," he admitted. "It isn't any FBI acronym that I've heard of."

She pressed her fingers against her lips, clearly distraught. "Why did he have to talk in riddles? I can't stop him from killing if I don't know who's at risk."

He felt as if he were letting her down by not being able to figure out more of Forrester's comments. Except he didn't owe her anything, apart from keeping her safe.

But Claire's wasn't the only life at risk.

He headed for the hall to call Gene, but at the doorway, he happened to glance back. Claire's green eyes were fixated on his body, her lips parted as if breathing were an effort.

He stopped, paralyzed by her hungry stare. A blast of warmth licked along his shoulders and spread through his chest. The burn turned south, traveling into his belly, then lower…

She blinked and looked down at the table. As she gathered up the headset, recorder and tape, he checked her hands. Rock-solid steady. No telltale tremors of arousal. He'd been wrong. She hadn't been throwing out all that heat. He turned back toward the hall, irritated that he'd misread her so completely. But he'd only moved a few strides when he heard something clatter to the floor.

Hah. Her hands weren't so steady, after all.

No longer irritated, he called Gene. Having already informed his supervisor of the shooting at Claire's house last night and their safe arrival at the cabin, his words were brief and direct. "I want to search Forrester's place."

As usual, Gene was all over the situation. "I had the warrant drawn up right after he escaped from Ridsdale. There's a surveillance team watching his house, in case he shows up. I'll let them know to expect you and Claire."

Hold on. His plans hadn't included Claire tagging along. "I think I should go alone."

"And leave Claire on her own?"

"She's safe here."

"What if Forrester saw you last night?"

"No amount of digging will connect me to the cabin. It's still registered to that offshore holding company Sanderson set up." His mentor had been fanatical about privacy after a suspect had killed a colleague in her home.

"Claire should remain with you."

"Gene—"

"That point's not negotiable. The only reason I'm letting you go is because the department's short three agents. If you want to check out his house, you take her with you."

When Gene pulled rank, no amount of arguing could change his mind. "What's the address?"

Gene gave it to him. Also, a description of the surveillance team's vehicle and both agents' cell numbers. He added, "I'll update them. What's your ETA?"

"Tell them to expect us around noon," Brent said, and disconnected.

Damn. He'd planned on giving Claire a wide berth today. Instead, the trip to Forrester's meant they'd be together for most of the afternoon.

Plenty of time for her to try poking around his brain.

Plenty of time for him to try figuring out if the attraction he felt for her was mutual.

Who would end up with the most interesting revelations?

Claire might have the psych degree, but he'd interrogated lots of tough suspects over the years. If nothing else, it should make for an interesting trip.

He smiled for the first time that morning.

HOW MUCH DID DR. LAMONT really know? Enough to jeopardize his plan?

The psychologist excelled at drawing out thoughts and feelings. No easy feat considering the tough-minded agents who were her patients. And it wasn't as if many of them sought her out on their own. Supervisors usually had to order their staff to meet with her. At least the first time.

Then a lot of the guys figured out there were worse ways to pass the time than hanging out with the lovely Claire Lamont. So they signed up to see her again and again, assuming they could stonewall her.

But she didn't tolerate idle talk for long. She wanted to know it all—the good, the bad and the ugly. Who'd have guessed a few conversations would cause so much trouble?

He should have put an end to it sooner.

That miscalculation had placed the whole operation at risk.

Next time he set out to kill her, he'd do it right.

Chapter Three

Jim Sharratt had lied to the FBI.

The joints in his hands throbbed as he watched his six-year-old granddaughter, Amy, play on the swings at Cambridge Park. He could call them and come clean, but he knew he wouldn't. If his family and friends found out what he'd done, they'd lose respect for him. His son might never allow him to take Amy for another outing.

"See me go really high, Grandpa," she shouted, her skinny, pale legs stretching forward. "I'm flying."

"You sure are, angel." He smiled at her even though he felt like crying. These moments were what he lived for. He couldn't bear to have them taken away from him.

Telling the truth would destroy his life. All because he'd made one terrible error in judgment. Thank God his wife, Jeannie, would never know the man she'd married was capable of such wickedness. He missed her so much. For decades he'd worked eighteen-hour days, six days a week. Jeannie hadn't complained through the lean years, but later on she'd grown unhappy with rarely seeing him. She hadn't wanted more houses or cars or money. She'd wanted more time with him. He'd told her to hang on, just a few more deals…

His retirement had come too late for them to enjoy it. A month before he'd sold off his businesses, Jeannie had caught a virus that became pneumonia and took her life. They couldn't travel the world or laze on the beach or visit with friends as he'd promised her. And all the wealth he'd accumulated over the years couldn't ease his crushing grief and loneliness.

If only Jeannie hadn't died, he would have stayed strong, not become weak and vulnerable to temptation.

Amy giggled, the sound jerking him out of the past.

She swung in a wide arc, her face tilted toward the sun, her fine hair streaming down her back like liquid gold. "Are you thinking what I'm thinking?" she called out to him.

"What's that?"

"Ice cream!"

"Butterscotch ripple, two scoops?"

She beamed at him. "You got it, Grandpa."

He watched her slow the momentum of the swing. Her sneakers skidded to a stop in the loose dirt, then she was racing toward him. A moment later, he swept her up in his arms and breathed in the scent of sunshine and innocence.

Did he have to lose everything because he'd messed up once? No, he refused to believe that. He would carry on as though nothing had happened. As long as he remained silent, that might be possible.

CLAIRE STARED out the passenger window at the trees whipping past. She'd been surprised to learn they were returning to Cincinnati to search Forrester's house. She had just assumed they would wait at the cabin until he was arrested. Apparently Brent wasn't content to do that. In addition to protecting her, he was determined to uncover Forrester's other target.

She glanced sideways at her companion. His straight, black hair was cut short in a no-nonsense style that matched the expression in his brown eyes. Even though she knew better, his digs about her profession had stung. What had happened to make him feel so negative toward psychology? Had a suspect he'd arrested gotten off because of a psychologist's testimony? Had a friend's mental illness been misdiagnosed?

If she knew the basis for Brent's hostility, she might be able to help him reevaluate the experience. Of course, getting him to open up wasn't going to be easy. But then, few agents arrived at her office ready to pour out their hearts and souls. She had to build trust slowly.

"Most of the agents I know dreamed of a career with the Bureau when they were young," she said. "Was that the case for you, too?"

"Pretty much," he admitted.

"How long have you been an agent?"

"Seven years."

She judged him to be in his late thirties, so his answer surprised her. "Why did you wait so long to apply?"

He frowned. "Who says I waited?"

"Well, I'm guessing you were older than the average recruit when you joined. There must be a reason for that."

"Oh, there's a reason, all right," he muttered.

She waited for an answer that didn't come. Finally, she prompted, "Are you going to give me a hint?"

Silence from the other side of the car.

She'd wanted to get him talking but had struck a nerve instead. Nice going, Freud.

"Let me ask you a question," he said. "When you were a kid, did you dream of becoming a shrink?"

She wasn't fond of the word *shrink,* but maybe if she volunteered some information, he'd reciprocate. "Actually, I dreamed of becoming a veterinarian."

"What made you change your mind?" he asked.

Her brain responded immediately, but she pressed her lips together so her secret couldn't slip out.

"Claire?"

She drew in a deep breath and held it, waiting for the sharp pang to recede to the more familiar ache she'd learned to live with. Oh, God. The loss shouldn't hurt so much. Not after all these years. But it still did.

She made a fist in her lap, released her breath slowly. "I lost interest."

"Why psychology?" he prompted, braking for a slow-moving vehicle.

Leave it alone. But she knew he wouldn't. "I wanted to help people cope with the challenges in their lives."

How idealistic she'd been at twenty. How discouraged she felt at this point in her career.

"Do you think you have?" Brent asked.

She'd been struggling with that question for almost a year. *Was* she having a positive impact on her patients? If she accepted that job in Minneapolis, she wouldn't have to agonize anymore. In the meantime, she wasn't about to broadcast her doubts to someone who was already pre-disposed to think badly of her profession. "I think I've been successful with many of my patients."

"Like Forrester?"

Her temper rose. She ignored it, reminding herself that Brent was only doing what she often did: ask probing questions. "By committing Forrester to Ridsdale, I gave him the opportunity to be thoroughly assessed. I also ensured his safety as well as that of his intended target. Now that he's out, who knows what might happen."

"You're not responsible for Forrester's actions," Brent said quietly.

Leaning her head back against the headrest, she closed her eyes. "I'm sorry about earlier. I wasn't trying to pry."

"What were you trying to do?"

She didn't want to admit her real motive so she said, "Make conversation."

"Are you sure that's all?"

She opened her eyes. "What do you mean?"

"You ask a lot of personal questions."

"I'm curious about you."

He changed lanes to pass a blue minivan. "I think it's more than curiosity."

"Like what?"

His soft chuckle made her mouth go dry. "Like maybe you're hot for me."

Her jaw dropped, and heat crept up her neck. "You are so wrong."

"Then explain why your pulse races when I touch you."

"If you're referring to last night at my house, don't forget I thought you were Forrester."

"Only for a couple of seconds. Then you knew it was me, and your heart beat even faster."

Damn, he had noticed. The fact that he spoke the truth only made her more determined to deny it. "You misinterpreted what you felt."

"Is that so?" His hand left the steering wheel and settled on her forearm.

His fingers slid down toward her wrist in a gentle caress. Even though she knew his move was calculated, she couldn't control her accelerating heart rate. Why was she reacting so intensely? He was hardly touching her.

She willed herself to ignore him and focus on the scenery rushing past the car.

A moment later, he turned his head and spoke in a husky voice. "How about we pull over…"

And do what? Her heart went wild at the possibilities.

"…and check out that pulse of yours?"

Shrugging off his hand, she said more sharply than she intended, "Watch the road. I saw a deer-crossing sign a few yards back."

She stared straight ahead, hoping he'd take the hint.

"Sooner or later you're going to run out of excuses to avoid the attraction between us."

His self-satisfied tone irked her. "Are you familiar with the term 'delusional'?"

"Are you familiar with the term 'coward'?"

Her head whipped around. "What?"

"Why can't you be honest about your feelings instead of hiding behind that psychobabble?"

"Psychobabble?" she said. "Why on earth would I be attracted to somebody who disparages what I do for a living?"

He had the gall to smile. "I don't know."

The man was impossible. No matter how much she denied the sparks between them, he wouldn't believe her. But maybe she could convince him that the point was moot. "Even if I were attracted to you, nothing would happen between us."

"Why not?"

"Given my position, it would be wrong to become personally involved—"

"—with a patient. I'm not a patient."

"Not now."

"Not ever," he amended tartly.

"Doesn't matter. I consider all agents to be off limits."

He gave her a penetrating stare. "Why?"

"I have a rule about it."

"Haven't you heard? Rules are made—"

"—to be broken." She shook her head. "Hardly reassuring words coming from a federal agent." But she couldn't prevent the hint of a smile that curved her lips. "You're supposed to enforce the law."

"Hey, I follow the rules in my job."

"Like breaking and entering my house?"

He grinned. "Sometimes the rules require liberal interpretation."

"Does Gene know that?"

"Gene knows I'd never cut the wrong corner."

"Glad to hear it."

"My personal life is a different story," he told her. "There, I don't worry about rules. I go with my impulses."

And what impulses would those be? she couldn't help but wonder. It would be better not to speculate. She was already finding him dangerously appealing. "I commend your flexible approach. But it doesn't change how I feel."

"Maybe you're harboring resentment against *my* profession. And that's the real reason you don't date FBI guys."

"You're entitled to your opinion," she said with a shrug. "However wrong it may be."

A sign appeared on the side of the road, indicating they'd arrived at the outskirts of the city.

The last few minutes had distracted her, but now a shiver ran up her spine. Until Forrester was in custody, she wouldn't feel safe here. But her fear didn't matter. What mattered was tracking down his target before he did.

She only hoped they weren't already too late.

BRENT DRUMMED HIS THUMBS on the steering wheel. Claire's conviction not to get involved with an agent intrigued him. What was she hiding? Because he was certain she was hiding more than her feelings for him. Had she been burned before, maybe in a relationship with one of his colleagues? The possibility made him uncomfortable. He didn't go for long-term relationships, but a woman who became involved with him did so knowing the score. Lots of men made promises they had no intention of keeping. Is that what had happened to make Claire wary?

Or maybe her "rule" was just a smokescreen? A way of not having to admit she was attracted to him. What did psychologists call that? Denial?

He, on the other hand, had no problem owning up to the attraction he felt. Their disagreements revved his engine because she was smart and focused. Her mouth looked infinitely kissable, and her thick, blond hair was sure to feel amazing against his bare skin. Last, but certainly not least, her curves had him hungering to learn every contour.

She didn't know him well enough to realize that telling him about her "rule" had been a tactical error. He never accepted rules at face value. They always had to make sense to him. This one didn't. This one seemed more like a challenge. And he never backed down from one of those.

Thinking of challenges reminded him of Forrester's comments on the tape. What had happened to bend the bastard so out of shape? And whose life was in danger? Of course, the most pertinent question right now was, would a search of his house be productive or a colossal waste of time?

As he turned the corner onto Forrester's street, he counted a dozen vehicles parked along the curb, including the one assigned to the surveillance team. He pulled into an empty spot and called the number Gene had given him.

"Riley Harris," a voice answered.

The name wasn't familiar, but frequent transfers made it hard to keep track of everyone in the Cincinnati office. Brent identified himself.

"Gene said you'd be checking in," the other man said. "Any sign of Forrester?"

"Negative. McKenna's walking the perimeter. If Forrester shows up, he'll attempt to talk him into giving himself up."

It was worth a try, Brent supposed. And Alec McKenna had been around long enough to know not to let down his guard.

"I'll let McKenna know you've arrived," Harris said.

Brent closed his cell phone and turned to Claire. She hadn't spoken since they'd reached the city and was hugging her arms to her body even though it wasn't cold in the car.

"Don't worry," he said. "The surveillance team hasn't seen any sign of Forrester."

She nodded, but her arms remained locked across her torso.

He cupped her shoulder with his palm, drew her gaze to meet his. "If he shows his face, you have me and two other agents to protect you. But it's more likely he's gone to ground miles from here." He didn't know if that was true—all he knew was that he felt compelled to ease Claire's tension.

"I hope you're right," she said. "Leaving town may force him to postpone going after the person on the tape."

He checked his gun just in case he was wrong. "Let's go."

They didn't encounter Alec McKenna on their way to the back of the house, but Brent hadn't expected to. The agent would be focused on watching out for Forrester, and their presence couldn't act as a distraction.

At the house, Brent picked the lock on the front door, then he and Claire ventured inside. The main level consisted of a galley-style kitchen and an L-shaped living-room-and-dining-room area. A quick search through the stacks of opened mail on the coffee table revealed utility bills and junk mail, certainly nothing of interest. He checked the garage next. Empty. Wordlessly, he motioned for Claire to proceed to the second floor.

"What a mess," Claire murmured, advancing into the room at the top of the stairs.

The space, which had been set up as a home office, overflowed with books, magazines and loose papers. Suddenly, he was glad Gene had made him bring Claire along. Two people could search through this pigsty faster than one.

The office door slid shut.

Claire crossed the room to reopen it. "Where do you want me to start?"

"Try the stack of paper next to the bookcase," he said, his attention caught by the framed photo of Forrester on the desk. Sporting a wide smile, the agent stood next to a shiny classic Trans Am.

The door closed again due to the sloped floor, and this time Claire gave up and left it that way.

Opening the top drawer of the desk, Brent leafed through its contents which included an address book and six months' worth of bank statements. He flipped to the most current one. No immediate red flags. All the deposits and withdrawals appeared to be of reasonable magnitude. Setting the statement aside, he turned to the next one.

Paper rustled in the vicinity of the bookcase. Claire let out a sigh.

"Find anything interesting?" he asked.

"Only if car specifications and parts catalogues float your boat. Forrester mentioned in one of our sessions that classic cars were his hobby, but it looks more like an obsession."

Brent moved on to the bottom drawer where he found a nearly empty briefcase and a stack of credit-card receipts. It would take hours to review all the receipts, and he didn't want to spend that much time here.

He placed the address book, credit-card receipts and bank statements inside the briefcase, then added the photo from the desk.

"It's getting stuffy in here," she murmured, moving past him.

She unlocked the room's solitary window, then tugged on the handles without success.

"The house is old. It's probably been painted shut," he commented.

She headed for the closed door as he added more items to the briefcase.

A sudden cry jolted him like an electrical charge.

"The knob's hot," Claire said, regarding her upturned palm in disbelief.

In a heartbeat, he stood beside her, pressing his ear against the door. From the other side came a crackling sound. His gaze shot to the woman who should have been safe at the cabin, but was trapped here with him instead.

He answered the unspoken question in her eyes with a single word.

"Fire."

Chapter Four

Claire stared at Brent in stunned disbelief. The stinging in her hand receded under a wave of fear as he pulled out his cell phone. He pressed only three buttons. 9-1-1.

Fire. They had to get out.

Instinctively, she reached for the doorknob again.

"No," he yelled, jerking her back against him. "The fire's right outside. If you open the door, it'll explode into the office."

Oh, God. He was right. Hungry for oxygen, the fire would gravitate toward any new source. They had to find another exit. The window.

"Help me," she said, heading for it.

This time he didn't suggest reasons why it wouldn't open. Turning on his heel, he made it there ahead of her. She watched anxiously as he yanked and pulled.

"It won't…budge," he said, his words interrupted by coughs.

Her own throat felt raw and scratchy. Smoke seeped under the door like fog in a horror movie. She tugged at Brent's arm in alarm.

He glanced over his shoulder, then cursed softly and stripped off his shirt.

The sight of his rippling muscles and bronzed flesh had her mouth going dry—or maybe she was just reacting to the heat building inside the room. She couldn't tear her gaze away as he dropped his shirt to the floor and used his foot to wedge it against the crack. It wasn't going to stop all the smoke, but it might keep out enough so they could breathe for an extra minute or two.

Unless the door went up in flames.

A mighty crack sounded in another part of the house. Could it be the support beams collapsing? She had no way of knowing, and no intention of staying inside long enough to find out. She looked around for a heavy object to break the window, but Brent was already wheeling the oak desk-chair toward her. Lifting it by the arms, he thrust the chunky legs at the window pane repeatedly.

A spray of glass shards rewarded his efforts. Cooler air from outside rushed into the oven the office had become. Claire almost wept with relief as she moved forward, eagerly breathing in the fresh air.

Brent dropped the chair and blocked her path. "Stay away from the opening."

"Why?" All she wanted was some air to ease the burning in her lungs and the stinging in her eyes.

"Because the house didn't burst into flames on its own. The arsonist could be trying to smoke us out."

She instinctively took a step back, away from the window.

"The surveillance team—"

"He must have got past them to torch the house. I don't want to take the chance he picks us off as we leave."

Oh, God. If Brent was right, their only escape route exposed them to another kind of danger.

A gray haze of smoke soon filled the office.

Dragging the neckline of her tank top up to cover her mouth, she sucked air raggedly through the fabric. Her throat was already so raw that every breath she took hurt more than the last. She swayed to one side, dizzy from lack of oxygen. Losing consciousness wasn't far off. And even though her stomach churned at the possibility of being shot, she decided a bullet wound couldn't feel worse than this slow suffocation.

She eyed the narrow opening, psyching up to plunge through it, no matter what she'd encounter on the other side.

Brent must have sensed her intent because he moved to trap her against the wall.

"Trust me," he murmured. "I'll get you out of this alive."

She wouldn't have believed those words from anyone else, but last night this man had proved he could protect her. So even though her instincts screamed for her to shove him out of the way, she didn't surrender to them.

She closed her eyes, breathed shallowly.

Despite the dire situation, she was supremely conscious of his naked chest. The smooth skin…taut muscles…tangy masculine smell. As his body pressed against hers, his labored breathing mirrored her own.

"Hold on," Brent said. "We'll leave when the emergency crews arrive. Whoever set this fire won't risk being spotted."

She nodded to show she understood and struggled to stay alert, knowing that her survival depended on reacting quickly to changing circumstances.

Hold on. Hold on.

The words were a mantra in her mind. She clung to them for comfort. Belatedly, she realized that she was also clinging to Brent, her arms locked around his waist. She knew she should release him. She also knew she should be mortified. She had no business touching him, especially after denying her attraction to him in the car. But this wasn't about attraction. This was about need. She needed to be close to him right now. She needed to share his strength, absorb his courage. His lack of fear was the only thing keeping her from full-scale panic.

He didn't seem to mind or even be aware of her fierce embrace. His gaze was directed outside, scanning the area around the house.

Sirens wailed nearby.

"Let's go," he said abruptly.

Claire felt her legs go weak. Finally.

But her relief evaporated when the tongues of flame began to lick at the frame of the door. The spark and crackle of the fire was so close. It wouldn't be long before it had consumed everything in its path.

Brent stepped in front of the window, then paused for a long moment before he grasped her by the waist and hoisted her through the opening in a single, smooth movement. Only when she was kneeling outside on the roof of the garage did she realize why he had stopped in front of the window first—to offer himself as a target. The reminder that Brent would take a bullet for her made her grateful that he was protecting her, and worried what could happen to him.

She waited, expecting him to join her immediately. When he didn't, fear stabbed her. Had he been cut off by the fire? Or had he passed out from smoke inhalation? The thought of climbing back into the burning office terrified her, but she couldn't leave him to die. She gripped the window frame, anxious that she might not be strong enough to drag him to safety.

He appeared in the opening, brandishing Forrester's briefcase like a trophy.

Her happiness at seeing him turned to anger. "You risked your life for a briefcase? Are you crazy?"

He swung a leg out the window. "I didn't think shrinks liked that word. Too derogatory."

Flames leapt behind him as the fire advanced into the office. So close. Too damn close. The man was in denial about his own mortality.

"I know a lot more derogatory words than 'crazy'," she said, through gritted teeth.

"I'll bet," he said, with a grin. "You can enlighten me later."

He pointed to the street where half a dozen men in protective clothing swarmed around a fire engine. "Those hoses look set to go. Unless you want an impromptu shower, I suggest we get off this roof right away."

Following his lead, she crawled over the shingles to the far side of the roof. But when she saw him swing over the edge, hang by his fingers for a moment, then drop to the ground, she groaned inwardly. There was no way she could do that. Her burned hand hurt so much, she'd probably faint from the pain.

"Throw me the briefcase," he called out.

She did, using her left hand.

Brent looked up at her, waiting. "I know it seems like a long way down, but it's not that far. Jump and I'll catch you."

He obviously thought she was afraid of heights, and she didn't bother to contradict him. Her injury was nothing compared to the ones he'd likely collected over the course of his career.

Rolling onto her stomach, she pushed off the roof. As promised, he caught her before her feet hit the grass.

"Thanks," she said breathlessly. Was it her imagination or did his hands linger on her?

"No problem," he said, releasing her.

Seconds later, a fire hose spewed jets of water onto the east side of the house.

They sprinted across the lawn, then headed for the fire engine, where Brent let the crew know that the house was empty and the fire had likely been started by its owner, who was wanted by the FBI.

Reminded of the surveillance team, Claire murmured, "Where do you suppose your colleagues are?"

"I don't know," Brent said grimly, "but I intend to find out."

He strode along the street past numerous parked cars

until he reached a green Chevy Impala. Peering through the window, he let out a guttural curse.

"What is it?" Claire said, unable to see past him into the car.

"Harris has been shot." He opened the door and reached inside.

She glimpsed bloody clothing and a slumped-over body before she turned away, sickened. "How bad is it?"

"He's dead."

Oh, God. She swallowed. "Where's McKenna?"

"Let's go find out."

For the next ten minutes, they trekked through the surrounding yards, climbed over fences and checked behind hedges. Nobody objected to their presence, perhaps because those who might have were distracted by the fire engine in front of Forrester's house. With every step, Claire felt a deepening sense of dread. A few minutes later, they rounded the corner of a garage and found a man lying face down on the grass. Blood oozed from his scalp, matting his dark red hair.

She held her breath as Brent knelt beside him and touched the side of his neck.

"I feel a pulse," he said.

McKenna's eyelashes flickered and the lips under a generous mustache uttered a groan. "What the hell?" he muttered.

"I was hoping you'd tell me," Brent said.

"All I know is my head feels ready to explode."

"You're lucky to be alive. Harris isn't."

"Sonovabitch." The agent sat up gingerly. "Did you see who did this?"

Brent shook his head. "I just came from the house." He explained about the fire and how he and Claire had escaped onto the roof of the garage.

McKenna exhaled heavily. "How the hell did he get past me?"

"Forrester knows all the tricks."

"I can't believe he'd do this. I've worked with him a few times, and I liked him."

"That probably explains why you're still alive," Brent said. "He knew you, but Harris was a stranger to him."

"Being locked up must have messed with his mind," McKenna muttered.

"You believe he'd kill a fellow agent because of two days at Ridsdale?" Claire asked incredulously.

McKenna treated her to a long, hard stare. Did he resent her for confining Forrester to a psychiatric facility? After the roller-coaster events of the last hour, she was uncertain how to interpret his expression.

McKenna fingered his bloody scalp.

"You should see the paramedics," she said.

"Nah. A couple of Tylenol, and I'll be fine."

She wasn't surprised he'd refuse medical treatment. He was, after all, a G-man. Too stubborn and proud to admit to any human frailties. Just like her father had been before his breakdown.

The memory of her father had her clenching her fists. But the pain it dredged up was superceded by a more immediate one: the blistered skin on her right palm. She relaxed her hands immediately and bit her lip to keep from voicing her discomfort.

"You'd better head to the hospital," Brent said to the

injured agent. "Gene won't let you get back to work without a doctor's okay."

"Waste of time, in my opinion, but you're right."

"While you're doing that, I'm going after Forrester."

"If you find him, don't underestimate him."

"I'm not the one with the concussion," Brent said.

McKenna grimaced. "Good point."

As Claire walked with Brent back to his car, she asked, "Why would Forrester set fire to his own home?"

Brent laid the briefcase in his trunk and rummaged through his gym bag for a T-shirt. "There must have been something inside he wanted destroyed."

She watched the muscles in his bare back shift with his movements, remembering the feel of his supple skin, the tangy scent of his sweat. As he raised his arms to tug on his shirt, her mind stalled out, and she had to shake herself mentally to restart it. "You mean us?"

"Or incriminating evidence."

"I think he's too smart for that."

"He didn't expect you to commit him to Ridsdale."

"He's an experienced agent. He knows to be prepared for the unexpected."

"You have a better theory?"

A full minute ticked by as she tried to come up with a plausible one.

"Not at this point," she admitted. "But I don't believe Forrester set fire to his home or killed Harris. The agent I interviewed wouldn't risk prison without a huge financial incentive."

Brent shrugged, then strode toward the neighboring house. She hurried to catch up.

A middle-aged couple stood in the driveway, watching the comings and goings of the firefighters with keen interest.

Brent introduced Claire and then himself.

The woman's pale blue eyes widened. "What's the FBI doing at a house fire?"

Brent sidestepped her question. "I didn't catch your name, ma'am."

"Jolene Blackburne. And this is my husband, Rod." She patted the sleeve of the man's yellow T-shirt with obvious affection.

Brent jotted down the information. "Are you well acquainted with the person who lives next door?"

"Andy Forrester keeps his grass cut and his trash inside till garbage day. Got no complaints with him. Unlike some others around here." Lips twisted in disgust, she glared at the house directly across the street.

"When did you last see him?"

Jolene turned to her husband. "A couple of days ago, right, hon?"

Her husband nodded.

She heaved a sigh, her gaze resting on the still-burning hulk that was Forrester's residence. "A terrible thing for him to come home to. Do you know how it started?"

Claire figured Brent would plead ignorance, so his next words surprised her.

"Looks like it might be arson."

"Arson? Oh, my God. Did you hear that, Rod?"

The man rolled his eyes. "I'm standing right here, Jolene. Of course I heard."

The woman pressed her fingers to her lips. "That

could have been our house up in flames. All our furniture, photographs, my mother's Royal Doulton china, every last thing burned to a crisp." Her distraught expression changed to angry speculation. "Was it kids playing with matches?"

"I don't think so," Brent said. "Did you see anybody around his house today?"

Rod scratched under his baseball cap. "Nope. But I worked the late shift last night so I was sleeping until the sirens woke me up."

"And I was doing laundry in the basement all morning." She added, "What about his fancy car? Did it go up in flames, too?"

"You know he doesn't keep that one in his garage," Rod reminded his wife. "He only brings it home on Sundays to shine her up and show her off."

"What kind of car is it?" Claire asked.

Rod grinned. "A sixty-nine Trans Am."

"That man sure does love his car," Jolene added.

"His prize possession, huh?"

Brent made a quick notation on a business card and gave it to the man. "Thanks for your cooperation. Please call if you see Mr. Forrester or if you remember anything else that might help our investigation."

He headed down the driveway to the street.

Claire waited until they were out of earshot of Forrester's neighbors. "Too bad they didn't see who set the fire."

He stared straight ahead, but she wasn't sure whether he was deep in thought or ignoring her.

"Brent? Are you okay?"

His pace quickened. "I'm not comfortable with this setup. You're supposed to be under protection, not out in the field interviewing contacts."

"I barely took part in the conversation." She lengthened her strides to match his. "The car is worth following up on, don't you think?"

"Maybe," Brent admitted.

When she started to speak again, he cut her off. "Look, I appreciate your wanting to help, but this isn't your concern."

Her temper flared at his tone, and she stopped walking abruptly. "Anything that could help the FBI locate Forrester *is* my concern."

"Let me rephrase that. You did your job. You determined that Forrester was a threat and sent him to Ridsdale. Now you have to trust Gene and me to do our job, which is to ascertain his whereabouts and apprehend him."

"I thought your job was to protect me."

He locked gazes with her, and she suddenly felt lightheaded. A delayed reaction to nearly suffocating earlier, she decided. It was *not* because his dark, thick-lashed eyes took her breath away.

"You are my primary responsibility," Brent said, "but I intend to participate in the search for Forrester."

Was that annoyance she heard in his voice? Did he feel that safeguarding her was diverting him from a more important job?

She forced her thoughts back to his last comment. "I'm sure he'll be caught faster if you participate."

He nodded. "I'm glad we agree on something."

She smiled at the first sign of accord between them. It lasted until he spoke again.

"You can forget about my discussing field operations with you. As I said before, that's not your concern. The only thing you need to know is that the Bureau will do everything possible to bring Forrester into custody."

Easy for him to say. He wasn't expected to wait passively for the situation to be resolved.

Watching others act while she did nothing went against her grain. Especially when it looked to her like Forrester's arrest was far from imminent.

Chapter Five

Brent kept a tight rein on his frustration until he was behind the closed door of Gene's office. "Claire shouldn't have been at Forrester's."

"Her being there wasn't the problem," his boss countered, shoving a handful of papers into his out tray. "The problem was the surveillance team that failed to stop a perp from torching his house."

"They followed Bureau procedures that Forrester, being an insider, is completely familiar with." He wasn't making excuses for his colleagues, just pointing out the extenuating circumstances.

Gene glanced up, his pale eyes unyielding, his salt-and-pepper hair reminding Brent that the man had thirty years of experience dealing with tough situations. "The team's failure endangered lives."

There was one life that had been placed in jeopardy needlessly. "Harris and McKenna didn't veto Claire remaining at the cabin. That was you." The decision had almost had fatal consequences, and he wanted his boss to admit he'd made a mistake. "Dammit, she could have died in that fire."

The other man's eyes narrowed and his voice boomed like a drill sergeant's. "She escaped without a scratch. You know why? Because I assigned the right damn agent to watch over her."

It was a new experience to be yelled at and complimented at the same time. Before he could shift gears and respond, Gene barked out, "Until I'm convinced she's not in danger, Claire isn't to be left alone anywhere, anytime. No exceptions. If you're not happy with bodyguard duty, I'll assign somebody else."

Another agent taking care of Claire?

His reaction was visceral, involuntary. "Don't even think about replacing me," he ground out, fists clenched at his sides. "She's my responsibility."

Gene stared at him hard. Then he dropped his gaze and carried on with organizing his desk. "Fine. She's yours for the duration."

His satisfaction with Gene's decision was diluted by annoyance that he'd admitted possessive feelings toward the department's psychologist.

"Where's Claire now?" Gene inquired.

"With Lisa."

"Tell me what you found at the house."

Brent opened Forrester's briefcase and withdrew the photo of the agent with his cherished Trans Am. "I thought a candid shot of Forrester would be useful when I canvassed his neighborhood. However, it turns out the vehicle in the picture is very important to him."

"Are our tech guys working on it?"

"The car wasn't at the house. His neighbors don't know where he keeps it."

"I'll have Mickey look for it," Gene said, jotting down a note. "What about Forrester? Any leads on him?"

"I snagged his address book. Only a few names to check out."

"I'll free up some manpower to do that. What else?"

"Forrester's Trans Am is a classic. Extremely expensive. I'm wondering how he had the money to buy it."

"Maybe he borrowed big. Or has a rich lady friend who likes to buy him gifts. He could have a source of income apart from his Bureau wages. Possibly illegal," Gene mused.

"We have his bank account and credit card statements. They might give some insight into his financial situation."

Gene frowned. "I'm not optimistic we're going to find him with our usual methods. He knows how we search for a fugitive—who we contact, what we look for, how we process info."

"He has an unpredictable streak," Brent agreed. "He's already demonstrated that."

As well as a willingness to kill.

If they didn't catch him fast, he would surely up the body count.

THROUGH THE CLOSED DOOR of Gene's office, Claire could hear the sound of loud voices.

Lisa Conrad, Gene's admin assistant, glanced up from her computer monitor. "Don't look so worried. Gene and Brent get riled up from time to time."

Claire nodded, then sipped the coffee she'd bought from the vending machine around the corner.

Leaning across her workstation, Lisa lowered her voice to a conspiratorial whisper. "So what's it like staying alone with Mr. Tough Guy?"

She feigned nonchalance. "Fine."

"That guy's hot," Lisa said, with a grin. "Or haven't you noticed?"

When Claire didn't answer, Lisa winked. "Oh, yeah, you've noticed. Heck, you'd have to be blind not to. The question is, what are you doing about it?"

Claire finished her coffee and tossed the cup in the wastepaper basket. "Agent Young has been assigned to protect me. There's nothing personal between us."

"Then you're wasting a golden opportunity, girl. Most of the women on this floor would be delirious to swap places with you."

Oh no, they wouldn't, Claire thought. Not if they knew she'd almost died twice in the last twenty-four hours. "I didn't realize he was in such high demand."

"Yeah, well, it's not like he even notices. That hunky man shows zero interest in the female staffers around here."

Lisa's words pleased her more than they should have. "Maybe he wants to keep his professional and personal lives separate."

"Could be," Lisa said. "But I bet he'd make an exception for the right woman."

What type of woman would Brent go for? Claire wondered. Certainly not her. She was too intense, too opinionated, too—

She stopped, annoyed that she'd been speculating about him.

"You could be that woman," Lisa continued.

She shook her head. "I don't think so."

"Of course, he'd be a challenge. But your line of work makes you good at connecting with people."

"I haven't had much success with him."

"The other agents like you a lot more than Dr. Telso."

Claire had heard rumors about her predecessor's unpopularity, but she knew for a fact that Brent didn't consider her an improvement. Whenever she touched on subjects of a personal nature, he shut her down or stalked away.

"I appreciate the vote of confidence, but Brent and I are too different to have a relationship."

"Relationships are overrated." Lisa wiggled her eyebrows suggestively. "I was talking about sex."

Claire couldn't help but laugh. "I just met the guy and you think I should fall into bed with him?"

"Fall?" Lisa shook her head. "Hell, honey, I'd jump into bed with him."

"Jump into bed with whom?" Gene asked, bearing down on Lisa's workstation with Brent close behind him.

Claire felt her cheeks flame.

"No one," Lisa said, winking at Claire before she turned her attention back to her monitor and settled her fingers on the keyboard.

Claire felt Brent's gaze on her, but kept her own averted. If she looked at him, he would surely guess they'd been discussing him.

Gene came closer, a concerned expression on his face. "How are you holding up, Claire?"

"Okay," she said, although her hand stung as if she'd stuck it in a beehive. "I'd like to meet with you for a minute, in private."

He turned to Lisa. "While Claire and I are talking, please scan the material Brent gives you so he can load the files onto his laptop."

Gene escorted her into his office and closed the door. "What's up?"

"I heard you and Brent going at it. I couldn't hear what you were saying, but I'm concerned. Was it about me?"

She knew her speculation was on target when Gene hesitated.

"You should know," she went on, "that it's okay with me if Brent wants to be reassigned. He's done a great job, but you shouldn't force him to continue—"

"You've got it all wrong, Claire."

She'd expected the denial, but Gene sounded sincere. "Are you sure?"

"Brent was upset about what went down at Forrester's house. He wants to keep on protecting you. Most definitely."

Relief flooded her. Because no matter how infuriating Brent could be at times, he had saved her life twice and she trusted him to do it again.

"What happened today," Gene said, "was terrible, but you seem to be handling it well."

Mostly because she'd been blocking it out of her mind. And although part of her was still horrified and shaken, another part was keenly aware that the outcome could have been far worse. Even so, Gene had lost one of his men.

"I'm very sorry about Harris," she said.

Gene looked down at his desk. "He was a new agent. Showed a lot of promise."

"You couldn't have prevented what happened."

Gene's solemn gaze lifted to meet hers. "Thanks for your concern, Claire, but I've had men die under my command before. I can deal with it."

"I know you can." She was the one who felt out of her element.

"We'll get Forrester," Gene promised, and the fierceness in his tone left her in no doubt that it would happen.

She cleared her throat. "What about my patients?"

"You're not meeting with anybody until the situation with Forrester is resolved."

"But I have appointments every day."

"Give me your BlackBerry. Lisa will check your schedule and cancel the ones for the rest of this week."

"But—"

"We need to eliminate the risk that Forrester can trace your calls. Lisa will give you a disposable cell phone on your way out."

"I don't care about phones. I care about my patients."

"Until we rule out the possibility that someone internal is involved with Forrester, I'm not letting you meet with anyone."

She knew Gene was only trying to keep her safe. Still, it was hard to accept not working until Forrester was arrested. What if he eluded them for weeks? Some of her patients were just beginning to trust her. Months of effort could easily slip away. Of course, if she accepted the job offer in Minneapolis, her patients would have to adjust to her absence on a permanent basis.

Gene got to his feet. "Try to make the best of this break, Claire. And know that we're working hard to end it soon."

AS BRENT UNLOADED the groceries onto the cabin's kitchen counter, it occurred to him that his companion was uncharacteristically quiet. She stood in front of the fridge, a blank expression on her face.

"Claire?"

He couldn't be certain from this distance, but it seemed as if she was trembling. He should probably say something to settle her down but couldn't think of the right words. Besides, talk was overrated. He was a man of action. But what action was called for?

He eyed her slender frame. If he held her, would the trembling stop?

He remembered the last minutes at Forrester's house when Claire had plastered herself to him like wallpaper. Even now, he could feel her arms around his bare torso, her breasts crushed against his chest, the softness of her skin and the silky texture of her hair. His body began to respond, and he knew he had better avoid physical contact with her.

She blinked several times, on the verge of tears.

Her damp eyes surprised him. She had acted so levelheaded during the fire and the discovery of Harris's body, it was easy to forget how overwhelmed she might be feeling. Wanting to offer some kind of comfort but not trusting himself to embrace her, he reached for her hand.

She cried out, jerking it away from him.

Damn. He'd forgotten all about her touching the hot doorknob—probably because she hadn't drawn attention to it. That type of stoicism was a refreshing change from his last girlfriend, Patty, who had complained about everything: the weather, PMS, his job. Why was he comparing them? He wasn't looking for another girlfriend—no matter how much Claire's hug had turned him on.

"Let me see," he growled, annoyed by his meandering thoughts.

She hesitated for a moment, then extended her right hand to him, palm up.

As he stared at the red, blistered skin, a wave of regret hit him. It was his job to protect her. Not just to keep her alive but to keep her safe. He'd failed her.

That must never happen again.

He guided her over to a kitchen chair, then retrieved the first aid kit from the cupboard above the stove.

"What's that?" Claire asked, peering at the capsules he extracted from the kit.

"Aloe vera." Breaking them open, he spread the gel over the burned area.

He didn't want her to have a scar. When this was all over, he wanted her to forget about Forrester, not carry a reminder of the violent patient who had tried to kill her.

She bit her lip, obviously hurting, and he spoke to distract her. "I'm surprised there's any of this stuff left.

Sanderson used to singe his fingers every time he grilled—" He stopped abruptly.

A very loud silence ticked by.

"It must be difficult to be here without him."

He jerked his shoulder in an awkward shrug. He should know better than to talk to a shrink. She'd immediately zeroed in on his pain.

As he carefully wrapped gauze around her hand, he braced himself for more of her questions.

She surprised him by saying, "You'd make a good paramedic."

His mother was a nurse and had taught him how to bandage cuts, set broken bones. Important skills for a skinny kid who had been beaten by the bullies at school because he sucked at team sports and had no father. "I fought like hell to become an FBI agent. I'm not about to switch careers anytime soon."

"I didn't say you should be a medic. Just that you could be."

Should. Could. Typical shrink double-talk. But instead of ignoring her comment, he heard himself asking, "Why?"

"You stay calm and focused in a crisis." Her voice took on a husky undertone. "And you have a gentle touch."

She dropped her gaze to her bandaged hand, but a telltale pink stained her cheeks.

He smiled as he applied adhesive tape to secure the bandage. So she thought he had a gentle touch, did she? Maybe she'd enjoy it somewhere other than her hand. He traced his fingers from her wrist to her elbow. Her arm was lightly tanned, muting the network of veins under her skin. He thought about tracing those veins with his tongue, then licking places on her body with no tan.

Claire had said she wouldn't get involved with an agent. But she was going to make an exception. For him.

He heard her breath catch as his fingers moved toward her shoulder, and he smiled again. Did she have any idea what he was thinking? What he wanted to do to her? What he wanted her to do to him?

He still distrusted psychologists. But he was making an exception. For her.

Moving closer, he kissed her full on the mouth.

CLAIRE'S MIND SPUN like a kaleidoscope. Feelings she barely recognized swamped her. Feelings of longing. Of need. Of desire. No matter how much she pretended otherwise, Brent's every look, his every touch sparked an intense awareness in her. The chemistry between them was volatile as nitroglycerine, and she had no doubt his kiss was the prelude to a sweet explosion.

Opening her lips, she welcomed the thrust of his tongue. She'd never been kissed so thoroughly. Her last boyfriend had been a main-event man, with little interest in foreplay. Despite her attempts to guide him otherwise, he'd remained stubbornly fixated on the cul-mination of the act. That destination-over-journey pref-erence had only been one of the differences that had led to their breakup two years ago.

Brent seemed to be more attuned to her. She rewarded him by kissing him back with enthusiasm, angling her mouth to deepen the kiss and show her approval for his slow, unhurried pace. He let out a low groan. The vibration rippled through every one of her nerve endings.

She wanted to get closer to him. As she moved forward, her breasts brushed against his T-shirt and her nipples puckered. She gasped, thrilled by the sensation.

He kissed her again, then slipped his hand beneath her tank top and stroked the swollen peaks through her bra.

Oh, yeah. That felt good. Better than good. Phenomenal.

But was *phenomenal* enough of a reason to keep going?

This morning Brent had made it clear that he despised psychologists. And during the intervening hours, he'd given no indication of having altered his opinion. So how come she was letting him feel her up? Not only letting him but *encouraging* him? And enjoying herself to boot? The fire at Forrester's place had done more than burn her hand. It had fried her brain.

Brent's fingers traced her spine, en route to the clasp on her bra. Within seconds, he'd have it unfastened and touch her bare breasts. And though her body yearned for exactly that, her brain was struggling to give her a different message. Something about not letting a man she barely knew strip her naked.

She jerked back and dragged her top down.

"What's wrong?"

"What's happening between us," she said.

He shot her a look of disbelief. "You don't want me touching you?"

The lie stuck in her throat, and she swallowed around it. "You're missing the point."

"Which is?"

"We don't even know each other."

He reached for her. "We can fix that soon enough."

"By having sex?"

His eyes narrowed before his mouth relaxed into a smile that took her breath away. "Well, I'm not usually a first-date kind of guy, but for you, I'm willing to be flexible."

She wasn't sure whether to laugh or slug him. "You're being obtuse."

"No, I'm confused." He rubbed the side of his face. "Although, on second thought, maybe I do understand. You enjoyed me kissing you. But you got cold feet when you realized I wanted that bra gone—"

"Do you like me, Brent?"

He looked taken aback. "What kind of question is that?"

"A perfectly legitimate one," she answered, feigning a calmness she didn't feel.

"You think I'm in the habit of making out with women I dislike?"

"I think you're attracted to me physically, but you don't know me well enough to like me or not."

"That's not true."

"What do you know about me?"

He considered her for a long moment as if she were a meal he wanted to devour. "When I was inside Forrester's house, you came back for me even though you were terrified of the fire. And when we found McKenna, you suggested he seek out the paramedics. So I'd say, based on your actions, I like you fine.

"And I'm attracted to you," he continued. "In fact, I'd like nothing more than to pick up where we left off. But I don't put the moves on a woman who isn't interested. So it's my turn to ask a question, Claire. Are you interested—or not?"

Of course, she was interested, and that was the problem. If he touched her again, she'd abandon all common sense for the pleasure she would find in his bed. And mixing it up with an agent, however temporarily, would be a huge mistake.

The solution was simple. Kill his interest in her. "Nothing's changed since this morning. I'm still a psychologist."

He had the audacity to shrug. "Which is why you're talking this whole thing to death instead of admitting you want me."

She gritted her teeth. "You're projecting—"

He laughed low in his throat. "If you think resorting to shrink lingo will put me off, you're wrong. You kissed me back."

"You surprised me."

"For a few seconds," he conceded. "After that, you were enjoying yourself. A lot."

She hated the smugness of his tone, hated even more that the words he spoke were true. "So what if I enjoyed kissing you? That doesn't mean... You're practically a stranger."

"We can discuss our favorite foods and movies later. For now, stop analyzing and go with the flow."

She folded her arms. "As far as I'm concerned, the flow has stopped."

He looked disappointed, but philosophical. "There's always next time."

"There won't be a next time," she said, in an effort to convince herself as much as him. "We have to stick together until Forrester is apprehended. Then we go our separate ways."

He frowned, as if tired of arguing with her.

She tucked her tank top into her jeans. "I'm sorry I gave you mixed messages. I just don't want to act on an impulse that I'll regret afterward."

But as she left the room, a voice inside taunted her with a different possibility—that she might later regret *not* acting on the impulse.

She fervently hoped that voice was wrong.

CLAIRE WAS RIGHT, Brent decided. Sleeping together would make an already complicated situation even more so. He should be grateful her common sense had nixed their passion. But he wasn't. Her exotic taste still lingered on his lips, her sweet fragrance still filled his nostrils and her excited gasp still rang in his ears. If she hadn't left the room, he'd have been hard pressed to keep his hands to himself. Because despite the arguments she'd made, he was sure he could make her forget logic and respond to him.

He cursed softly. He needed to stop thinking about her and start thinking about Forrester.

Firing up his laptop, he opened the file containing the scanned material from the house. But after twenty minutes of reviewing bank statements, he pushed back from the table in disgust. If Forrester had acquired illegal funds, he wasn't stupid enough to deposit them into this account. So where were they?

Maybe he'd call Pete to brainstorm—

Except his buddy wasn't available to take his call. Ever.

Dammit, Pete. Why did you have to get yourself killed?

He sucked in a breath, braced himself for the on-slaught of familiar questions. Why hadn't Pete waited for him to return from training in Quantico so they could go together? Or secured other backup? Why had a guy, whose Bureau nickname was the Bloodhound, failed to smell a setup at the Enbridge warehouse? Why had he—

Stop it.

He couldn't change what had happened. He couldn't turn back time and reorder events the way he wanted to. He had to stop wishing, stop wondering, stop feeling.

Numb was the only way he could hold it together until Pete's killer received justice—a life sentence to rot in prison. And that sweet retribution would lessen his bitter loss.

Chapter Six

An hour later, Claire left her room and ventured into the kitchen. At first, she thought Brent was working on his laptop, but then she realized the screensaver was on, and he was staring into space.

Was he thinking about Forrester, mulling over leads to pursue? Or was he preoccupied with memories of the friend who had used the first aid kit that lay open on the table? She guessed it was Sanderson on his mind, and her heart went out to him. Brent gave the impression of being so strong it was easy to forget he'd sustained a terrible loss only two weeks ago. Did he have any family or friends he felt close enough to talk to? She suspected he hadn't opened up to anyone. He struck her as a loner, a man who would bury his pain, figuring it would cease to exist if he ignored it.

If only that were true.

In her experience, negative feelings that weren't acknowledged could turn corrosive, toxic. Her father's guilt had ripped him apart, destroyed his life. And she hadn't realized until it was too late that his failure to communicate had intensified his suffering.

Brent had saved her life. The least she could do was to offer him a sympathetic ear.

"How long had you known Sanderson?" she asked softly.

His eyes snapped into focus. "Why do you ask?"

"I want to get to know you better."

His lips thinned. "I remember saying we could discuss favorite foods and movies. I don't remember any mention of dead friends."

He was trying to shock her into silence, but there was too much at stake for her to give up. "I think the people we spend time with tell more about us than what we eat or watch."

He shrugged.

"Sometimes it helps to share your feelings—"

"—and sometimes it doesn't."

"How do you know? Have you tried to talk to anyone about them?"

"That's none of your business."

Damn, he was stubborn. He was also hurting. If she could only find the right words.

"On second thought," he said, "I guess that *is* your business. Pushing people to unload their personal baggage. Manipulating them into—"

"Insulting me won't take away your pain," she observed.

"The only pain here is the one you've become." He stood and moved away from the table.

"I don't mean to upset you. I just want to—"

"You just want to add me to the list of people you've psychoanalyzed." His lips twisted into a sneer. "Give it up, Claire. I won't ever bare my soul to you."

He went to the sink, splashed water over his face. Then he braced his hands on the counter and stared out the window.

Disappointed that he'd shut her down, she switched to a neutral topic. "Gene mentioned Forrester might have had inside help to get out of Ridsdale. Has the staff there been questioned?"

He nodded. "Gene sent agents to the hospital to interview every employee. Nobody admitted to knowing anything."

No surprise there. "When did the interviews take place?"

"The night of his escape."

"At that point, Harris was alive."

"So?"

"You could use his murder as a reason to speak to them."

"But you don't believe Forrester killed him."

"It doesn't matter what I believe. It's what the person who helped him believes. Believing you're an accomplice to a murder would shake up most people."

Brent folded his arms over his chest, reluctant to admit that she had made a valid point. He would conduct the second round of interviews at Ridsdale himself. This time it made sense to take Claire with him. She was familiar with the facility and its operations, knew the rules and protocol. And although he didn't believe her professional training gave her any special insight, two sets of eyes and ears were better than one.

"We'll go tomorrow."

As she nodded her agreement, her blond curls fell over her shoulder. He fought a sudden urge to tangle his fingers in her hair. It would be soft, just like her lips. If he tugged her closer and nuzzled the corner of her mouth, maybe he could change her mind about kissing him again.

He tensed, his fingers itching to move.

But she would hardly welcome his touch after the way he had snapped at her. He hadn't intended to be mean. He just couldn't keep his emotions locked down if he talked about Pete.

He relaxed his fingers.

The trip to Ridsdale was important. Not only because it might result in a lead to Forrester, but because the less time he spent alone with Claire, the better.

THE STAFF MEMBERS at Ridsdale Psychiatric Hospital weren't happy about being interviewed again. They'd already told the FBI what they knew about the evening that Forrester had escaped. Being questioned again and by another agent suggested that one or more employees was suspected of lying—or at least withholding information. So Claire wasn't at all surprised by the interviewees' range of reactions—defensiveness, belligerence, confusion and resignation. Unfortunately, those differing attitudes made it tricky to spot deceit.

Brent had started the second round of interviews with the employees identified by the original investigators as top suspects. Five had been flagged either because of their conduct during the initial questioning or the results of the subsequent background check.

He turned to Maria Gomez, a petite thirty-two-year-old nurse and mother of two young children, who was the last of the staff to be questioned.

"You have previously discussed the escape of a Ridsdale patient, Andy Forrester, with one of my colleagues."

"That's right."

Claire watched the woman's fingers twist together in her lap.

"I'm here today to ask if you've remembered anything else that might be pertinent to our investigation."

"No, I haven't."

"At the time Forrester was admitted, he hadn't committed any crimes. The person who helped him escape might not have believed he was dangerous."

The nurse's fingers twisted faster.

"He can be persuasive," Brent said. "It's possible he convinced someone that a mistake had been made, that he shouldn't have been confined."

Claire liked Brent's strategy. He was providing the woman with justification for her actions—if she was, in fact, involved.

"It doesn't matter what you told the other agent," he prodded. "All that matters is what you tell me now."

"You think I was lying when I talked to that other guy?"

Claire noted the tension in her shoulders, the pallor of her skin. Were they signs of indignation or guilt?

"I think that you may have been worried about the consequences," he allowed. "And no one could have guessed that, once out, Forrester would kill one FBI agent and injure another."

Maria's gaze dropped to her lap, where her white knuckles stood out against her peach uniform. "Is that really true?"

He nodded. "He tried to kill Dr. Lamont and me, too. Whoever helped him get out of here could be charged as an accessory to those crimes unless he or she cooperates with the investigation."

She remained silent.

"If you have any idea where he is, you need to tell me. Before he hurts anybody else."

"I have nothing to say."

Brent's gaze grew steely. "It's just a matter of time until Forrester's caught. When he is, the identity of his accomplice will come to light."

Marla raised her chin. "I have to go now. My kids are waiting for me at the sitter's."

After the nurse left, Brent asked Claire, "What do you think? Did Forrester have inside help?"

"I can't imagine how he escaped otherwise. The security procedures are excellent."

But helping Forrester leave Ridsdale was a far cry from arson or murder. She didn't see any of the five she'd met today participating in that. Certainly not Maria Gomez. But something about the petite nurse had Claire's internal radar pinging. "I think Maria Gomez was involved."

Brent frowned. "My prime suspect is Wayne Bonsall."

"Why?"

Brent pointed to files he'd collected from the Bureau

office. "The background info shows his charge cards are maxed out. Given his orderly's wages, it'll take him years to pay them off."

"You think Forrester bribed him?"

"Yeah, I do."

Bonsall's resentment over being paid less than the nurses had been evident early in the interview. So why was her intuition still pointing her in the nurse's direction?

"What happens next?" she asked.

"I'm going to recommend surveillance."

"For whom?"

"Wayne Bonsall…and Maria Gomez."

She could have sworn her heart skipped a beat. Damn, there was something about the man that got her worked up.

She shifted her gaze away from the sensual curve of his lips to the moss-green wall behind him. But her eyes rebelled, sliding back to study the man across from her, drawn to him by an invisible force that was stronger than her ability to resist it.

Sprawled in a chair, his body appeared lax, almost lazy, but she knew only too well the steely strength of the muscles that lay beneath his cotton shirt. She'd felt the power of those muscles when he'd lifted her through Forrester's office window. It wasn't just his physique she found tantalizing. Her mouth tingled with the memory of his kiss. Just the right amount of pressure, just the right amount of tongue. In fact, everything about it had been perfect. She wanted to clear the table of those files, push him down on top of it and have her way with him.

She clasped her damp hands together, told herself that her fantasy was wildly inappropriate. This was a hospital, for crying out loud.

Besides, did she really want to set herself up for heartache by becoming involved with a man who was emotionally distant and dismissive of her profession? Far better to disappoint her raging hormones now than have to live with hurtful memories later.

So she didn't jump Brent but waited patiently while he loaded files into a black case. Clearly, she was the only one whose thoughts had strayed to sex. His focus was on arranging surveillance and locating Forrester.

Or so she thought, until he asked, "How come you work mostly with federal agents?"

It was a question she'd been asked before, so she had a pat answer ready. "My dad worked for the Bureau, so I'm familiar with the pressures of the job and its impact on families."

His response was immediate and unequivocal. "Agents shouldn't have families."

"Why not?"

"The job requires one hundred percent commitment."

Did he really believe he had to sacrifice a personal life for the sake of his career? "Lots of agents have families."

"And lots of them end up as single parents and rarely see their kids."

"That doesn't have to happen."

"You can't tell me that divorces aren't more common for us."

She hesitated, loath to concede the point but knowing she had to. "It's true that certain professions—"

"—law enforcement, the military—" he supplied helpfully.

"—have higher rates of divorce than the general population," she persevered. "But that doesn't mean people in those careers should avoid getting married or forming close attachments. In fact, the opposite is true. The extraordinary demands of the job mean they need more, not less, support." Although she spoke in general terms, her thoughts centered on one man. Her father. He had had the support of a loving family but had still come to feel adrift, disassociated, alone. Her desire to be a psychologist had sprung from wanting to understand how depression had taken hold and dragged him into a downward spiral of despair.

Brent leaned back in his chair. "I'm not the only agent who thinks a family is a bad idea."

She forced her thoughts from the past to the present. "You're obviously not talking about Gene. He's been married for a long time and has three kids. So I'm guessing it was your friend, Pete Sanderson, who shared your view."

Brent frowned. "As a matter of fact, he did. Although he didn't start off that way. He married his college sweetheart the year after he joined the Bureau."

"And divorced a short time later, right?" Such an experience would explain his negative view.

"He told me the breakup of his marriage hurt him a hundred times more than any injury he got in the field."

"So you've decided not to risk it."

His eyes narrowed. "I only take calculated risks. There's no way to figure out the chances of a marriage lasting."

True. Marriage wasn't a logical decision reached by the brain. It was a leap of faith taken by the heart in love. She hoped to take that leap herself someday. "Did you always think this way?"

"I was engaged once," he admitted. "After I was accepted at the Bureau, I left for my sixteen weeks of training at the Academy. When I came home, I found Sylvia, my fiancée, pregnant with another guy's baby."

He was talking dispassionately, but Claire suspected that betrayal was the reason he had no interest in a close relationship. Her heart went out to him for the hurt he'd suffered and evidently not recovered from. "I'm sorry, Brent."

"It's ancient history," he said, with a shrug.

Their conversation had been enlightening—and disappointing. For an agent as driven as Brent, his job would come first and last. A woman would never mean more to him than a temporary diversion.

No matter how insistently her hormones clamored, she mustn't indulge them.

Chapter Seven

Brent rubbed the back of his neck in frustration. Two days had passed since the trip to Ridsdale, and neither suspect under surveillance had made contact with Forrester. When Brent's cell phone rang, he answered it immediately, hoping for a break in the investigation.

"We found the dealer who sold the Trans Am to Forrester," Gene said. "His name is Fergus Lyons, and he remembers our suspect paid eighty thousand cash for the car. And get this. Forrester asked him to keep his eyes open for a sixty-five Cobra Roadster in mint condition."

"Where the hell is he getting the cash?" Brent asked.

"No leads on that yet."

"Any luck finding the Trans Am?"

"Langdon is contacting local garages in case it's being repaired."

"If nothing turns up there, tell him to widen the search to storage units."

"Anything else?"

"I found a sales slip for the laptop Forrester bought

in the spring, but I didn't see it at his house." He glanced out the window at the lake shimmering in sunlight.

"It wasn't among his belongings when he was admitted to Ridsdale."

"Great. So now we're looking for his car *and* his laptop."

"I'll be in touch," Gene said.

Brent closed his phone, his gaze still on the view outside. A boat bearing two men with fishing poles chugged past the dock.

That should be Pete and me.

The thought hit hard—a sucker punch to the gut. Sanderson was dead while his killer roamed free. The wrongness of the situation seared like acid. He needed to know what was being done to catch Sanderson's killer. And Ian Alston, an investigator with the team, owed him a favor.

A PHONE CALL, a quick trip to Cincinnati and Brent had a flash drive containing all the pertinent info on the investigation. As he waited for his laptop to boot up, Pete's image came to mind. The blue eyes that had danced when he hooked a big one. The wide mouth that had belted out country tunes off-key. The strong arms that had carried him to safety after he'd been stabbed… Oh, God.

He sucked in a breath, waited for the pain to dull. Then he plugged in the flash drive, opened the first file and began reading.

He already knew the basics. Sanderson's body had been discovered at 11:30 p.m. at the Enbridge warehouse located at 15 Duke Street. Cause of death: the second of two bullets he'd taken in the chest.

A review of Sanderson's PDA indicated a meeting at 9:00 p.m. with one of his snitches, Marty Adey, who claimed he hadn't set foot in the warehouse. He'd received one thousand dollars to act as a go-between for a third party. His alibi for the time period was solid; he had been picked up for DUI at eight and spent the night in jail. Adey had spent half of the money he'd been paid, but the remaining bills had been confiscated as evidence and dusted for fingerprints. None matched the Bureau's database of felons.

The next file was a photo of Sanderson's naked body lying on a metal table, awaiting autopsy. He refused to let himself look away, refused to spare himself the hurt of seeing his friend that way. Because he knew Sanderson had endured an agony a thousand times worse when those bullets had drilled into his chest.

A horrified gasp had him pivoting around in his chair.

"That's your friend, Pete Sanderson, isn't it?" Claire asked from the doorway.

He closed his laptop, letting her draw her own conclusion.

She approached slowly as if she knew she was intruding but couldn't stop herself. "Has a suspect been identified yet?"

He avoided looking her in the eye. "Nope."

"This must be so frustrating for you."

He heard compassion in her voice and had the sudden urge to go to her, bury his face in her hair, breathe in her scent. She would be surprised, even astounded, but he was pretty sure she wouldn't deny him the comfort he craved.

He steeled himself against the impulse. *Numb is the only way to hold it together.*

"Investigations take time." A stock phrase used at the Bureau, but the words tasted like ashes in his mouth.

She came farther into the room, her hands shoved in her jean pockets. "You'd like to help with it, wouldn't you?"

"That's against the rules," he mocked.

"Because you and Pete were friends." She leaned a hip against the counter. "I understand the reasoning, but it doesn't seem fair, somehow."

"It *isn't* fair."

"But you'll abide by the rules, right?"

That was his cue to stop talking. If she guessed he had unauthorized access to the case files, she'd feel obligated to warn him of the consequences—disciplinary action courtesy of the review board.

His cell phone rang, a welcome interruption. He glanced at the caller ID display. "It's Gene."

She moved away. "We'll continue this conversation later."

Oh no, we won't.

He flipped open his phone. "What have you got, Gene?"

"A guy at U Lock It saw a white Trans Am being driven into one of his units a few weeks ago. Our agent showed him a photo of Forrester and confirmed that he's renting the unit. I should have a search warrant signed off soon."

Brent straightened as a fresh rush of adrenaline pumped through his system. "I want to be on-site when it's opened."

"You can take the warrant to the storage facility. Mickey Langdon is watching the unit."

Brent disconnected and pocketed his phone.

Sanderson's files would have to wait. Because no matter how badly he wanted to solve his friend's murder, his first priority was to locate Forrester and stop him from killing again.

THE U LOCK IT storage facility sprawled over a sizable stretch of industrial park just west of the city. Claire leaned forward in her seat, checking for the main entrance.

"Turn there," she said, pointing to the next driveway.

Brent spun the wheel to the right. "There's supposed to be an agent waiting for us."

A prefabricated office structure faced a long row of gray storage units with eight-foot-high blue garage doors. Brent flashed his headlights twice, then parked adjacent to unit 5.

A man with a crew cut and a bodybuilder physique materialized from the side of the building. He loped over to the car and pressed his credentials against the glass.

Brent lowered his window. "Good to meet you, Langdon."

"Likewise." The agent switched his gaze to the passenger seat. "Hey, Claire. You trade in your couch for fieldwork?"

She smiled at his teasing remark. Last November, Mickey Langdon had found it hard to get out of bed, much less tease anyone. He had come to her after his twin brother had died of lung cancer. The disease ran rampant in the Langdon clan, and Mickey was obsessed with the idea that his own death was imminent. After several sessions, she managed to convince him to go to his doctor, who ordered a complete medical workup and prescribed the patch to help him quit smoking. Mickey had called her afterward to say all tests had come back normal, and he was cigarette-free for the first time since high school. He took Zoloft for depression but was fully functional.

"Brent brought the search warrant," she said, shoving up the sleeves of her cardigan sweater.

"He brought more than that," Mickey replied. "He brought my favorite psychologist. Thanks to you, I'm back at work."

"Speaking of work—" Brent began.

"I'll talk to the manager." Mickey jogged toward the office building.

Brent turned to her. "You have a fan."

She smiled. "Not everybody at the Bureau tries to avoid me."

He hooked his thumbs over the steering wheel, his blue shirt rippling like water over his chest. "Oh, I believe that."

She detected an edge in his tone. "You think guys like Mickey want something other than counseling when they come to see me, don't you?"

His eyes narrowed. "I think some people can't resist dumping their problems onto others."

"But you're an island."

His smile sent an arrow of awareness straight through her. "You got that right, doc."

A door banged in the distance. A tall, lanky man crossed the pavement toward them.

Brent left the car, and Claire heard Mickey introduce him to Kevin Curtis.

Brent held out the search warrant. "We're authorized to search unit number five."

Curtis glanced at the document. "I've never seen one of these before, but it looks official."

"Mr. Curtis just told me that he saw a guy hanging around here early this morning," Mickey said.

"Forrester?" Brent asked.

Claire felt her stomach knot.

"I can't be sure," Curtis said. "He had his back to the office. When I came outside, he got in his car and took off like a bat out of hell."

"Did you notice the make and model of the vehicle he was driving?" Mickey asked.

"Nah, I was barely awake. It wasn't the Trans Am, that I do know."

Brent turned toward the unit. "We'd like to get started."

"How long is this going to take?" Curtis asked, retrieving a key from his pocket.

"Depends on what's in there."

"Well, if you think you might be a while, you need to move your car. I got three moving vans coming to unload this afternoon, and they can't do it with you parked there."

"Where to?" Brent asked, opening the driver's door of the Mustang.

Curtis pointed. "Down at the end should be okay."

Brent pulled around and reversed into the space Curtis had indicated.

"You might as well wait here," he told Claire. "I can keep an eye on both you and the exterior of the building while Langdon does the first sweep of the unit."

Brent headed out, and she caught herself admiring the quick, powerful movements of his legs. Damn, even the man's walk was sexy.

She glanced away, settled deeper into the Mustang's leather seat.

A moment later, a loud boom shook the car.

She bolted upright. A dark form lay prone on the asphalt twenty feet from the office.

Brent.

Flinging open the door, she raced toward him, sucking in a breath only when she saw him stir. He was on his feet by the time she got to his side, and he was—thank God—seemingly uninjured. Relief flooded through her so strongly, she nearly sank to her knees.

A gut-wrenching scream came from the storage units.

She turned her head, then gasped in horror. The blast had blown off Mickey's right hand. Blood sprayed from the severed limb onto the asphalt.

The manager of the facility lay sprawled a few feet away. There was no blood, but his leg was bent at an awkward angle, probably broken. He appeared to be unconscious.

"Claire!" Brent yelled.

She looked toward him mutely.

"Call nine-one-one." He tossed his cell phone to her.

She caught it and started punching in the numbers as he raced toward the men.

By the time she'd completed the call and joined him, Brent had cinched his belt around Mickey's forearm. "Easy, man. Help's on the way."

Claire stripped off her sweater and used it to staunch the gaping wound. Her stomach churned as the blood soaked through, turning the garment and her hands crimson. The metallic smell of blood flooded her nose, and it took a supreme act of will-power not to gag.

"Why?" the wounded agent panted.

"Good question," Brent said grimly, glancing toward the smoking hole in the unit.

"Search it…before the cops come."

"I'm not leaving you." Brent checked under the sweater, testing the belt to ensure it was choking off the blood flow.

Mickey shoved at him weakly with his remaining hand. "Claire…can stay."

She made shushing noises as she stroked his forehead. "I'm here, Mickey. Don't try to talk."

His head thrashed from side to side. "Go. Hurry."

She glanced at Brent, sick with worry. "I think you'd better go. He won't rest until you do."

Brent began to argue, but one look at his colleague's pleading eyes had him rising to his feet. "I'll be right back."

She watched, feeling strangely bereft as he set off for the damaged unit.

Mickey moaned in pain. "Always figured...I'd die from the big C."

"You're not going to die," she said fiercely. "You're a tough hombre."

"Hurts." He spoke through clenched teeth.

"You'll get something for the pain, just as soon as the ambulance arrives."

His torso jerked off the pavement suddenly.

She cradled him in her arms. "Lie still, Mickey. Please."

He didn't respond, and she realized it was because he was no longer conscious. Looking at his closed eyes, slack mouth and gray skin, she experienced a helplessness that she'd never known before. He was one of the few agents who had ever appreciated her assistance, and he was counting on her. She would *not* fail him.

"Where's the damn ambulance?" she yelled in frustration.

She turned her head, hoping to see Brent on his way back to them, but he was still inside the storage unit.

She stared intently at its jagged, blackened entrance, her anxiety escalating. Surely, she should be able to catch a glimpse of his pale T-shirt or hear him moving around in there.

What if another bomb had been hidden inside? What if Brent were attempting to disarm it?

Scared and covered in blood, she fought the urge to scream.

Chapter Eight

Brent hurried through the debris that littered Forrester's rented storage unit, knowing that he had only minutes to search.

When the cops arrived, they'd secure the crime scene, and no one would be permitted inside until the CSI guys had completed their painstaking evidence-gathering process. Then more time would be wasted while the Bureau and the local police department wrangled over jurisdiction.

The acrid smell of smoke and chemicals invaded his nostrils and burned his eyes. The Trans Am stood directly ahead of him, its trunk empty and cleaved in two by a blue metal projectile that had once been part of the storage unit door. The fender looked like crumpled aluminum foil. All the windows had shattered, dusting the vehicle with a layer of sparkling crystals.

He edged around the side of the car. The driver's door hung ajar from the force of the explosion.

Tugging on his driving gloves, he proceeded to

search the interior. The glove compartment contained a Trans Am owner's manual and a flashlight. He thumbed through the manual, then unscrewed the top section of the flashlight, removed the batteries and peered inside the empty cylinder.

Next, he flipped down both sun visors and checked the pockets on the driver and passenger doors. Using the flashlight, he went over the front seats and carpet, trying not to disturb the glass shards while he examined every damn inch. Then he moved to the backseat and repeated his search.

Nothing.

That left the interior of the roof. His fingers ran back and forth, feeling for any irregularity in the fabric. After several passes, he detected a raised section near the overhead light. He traced the shape with his fingers, then blasted the area with the flashlight. The fabric had been neatly sliced and something inserted. He coaxed the thin, ragged-edged item from its hiding place.

A key.

Too small for a vehicle or door lock, it seemed about the right size for a locker or trunk. He exited the car, trying to remember if he'd seen anything the key might fit at Forrester's house.

The flashlight lit up the back wall of the storage unit, revealing a multidrawer metal cabinet. He went over and tugged on the top drawer. When it wouldn't open, he tried the key, which quickly released the locking mechanism. The cabinet drawers held numerous automotive tools.

Why would Forrester bother to secure them separately when he had a locked storage unit?

After extracting all five drawers from the cabinet frame, Brent knelt down, reached inside and felt along the back and both sides. Then, remembering the car, he touched the top of the cabinet. His hand made contact with a half-inch ridge in the shape of a square. The flashlight showed a CD case taped to the underside.

As he removed the case, the ripping sound was followed by the muted wail of emergency sirens. He pocketed the CD and strode out of the storage unit.

"How's he doing?" he called out, crossing the parking lot.

"Not good," Claire said, strain evident in her face. "He passed out a few minutes ago, and his color's been getting worse ever since. Those sirens had better be his ambulance."

When she touched the side of Langdon's neck for his pulse, Brent saw her hands were shaking and blood-stained. "I'm sorry you had to deal with this."

She glanced up, squinting in the bright sunshine. "Did you find anything?"

"An unlabeled CD."

As the sound of the sirens grew louder, he added quickly, "My gut tells me it's important."

An ambulance swung onto the U Lock It property and drove up the laneway toward them, followed closely by a police cruiser.

"Let's hope your gut is right," she said.

THE PASSWORD protecting the unmarked CD was a clear sign to Brent that Forrester didn't want others accessing it. He made attempt after attempt to type the right combination of letters and numbers in the password box. He tried the man's birth date, his Social Security number and his employee number. Then his middle name, his mother's maiden name and all of the names listed in his address book. Within an hour, he was grinding his molars. The Bureau's tech guys had more practice unlocking protected files than he did, but it would take too long to go through official channels.

After another fifteen minutes, he was out of ideas— and caffeine.

Claire wandered into the kitchen as the coffee finished brewing. He poured two mugs and handed her one.

"Thanks." She lifted the cup to her lips and sipped. "I've never had this much free time. I feel restless."

"You could take the canoe out. Or go for a swim." An image popped into his head of Claire wearing a skimpy bikini, her curves covered by only scraps of material, her skin soft and bare—

He gulped down the hot coffee so fast his throat burned.

She strolled to the window, oblivious to the fantasy torturing him. "Anything creepy in the lake?"

He tried to settle himself down, but his voice came out hoarse. "Nothing but minnows near the shore. The last few days have been sunny so it should have warmed up a little."

She smiled. "Cold water doesn't bother me."

It didn't bother him, either. In fact, his body temperature could use lowering. But taking a dip in the lake with Claire wouldn't have the desired effect. It would only increase his desire for her.

"Do you want to join me?" she asked.

Of course he did. But until he cracked the password, he had no business doing—or thinking about—anything else.

He returned to the couch. "I'm still working on the CD from Forrester's car."

Her smile faded. "Of course."

He knew his words had reminded her of the incident at the storage unit, and he regretted that. Claire had made several calls to the hospital to check on Mickey's condition but hadn't been given much information.

He turned back to the computer on the coffee table. What should he try next? Forrester's driver's license number? He checked the info in the file Lisa had downloaded at the office, then entered the necessary keystrokes.

Access denied.

"How long have you been at that?" Claire asked.

"Too long," he muttered.

"What are you trying to do?"

Brent rubbed the back of his neck. "Figure out his password. Most people pick something easy to remember."

"I use my zip code," she admitted.

"If Forrester had, I'd have cracked the sucker in ten minutes."

He leaned back, rolling his shoulders to work out the kinks. "Why don't you take a stab at it?"

Her eyes widened. "Me?"

He'd spoken on impulse but now decided that getting her involved wasn't a bad idea. "Hey, you've spent more time with this guy than I have."

"That doesn't mean I can help."

"Well, I'm out of ideas. It's your turn to get frustrated."

She sat beside him. "Forrester's passion is classic cars. Have you tried the Trans Am's license plate number?"

"Puh-lease," he said, rolling his eyes.

"Sorry. What about the year of the car?"

"It's worth a shot." He typed in "1969," hit Enter and checked the screen.

Access denied.

He was beginning to hate those words.

"Forrester has a nickname for his car that he mentioned during one of our sessions. It's Beauty."

Brent typed in the six letters, just to humor her.

The empty password box disappeared, and the image of a Trans Am loaded onto the screen. He was in.

Beauty, indeed.

Claire peered over his shoulder. "Hey, it worked. Are you happy?"

He was *very* happy. And damn grateful she hadn't taken his suggestion and gone swimming. He leaned over and pressed his mouth against hers.

What started as a kiss of gratitude quickly became more. As soon as his lips made contact, he forgot everything but how much he wanted her. He kissed her again, not caring that there were reasons he shouldn't. He'd been holding back too long, stifling urges that were demanding to be acted on.

She sighed and kissed him back.

Last time, he'd misjudged her comfort zone by moving too fast. He wouldn't make that mistake again. It wasn't a damn race, it was an experience to be savored.

She was an experience to be savored. And he intended to show her he understood that.

He had to be doing something right because Claire kept up with him, kiss for kiss. Then she wrapped her arms around him. As her fingertips massaged his heated flesh through his shirt, he moaned in pleasure.

He was damn well going to make her moan, too.

He nibbled a trail of kisses along her jaw, then down her neck to her collarbone, marveling at the softness of her skin and her tantalizing fragrance. Near the swell of her breast, he slowed, not wanting to assume too much, but she threaded her fingers through his hair and urged him to move lower. Her breathing quickened in anticipation, and his heart-beat did the same.

She was beautiful, vibrant and passionate. And so very responsive to his caresses. Her nipples pebbled under her tank top, and she strained against his body so that he hardened until he ached.

His lips nuzzled her breast through the thin cotton. He slid a hand under her top and stroked her stomach.

It's wrong to be making out with Claire while Sanderson's killer is on the loose.

He sucked in a breath and pressed his hot face against her neck. Although he desperately wanted to keep touching Claire, the voice inside his head couldn't be ignored. He had more important priorities than to satisfy his desires.

Before he could change his mind, he moved away.

Claire swayed in her seat, her mouth swollen from his kisses, her skin flushed with excitement.

"Thanks for cracking the code," he said, keenly aware that his words sounded brusque and impersonal. "I have to get back to work now."

She looked away, but not before he saw the hurt and confusion in her eyes.

Disgust lodged in his stomach. He shouldn't have touched her, shouldn't have allowed himself to forget— even for a moment—that his energies had to be directed elsewhere. She might not appreciate it now, but he'd done her a favor by stopping. He couldn't give her the attention she deserved—even in the short term—and he'd never been a long-term kind of guy.

From this point on, he had to focus solely on catching Forrester and identifying Sanderson's killer.

CLAIRE GRIPPED the sides of her chair, struggling for composure. The last time she'd felt like this, she'd been riding a friend's horse when it had spooked and thrown her to the ground. Then as now, having the breath knocked out of her wasn't the worst part. It was the sense of complete disorientation.

Why had Brent withdrawn from her just when things were getting interesting? To pay her back for shying away from intimacy before? Or had he decided making love to her would be a mistake? Both possibilities upset her. She'd finally accepted their relationship for what it was: an exciting, sexually-charged connection. That fell short of all that she wanted, but maybe it would grow into more if she took a chance.

Apparently, he wasn't going to give them that chance.

Outside, the sun was setting, painting the lake and beach a glittering gold. Despite the turmoil in her life, she couldn't remember a more peaceful setting. No wonder Brent and Pete had enjoyed coming here. Maybe if her father had had such a place to unwind, things would have turned out differently.

The old ache rose up, but she ruthlessly pushed it back down. The past was done, and no amount of speculation could change it.

Even though a relationship between her and Brent was a no-starter, she was worried about him. He had so much on his mind that he could delay coming to terms with his loss. But eventually there would be a lull, and then the pain and grief would strike him like a tidal wave. She hoped, when the time came, he had somebody to call on for support.

Too bad he wouldn't allow that *somebody* to be her.

UNABLE TO SLEEP, Brent lay in the darkness, his mind jumping from one thought to another. The discovery of Forrester's password had allowed him to open the CD's files, but then he'd hit a wall. The contents were strings of letters and numbers whose meaning eluded him.

What he wished would elude him was his awareness of Claire. It didn't matter how often he told himself to ignore her, he simply could not shut her out. Every move she made, every look she sent his way, fed his attraction to her.

He wanted to taste her and touch her again—not just her lips, but every inch of her. It was an urge he'd been feeling since they'd met, an urge that was harder to resist with every minute they spent together. Today, she had responded with heat and passion…until he'd shoved her away.

That seemed like such a stupid, hurtful move now.

He didn't want her spending the night alone next door. He didn't want a wall separating them. He wanted them to be in the same room, in the same bed, where he'd soon take away her hurt and make her feel like the most desirable woman in the world.

Stop it.

He'd lost sight of his assignment. He was supposed to protect her, not lust after her. Besides, she wouldn't be content with a fling, and he couldn't offer her anything more.

His stomach grumbled, and he decided a quick trip to the fridge might help him sleep. He padded barefoot through the hall but stopped when he reached the living room. Moonlight streamed through the window, showcasing a blanketed form huddled in a chair. Evidently, Claire couldn't sleep, either.

He debated beating a retreat, but that was a coward's way. He had to face her and tell her she hadn't done anything wrong earlier. He just wasn't the right man for her.

As he advanced into the room, only the soft curls of her hair and pale oval of her face were visible above the blanket.

"How long have you been awake?" he asked.

"An hour," she admitted. "I can't stop thinking about Mickey. One minute, he was standing there, perfectly fine. The next…" She pressed her fingers to her mouth. "I wish they'd let me ride in the ambulance with him."

"He wouldn't have known you were there," Brent pointed out. "And once he reached the hospital, the doctors would've sent you away while they worked on him."

"I know you're right." She let out a weary sigh. "I just wish I knew how he's doing. The hospital won't tell me much."

"Gene called after you went to bed," Brent said. "Langdon's scheduled for surgery the day after tomorrow."

"Why?"

"He has to have a few inches of bone removed so the skin can cover the stump."

She shivered, and drew the blanket more tightly around her. "Poor Mickey."

"His doctor said the prognosis is good. There's no sign of infection, and he should be out of surgery in a few hours."

"Thanks for telling me," she said, her lips curving softly.

Maybe this was his chance to make amends. "Do you want to go to the hospital tomorrow? You could visit with him, maybe meet his fiancée. Gene said she wants to thank you in person for calling the ambulance and staying with him until it arrived."

Her eyes glowed in the moonlight. "Thanks, I'd like that."

Her gratitude sent a rush of warmth through him. Actually, her company often had that effect on him—and not only when he was kissing her.

The thought brought him up short. The late hour was probably to blame, but even so he shouldn't be thinking along those lines. It didn't matter what he felt when he was around Claire. It only mattered that he kept her safe until Forrester was in custody.

"We'll go after breakfast," he said.

Before Claire could respond, the ring of his cell phone intruded.

He glanced at the illuminated display, frowning when it showed Gene's home number. He flipped it open. "What's up?"

"It's Langdon," Gene said. "There was a blood clot."

He swore softly. A blood clot could mean a dozen different things—none of them good. "How is he?"

"He died an hour ago."

Chapter Nine

The next morning Brent was up early, having spent the night tossing and turning. Langdon had died because Forrester hadn't wanted anybody to discover the CD. What made the damn thing worth killing for?

He opened the first file and stared at the contents. The letters and numbers had to be a code. But how could he decipher it without knowing the key?

His cell phone rang. It was Ian Alston, the agent who had given him the flash drive. "You were right to question that ballistics report. The two slugs that were tested weren't the ones that came out of Sanderson."

"How the hell could that happen?"

"Somebody at the lab screwed up."

"So the team has spent weeks searching for the wrong caliber gun?"

"Afraid so."

He swore. "Let me know when the new results are available."

"You got it."

"Has anybody figured out who No Neck is?" The nickname had shown up on Sanderson's PDA.

"He was a homeless junkie," Ian said.

"Was?"

"The guy died last week. Massive organ failure."

Brent crossed out his "interview pending" notation.

"There's something else you should know," Ian said. "During the Eddie Hola investigation, Sanderson ran surveillance on a guy named David Cantrell. Sanderson caught Cantrell cheating on his wife on film."

"How is that relevant?"

"Cantrell received copies of Sanderson's photos in mid-April. Soon afterward, he withdrew seventy-five thousand dollars from his bank."

"What are you saying? That Sanderson was black-mailing him?" The idea was ludicrous.

"Lots of agents had access to the Hola files," Ian said in a conciliatory tone.

"Has anyone talked to Cantrell?"

"He's dead. Shot at close range. The money's missing. A team is coming from the Oklahoma office to investigate."

"Who's under suspicion?"

"I was given a gag order on the names, but I think you can guess one of them."

"Forrester." The agent who had paid eighty thousand cash for the Trans Am. The agent who had already killed a colleague and wounded another.

"I'll call if I hear anything else," Ian said, and disconnected.

Brent returned to staring at his laptop screen. Could the strings of gibberish relate to payoff amounts? Partway down his laptop screen, he saw one ending with 75.

Ian had said that Cantrell had been blackmailed for that amount.

Could this be the key he had been looking for?

He wrote "David Cantrell" on a sheet of paper, circling the two *D*s, two *A*s and two *L*s. Next he copied the letters from the string. NKFSNMKXD-BOVV. The presence of two *N*s, two *K*s and two *V*s confirmed his suspicion. Forrester had transcribed Cantrell's name by replacing the D with an N, the A with a K, and so on.

He spent the next ten minutes unscrambling the names in the files. Then he came to one that looked familiar. Jim Sharratt. How did he know that name? It took him an hour to locate the name buried in a report. Sharratt and Sanderson had met for an hour in late May.

Why would a name on Forrester's CD match with someone Sanderson had contacted shortly before his murder?

He phoned Ian. "I need you to run the name Jim Sharratt through our databases."

Ian checked the spelling, and Brent stayed on the line while the other man completed the search.

"Okay, here's what I found," Ian said. "Last year, the Bureau was tracking visitors to child-porn Web sites. Sharratt was on the list."

"What happened?"

"Only those suspected of direct involvement with minors were arrested. Sharratt wasn't one of them."

"Who were the investigators?"

There was a short pause and the sound of keystrokes. "Heydon, Mills and Forrester."

No surprise there. "What kind of background info do we have on Sharratt?"

"Born in 1934," Ian said. "U.S. citizen. Owned a dozen successful companies but retired a few years ago. He's worth megabucks and had a squeaky clean record prior to the Internet porn operation."

Internet Porn Operation.

IPO.

Brent exhaled in a rush as Forrester's cryptic remark finally made sense. "Thanks," he muttered, and hung up.

A rich old man like Sharratt could afford to pay to bury his indiscretions. Had Forrester accepted money to keep him from being charged? Then there was Sanderson's meeting with Sharratt. How had that come about? Had the Bloodhound uncovered new information about the case and questioned him? To stop further digging, Sharratt could have arranged for Sanderson to be killed.

Brent rolled his shoulders, trying to work out the aches in his tight muscles. Conjecture was only a starting point. What he needed was evidence.

As he was shutting down his laptop, Claire appeared. "Any progress?" she asked.

"Yes, but first I want to tell you that I made a bad decision yesterday. I should have gone with Langdon to open the unit."

She looked horrified. "Why?"

"I might have noticed the lock had been tampered with." Then he could have stopped Langdon, and the guy would still be alive.

"But if you'd missed it, the explosion could have killed you, too."

She had a point. And if he died, he couldn't protect her from Forrester.

"It just doesn't make sense to me," she said.

"What? Mickey's death?"

"No, the bomb."

"Looks cut-and-dried to me. Forrester didn't want anybody to find the CD."

"Then why not choose a different hiding place for it?" She moved to sit on the couch. "According to his neighbors, that car was Forrester's pride and joy. Why would he risk destroying it? Especially when he paid a small fortune for it?"

"Okay, maybe the CD wasn't his only concern," Brent said. "Maybe he couldn't tolerate others gaining access to his Trans Am. So he rigged the unit to explode if it was opened."

"That's a really extreme thing to do."

"Fits with his other actions. Arson. Murder—"

"We can't prove he did anything except escape from Ridsdale," she pointed out.

"He's the only logical suspect." Claire's reluctance to accept Forrester's guilt irked him—as did the agent's skill at covering his tracks. "This time he got sloppy. The bomb squad reported there was enough explosive material to blow up the whole storage facility and a chunk of the parking lot, but the bomb wasn't properly rigged."

"Does Forrester have explosives experience?"

"Yes, he took special training last year. But remember the manager said he saw someone take off when spotted. Maybe Forrester botched the job because he was rushed."

"Or maybe it wasn't Forrester. Maybe someone wanted to kill him and got Mickey instead."

"That theory is a tough sell without corroborating evidence."

She was silent for a long moment. "You said you'd made some progress."

"I've figured out what IPO means," he said, "and I have a suspect for Sanderson's murder."

CLAIRE LISTENED intently as Brent explained the files on the CD related to suspects in an FBI Internet porn operation.

"Forrester was part of the IPO team," Brent added, "so he could have manipulated evidence to keep certain individuals from being prosecuted. I'm convinced he did that—for a payoff, of course."

"But how does that relate to Sanderson's murder?"

"One of the suspects, Jim Sharratt, met with Sanderson a few days before his murder."

"I still don't see the connection."

"Sanderson must have sniffed out something and contacted Sharratt. Alarmed by what Sanderson knew or might figure out, Sharratt had him killed."

"By Forrester?" she asked.

"That's a definite possibility. Forrester wouldn't have wanted his payoffs to be exposed." He pulled out his cell phone and punched in numbers.

"Who are you calling?"

"Sharratt."

"Wouldn't your colleagues have talked to him already?"

"I know they have," he agreed. "But the agents who interviewed him didn't know about his tie to the Internet porn case or Forrester."

He paced in front of the window, then spoke into the phone.

She heard him arrange to meet with Sharratt the next day. And although she knew she should feel optimistic about this new development, Forrester's whereabouts were still unknown. That meant spending more days—and nights—with Brent.

She should be indifferent to his presence. He appeared to have no trouble shutting her out. Even if that changed, a relationship with him—no matter how exciting and thrilling—would ultimately lead to a dead end. Her awareness of these facts should act as armor, making her immune to his appeal.

And yet…

In spite of every argument her logical mind brought forward, she still wanted to be with him.

Explain that, doc.

JIM SHARRATT'S country estate included a sprawling stone house with elaborate gardens in the front and a swimming pool and tennis court around the back. Most people dreamed about retiring like this, Brent thought as he waited with Claire on the multitiered deck for their host to return with drinks. Still, most people would think twice about switching places with the guy if they knew he was an FBI suspect.

"I hope you don't mind cranberry juice," Sharratt said, as he emerged from the back of the house holding a tray. "I seem to be out of sodas."

"Cranberry juice is fine," Claire said, shading her eyes against the sun.

Sharratt set the drinks on a glass table, then lowered himself gingerly into a deck chair. "Ten years ago, I was strictly a Scotch man, but my doctor kept harping at me to take better care of my health. When I retired, I cut out booze, started eating right, and now I play tennis five times a week, although my knees have been giving me trouble lately." He gave Brent an apologetic look. "But you didn't come to hear me grumble about the hassles of getting older. You came to talk to me about Pete Sanderson."

Brent nodded. "You told the other agents that you met with him May twenty-seventh."

"That's right. We shared ideas for reducing costs at the Last Resort Food Bank."

"Did you discuss anything else?"

Sharratt frowned. "Like what?"

"Like sex videos?"

Two bright spots appeared high on Sharratt's cheeks. "What are you talking about?"

Brent leaned forward and stabbed the table with his finger. "Do the words 'Internet porn' clarify matters for you?"

"No, they do not." Sharratt's tone was indignant, his gnarled hands gripping the arms of his deck chair.

"What about bribes? The ones you paid to keep from being prosecuted?"

"Bribes?" he repeated. "I don't know where you're getting your information, but you are dead wrong."

"Speaking of dead," Brent said, "who did you hire to kill Sanderson?"

Distress showed clearly on the older man's face. "Stop right there. I considered Pete Sanderson my friend."

"Well, I'm thinking any friendship you had with him ended when he threatened to expose your cozy arrangement with Forrester."

"I don't know anybody named Forrester." Sharratt rose to his feet with difficulty. "Get the hell out of here."

"Not just yet," Brent said, remaining in his seat. "I have more questions for you."

"I don't care how many more questions you have. I'm not talking to you again without my attorney present." He shuffled toward the patio door, looking noticeably older than when he'd come outside.

"It doesn't matter how many high-priced sharks you hire," Brent said, pushing back from the table. "The truth will come out."

Sharratt stopped just inside the opening to the house. "You say that as if you know the truth," he stated quietly. "But your wild accusations prove that you don't."

Brent straightened to his full height. "Well, you're in my sights now. I'll be gunning for you."

He left one of his cards on the table, weighted down by an empty tumbler. "If you decide to cooperate, call me. Because I won't stop until you're held accountable for every one of your crimes."

BRENT'S CELL PHONE rang two hours later, as they drove along the expressway heading out of the city.

It was Sharratt requesting another meeting immediately. Surprised by the man's urgent tone, Brent agreed and turned the Mustang around. This time, Sharratt didn't offer them drinks or make small talk. He appeared subdued, shaken. "I've changed my mind about talking to you."

"I'm listening," Brent said.

"My wife died last year."

Brent didn't see how the man's loss was relevant, but he remained silent, waiting.

"I didn't know what to do with myself. So my son got me a computer, set me up with an e-mail address and access to the Internet. Within a few days, I was getting all this porn stuff in my e-mail box."

Obviously, his son hadn't installed a decent spam blocker. And for a man in his seventies, the concept of porn delivered to the home via personal computer was probably a strange—and titillating—experience.

"At first, I didn't even know what the subject lines meant, and I was shocked when I opened the first message. I immediately deleted it, of course, and so many others. But then…" His voice trailed off.

"But then what?"

Sharratt licked his lips. "I got curious."

Did the guy expect him to believe that he was only guilty of sneaking a few peeks? "So you checked out those smutty e-mails, right?"

"They came to me. I didn't go looking for this stuff." He glanced away. "At least, not at first."

Brent only raised his eyebrows.

Claire leaned forward, her expression sympathetic. "Then they invited you to check out some Web sites," she guessed.

He nodded. "And I did. Then I joined a chat room. I just wanted to look at some pictures, talk to some people."

"I doubt that would make you a suspect in an FBI investigation," Brent said.

Sharratt grimaced. "Well, I did a little more than that."

"Define 'more' for me."

"I ordered some movies."

"Kiddie porn," Brent said, unable to keep the disgust from his voice.

"I've never seen anything like it," the old man said. "Little girls being slapped around and forced to have sex." He shuddered.

"You understand that by ordering those movies, you encouraged the brutal exploitation of those children."

Sharratt flinched as if he'd been struck. When he spoke again, his voice wavered. "I swear, I didn't know. In fact, I was so horrified by what I saw that I threw the movies in the trash.

"I wish I'd never got involved. And that's what I told Pete."

"Let's back up," Brent suggested. "Did you know you were a suspect in an Internet porn operation?"

"Nobody ever questioned me about it."

If Sharratt's story was true, Forrester wouldn't have needed to manipulate or expunge evidence from his file. The Bureau had targeted dangerous predators, not porn viewers. "Tell me about your meeting with Sanderson. Who set it up?"

"I did."

"Why?"

The man's gaze shifted to the thick area rug in the center of the living room floor. "I was scared."

"Of what?"

Sharratt lifted his head, his eyes filled with anxiety. "The man who threatened to kill my granddaughter if I refused to pay."

CLAIRE DARTED A LOOK at Brent, whose only outward sign of surprise was a flicker of his eyes. He must be one heck of a good poker player. But then, she already knew what a challenge it was to read him. He had alternately intrigued and frustrated her.

"Who's blackmailing you?" Brent demanded.

"I don't know. I've never seen him. I just leave the money where I'm told. Last time it was a hundred grand."

Brent looked at Claire.

She wondered if he was remembering her insistence that Forrester would need a big financial payoff to risk prison. A single payment of a hundred thousand dollars would certainly fit her definition of *big*.

"At first, he only threatened to expose my secret," Sharratt said. "I just couldn't bear losing the respect of my children, my friends and the members of my church. After several sleepless nights, I sold off some investments and paid, hoping that would be the end of it."

"But it wasn't," Brent stated flatly.

Sharratt grimaced. "He phoned two weeks later, demanding more money. When I balked at paying, he threatened to murder my granddaughter. That's when I called Pete."

She saw a muscle in Brent's jaw clench before he asked, "Why Sanderson?"

"We've worked together on various charities over the years. And I figured as an FBI agent, he'd know how to handle a situation like this."

"What did he advise?"

"He urged me to report everything, but I told him I couldn't risk the consequences and I begged him to respect my decision. Eventually he gave up trying to change my mind and asked if I knew why the black-mailer had picked me to shake down."

"And did you?"

"No, but I certainly wondered about it. So the second time he called, I asked him straight out. He just laughed and said, 'Research is the key.' I still have no idea what he meant, but Pete seemed shocked."

Claire shivered. Anybody who had spent time with Forrester would recognize that expression as one of his favorites.

Sharratt spoke in a sad monotone. "Pete said he had a hunch he wanted to follow up. That was the last I heard from him."

Claire shot Brent a quick look, but nothing about him betrayed personal involvement. He had his feelings under complete control.

The old man passed a shaky hand over his face. "When the FBI contacted me, they said they were talking to everybody who had seen Pete recently. There was no mention of blackmail, so I figured no one knew what Pete and I had discussed. And I wasn't about to tell them."

Sharratt had no way of knowing his blackmailer was an FBI agent who would kill Sanderson rather than be forced to give up his "sweet deal."

"Did you pay the second time?" Brent asked.

"Yes, three weeks ago."

"Then what happened?"

"I heard nothing, and I hoped he'd forgotten about me. But he phoned today after you left, demanding another hundred thousand," Sharratt told them.

"When are you supposed to deliver the money?"

"He wanted it tomorrow, but I told him I couldn't liquidate my assets that fast, so he's given me three days to come up with the cash. He'll tell me the location later."

"How will you deliver it?" Brent said.

"He said to put the money in a black canvas bag. The bills are not to be sequentially numbered."

Forrester had made sure neither the money nor its container was unique enough to be identified at a later date.

Brent drummed his fingers on the arm of his chair, and Claire understood his frustration. Eventually, Forrester would be picked up. However, without Sharratt's positive ID of him or large amounts of unexplained cash, blackmail would be tough to prove. And the same was true of Sanderson's murder. To build a case against him, Brent needed evidence.

"If he contacts you again," Brent said, "call me immediately."

"You'll try to stop him?"

"I *will* stop him," he said, his jaw tight. "In the meantime, do whatever is necessary to get the money together. It's the bait we'll use to hook him."

Chapter Ten

Brent wasn't able to reach Gene until an hour after he and Claire had arrived back at the cabin. Sitting alone in the living room with the cell phone pressed against his ear, he decided it was time he was fully candid with his supervisor.

"There was a CD hidden in Forrester's vehicle," he told Gene when the other man finally came on the line. He quickly briefed him about decoding the information in the CD's files, matching a name to Sanderson's murder investigation and meeting with the blackmail victim.

When he was finished, Gene let out a low whistle. "As awful as this may sound, the Bloodhound's murder is finally beginning to make sense to me."

"Forrester must have figured out Pete knew about the blackmail scheme," Brent said. "He paid a snitch to set him up, and then he killed him."

Acid roiled in his stomach, and he shifted position, trying to ease the discomfort. Since the beginning, he'd been keeping Pete's loss at arms' length, telling himself he had to stay detached in order to solve the puzzle. But instead of feeling good that a crucial piece of the puzzle, motive, had slipped into place, he felt hollow, emptied out.

Gene cleared his throat. "Forrester's participation in the Bureau's Internet porn investigation means he had access to everything known about the suspects."

"That info helped him choose his targets."

"Nothing to stop him," Gene added.

"Until he picked the wrong one." The wrong one being Sharratt, longtime acquaintance of Pete Sanderson, who recognized Forrester's pet phrase.

"The blackmail drop is the best chance we have of apprehending Forrester," Gene said. "Let's meet tomorrow at nine to work on a plan."

"Sounds good."

"If the Bloodhound had lived a little longer," Gene added quietly, "he would have nailed Forrester's sorry hide to the wall."

"Damn right he would have."

"I'm sorry about Pete. I know I've said it before, but it always seems so damn inadequate."

Brent swallowed around the lump in his throat. Usually, he could come up with a glib response without breaking a sweat, but not right now.

After a lengthy pause, Gene continued, "I guess some things are just too big for words, huh?"

Brent cleared his throat and searched around for a way to lighten things up. "Don't let Claire catch you saying that. That woman believes talking can solve all the problems of the world."

"You should listen to her. She's a smart lady."

Smart enough to know he'd had a rough day and needed some space. She'd been quiet on the ride home, then made herself scarce as soon as they'd reached the cabin. He was lousy company tonight. And she was still upset about Mickey's death.

"When do you want to pick up today's reports?" Gene said, when Brent failed to respond to his comment about Claire.

Even though Brent needed to stay abreast of the team's efforts to locate Forrester, he couldn't face driving back into the city today. Not for the first time, he cursed the cabin's lack of Internet access.

As he tried to summon up the energy to get back in the car, an idea came to him. "How about faxing them to me at the marina near here?"

"The reports are confidential."

"I know the owner. I can be waiting at the fax machine when they come through."

There was a brief pause, then, "I'll have Lisa call when she's ready to send them."

It was a major concession, but Gene didn't give him a chance to thank him. "Read the reports, then get some rest. We've got a lot of work to do tomorrow."

As soon as the call ended, Brent felt his eyelids droop. At first, he was drifting, but then an image flashed in his mind. Sanderson, writhing in a pool of blood while Forrester stood over him, cold-bloodedly counting a wad of cash.

He jerked his eyes open, rubbed hands slick with sweat on the thighs of his jeans.

When Forrester was arrested, he was going to learn that money didn't buy cars in prison.

CLAIRE STUDIED BRENT'S blank face and slumped body. The professionalism he'd used as a shield seemed to have deserted him. He looked worn-out and depressed. She should leave before he noticed her. But over the past few days, her feelings for him had expanded beyond mere physical attraction to include something unexpected.

Friendship.

She must be a glutton for punishment to even consider talking to him. The last time she'd broached the subject of grief, he'd hit her with that "no trespassers allowed" stare of his and several biting comments. She turned to go, then hesitated as her mother's advice echoed in her head.

A true friend doesn't wait for an invitation to help. A true friend makes the offer and accepts the risk of being told to mind her own business.

With a sigh, she turned back.

"Are you hungry?" she asked.

It took Brent a full twenty seconds to switch his gaze from the lake to her. "No."

"Do you want a drink?"

He grimaced. "No more coffee."

"I wasn't thinking coffee. I was thinking beer or whiskey. If I hunt through the cupboards, will I find some left over from last year?"

"I doubt it."

"We should have stocked up before we left the city."

"Why? So I could get drunk?"

"You've had a rough day," she said, settling into the leather chair opposite him.

"I must be a sorry sight for you to be offering me that." His gaze slid from her face to her breasts and stayed there. "What else are you offering?"

Her breath caught as awareness shot through her. But despite his provocative words, she saw no lust in his eyes. Only despair.

"Not sex," she said quietly. "Friendship."

His gaze backtracked to her face. "Not a good idea to be my friend. Look what happened to Pete."

When she frowned, he waved a hand dismissively. "Forget I said that. I'm just being morbid."

"You can't hang tough all the time."

"Why not?" He shifted restlessly. "Hanging tough sure as hell feels better than hanging by a thread."

"Is that how you feel? Like you're just barely holding on?"

"I can't talk about this," he said in a low voice.

"Yes, you can," she said gently.

She was treading on sensitive ground so it wasn't surprising that he remained silent for a long time.

Finally, he looked at her, his eyes dark with anguish. "Pete died because Forrester's a greedy bastard."

"I know. I'm so sorry."

He shook his head in bewilderment. "I want a rewind button on life. But that's stupid. Pete's gone. End of story."

"It's perfectly natural to feel anger and frustration and grief."

His mouth tightened and his eyes flashed. "You think you know what I'm feeling?"

"Yes, I do."

"Why? Because you've read some psych textbook?"

She had a sense of déjà vu, of coming full circle to where they'd started, and the thought upset her more than she cared to admit. "I thought you were done with cheap shots against my profession."

"That wasn't a cheap shot," he said. "I'm trying to make a point."

"Which is?"

"You can't possibly *know* what I'm feeling because you've never experienced the violent death of someone close to you."

His bitter words stung like a slap in the face. "I understand more about tears and pain than you could ever imagine."

He crossed his arms over his chest, clearly unconvinced.

Should she tell him? She took a deep breath, then plunged ahead. "When I was eighteen, my father put his gun to his right temple and pulled the trigger. His note said it was the only way he could make the nightmares stop. Ten months earlier, he'd been involved in an investigation where innocent bystanders were killed, including a six-year-old girl. He couldn't stop thinking about her and second-guessing his actions. Had he reacted fast enough? Had there been a chance to save her that he'd missed?"

Brent's angry expression was long gone, but a dam had burst inside her and she couldn't stop. "The Bureau sent him to a counselor who was clueless about the complexity of the job, clueless about the kind of split-second decisions agents have to make and live with for the rest of their lives. My father went to a few appointments, then refused to go again. He blamed himself for that death. Six months later, he took his life."

Goose bumps rose on her arms at the memory. "You asked me why I changed my mind about becoming a vet. I did it because of my dad. I promised myself at his graveside that I'd learn enough so that one day I might be able to spare another agent's family the tragedy my mom and I had to endure."

"Claire—"

"Let me finish." She lifted her chin. "With the exception of Mickey, none of the agents I've treated has appreciated my concern and support. And tonight, you've shown me that you're also too closed-minded and cynical for me to help."

She swallowed. "It's hard for me to admit this, but I've been wasting my time. Not anymore. I'm leaving the Bureau."

For a moment, his poker face slipped, and shock took its place. But she didn't feel satisfaction, only sadness that it had taken her so long to see what should have been obvious all along.

She stood up. "Please don't mention my plans to Gene. He has enough on his mind."

"He'll want to know."

"I'll give him sufficient notice." She headed for the hallway, pausing only when she'd reached it. "The day Forrester is in custody, I'm starting a new life far from here."

WHEN BRENT AWOKE the next morning, he had a major hangover—without the enjoyment of having partied hard. Pete's death weighed heavily on him, and he was still reeling from Claire's revelations about her father and her future plans.

Claire had always seemed overly enthusiastic in her desire to help, but now that he knew her underlying motivation, he wished he hadn't given her such a rough time. His foul mood last night was no justification for the scathing remarks he'd made to her. But how could he have known she'd endured her own devastating loss?

It took a lot of courage to counsel others on grief and trauma, especially when doing so must dredge up painful memories of her own. However, Claire seemed to be someone who did what needed to be done, no matter how difficult. There were people who would say the same about him.

Much as he hated to admit it, he owed her an apology.

He took his time, washing, shaving and brushing his teeth. He didn't mind admitting that he was wrong so much as he hated *being* wrong. In a job like his, mistakes could cost lives.

When he could delay no longer, he left the washroom in search of Claire. Her bedroom door was open when he passed by, but she was nowhere in sight. He checked the main room first, then headed into the kitchen. Both places were empty. His heart rate picked up, but he could see his Mustang from the kitchen window so he knew she hadn't snagged his keys and taken off.

Before he could check outside, Claire came through

the front door, a turquoise beach towel wrapped like a sarong around her. Obviously, she'd been swimming, and her wet hair dripped onto her exposed left shoulder, leaving the bare skin glistening with moisture. He wondered what kind of bathing suit she was wearing—daring bikini? modest one-piece?—but the oversize towel was excellent camouflage.

Of course, he had no business thinking those thoughts after haranguing her last night.

"How was the water?" he asked.

"Refreshing," was her response.

Well, at least she was speaking to him. Although a one-word answer could hardly be construed as conversation. He decided to see if he could get a full sentence out of her. "Does that mean chilly?"

She gave him a rueful smile. "Yes, but I decided I needed the exercise even if my lips turned blue."

The word "lips" drew his gaze to her mouth like a magnet. Her smile faltered for a moment, and he realized he ran the risk of doing something utterly asinine—like kissing her—if he didn't focus on a different part of her anatomy quickly. He chose her left eyebrow.

"About last night…" He hesitated, unsure whether she'd accept what he had to say.

Her eyebrow rose toward her hairline as she waited for him to continue.

"I know you meant well, and I was being a jerk, but the thing is—"

"You're a very independent person who isn't used to confiding in anyone."

"Am I wrong to want some privacy?"

She took a moment to answer. "I believe it's a lonely way to live. However, that strategy appears to have worked for you."

Had it worked? Or was he just too hardheaded to try another way? Maybe he was ready for a change. The only problem was the person he felt most comfortable talking to was no longer alive. And Claire… Claire was the woman he wanted to share his bed with, not his problems.

She tugged at her towel, which had begun to slip. "I need to get dressed. I don't want to make you late for your meeting with Gene."

He'd assumed some serious groveling would be necessary to clear the air between them, but Claire apparently didn't believe in holding a grudge.

As she turned to go, he touched her arm. "I didn't get a chance to say it last night, but I'm sorry about your father."

"Thanks." She lowered her gaze. "I wanted you to understand why I can empathize about Pete's death, but I was wrong to hit you over the head the way I did."

He grimaced. "That's usually the fastest way to get my attention."

A smile tugged the corner of her mouth. "I'll keep it in mind."

He knew he should quit while he was ahead, but he needed to know something. "Are you really planning to leave the Bureau?"

She tucked a strand of hair behind her ear. "Yes, I've been offered a position in Minneapolis."

He thought she'd spoken rashly last night, but evidently the idea of resigning had been on her mind.

"I've been undecided," she added. "It took this situation to make me see things clearly."

Unfortunately, the situation she referred to was one involving him. Gene was going to string him up by his thumbs.

"Look, I know I've been...difficult. And last night, I was way out of line—"

"Don't worry. I'll make sure Gene knows my decision has nothing to do with you."

Was he so transparent?

Only to her.

He pushed the unsettling notion away. His concern about Gene's response had been a knee-jerk reaction. What really bothered him was the thought of Claire leaving town. He'd been telling himself that physical attraction was all he felt for her, but he knew now that was a lie. When Forrester was apprehended and the danger was over, he wanted to spend time with her. Watch movies. Go for walks. Make love with her. Show her with his hands and mouth and body the feelings he had so much trouble expressing in words. But none of that could happen if she moved to another state.

"With all the stress of the past few days, are you sure switching careers is the right decision?"

"I won't know if it's a mistake until I do it."

"By then, it may be too late to change things back the way they were."

"I have to take that chance." She captured his gaze, her expression more earnest than he'd ever seen it. "I need to know that my work has a positive impact on my patients' lives. That isn't happening at the Bureau."

He wanted to argue with her, but he didn't know enough about her experience with her FBI patients to be convincing.

Before he could think of anything to say, the ring of his cell phone intruded.

He expected the call to be from Gene, but it was Jim Sharratt.

"The blackmailer called to tell me the location," the older man said, anxiety evident in every word.

"His days of making demands are coming to an end," Brent reassured him.

As he gathered up his notes for the meeting with Gene, he felt the quick thrill of anticipation. Wherever Forrester arranged to pick up his blackmail money, the FBI would be waiting for him.

Chapter Eleven

The trap was set for four o'clock Thursday afternoon, less than two days away.

Claire watched from the sidelines as Gene and Brent worked feverishly to hammer out a plan to capture Forrester. Everything was complicated by the fact that they were after one of their own. They had to jettison their usual deployment and tactical procedures and come up with new ones, something Brent excelled at.

Forrester had instructed Sharratt to leave the money in the office of the Friedberg Book Manufacturing Company. A call to the company revealed the plant was shut down for the week. Gene wanted to tour the building on Wednesday, but Brent argued Forrester might be watching. They contacted the plant manager at home, who met with them to explain the layout of the building and give the locations of the equipment, shelving units, skids of paper and books in process—anything that might provide cover or a hiding place for the agents needed inside. Once the logistics were sorted out, they held a meeting to brief the dozen agents assigned to the operation.

Claire was to remain with Gene in the surveillance van parked at a neighboring factory. Brent would take cover by the Heidelberg six-color printing press and be the agent closest to the drop-off point.

A new ballistics report indicated that Sanderson had been killed by a weapon previously used in an armed kidnapping by a felon named Hank Totten. The gun had been locked up in evidence storage but was now missing. Forrester had been involved in the initial arrest, making him a likely suspect in the theft. However, the storage facility's records showed that the agent hadn't been on the premises for several months. Brent was convinced that Forrester had visited more recently, so he asked the supervisor to double-check and get back to him.

The only break in preparation came on Wednesday when the team and Claire attended Mickey's funeral. Agents from offices all over the country came to show their respect for Mickey's sacrifice. Claire noticed that even the most stoic among the attendees shed tears during the deeply moving eulogy, which Mickey's best friend gave. The image that stayed with her long after the service ended was of Mickey's fiancée and his mother clinging to each other.

Then it was back to the Bureau to review the plan again.

By late Wednesday night, the last few details of the operation had been finalized. There was nothing left to do but wait.

Claire kept telling herself that every contingency had been anticipated and dealt with, but her nerves were vibrating like a power line in a storm. After a week on the run, Forrester could be so strung out that he'd rather kill than go to prison. And as the agent nearest the blackmail money, Brent would be in the most danger.

"You're going to wear out the carpet," Brent said, glancing up from his laptop.

She stopped in midpace, flopped into a chair. "I wish it was over. Doesn't the waiting get to you?"

"Sometimes." He stretched his arms above his head, settled deeper into the cushions of the couch. "Pete and I used to trade sports trivia to keep from climbing the walls."

"Sports trivia, huh? I wish I knew some."

"I thought psychologists were trained in sophisticated relaxation techniques?"

His voice was slightly mocking, and she finally asked him what she'd wanted to know since they'd met. "What *is* your problem with psychologists?"

His eyes drilled into hers, but she held his stare and didn't look away.

"You really want to know?" he asked.

"Yes, I do."

"You remember asking why I waited so long to join the Bureau?"

She nodded.

He braced his hands on his muscled thighs. "The fact is I applied right after college. Aced every interview. Beat out hundreds of applicants to make it to the final round. Last hurdle was the psych testing…."

Her mouth went dry, but she managed to ask, "It didn't go well?"

"Dr. Telso made it clear that he wouldn't recommend hiring me at the Bureau. *Ever.*"

"Did he explain why?" she murmured.

"He said my temperament was incompatible with being an agent. The word *reckless* came up in the conversation."

That didn't fit with the Brent she knew. He weighed the risks before he took action—even in relationships. But maybe he'd been different back then. "If Dr. Telso was against your being hired, how did it happen?"

"A few years after we met, I was at a convenience store when two thugs armed with shotguns strutted up to the counter and started terrorizing the teenage clerk. If they'd only wanted the money in the till, I wouldn't have intervened. But one of them grabbed the girl by the hair and started dragging her toward the storage room."

Claire felt her stomach drop to her feet. "What happened?"

"I grabbed a can of peaches, nailed the bastard in the head, then tackled the other guy before he could get a shot off."

"That was very brave of you." And dangerous. What if he had missed with that can of fruit?

He shrugged. "Yeah, the local media called me a hero. When I mentioned my dream was to work for the FBI, pressure mounted until Telso caved, and I was allowed into the training program."

"I'm guessing you worked harder than the other recruits to prove you belonged there."

He grinned. "Yeah, I did."

"Are you still trying to prove something? Is that why you nearly went up in flames to rescue Forrester's briefcase?"

His grin disappeared. "You worry too much."

"I'm worried about tomorrow," she admitted.

He leaned forward, his gaze serious. "Tomorrow should run as smoothly as these things ever do."

"I don't like that qualifier," she said, stiffening.

"Complications happen, but the plan's solid. It'll turn out okay."

She knew he was trying to reassure her, but her imagination kept coming up with scenarios in which he was injured or—God forbid—killed. "Why not arrest Forrester as soon as he shows up?"

"And charge him with what? Trespassing?" Brent crossed his arms over his chest. "We don't have a single witness who can place him at the scene of the crimes he's committed this past week. We need to catch him red-handed with Sharratt's money."

"You think that will be enough to connect him to Sanderson's murder?"

"I think we can make the case that Sanderson could have identified Forrester as Sharratt's blackmailer by what he said to his victim so Forrester killed him to protect a lucrative stream of income. That's a motive the jury can understand and feel good about convicting on."

"How far are you willing to go to make that happen?"

A muscle twitched in his jaw. "Really far. I want to see Forrester in prison."

She couldn't stop herself from saying, "Please be careful."

He nodded, then gave her a sideways glance. "What will you do when we finally lock him up?"

That was easy. "Get on with my life."

"In Minneapolis?"

She tried to read his body language and tone of voice. Did it matter to him if she stayed or went? Would she let his opinion sway her one way or the other? She gave herself a mental shake. She'd already made her decision.

"Yes," she said, then, if only to clarify in her own mind, "in Minneapolis."

His expression gave nothing away, so she asked, "What are the chances that Forrester won't show?"

"He'll show," Brent said firmly. "He wouldn't have contacted Sharratt if he had any inkling we've discovered his blackmail scheme. And he hasn't used his credit cards since he escaped from Ridsdale so he's probably running out of cash."

Cash. The reason he'd murdered Pete Sanderson. The reason he'd threatened Sharratt. Forrester had to be stopped. And no amount of worrying on her part could keep Brent safe.

She had no choice but to trust in tomorrow's plan.

GRIPPING THE SIDES of the printing press's control panel, Brent stretched to restore circulation to his cramped legs. Sharratt had made the drop forty-five minutes ago. Outside, several mobile units were watching for Forrester. When he arrived, Gene would relay the news to the agents waiting inside the plant. In the meantime, Brent concentrated on keeping his muscles limber and his nerves steady.

His thoughts wandered to the previous night's conversation with Claire. He'd never talked to anyone, not even Pete, about his run-in with Telso. The rejection had ripped into him, made him feel weak and stupid and worthless—just like the vicious bullying he'd endured as a kid. He had tried to reason his feelings away, but they had hardened like cement. So he buried them, never anticipating he'd have to deal with a psychologist again.

Then Claire had come into his life.

She was nothing like Telso, but he'd turned his seething animosity for the man on her. She had stood up to him. She had tried to get to know him. She had made repeated attempts to help him.

After everything she'd done, how could he let her walk away?

Screw Minneapolis. She might claim to want a career change, but he knew her decision was motivated by insecurity. And that issue could be dealt with separately from their future. Could he convince her to stay? Maybe. Did he want her to stay? Definitely. But was it fair to ask her to turn down a job offer when he wasn't sure he wanted— or was even capable of—a long-term relationship?

Claire was the first woman to really interest him since his fiancée had left. He didn't want to miss out on something terrific with her, but he also didn't want to have his heart shredded again.

His earpiece suddenly resonated with Gene's low voice. "Suspect spotted on Elm, driving a light blue Camry sedan, and is headed for the target location. ETA five minutes."

Finally.

Brent murmured into his mouthpiece, confirming that his colleagues inside the plant were in position and ready for action.

The seconds ticked by.

"Everybody, listen up," Gene said. "Emotions are running high tonight, but if anybody's contemplating a lone-wolf takedown, he risks endangering himself and his fellow agents. This is a team operation, and nothing else will be tolerated."

Gene had directed his remarks to the entire group, but Brent suspected it was a personal warning. If the others hadn't been listening in, he would have told his boss not to worry. He had rehearsed this operation countless times in his mind and believed its success depended on all of them executing their assigned tasks. He had no intention of deviating from the plan to settle a personal score with Forrester.

He felt the tension in the room mount as Gene continued his running commentary.

"Suspect is approaching our location."

Half a minute later, *"Suspect is pulling into the parking lot."*

Then, finally, *"Suspect has left his vehicle."*

Brent withdrew his semiautomatic pistol from his holster and rested it against his jeans-clad thigh. Adrenaline raced through his veins. He forced his breathing to slow, his mind to focus. Soon he'd be face-to-face with the man who had murdered his mentor and best friend, Pete, as well as Harris and Langdon—both agents with promising futures—and who had almost killed Claire and himself.

Forrester's threat to Claire was going to end tonight. He gripped his weapon tightly and waited.

The door on the south end of the building opened, and a funnel of light pierced the darkness. Forrester took his time directing the beam of his flashlight in a wide arc around him. The light moved methodically to each section of the plant. When the beam hit the printing press, Brent's pulse leapt even though he knew he was well concealed and would cast no betraying shadow.

After a few minutes, Forrester seemed satisfied nothing was out of place and redirected the light to his destination: the office. Footsteps—quick and determined—echoed in the cavernous building.

Brent counted the steps until he heard the office door opening. The plan called for him to wait for Forrester to pick up the money and make it halfway back to the exit. At that point, Brent was to spring the trap. Forrester would be caught out in the open, unable to retreat into the office for cover or escape to the exterior.

Brent illuminated the face of his watch and monitored one minute ticking by and then another. What was Forrester doing? he fumed silently. Counting every damn bill?

Finally, the footsteps started again, more quickly this time. Now that Forrester had the money, he was obviously in a hurry to get the hell away.

At the count of twenty-five, Brent spoke into his mouthpiece, "Now."

Ian Alston, who was responsible for rigging the breaker panel, responded by hitting the lights.

Forrester was illuminated in midstride, flashlight in

his left hand and Sharratt's canvas bag slung over his shoulder. His right hand immediately went for the gun holstered on his hip.

Stepping in front of the trapped man, Brent aimed his SIG Sauer. "Stop right there, Forrester."

The guy let out a stream of expletives.

Five more agents, all with weapons drawn, fanned out around him.

Like a fish in a net, Brent thought with satisfaction. Forrester's capture was worth every second of planning and waiting.

"You getting this, Gene?" he asked. Alston had set up a camera with the feed going to the surveillance van so Gene and Claire could witness the events playing out inside the plant.

"Oh, yeah."

Brent directed his next words to Forrester. "You know the drill, but I'll say it for the record. This is the FBI, and you are ordered to raise your hands above your head."

Forrester didn't move.

"I said raise your hands, you sonovabitch," Brent said, advancing toward him. "Unless you want to add resisting arrest to the charges of extortion, murder, attempted murder and—"

"What the hell are you talking about?" Forrester interrupted. "All I did was break out of that damn psych hospital, which I should never have been sent to in the first place."

"I'm talking about what you've been doing since you left Ridsdale."

"I've been lying low."

"Arson and bomb-setting are hardly lying low."

"What am I supposed to have set on fire?"

"Your house."

"What?"

Brent hadn't expected a confession, but this I-don't-understand act infuriated him. Did Forrester really think he could con his fellow agents?

"I was there. When the office caught fire, I nearly went up in flames, and Dr. Lamont suffered serious burns to her hand." The memory of those burns—and the blisters they'd turned into a few days ago—made him even angrier.

"Whatever happened had nothing to do with me. I haven't been able to get home for a week."

"Then who knocked out McKenna and put the bullet in Harris's brain?" he challenged. "Who blew up your rental unit?"

Forrester faltered for a moment, then shot back defiantly, "I have no idea."

"Save it for the jury," Brent said. "Now set your gun down on the floor and kick it toward me. Agent Starr is going to remove any other weapons you're carrying."

Brent saw Forrester glance at the man assigned to search and disarm him, a man he'd worked closely with. Obviously, Starr was thinking the same thing because he said, "I remember when you came to see me and my wife when my baby girl was born. You said I should spend more time at home, raise my daughter right. Now you've left Harris's kids to grow up without their father."

"You can't believe that," Forrester protested.

"Believe you'd turn against one of your own?" Brent interjected, wishing he could continue the interrogation in a locked room with no witnesses. But there was too much at stake to risk the consequences of breaking the rules. "Why not? Harris wasn't even your first victim— Pete Sanderson was."

"I didn't murder him."

"I'm not buying this innocent act."

"You've got it all wrong…." His words trailed off as the exterior door opened.

Brent shot a quick glance in that direction to find Alec McKenna striding into the plant, his gun aimed squarely at Forrester. The agent's arrival was unexpected, as he had been assigned to one of the mobile units tracking Forrester's progress.

"I heard you were having some trouble, and I thought I might be able to help out," McKenna offered by way of explanation. Then, to Forrester he said, "There's no way out, Andy. It's over."

Forrester's gaze darted from McKenna to Brent to the other armed men surrounding him. Brent had seen the same expression of fear and panic in the eyes of other criminals he'd arrested. Fight or flight usually followed.

"Don't do anything stupid, Forrester."

Forrester shook his head. "There's so much you don't know."

A sense of unease skittered along Brent's nerve endings. "We'll talk about it later."

If Forrester heard him, he didn't give any indication. Instead, the man ran straight at him.

Shots rang out. Somebody shouted a warning.

Too late.

A bullet slammed into Brent's chest.

As he fell to the ground, there was only one thought in his mind: Getting shot wasn't part of the plan.

Chapter Twelve

Claire cried out as she watched Brent go down. Her gaze had been avidly fixed on the closed-circuit monitor in the van throughout the operation, and while she'd sensed the mounting tension in the factory, she hadn't been prepared for Forrester's decision to bolt or the terror that struck her heart when Brent was shot.

Everything had happened so fast. She wasn't even sure who had pulled the trigger or how many bullets had been fired in the warehouse. The only thing that mattered to her was that Brent had been hit.

Her stomach churned and bile burned her throat, but she couldn't tear her gaze away from the horrifying image on the monitor. Brent lay on the factory's concrete floor, possibly dying, and she was trapped in this van, too far away to do anything. She couldn't hold him in her arms or look into his eyes or tell him she loved him.

Her heart skipped a beat. Oh, no. No way could she have fallen in love with Brent. She knew better. At least the logical part of her did.

No, she wasn't in love with him. She was just shaken up by what she'd seen, and yes, worried about him. He'd saved her life twice. Now he could be dying, his blood—

Her heart skipped another beat as she squinted at the monitor. In the back of her mind she was sure she hadn't seen any blood, but the other agents were crowded around Brent, obscuring her view.

"Claire."

She felt a hand on her shoulder, making her start.

"Brent's going to be fine," Gene said, searching her eyes.

"How do you know? He's not moving."

"He's wearing a Kevlar vest under his jacket."

"What?" The words took a moment to penetrate her fear.

"It's standard gear in this kind of operation."

"But he went down so hard—"

"The force of the bullet."

Gene's gaze shifted away from hers, and his next words indicated he was listening to a report over his earpiece. "Ian says Brent's going to have a beauty of a bruise, that's all."

She didn't know whether to laugh or cry. "You're sure he's all right?"

Gene nodded. "I took a bullet that way about two years ago, and while it's not fun, it sure as hell beats the alternative."

"No kidding," she said wryly.

She glanced back at the monitor in time to see one of the other agents help Brent to his feet. He turned to look at something behind him.

At first, she saw only a pool of dark liquid. Blood, she realized, and felt her stomach churning again. It was apparent from the size of the pool that someone had taken a bullet somewhere the vest didn't protect. Either that, or someone had failed to wear one at all.

When Brent moved aside, she saw that it was Forrester who lay motionless on the concrete floor.

And she knew from his open, unseeing eyes that he would never threaten her—or anybody else—again.

BRENT HAD IMAGINED dozens of scenarios in which Forrester was captured, but he'd always expected the bastard to go to prison, not wind up dead. Not that he was sorry. Forrester was a cold-blooded murderer who had ended the lives of men better than himself. If he hadn't died, he would have retained a clever lawyer and challenged every piece of evidence against him. Now that wouldn't happen. Now there was no chance Forrester would get away with his crimes.

So why wasn't he satisfied with tonight's outcome?

He glanced at Claire, who was driving the Mustang, then back at the winding road. A recent rain had washed away most of the gravel, making the last few miles of the ride uncomfortably bumpy. The jarring motion aggravated the bruise on his chest, and he was glad there wasn't much farther to go.

It was almost midnight when he and Claire reached the cabin, but neither of them was in any mood to sleep. They settled themselves on the couch in the living room.

"Forrester was completely surrounded," Claire said suddenly. "Why would he think he could escape?"

Brent had been wondering the same thing. Because as much as he couldn't regret Forrester's death, he didn't fully understand the circumstances surrounding it. "Maybe he just flipped out. I've seen it go down that way before. A guy suddenly realizes it's the end of the line for him, and he can't cope."

She shivered. "And you got caught in the crossfire."

"It happens." That didn't mean he hadn't felt a moment of stark terror when the bullets started flying and he was hit.

"I didn't even see who fired," she admitted.

"McKenna and Metzger both did."

"Who hit you?"

"McKenna claimed it was him, but he could be covering for Metzger, who's only been with the Bureau for a short time. Their guns have been collected, and Ballistics will determine the owner of the bullet that hit me and the ones that killed Forrester."

During the mandatory investigation that followed the discharge of an agent's weapon, both McKenna and Metzger would be called upon to defend their decisions to use deadly force.

"If Forrester had given up his weapon when I first ordered him to," Brent said, "he'd still be alive tonight."

"He must have known it was dangerous to hang on to it."

"Maybe it's a case of 'suicide by cop.'"

"You think he wanted to die? Why?"

"I'm guessing he couldn't stand the thought of going to prison."

If he was right, Forrester had executed one last

selfish act before his death. Agents who killed in the line of duty often suffered from guilt. McKenna was a seasoned agent with years of experience, but Metzger wasn't. How would Metzger cope, especially if the investigation concluded that Forrester had meant no harm to anyone but himself?

Brent immediately thought of Claire. Her job was to support agents through such difficult times. That's what she'd been trying to do with him. Yet he'd rejected her every effort.

That was going to change, starting now.

"Tonight didn't turn out the way I expected at all," he said, "and not just because I was shot and Forrester died. I thought apprehending Pete's killer would make me feel triumphant or at least satisfied that he hadn't gotten away with murder."

"How do you feel?"

He scrubbed at an ink spot on his jeans. "Disappointed, cheated somehow." He glanced over at her. "Does that make sense?"

She nodded. "For the past week, you've been concentrating so hard on capturing Forrester that I think you may have lost sight of something."

At his quizzical look, she smiled sadly. "Punishing him won't bring back Pete."

He felt his throat burn. She was right. Vengeance wasn't as sweet as people said. The pain didn't magically disappear or even lessen. But talking relieved some of the pressure.

"The day I met Pete was the luckiest one of my life. Not just because he had my back when I was new and inexperienced, but because he came to be my best friend."

"It's wonderful you two had such a close relationship."

"Some days we'd shoot hoops at his house, whooping and hollering like lunatics. Other days we'd fish in the lake, enjoying the silence and solitude." He struggled for control for a long moment, before continuing in an unsteady voice. "He was more than my best friend. He was the father I never had."

"I'm so sorry, Brent." She shifted closer and lay a comforting hand on his shoulder.

"I'm not sure I can accept him being gone yet." He closed his eyes, rested his head on the back of the couch.

"There's no timetable for grief," she said. "You can't rush it, you just have to deal with it when you're ready."

Her words sounded wise, but right now he was content just listening to her voice. It reminded him of a summer breeze, soft and relaxing. He felt himself unwind for the first time since the beginning of the stakeout for Forrester.

"It took me six months to accept my dad was lost to me," she said unexpectedly. "I kept telling myself he was on assignment and would show up in the kitchen and ask me to bake tiger brownies for him."

Brent opened his eyes and waited, hoping she would continue.

After a moment, she did. "I couldn't deal with the way he'd died. And I was angry and upset about the note he left for me." She stopped, bit her lip.

Brent looped his arm over her and drew her against his side. "Tell me about it," he murmured.

"I've never told anyone," she admitted softly. "Not even my mom."

He remained silent, letting her decide.

She inhaled deeply, then expelled the breath in a sigh. "He wrote that every time he looked at me, he remembered that little girl—the one who had died during the airline hostage rescue. Her family had been deprived of seeing her grow up, attend college, get married. And although he loved me and wanted the best for me, it was impossible for him to watch me enjoy those experiences." Her lips trembled, but she kept on doggedly. "He took his life because he couldn't stop obsessing about somebody else's daughter."

Brent held her closer, incredulous that a father could be so lost in despair, he wouldn't realize the agony his suicide would inflict on his child.

"He needed help," she said, "and he didn't get it. I couldn't let the same thing happen to another agent, another family."

Brent brushed her hair back from her eyes. "He'd be proud of you, Claire."

"I like to think so."

"How could he not be?" he said quietly. "You're sensitive and caring. You try to help people. You've helped *me* despite my making it difficult for you."

If someone had told him ten days ago that he would be having this conversation with a woman—especially one who was a psychologist—he'd have scoffed. But a lot had happened in the interval, and the best part was Claire.

"Your patients are lucky to have your special insight."

She looked away and traced the edge of the couch with her fingertips. "You really think that I can make a difference?"

"I know it."

The tentative smile that curved her lips gave him hope that she might stay.

CLAIRE HUGGED her arms to her body.

Brent had finally let down his barriers. He had shared his grief and loneliness over Pete's death with her. And his openness had, in turn, made it possible for her to reveal things about her father's suicide that she'd never told anyone before. She felt purged, released, and closer to Brent than she'd ever imagined.

She didn't realize she was crying until he reached over and brushed a tear from her cheek. It was a gentle, fleeting touch. Yet somehow the brief contact charged the space between them. She met his gaze. His eyes reflected the same desire that she felt. For days, she'd been telling herself that physical intimacy with Brent would be a mistake because they weren't emotionally close. But their relationship had undergone a transformation. Honesty had forged a unique rapport, drawing them together, leading them relentlessly to this moment when the attraction between them needn't be denied any longer.

Having already shared pain, they deserved to share pleasure, too. And she couldn't imagine a pleasure more intense, more joyful, than making love with Brent. This time, there would be no denying impulses, no stopping in the midst of passion.

With hungry eagerness, she pressed her lips to his throat…his jaw…his mouth….

BRENT DREW AN UNSTEADY breath, confused—and aroused—by the blatant sexuality in Claire's kisses. He was hanging on to control by a rapidly fraying rope. "This isn't a good idea."

"Sure, it is." She ran her hands up his shirt front, immediately pulling away when he sucked in a sharp breath. "What's wrong?"

He'd wanted her hands on him for so long. Now that she apparently wanted the same thing, he was frustrated that her touch had made him flinch. "I'm just a little sore where the bullet hit," he told her.

"I was terrified when I saw you fall," she admitted, as she unfastened the buttons on his shirt.

Pushing the fabric aside, she gasped at the starburst of red and blue and purple that marked his skin. He wondered if she was repulsed by the sight of his bruise, but then she tipped her head and kissed his chest.

Her lips whispered gently over the tender skin, tracing the outline of the bruise.

"What—" He swallowed as her mouth cruised lightly over his nipple. "What are you doing?"

"Kissing it better." She glanced up at him, a smile teasing the corners of her mouth. "Is it working?"

"Yeah. I…think it is."

Her smile widened. "Good."

Her mouth moved against his skin, tracing his collarbone, skimming up his neck until her lips brushed against his.

"Nothing's changed since last time we kissed," he said thickly.

She pushed his shirt over his shoulders. "You don't really believe that, do you?"

No. No, he didn't. He had bared his soul to Claire tonight and had no regrets about it. His only regret was that she had plans to leave town.

But maybe those plans weren't definite. Maybe she was still mulling over her options. Why else would she be willing to make love with him? She wasn't a one-night-stand kind of woman. Her actions suggested that she, too, wanted to give their relationship a chance.

Then again, coherent thought was next to impossible when she was touching him.

She smiled as if she understood. "One thing that's changed is my mind."

"Woman's prerogative?"

She tossed her blond head. "Don't look a gift horse in the mouth."

He studied her. "You are a gift. A beautiful, sexy gift—"

"—who's waiting to be unwrapped," she finished boldly.

His mouth turned dry as chalk. "Are you sure?"

It was his last attempt to resist her—although he could no longer remember why he had ever believed he should.

"I'm absolutely sure." She stroked her fingertips down his arm. "Unless your injury—"

"What injury?"

She gave him another dazzling smile, a wordless reassurance that she wanted him as much as he wanted her.

He kissed her, deep ravenous kisses that left them both panting for more. Their tongues collided. Their teeth nipped at each other. Their tastes mingled to become one.

Eventually, with her eyes encouraging him, he reached for the hem of her blouse. He eased it over her head, then undid her bra and freed her lovely breasts. Her nipples were just as sensitive as he remembered. They hardened immediately, stimulated by his admiring gaze. He bent his head so he could suckle her, his tongue swirling over one peak, then the other.

She gasped, her blond hair tickling his wrists. He pressed his lips under her left breast, where he could feel her heart beating fast. He wanted to drive her wild. Make her burn for him. As he burned for her.

He shifted position until she was lying on top of him. As he threaded his fingers through her luxurious, thick hair, he marveled at how beautiful, how desirable she was. How had he ever managed not to touch her?

The mating of their mouths made him hunger for a more intimate coupling, but he wasn't about to rush her. She would let him know when she was ready.

After a moment, she eased into a kneeling position astride him. Bracing her hands on his biceps, she moved her pelvis provocatively against him. He felt himself grow harder. He was tempted to crush her to him, but he resisted to savor every delicious sensation. He traced the features of her lovely, flushed face. She parted her lips and sighed his name. He caressed her neck, her shoulders, her beautiful breasts. She slipped her hand under the waistband of his jeans.

He caught his breath. Felt her touch him through the cotton of his BVDs. Anticipation was an exquisite torment—one he wasn't sure he could endure for very long. He breathed in the fragrance of her skin, her hair. She was an erotic dream come true. Her soft, sweet mouth made him ache. Her seeking hand drove him mad. He couldn't remember ever wanting a woman so desperately. When her fingers closed over him, he felt as if he were going to explode.

Gritting his teeth, he fought for control. No good. He'd yearned for her too long. With a groan, he pulled her to him and rolled until they lay on their sides.

"Hey," she said.

"Protection," he panted, reaching for his wallet.

She tugged down his zipper. "Looking out for me yet again," she murmured.

He kicked off his jeans and underwear, while she did the same, then he quickly covered himself with the condom. He rolled back on top of her, exhaling deeply as their legs tangled together. Damn, she felt good. So good. So right.

She urged him closer. Her mouth nibbled a wet path along his shoulder, her fingers gripped his back fiercely as she whispered passionate entreaties against his skin. "Please…I can't…wait…anymore."

"Look at me," he murmured.

She opened her eyes. They were dark with desire, clouded with passion.

"I want to see you," he said. "And I want to know you see me."

She smiled. "I want you inside me."

It was what he wanted, too, more than anything. He entered her slowly, prolonging the moment, heightening the pleasure for both of them. Then he began to move, responding to her excited breathing and caresses.

She twisted under him as he alternated shallow, controlled thrusts with deeper, wilder ones. She squeezed his buttocks and rubbed her breasts wantonly against his chest. Her uninhibited responses quickly shattered his rhythm—and his willpower. He didn't want this union to end, but the need for release became overwhelming.

She seemed to share his sense of urgency. "Now," she gasped, lifting her hips off the couch.

"Now," he breathed, plunging into her fully.

Her body went rigid. A heartbeat later, tremors convulsed her, and her inner muscles contracted around him. She expelled her breath in a deep, satisfied moan. The sound resonated inside him, and his control snapped. As his climax hit hard and fast, a shout escaped him. Then he collapsed on top of her.

"I wouldn't have guessed you were a screamer," she said a moment later, but her voice held no censure, just a purring contentment.

"I'm not," he mumbled.

"So what happened?" She rubbed her toes along his leg.

He cracked open one eye. "You."

"I'll take that as a compliment."

"It was intended as one."

She pressed her lips to his shoulder. He didn't want her to let him go. Not now. Not in an hour. Not anytime in the foreseeable future. His heart skipped a beat at the disconcerting thought. It wasn't his way to think long term. Life was too uncertain. Situations tended to be fluid, and he had learned to go with the flow.

But Claire wasn't comfortable with uncertainty. She liked to know what to expect next, liked to make plans. She had made a plan to leave the Bureau.

Tonight had proved their relationship deserved more time. Claire was the first woman he'd felt sexually *and* emotionally compatible with, and he wasn't about to be cheated out of her company because she was having second thoughts about her career.

Tomorrow, he'd convince her to make a new plan that included him.

Chapter Thirteen

Whistling under his breath, Brent dug through the kitchen cupboards for coffee supplies. This morning he didn't need caffeine to clear his foggy brain. Claire had done that with a few suggestive words and some bare skin. He definitely liked her way of waking up better.

He found the filters, and soon the smell of freshly brewed coffee filled the kitchen. As he poured the hot, dark liquid into two stoneware mugs, he heard footsteps. He glanced over his shoulder.

Claire wore black shorts and a bright red T-shirt. He let his gaze skim over her, from her bare toes, up the length of her shapely legs, to slim hips, a slender waist, perfect breasts and graceful shoulders. Her skin glowed, and her lips looked slightly swollen from his kisses. She made appreciative noises about the coffee, but he noticed her gaze slid away from his quickly.

Uh-oh. Regrets?

Her reaction stung more than he wanted to admit. Their lovemaking shouldn't be something she regretted. She had been the one to come on to him last night, not the other way around. And again this morning.

Turning to face her, he planted his butt against the counter and folded his arms across his chest. *What was her problem?*

She glanced at Forrester's CD on the kitchen table.

His anger vanished in sudden understanding.

With him next to her, she'd been able to forget what had brought them together. But left alone, she'd remembered the threat to her was gone, and Brent was no longer responsible to protect her. There was no reason for them to stay at the cabin any longer. No reason for them not to go their separate ways. No reason unless they wanted to be together.

Closing the distance between them, he pulled her into his arms.

AFTER A MOMENT'S hesitation, Claire relaxed against the solid wall of Brent's chest. Her worries had been for nothing. Brent showed no signs of wanting to cut and run.

She eased back from him. "How about I make pancakes to go with that coffee?"

He stroked her hair with his fingertips. "I wish I could stay, but a debriefing meeting is scheduled at ten."

"Call me when you're free." She remembered her mother saying the exact same words to her father more times than she could count. Of course, this situation was different. Brent didn't owe her an update on his activities—or anything else.

He frowned. "Before I go, there's something I want us to talk about."

An uncomfortable suspicion niggled at her. Was he concerned that she'd have unrealistic expectations about the two of them because of their lovemaking? *Did* she have unrealistic expectations?

"What is it?" she asked.

He hesitated, and her uneasiness grew.

"I don't want you to leave the Bureau," he finally said.

Definitely not what she'd been expecting.

He must have seen her confusion because he blew out a frustrated breath. "I think we're good together. I want to see more of you. But if you take that job in Minneapolis, this will be over before it really gets under way."

Happiness welled up inside her because he wanted to keep seeing her, but she held it in check. What kind of relationship did he have in mind? Casual? Or serious? It was too soon to know if they could be soul mates, but she didn't want to get in any deeper if his attitude toward commitment hadn't changed.

"You want us to date?" she asked cautiously.

He nodded.

Disappointment butted up against the blossoming hope. "Does our dating stand a chance of becoming anything more?"

He eyed her warily. "What do you mean?"

"You told me you didn't believe that people in your line of work should get married or have kids."

His whole body stiffened. "I know we've come a long way in a short time, but don't you think discussing marriage is kind of premature?"

"Of course it is."

He relaxed noticeably.

"You're asking me to turn down a terrific career opportunity, and I'm not willing to do that for a date or two."

"Claire—"

"What if I stay here and fall in love with you? What then?" She wasn't about to admit to him that it had already happened.

He shifted uncomfortably. "I don't think we can predict the future."

"I know that," she said, her voice rising in exasperation. "I'm not asking for guarantees. Just some reassurance that your heart isn't completely closed."

His eyebrows slammed together. "I'm surprised you didn't ask me this before we got naked last night."

Now she was the one who felt uncomfortable. "I don't regret making love, if that's what you mean. Being with you was an incredible, unforgettable experience." She smiled even though part of her felt like crying. "But I want to know if there are limits on our relationship. Is that so unreasonable?"

He shook his head. "You deserve to have what you want."

Could he be the man to give it to her? She didn't dare ask him. Instead, she said, "What do *you* want?"

He hesitated. "I thought I knew, but now…I'm not sure."

He could have told her what she wanted to hear, but he was too honest to take the easy way out. It was one of the things she admired about him, but the hurt made it difficult to continue the conversation.

"You're going to be late," she murmured.

"Do you want to come with me?"

She shook her head. At this point, they could use the time apart to sort through their feelings.

"I'll be back as soon as I can," he said.

"I'll be here."

He started toward her, as if he intended to kiss her good-bye, but she turned away. As much as she'd enjoyed his embrace earlier, she was feeling too raw and vulnerable to let him touch her now.

"This isn't finished," he said from the doorway.

He was right. Nothing had been resolved. Even so, she felt a sense of relief that their conversation would be postponed until later. Hopefully, she'd know what to do then.

AN HOUR LATER, Claire stood gazing out at the lake. The sun had disappeared behind the clouds, but its absence didn't detract from the beauty of the place or the peace she had come to know here. She was going to miss this view. But much more than that, she was going to miss Brent.

She'd reached a conclusion, one that was hard to accept, yet ultimately realistic. Despite everything that had happened between them, they weren't destined to be a couple. No amount of discussion was going to alter his attitude toward commitment. If he promised her anything more now, it would only be because she'd pressured him into it. Her heart would end up broken when he realized a long-term relationship wasn't what he truly wanted.

Having made a decision about Brent, she now needed to do the same about her career. If she remained at the Bureau, Brent's presence would be a constant reminder of what she wanted but couldn't have. Only a masochist would subject herself to that kind of pain, especially when there was a ready alternative. She would take the job at Balanced Life Consulting Group and move to Minneapolis. Once there, she'd be so busy adjusting to her new environment, she'd have little time to brood about Brent.

She was tempted to call Marcy Dearborne, CEO of the company, knowing if she made that commitment, she wouldn't back out of it. But she felt she owed Gene the courtesy of quitting her job with him before accepting another.

She punched in his number, then chewed on her fingernail as she waited for the call to connect.

When Gene came on the line, she cleared her throat. "It's Claire. Do you have a minute?"

"Yeah, I'm between meetings."

She knew this wasn't the ideal time to break her news, but she wanted it over with. "I've decided to resign from my position at the Bureau."

"What the hell are you talking about?"

She cringed at the harshness of his tone. "I've given it a lot of thought, and I don't think the Bureau's the right place for me anymore."

"Why not?" Gene demanded.

Because Brent works there. She couldn't say that, and it wasn't the whole story, anyway. She'd been dissatisfied for months. "I don't feel that I'm helping anybody."

"You know these guys, Claire. They don't wear their hearts on their sleeves, but they still have problems. You're great at getting people to open up to you."

"Maybe in the past," she conceded. "But right now, I'm burned out."

There was a pause at the other end of the line. "This is Brent's doing, isn't it?"

"I was thinking about quitting before I ever met Brent."

"Why don't you come in tomorrow so we can talk—"

"There's no point," she interrupted. "I've made up my mind."

Silence stretched between them.

When Gene finally spoke, the bewilderment in his voice was nearly palpable. "Are you sure you're leaving for the right reason?"

She should be able to answer his question without hesitation, but the words wouldn't come. Her thoughts about Brent and the Bureau had become hopelessly intertwined, and she couldn't seem to separate one from the other. Would she look back one day and realize she'd left a job she was uniquely qualified to do simply because of a failed romance? Or was she only second-guessing what she knew in her heart to be the right decision because of her feelings for Brent?

"I…I have to go now," she said, her voice hoarse with suppressed emotion. "I'll call you later to finalize the details."

Intending to be on her way soon, she packed her carry case and set it by the front door. It was hard to believe only a week had passed since she'd caught her first glimpse of the cabin. In that short time, she'd grown surprisingly attached to the place, but it was an attachment she knew she had to let go of. Just as she knew she had to let go of Brent.

It wasn't easy. She still felt a lingering hope that somehow she and Brent could resolve their differences and become a couple who laughed and loved and shared life together. But she knew better. She would never marry Brent. She would never raise a family with him. Part of her rebelled against such defeatist thinking. Other people managed to turn their dreams into reality. Why couldn't she?

Brent had the capacity to love deeply. His feelings for Pete proved that. Was she naive to think he would one day fall as irrevocably in love with her as she had with him? What if he never realized their relationship was worth committing to? She'd have squandered a great job opportunity. At least her new job wouldn't require patient assessments, so she couldn't mess up as she had with Forrester. Misreading him was the biggest mistake she'd ever made. For her own peace of mind, she needed to figure out where she'd gone wrong. Only then would she be able to move on.

She thought back to her sessions with him, and to last night at the manufacturing plant when she'd watched him on the monitor. What was she missing? Why did she believe him guilty of blackmail, but not the other crimes? Was it professional pride obscuring her perception? A reluctance to accept that Brent had been right and she had been wrong?

No. It was Forrester's shocked expression when accused of attempted murder, arson and bomb-setting. But his denials had been cut short by McKenna's arrival on the scene. She remembered Gene cursing beside her in the van. Despite specific orders to his team, one member had flown solo. After that, chaos had reigned.

She'd been terrified for Brent at the time, but now she was able to consider the events objectively.

Why *had* the plan gone to hell? Because Forrester had panicked.

What had set him off? Brent believed he'd been over-whelmed by the prospect of prison, but there could be another explanation. Maybe Forrester had realized he'd been set up to take the fall for crimes committed since his escape from Ridsdale and that the person respon-sible wouldn't let him stay alive to defend himself.

Who had worked other operations with Forrester? Who had survived the attack at his house with only a bloodied scalp? Who had left his surveillance position to come to the plant, then taunted Forrester with the words, "It's over," before firing his weapon?

McKenna.

No wonder she'd experienced uneasiness when she had met him. Her subconscious had been warning her to beware.

She considered calling Gene again, but her suspi-cions concerning McKenna would likely be met with the same skepticism as her doubts about Forrester. For the FBI to launch an investigation into one of their own, she needed proof.

How could she possibly come up with that proof?

No physical evidence or eyewitness had been found for any of the crimes committed after Forrester's escape from Ridsdale—

The escape from Ridsdale.

McKenna couldn't have engineered that alone. Someone inside Ridsdale must have been involved. And her internal radar had already zeroed in on the staff member responsible.

She called the facility and requested that Maria Gomez pick up a personal call in the office on the second floor, away from her regular workstation.

A few minutes later, the nurse came on the line. "Hello?"

"My name is Dr. Lamont. I'm the psychologist who was with Brent Young, the FBI agent you spoke with a few days ago."

"How can I help you?" Maria asked coolly.

"First, I want to assure you that I'm calling on a disposable cell phone so there's no way anyone can listen in. Second, you should know that Andy Forrester is dead."

"What?" The coolness was gone from her voice.

"Your former patient, the one you helped to escape, was shot and killed last night."

"You heard me tell that agent I had nothing to do with him getting out." There was desperation and anxiety in her voice, confirming for Claire that her initial suspicions had been correct.

"I think you said that because you were scared. Scared of the man who pressured you into getting involved in the first place. You now have a chance to stop being scared and fight back."

The nurse took a moment to respond. "Why should I listen to you?"

"Because you can get this man locked up. All you

have to do is identify him for the FBI and tell them that
he threatened you."

"He did worse than that," Maria said, her voice trembling with emotion. "He threatened my children."

"Tell me about it," Claire murmured.

"The day after Forrester was admitted to the hospital,
a stranger stopped me in the parking lot. He knew a lot
about my kids—their ages, their babysitter's name and
address. Then he told me if I wanted to keep them safe,
I'd better think of a way to get Forrester out."

Claire closed her eyes, imagining the young mother's
terror.

"Those kids are my life," Maria whispered. "I couldn't
risk something happening to them that I had the power
to prevent."

"I understand," Claire assured her. She didn't know
of any parents who could withstand that kind of pressure.

The other woman let out a sigh. "When I heard how
many people Forrester had hurt since his escape, I had
second thoughts about what I'd done. But it was too late
by then, and I was still so afraid for my family."

"I don't believe Forrester was responsible for any
of that. I think he was framed by the same man who
threatened you."

"Do you know who that man is?"

Claire hesitated. If she revealed McKenna's name,
Maria's positive identification of him might later be
challenged in the courts. But the media had been all over
the plant within minutes of the shooting. If McKenna
was visible in their footage of the event and Maria
picked him out on her own, there wouldn't be a problem.

"Are you near a TV?" she asked the nurse.

"There's one across the hall in the lunchroom."

"Turn on a news channel. See if there's any coverage of Forrester's shooting."

A few minutes later, Maria Gomez returned. "He was there, the man who threatened my children. His name is Alec McKenna and he's an FBI agent." She sounded shocked by this realization, and even more terrified.

"FBI or not, he will pay for what he's done if you're willing to come forward and tell your story." A long silence followed her words.

"I'll do it," the nurse responded finally. "I want him locked up. That way, I'll know my children are safe."

Claire agreed wholeheartedly with her reasoning. "You need to talk to his supervisor, Gene Welland, at the Bureau. Call him immediately, tell him who you are and everything that you just told me."

THE DE-BRIEFING seemed to last forever. McKenna, Metzger, Alston and Howard recalled hearing a warning shout before the first shot was fired, Brent, Starr and Cobb remembered hearing it afterward, and the rest thought the two had happened simultaneously. Fortunately, the recording from the van was available to settle the matter. McKenna had shouted a warning a split second *after* he'd opened fire.

Brent was grateful when Gene called a short break to deal with an operational issue.

Twenty minutes later, they reconvened in the meeting room.

"We're missing someone," Gene said, looking around the table.

"McKenna," Metzger supplied.

Brent glanced through the open doorway in time to see McKenna being hailed by Lisa Conrad, Gene's administrative assistant. The agent made a quick detour to her desk, where she passed him a slip of paper.

Brent saw him look down at the note as he headed toward the meeting room. His steps faltered, and his mouth tightened into a thin line. Whatever he'd seen had obviously displeased him, but he made no mention of it when he rejoined the group.

"Okay, let's see if we can reach a consensus," Gene said.

When Brent glanced around the table, he noticed McKenna staring at him intently. Something in the other man's expression made the hair rise on the back of his neck. Then McKenna looked away, and Brent figured the man simply had a lot on his mind.

Several minutes later, McKenna clutched his stomach. "I think the pizza I ate last night was rotten. My gut's been killing me all morning."

Excusing himself, he headed for the door. "If I don't make it back, you know I went home to puke in my own toilet."

"More information than we really needed to know," Metzger said, rolling his eyes.

Brent doubted McKenna's exit had anything to do with food poisoning. More likely the agent was sick and tired of the whole debriefing process and wanted to skip out. As Gene launched into more discussion of the prior night's events, Brent wished he could escape, too.

Finally, Gene ended with, "I want reports from everybody on my desk tomorrow."

Tomorrow worked for him, Brent thought. He had things to do today—like picking up flowers for Claire and making dinner reservations for them at Gencarelli's, his favorite Italian restaurant. After a terrific meal and a few glasses of red wine, he'd explain that he'd never felt more optimistic about a relationship, and he couldn't see it ending anytime soon. Hopefully, Claire would see that as a positive sign and put the brakes on her moving plans.

Gene's next words nixed his plans. "I'd like you to hang back after the meeting's over, Brent. There's something we need to discuss."

ALEC MCKENNA strode angrily through the Bureau's parking lot.

He should be feeling good today. Forrester was dead, killed before he could implicate him in either the blackmail scheme or Sanderson's murder. Not his original plan, which had called for Forrester to be blown up when he visited his beloved Trans Am at the storage unit. Instead, Langdon had triggered the bomb and Young had found Forrester's backup copy of their blackmail files.

In hindsight, he should never have arranged Forrester's escape from Ridsdale. But he didn't know what Forrester might let slip if they used drugs on him. And he no longer trusted a partner whose conversations with the Bureau psychologist had led to his being locked up.

With Forrester at large, he became the prime suspect for the attacks on Claire Lamont and he would have been blamed if she had been killed. Now that he was dead, the psychologist would have been safe—if the nurse at Ridsdale had stayed scared and silent.

When he reached his car, he reread Maria Gomez's message that Lisa had asked him to deliver to Gene. "Claire Lamont recommended that I contact you about an urgent matter." The nurse probably thought that mentioning the name of the Bureau's psychologist would lend more credibility to her request.

His risk of exposure had never been greater.

Two women were to blame for that.

Neither of them would live to see another dawn.

Chapter Fourteen

"What did you want to talk to me about?" Brent asked, as he followed Gene into his office. Although he could hardly refuse his supervisor's request for a private meeting, he was anxious to get back to the cabin—and Claire.

"Close the door," Gene said.

"This sounds serious."

"Claire's given me her resignation."

Brent frowned as he lowered himself into a chair. Claire had said she was in no hurry to tell Gene she was quitting.

"When did you talk to her?" he asked.

"She called me this morning before you arrived."

Brent's mouth went dry. He'd thought he and Claire were in the negotiating phase. How could she have acted without talking to him?

Gene was watching him, so he added quietly, "Maybe she'll change her mind."

"I don't think so. When I spoke to her, she was adamant about leaving. I probably shouldn't be discussing this with you, but I've known Claire a long time, and this has come as a big shock to me. If you have any ideas about how to convince her to stay, I'd like to hear them."

He resisted the urge to squirm in his chair. "Did she say why she's quitting?"

"She said she didn't think her counseling was doing the men any good." Gene leaned his elbows on the table, made a steeple of his fingers and regarded Brent over them. "I'm not convinced that's the real reason."

"She's mentioned her doubts to me, too."

"Then she's wrong, plain and simple," Gene said. "Anybody who has ever dealt with her professionally has benefited a lot."

Brent wasn't surprised. How many times had he rebuffed her? And yet she'd continued to offer him her empathy and support.

"In fact," Gene continued, "that's one of the reasons I suggested you use your cabin as a safe house for her."

Brent felt as if he'd been sucker-punched. "You're saying you set me up?"

"In the best possible way," his boss assured him. "I knew you were tangled up about Pete's death but too stubborn to go for counseling. And Claire needed protection from Forrester. I figured that if I threw you alone together in a secluded place, you'd both get what you needed."

Brent didn't know about Claire, but he had certainly gotten more than he needed. Making love with her and waking up beside her had been two of the sweetest experiences of his adult life. He wanted to share intense conversations and comfortable silences with her. He wanted to come home to her at the end of the day.

The thought pulled him up short, but he had no time to dwell on it because Gene had started speaking again.

"I can't tell you how disappointed I am that she's leaving. She's been a valuable resource to the agents in this office."

"She doesn't believe that," Brent reminded him.

"She's wrong. Last year, our departmental budget was tight, and the finance guys really pushed hard for me to cut in-house counseling."

"They wanted you to fire Claire?" He couldn't help but feel indignant on her behalf.

"I was dead set against making the cut," Gene said, "but I knew I'd have to defend my position so I e-mailed every agent I'd sent her way. I asked them for their input, whether they'd found talking to her helpful or not. Their response was overwhelmingly positive."

"Did you keep those e-mails?" Brent asked.

"As a matter of fact, I did." Gene rummaged through the bottom drawer of his credenza, found what he was searching for and pulled out a thick envelope. "I had planned to show them to her at her next performance review, but it doesn't look like I'll get that chance."

"She needs to know she's made a difference."

"I agree." He passed the sealed envelope across the desk. "I don't know that this will change her mind about leaving, but I don't want Claire doubting the impact of the work she did here."

Brent nodded. "I'll be sure to give this to her."

"You can also tell her that I'm grateful—not just for what she did for those agents, but for what she did for me. Without Claire, it's unlikely I'd be celebrating my anniversary tomorrow."

Gene's admission was surprising because the supervisor rarely mentioned his personal life. Brent rose to his feet, anxious to take the file to Claire.

"I still think there's more to her decision to leave than job dissatisfaction," Gene said. "And if it has anything to do with her relationship with you, I want you to think long and hard about how to fix it."

Brent bristled instinctively at the accusatory tone. "You're assuming whatever's wrong is my fault."

"That's right, I am." Gene folded his arms over his chest. "Claire was terrified for you last night when the bullets started to fly. It's obvious to me that she's in love with you and has acted on her feelings. I'd like to think it's not only lust on your side."

"Gene—"

"I'll trust you not to screw this up."

"I'll do my damnedest not to."

He spoke with a confidence he didn't quite feel. Although he had ammunition to prove to Claire that she'd succeeded in her work, he wasn't sure that would be enough to convince her to stay. She needed a compelling personal reason. She needed him to say that he was open to the possibility of loving her.

For Claire, he could do that. He could let go of the past and embrace a future with her.

If he hadn't already lost her.

THE BREEZE PICKED UP off the lake, sending Claire's list of moving reminders flying. She scrambled to retrieve it, then retreated indoors where she wandered restlessly into the kitchen. She should be making phone calls, making arrangements, getting ready to move on with her life. A life she would continue in Minneapolis— without Brent.

"Hello, Dr. Lamont," a voice said behind her.

Her heart slammed against her rib cage as she whirled around to find Alec McKenna lounging casually in the kitchen doorway.

A single thought broke free from the chaotic jumble in her mind. "H-how did you find me?"

His lips curved, but the smile didn't reach his eyes. "It took some prompting, but Gene's admin assistant remembered faxing papers for Brent to Weir's Marina. When I showed up there asking for directions, the owner was more than willing to help me out." His gaze moved over her T-shirt, lingering on her breasts in a way that made her feel sick.

"Why are you here?"

"Just tying up some loose ends."

She swallowed. "I thought that's why you were meeting with Gene and the other agents today."

"These are non-FBI loose ends."

She didn't have to feign ignorance. "What are you talking about?"

"Maria Gomez's phone call to you."

How could he know that the nurse had phoned her? Even as the question formed in her mind, she realized the reason didn't matter. All that mattered was the fact that he did. "Forrester's nurse did call me today," she admitted. "She was upset by news reports of his death."

McKenna's eyes narrowed. "And that's all you two talked about?"

"She was the last one to see him the night he escaped. I did my best to calm her down, but she kept repeating that if he hadn't gotten out of Ridsdale, he'd be alive today."

"She called Gene, too," McKenna said, "and left a message with Lisa, which I was lucky enough to intercept. Now how do you suppose she knew his name?"

Was McKenna toying with her? "Maybe she lost my phone number, called the Bureau and got redirected to his line."

He shot her a disgusted look. "Her message said *you* had told her to call. Why would you do that?"

She grasped at a possible explanation. "I thought Gene should know that she was feeling some guilt about Forrester's death, and he might want to ask her more questions about that night."

"Don't lie to me, Claire."

She held his gaze without blinking.

"I think she saw my picture on the news and spilled her guts to you." He added slyly, "Of course, she regrets that decision now."

"What have you done to her?"

"Nothing…yet. Before I left the city, I called to remind her how easily her three-year-old could disappear if she opens her big mouth about me to anybody again."

Relief that the nurse hadn't been harmed was cut short by his next words.

"I'll deal with her…after I've finished with you."

A trickle of sweat ran between her breasts, and she racked her brain for a way to save herself and the young nurse. "Brent knows that you coerced Maria Gomez into helping Forrester escape. If something bad happens to her or me, he'll know you were responsible."

"Brent doesn't know anything and neither does Gene. I just came from a meeting with them—"

"I talked to Brent *after* the meeting."

He looked skeptical.

"When we spoke," she continued, "he was more than halfway here."

Suddenly, she found herself staring at a wicked-looking ten-inch blade. Backing away, she made a last-ditch attempt to convince him not to kill her. "If you leave right now, Brent won't be able to catch up to you."

"You think so?" His tone was rhetorical. "Well, it's time you and I left, anyway."

Did he intend to kidnap her? Or was that just wishful thinking because death was the alternative?

"Where are we going?"

"I rented a speedboat at the marina and docked it not far from here."

"Brent will come after us," she warned, "and he won't stop until he's arrested you."

He turned the knife in his hand, carefully studying the blade. "I'd like to see him try."

A moment ago, his tone had been casual, almost dispassionate. Now both his voice and body language conveyed an eagerness that terrified her. Desperately, she jerked her gaze away from the knife and scanned the kitchen, searching for something she could use to fight him off. In movies, there was always a butcher block of knives close at hand or a heavy cast-iron frying pan on top of the stove. But reality wasn't like that. Reality was a plastic spatula in the dish drainer.

She pressed her fingers against her temple, which had begun to throb.

He gestured toward the hall. "After you."

She walked past him, shoulders slumped, outwardly obedient. But as soon as she pushed open the front door, she leapt off the porch, hitting the ground so hard she bit the inside of her cheek. The taste of blood spurred her on. If she didn't get away, he would shed more of it with that lethal blade he carried.

Sandals slipping on the grass, she darted around the side of the cabin and raced for the trees.

A surprised shout rang out behind her, followed by pounding footsteps and ragged breathing. She pushed herself to run faster. The uneven ground made it risky to lengthen her stride. If she twisted an ankle, he'd be on her in a heartbeat. She had to make it deep into the woods where there might be a place to hide.

She could tell he was closing the distance between them. She dodged left, then scrambled over a fallen log, her lungs burning, her muscles screaming. The denser part of the woods wasn't far off now—

McKenna tackled her.

She sprawled onto the ground with him on top of her, unable to move, unable to breathe. The weight of his body—and her fear—threatened to suffocate her. He would kill her now. Plunge the knife into her and leave her body here, where it would be devoured by scavengers.

He surprised her by grabbing her arm and jerking her to her feet. "That wasn't a smart move." He spat out the words through his teeth, his breath coming in short gasps.

She struggled to catch her own breath, stumbled twice as she tried to regain her footing. She had lost this chance to escape. It wouldn't be so easy to find another. As he navigated back through the trees without difficulty, she realized he must have scouted out the area earlier.

He propelled her down the hill toward the water. Her footsteps slowed instinctively, until he laid the cold steel of his knife against her throat. She resisted the urge to shiver. "Where are we going?"

"We're taking a ride in the canoe I found in the boathouse."

When they reached it, he opened the door. But instead of going inside, he pushed her ahead of him toward the dock where the canoe was already waiting.

"Why did you leave the door open?"

"Just thought some crumbs would be helpful."

He was setting a scene. When Brent returned to the cabin and didn't find her inside, the open door would automatically lead him to the boathouse and the missing canoe. That's why McKenna hadn't used the knife on her. He wanted to make her death look like an accidental drowning.

She stiffened her spine—no way was she going down without a fight.

The blade fell away from her neck as he pointed to the canoe. "Step in," he ordered. "Sit in the front."

If she dove into the shallow water, McKenna would be on top of her in an instant. Better to wait for another opportunity. She gingerly set one foot, then the other on the wooden slats. The canoe bobbed in the water, giving her an idea. When they reached the middle of the lake, she'd hammer him with a paddle, then dive overboard and escape.

"Let's go," McKenna said.

She dipped the paddle into the water. With her heart pounding and her muscles quivering, it wasn't easy to move them away from the dock.

"Don't get any bright ideas about using that thing as a weapon," he warned. "I still have my knife, and I won't hesitate to kill you."

She didn't doubt him. He pointed to a rocky outcropping in the distance and instructed her to move in that direction.

She was safe as long as she was paddling, so she made a determined effort to delay reaching their destination. Since she hadn't been in a canoe in years, it took little pretense to be awkward with her paddle. Alternating the paddle from side to side, she barely kept the boat going in a straight line.

Fifteen minutes later, they hadn't made much progress.

"Pick up the pace," McKenna ordered.

She swung her paddle out of the water. In her peripheral vision, she saw a flash of wood—the other paddle.

Oh God. She was too slow, her paddle too heavy from the water—

"So long, Dr. Lamont," McKenna said.

A searing pain turned her world black.

Chapter Fifteen

On his way back to the cabin, Brent mentally rehearsed what he was going to say to Claire. He wanted her to understand that his aversion to commitment was a self-defense mechanism. Sylvia's betrayal had cut so deep, he'd relegated his heart to the deep freeze to protect it. Only Claire—with her warm and caring personality—had succeeded in melting away his defenses. Now he was ready to commit unconditionally to their relationship.

His cell phone rang, and he answered it immediately, hoping Claire was on the line.

"Erik Norman here. Sorry it took so long for me to get back to you. I double-checked, and Forrester hasn't been to evidence storage since February eleventh."

That was months before Sharratt had contacted Pete, months before Forrester had known his sweet deal was threatened. Why would the guy have risked stealing Totten's gun back then? It didn't make sense.

"Any chance he could've slipped in unnoticed?" Brent asked.

"It's a secure area. The only way for an agent to gain

admittance is to swipe his card, which automatically produces a computer record of his visit."

"Could the records have been tampered with?"

"The Bureau has spent a fortune on security software to prevent that from happening," Norman said.

But if Forrester hadn't been to evidence storage since February, how had he acquired that weapon? Maybe he really did have a partner—one who had known about Totten's gun.

"Who else was involved in taking down Hank Totten?" he asked.

The sound of rapid keyboarding was followed by, "Feltz and McKenna."

McKenna.

The agent who had survived the conflagration at Forrester's house with only a bump on the head. The same agent who had shown up unexpectedly at the factory, claimed to see Forrester threaten Brent and shot the man dead.

"See if there's a record of Alec McKenna visiting evidence storage in the past six weeks."

As he waited for Norman to run the query, Brent became even more convinced that McKenna had been Forrester's partner in crime. Which one of them was responsible for killing Sanderson and shooting through Claire's window? Had McKenna passed Totten's gun on to Forrester or had he used it himself?

"Bingo," Norman said. "McKenna was here on May thirtieth."

The day before Sanderson was shot. Too much of a coincidence.

He thanked Norman, disconnected, then called Gene and explained what he'd discovered.

"I'll bring McKenna in for questioning," Gene said grimly.

"Can you ask Lisa about a note she passed to McKenna? He bailed on the meeting soon afterward."

"I'll check into it," Gene promised.

Brent had driven another ten miles when Gene called back.

"Lisa says she gave McKenna a phone message for me. She remembers Claire had recommended a woman named Maria Gomez contact me. Why does that name sound familiar?"

"Maria Gomez was one of Forrester's nurses at Ridsdale."

"I wonder what she wants."

"As soon as I reach the cabin, I'll ask Claire."

"I had Lisa ring McKenna's place. He's not picking up."

The uneasiness in Brent's gut escalated. McKenna had claimed he was going home when he left the meeting—so where the hell was he?

"Keep trying," he said. "And call me when you get in touch with him."

He increased the Mustang's speed, a sense of urgency growing inside him. McKenna knew from Lisa's note that Claire had talked to Forrester's nurse. Could he have left the meeting early to try to find Claire? He wouldn't find her. The only people who knew he and Claire were staying at the cabin were Gene and Lisa. Could McKenna have tricked Lisa into revealing the cabin's location?

He swore as he hit the cabin's speed dial number on his cell. One ring. Two rings. Three. Four.

No answer.

He tried not to panic, but his palms were slick on the steering wheel and his heart hammered against his ribs. Maybe she'd gone for a swim. Maybe she was sitting outside or had the radio cranked up. Whatever she was doing, she'd likely return to the cabin soon because the weather was turning nasty.

Dark clouds had rolled in, blocking out the sun. Whenever it rained, the dirt road near the cabin became treacherous so he pressed the accelerator to the floor, determined to beat the storm.

The last section of the trip seemed to take an eternity. Finally, he turned off the winding lake road into his laneway. As he caught sight of the cabin, the tension in his shoulders eased. Shutting off the engine, he scooped up the red roses he'd bought for Claire and Gene's envelope of e-mails and headed for the cabin.

The front door stood ajar. He wanted to believe she was just airing out the place, but his instincts warned him otherwise. He vaulted onto the porch, then headed inside, calling her name as he went. The living area, kitchen, both bedrooms and bathroom were all empty. Was she down at the lake?

After leaving the cabin, he set off down the hill, telling himself to calm down. She was fine. He was just on edge because of McKenna. A minute later, the shoreline came into view. Both Adirondack chairs on the dock were empty. However, the open door of the boathouse suggested she'd been there. When he checked inside, he saw the canoe was missing.

He turned toward the lake and glimpsed something on the water's surface.

A canoe, holding a lone figure. Although the paddler's back was to the shore, he could tell it wasn't Claire.

Oh, God. What had happened to her? His mind reeled at the possibilities.

A cross-current wave rocked the canoe sideways, and he caught sight of an arm trailing over the side. Someone lay face down in the boat, and he suddenly realized where Claire was.

He also got his first look at the paddler's face.

It was Alec McKenna.

BRENT DUCKED inside the boathouse, a murderous rage swelling inside him. He shook it off. Only clear thinking would help him catch McKenna.

Beside him, a shelving unit was piled high with fishing tackle and assorted swim gear. He grabbed a mask and snorkel, then kicked off his shoes and jammed his feet into a pair of fins. On an impulse, he pocketed a sizable fishhook. Wading into the shallow water, he quickly cleared the open end of the boathouse and struck out in a fast crawl.

His stomach churned, and his heartbeat pounded in his ears. He had to reach Claire, had to find out why she lay so still. She couldn't be dead. That belief alone allowed him to stay sane. The canoe hadn't made much headway while he'd been in the boathouse, and he soon discovered why. The lake was choppy because of the approaching storm.

Stroke, breathe.

He tried not to think as he swam, but his mind wouldn't shut off. The thought of losing Claire was unbearable—like fire consuming his flesh, the pain so intense he couldn't endure it. He'd discovered so much in the short time they'd had together. He'd learned to laugh and love, and he did love her—he knew that without a doubt now. Just as he knew a future without her would be barren and joyless.

Stroke, breathe. Stroke, breathe.

After several minutes, he checked on his progress.

The gap between him and the canoe had closed to fifty feet. McKenna seemed oblivious to being followed, but he could look behind him at any moment.

Not wanting to lose the element of surprise, Brent shoved the snorkel into his mouth and submerged his body below the lake's surface. Then legs and arms pumping like pistons, he propelled himself forward.

When he raised his head, he saw massive rock outcroppings jutting out into the water. The canoe soon disappeared around one of the rocky bends.

He kicked his legs harder, ignoring his aching muscles. He didn't use the snorkel again since the threat of being spotted had ended, and he could make better speed swimming on the surface of the water.

A few minutes passed before he came to the bend. His legs—and brain—stalled at the sight of a sleek, expensive-looking speedboat tethered to a dock less than twenty feet ahead.

What was McKenna up to?

Paddling up to the dock, McKenna carefully stepped onto the wooden platform. Then he tipped the canoe and dumped Claire's limp body into the lake.

Dragging air into his lungs, Brent dove deep, arms and legs straining toward the lake bottom.

A blur of red appeared below him.

Claire had been wearing red today.

The vibrant color had contrasted boldly with her blond hair, and the fabric of the T-shirt had molded softly to her curves. He wished he'd told her how great she looked in that red T-shirt. Dammit, he wanted another chance to tell her. He thrust his hands in front of him but couldn't reach her. Panic bubbled up inside him. She was falling too fast. He couldn't catch her in time. She was going to drown.

No! He could still save her. They could still have the future he wanted for them.

He kicked his legs harder and extended his arms until they felt as if they were pulling free from their socket joints. Come on. Just a few more inches...

His fingertips brushed her shirt. A second later, he was able to latch on it and stop her descent. He felt her hands weakly gripping his forearms. His heart rejoiced that she had regained consciousness, but the relief was fleeting. She had to be perilously close to drowning and so was he. The surface of the water was far above them, and his muscles were flagging from exhaustion.

Lungs bursting from lack of oxygen, he gripped her and with the last of his strength kicked toward the surface. The long shadow of the dock appeared above them.

Three more kicks. Two. One.

Their heads cleared the water in the same instant the speedboat's twin engines roared to life. The noise drowned out Claire's choking and coughing as well as his noisy gasps for air. He hooked a leg around one of the dock's support posts and wrapped his arms around Claire. Although he wanted to savor the moment, he wasn't about to let McKenna get away.

When he eased back to look at her, Claire's lips were moving.

The engines stalled, allowing him to hear what she was trying to tell him.

"McKenna…wants to kill…Maria Gomez," she said.

"I'm going after him."

She bit her lip. "He has a knife."

The engines started up again with an eardrum-piercing clamor. He swam around to the dock's ladder, discarded his fins and quickly climbed it. The craft was drifting toward open water, drawn by the current. As soon as McKenna shifted the boat into gear, there'd be no hope of catching him.

The speedboat surged forward, and Brent launched himself off the dock. By some miracle, he cleared the engines and came crashing down in the aft section of the boat.

McKenna, kneeling on the driver's seat, jerked his head around at the commotion. His surprised expression changed to one of fury. He yanked the steering wheel hard to the right. Brent tumbled sideways, his right shoulder slamming into the storage compartments. A dark cloud of agony blurred his vision. He must have dislocated his shoulder. He felt light-headed, but if he passed out, McKenna would make sure he never woke up.

Gritting his teeth, Brent lurched upright. The boat swerved violently again. The sudden movement sent a fresh wave of pain surging through his injured shoulder. Even so, he kept his footing by grabbing hold of the railing with his left hand.

Ahead of him, McKenna was groping for something on the floor near the passenger seat. Brent let go of the railing and retrieved the fishhook from his pocket. McKenna gave a triumphant cry and began to straighten.

Squeezing between the rear seats, Brent slipped his good arm around McKenna's neck and pressed the point of the fishhook against the other man's jugular vein. "Drop the knife."

McKenna erupted with a stream of profanity.

His shoulder ached so much he didn't know how long he could stay conscious—especially with the boat jarring him mercilessly as it plowed through the waves.

He nicked McKenna's skin next to the vein hard enough to draw blood. "Lose the knife now or I'll kill you."

The knife clattered to the floor of the speedboat.

The pain in his shoulder pulsed like a strobe light. He had the upper hand, but the situation could reverse in a heartbeat. He gritted his teeth, willing himself to stay conscious. "Take us back to the dock."

He kept the fishhook poised at McKenna's neck as the other man took hold of the wheel, made an 180-degree turn and sped back the way they'd come. Neither he nor

McKenna spoke during the trip. He had no inclination to ask questions, partly because he felt so lousy and partly because he wouldn't trust any answers that McKenna gave him, anyway. But he wondered what thoughts pre-occupied the other agent. Did McKenna feel guilt or remorse over anything he'd done? Or did he just regret getting caught?

McKenna would be charged and tried for the crimes he'd committed. But no matter what prison term the agent served, it wouldn't bring back Pete.

The speedboat pulled alongside the dock where Claire stood with her arms clasped around her shivering body.

"Sorry to keep you waiting," Brent called out.

She smiled at him. "No problem. I knew you were busy."

As she climbed aboard, the speedboat bumped against the dock.

He bit back a curse. His shoulder felt as if it was on fire, and he was afraid he might black out at any moment. "Grab a mooring line…and tie him up."

She eyed McKenna warily but moved quickly to bind their captive's wrists and ankles.

Brent shoved the other man into the aft section. When he turned back to Claire, he saw her eyes glistening with moisture.

She'd held up amazingly well considering every-thing she'd been through. But now a combination of shock and relief had her body trembling and tears sliding down her cheeks. He lifted his good arm around her shoulders and hugged her to his side, trying to impart both comfort and warmth. His own body burned from the pain of his injury. Unable to stop himself, he slumped into the driver's seat, pulling her down beside him.

"What's wrong?" Claire asked, her eyes wide with worry.

He tried to reassure her with a smile, but all he could manage was a grimace. "My right shoulder is dislocated."

He closed his eyes, sucked in a shallow breath.

Claire touched his cheek. "Is there anything I can do?"

He forced his eyes open. "Think you can pop my shoulder back in for me?"

She blanched.

"I guess not." As an afterthought, he added, "Pete was squeamish, too, until he got the hang of it."

"I'm sorry he's not here for you," she said in a low voice.

They exchanged a look of silent understanding.

"Can you drive the boat?" Brent asked.

"If you give me some pointers."

"I can do that."

They should have switched seats, but Claire wouldn't let him move. Instead she reached across him to the steering wheel, insisting she had to be on her feet to see over the bow properly.

He was in no shape to argue. All his energy was focused on coping with the pain.

"Where to?" Claire prompted.

He checked the compass on the console, then looked out at the lake, trying to get his bearings.

He pointed eastward. "The closest marina is five miles that way."

She reached over his shoulder and turned the key in the ignition. Nothing happened. She frowned and tried again.

"You need to set the choke," he told her.

She followed his instructions to start the engine, then looked at him.

"The throttle's over here," he said.

"Oh, yeah."

It was obvious she'd never operated a motorboat before, but with some coaching, she maneuvered the craft away from the dock and set off.

"Watch out for the marina's blue flags," he said, closing his eyes because keeping them open made him dizzy.

He couldn't have done this alone. If Claire hadn't been here to tie up McKenna and drive the boat, this day would be ending very differently. He and Claire made a great team. If only he could convince her to stay with him.

He came to when Claire's soft voice announced Weir's marina was ahead. He ground his teeth against the pain and opened his eyes to see the floating docks that formed the marina's boundary less than two hundred feet ahead.

Claire cut back on the throttle, steered between the orange buoys that marked the entrance and sought out an empty mooring spot.

"Nice driving," he murmured.

She sank down onto the passenger seat. "How are you feeling now?"

"Like someone's holding a blowtorch to my shoulder."

"I'll get help," she said, rising quickly.

"Good idea, sweetheart. But first—" he gave her a lopsided grin "—kiss me."

She tenderly touched her lips to his.

He needed this woman in his life. Each and every day. Forever.

And as soon as he was sure he wouldn't pass out in midsentence, he would tell her so.

Chapter Sixteen

Claire spent the next couple of hours exhausted and worried.

Gene arrived at the marina with half a dozen other FBI agents to take McKenna into custody, and Brent was hustled away for medical treatment.

She took a seat in the corner and waited while Gene showed two agents where to search for the canoe using the marina's wall map of the lake. He sent the others to look for McKenna's vehicle. Then he turned his attention to her—he wanted to know everything her attacker had said and done from the time he'd arrived at the cabin, yet found it hard to focus on the details. She knew that McKenna would be charged with attempted murder because he'd tried to drown her, but she almost didn't care. All she cared about was Brent.

When they'd taken him away, his face had been gray, his eyes bleary with pain. She needed to see him again, to know that he'd been taken care of. Much more than that, she needed to tell him what was in her heart.

Gene's voice interrupted her thoughts. "Claire, I have

to talk with the divers. Can I get you anything before I go? A warm drink? Something to eat?"

She shook her head, drawing the blanket she'd been given tighter around her body. "When do you expect Brent to be here?"

"I'm sure he won't be too much longer," he assured her.

She closed her eyes, relieved to be left alone. The blanket slipped down. Even though she was shivering, she didn't bother to adjust it. Only Brent's arms around her could ease the chill inside her. She tried to think positive thoughts, to remind herself that it was only a dislocated shoulder, and obviously not the first one for him. But she wouldn't be able to relax until she saw for herself that he was okay.

And then what? she wondered. When Brent got back, what would happen next?

She sighed, knowing that the answers to those questions would have to wait until she saw him again.

Then she opened her eyes, and he was there.

Her heart overflowing with relief, she dropped the blanket and ran to his side. She didn't hug him because his right arm was in a sling. Brent still looked tired, but his eyes were no longer glazed with pain, and his lips curved in a smile that was only for her.

"I like you in red," he said, his gaze sliding down to her T-shirt. "And no, I don't have a head injury. I just promised myself I'd tell you that when I got the chance."

She smiled. "How's the shoulder?"

"Back in its proper place," he said. "How are you?"

"Better, now that you're here."

She wanted to reach out to him, to touch him, but the presence of his colleagues made her hesitate.

Just then, Gene strolled over. "When can I expect your written report?"

Brent glanced down at the sling with a grimace. "That's going to take a while, since I'll be typing with one hand."

Gene grinned. "You're lucky you'll be able to type at all. I doubt McKenna would have hesitated to kill you, too. And by the looks of the knife we confiscated, it would have been quick work."

Claire shivered, remembering the cold metal blade pressed against her throat.

Brent wrapped his good arm around her and hugged her close. "Claire's help was crucial to his capture. After I wrecked my shoulder, she was the one who tied up McKenna, drove the boat here and contacted you."

Claire was surprised—both by his words of praise and the gesture of public affection.

"I've always said she was an asset to the Bureau," Gene said.

The two men exchanged knowing smiles that made Claire wonder what she was missing.

Gene beckoned to a tall, lanky man, who had been pointed out to Claire earlier as the marina owner. "Mac Weir's offered to give you both a ride back to the cabin."

"It's the least I can do for the people who brought my boat back in one piece," the other man said gruffly.

Claire was glad to finally be leaving—and even happier that Brent was coming with her, not staying behind with the rest of the team from the Bureau.

Outside, rain was falling heavily, reducing visibility.
The marina owner dropped them at the cabin. She and
Brent thanked him for the ride and hurried through the
rain to the door. As she stood inside the entry, brushing
raindrops from her clothes, Claire caught sight of a
long, white box on the coffee table in the living room.

"You brought me flowers?" she said, her heart swelling with pleasure at his thoughtful gift.

"Seems like a lifetime ago." With his sling-wrapped
arm cupped in his good hand, Brent slowly lowered
himself onto the couch and stretched out his long legs.

Claire removed the lid to find a dozen long-stemmed
red roses nestled in silver tissue. She inhaled their fragrance, then brushed a fingertip over a single velvety
petal. She swallowed around the sudden lump in her
throat. "They're beautiful. Thank you."

"I brought you something else, too," he said. "Something even better than flowers."

"Better than flowers?"

He pointed to an envelope partially obscured by the
florist's box.

"What is it?" she asked, bemused.

"Something I think you'll find very enlightening."

She shot him a quizzical look, but he wouldn't say
more, so she ripped open the envelope and scanned the
first sheet of paper.

By the time she'd finished reading the fifth e-mail,
she felt light-headed. The men who had authored these
e-mails had praised her so enthusiastically that she kept
forgetting to breathe. Prior to this, the most apprecia-
tion she'd received was an occasional thanks, muttered

in a barely audible voice. But the threat of her dismissal had prompted these intensely private agents to document for the record all the ways that her counseling had helped them.

Over the past few months, her confidence had taken a huge nosedive. Yet here in her hands was proof that she hadn't wasted her efforts, that she had, in fact, made a significant difference to her patients.

Brent was right. This was much better than flowers.

She blinked away the moisture that blurred her vision. "Why didn't Gene tell me?" she asked softly.

"He planned to do that at your next performance review, but then you told him you were quitting the Bureau."

She held the envelope against her chest. Did she really want to leave these agents whose wonderful words of support she would never forget? Did she really want to turn her back on a supervisor who would rally his troops to save her job?

"Gene also mentioned that it was your advice that saved his marriage."

She curled up next to Brent on the couch. "He really said that?"

"I'll take a polygraph if you want," he said solemnly.

She smiled. "That won't be necessary."

He reached for her hand. "I haven't thanked you properly for helping me. In light of all your other accolades, I guess one more hardly matters, but I wanted you to know."

"What you think matters a great deal to me."

He gazed at her in silence for a long time. Then, just

as she sensed he was about to speak, his cell phone rang. He made no move to answer it.

"It might be important," she pointed out.

"This is important," he said.

She nodded. "And we'll finish it after your call."

He released her hand and pulled out his cell phone.

While he spoke in a low voice, her thoughts wandered. Starting a new job had lost its appeal now that she felt validated in her current position. And tonight's short separation from Brent had shown her how much she wanted to be with him. Because she loved him.

She was going to tell him how she felt, confident they had a chance at a real relationship.

As for Balanced Life Consulting Group, they would just have to find somebody else to teach stress-management courses to executives.

Brent set down his cell phone. "That was Gene," he told her. "They found McKenna's car and have already torn it apart. Hidden inside the passenger seat, they found a gun that looks like the one that was used to kill Pete and shoot through your front window."

She shuddered. "I'm surprised McKenna didn't bring it when he came to the cabin. It would've been simpler—and quicker—than renting a speedboat and paddling to that dock."

"I think he wanted Forrester to take the blame for what happened before today. So your death had to look accidental—as if you'd paddled to the dock, then slipped and hit your head as you stepped out of the canoe."

"I hope he has a long time in prison to think about everything he's done," she said vehemently.

"He will. I'm sure the gun is only the first piece of evidence we'll find. He killed Pete and Harris—no one's going to let him get away with any of it."

"Pete would approve of everything you've done to bring McKenna to justice."

"I think so, too," Brent agreed. "But when I went after McKenna today, I wasn't thinking of Pete. I was only thinking of you. I wanted to kill him for trying to hurt you."

"You saved my life today."

He smiled. "And you saved mine."

Beyond the living-room windows, lightning streaked toward the lake in a jagged flash of brilliance, and the wind whipped the trees.

"Do you remember the night Gene sent you to get me—after Forrester had escaped from Ridsdale?"

He rubbed his nose. "How could I forget?"

She smiled. "There was a storm that night, too." But the terror she'd felt was gone. She was with Brent, safe and secure in his arms.

"I hope we'll see many more together," Brent said.

She glanced up at him and held her breath, almost afraid to hope.

He looked back at her, his eyes filled with an emotion she hadn't seen in them before.

"I think you know," he continued, "that I've never had a problem putting my life on the line. But putting my heart on the line? That's an entirely different story. No serious relationships means no way to get hurt, right?"

His mouth twisted in a grimace. "I don't want to play

it safe by limiting myself to work—and nothing else—anymore."

"What do you want?" Claire asked.

"I want you." He stroked her cheek with a gentle finger. "My heart nearly stopped when I saw McKenna overturn that canoe. In that moment, I finally realized how much I loved you. I'd have known it sooner if I hadn't been blinded by stubbornness, but nearly losing you made my feelings crystal clear. I love you, Claire, and I don't ever want to let you go."

Her heart expanded until she could feel it pressing against her ribs. "I love you, too, Brent. So much."

At last, he kissed her. He kissed her deeply, thoroughly, endlessly until her head was spinning. As always, she tasted passion on his lips, but this time there was a tenderness that warmed her soul.

She drew back to catch her breath. "Does this mean I can look forward to something more than a few dates in our future?"

"Definitely more than a few dates," he promised. "Maybe even marriage and children—if that's still what you want."

She was too overwhelmed to speak.

He leaned his forehead against hers. "I want to make a life with you, Claire. I want us to share our best and worst moments and be together always." He drew back and searched her eyes, his gaze reflecting the love his words had just expressed. "My gut tells me we can make that happen."

She gave him a tremulous smile. "My heart agrees."

"What about the Bureau?"

She realized she hadn't told him she'd changed her mind about leaving. Everything had happened so fast, she hadn't had a chance. "Do you think Gene will take me back?"

"You know he will. But is that what you really want? Because if it's not, I could ask for a transfer—"

She stopped him with a hand against his lips. "I appreciate your offer, but those e-mails—along with everything else that's happened in the past twenty-four hours—have given me a whole new perspective."

"I'm glad."

She wrapped her arms around his waist. "How long before your shoulder heals?"

He nuzzled her earlobe. "Doctor said that depends on how much I restrict my activity."

"What does that mean exactly?"

"I have no idea." He shifted her suddenly so that she sprawled on top of him. "But I do know how resourceful you can be in times of need."

"I need you," she whispered.

He brushed several strands of hair back from her face. "The feeling's mutual, sweetheart."

She slid her hands over the part of his chest not covered by his sling. "I don't want to hurt you."

"I'm willing to risk it if you are."

She caressed his sculpted cheeks and looked deep into his eyes. "Loving you is no risk at all."

"I was just thinking the same thing," he said sincerely.

"Then it's official. We belong together—"

"—in every way possible." Easing down the neckline of her shirt, he kissed the sensitive skin he'd uncovered.

Then he used his teeth and tongue and hands to explore the rest of her—in every way possible.

As much as his touch excited her, she was even more thrilled by the love she saw in his eyes. They'd both almost died today and joining their bodies together now felt natural and right. It was more than making love.

It was a celebration of life.

* * * * *

THE BRIDE'S BODYGUARD

BY
BETH CORNELISON

First published in Great Britain 2011
Harlequin Mills & Boon Limited,
Eton House, 18-24 Paradise Road, Richmond, Surrey TW9 1SR

THE BRIDE'S BODYGUARD © Beth Cornelison

ISBN: 978 0 263 88507 1

46-0211

Harlequin Mills & Boon policy is to use papers that are natural, renewable
and recyclable products and made from wood grown in sustainable forests.
The logging and manufacturing processes conform to the legal environmental
regulations of the country of origin.

Printed and bound in Spain
by Litografia Rosés S.A., Barcelona

Dear Reader,

I'm having so much fun writing the Bancroft Brides series! In *The Bride's Bodyguard*, Paige Bancroft is ready to walk down the aisle when a disaster beyond anything she could imagine throws her life into chaos. Orderly, organized Paige doesn't do chaos. Thank goodness she has ultra-hot, former Navy SEAL Jake McCall at her side, helping her dodge bullets! Paige is in for a wild ride and about to discover that love can bloom in the most difficult situations and with the person you'd least expect.

As I write this letter, I'm in the final stages of wrapping up book three (Zoey's book), and I admit, leaving these three sisters is going to be tough! Having grown up as the middle of three sisters, I pulled bits and pieces of my own experience into creating Paige, Holly and Zoey. Their love for each other, their widely different personalities, the occasional sibling rivalry … even the camping in a pop-up trailer come from memories of my youth.

I hope you enjoy Paige's story, and stay tuned for Zoey's book.

Happy reading,

Beth Cornelison

Beth Cornelison started writing stories as a child when she penned a tale about the adventures of her cat, Ajax. A Georgia native, she received her bachelor's degree in Public Relations from the University of Georgia. After working in public relations for a little more than a year, she moved with her husband to Louisiana, where she decided to pursue her love of writing fiction.

Since that first time, Beth has written many more stories of adventure and romantic suspense and has won numerous honours for her work, including the coveted Golden Heart award in romantic suspense from Romance Writers of America. She is active on the board of directors for the North Louisiana Storytellers and Authors of Romance (NOLA STARS) and loves reading, travelling, Peanuts' Snoopy and spending down-time with her family.

She writes from her home in Louisiana, where she lives with her husband, one son and two cats who think they are people. Beth loves to hear from her readers. You can write to her at PO Box 5418, Bossier City, LA 71171, USA or visit her website at www.bethcornelison.com.

To my sisters — Martha and Lenna. I love you guys!

And in memory of Nate. I miss you

Chapter 1

"Do you, Paige Michelle Bancroft, take Brent to be your lawfully wedded husband, for better or for worse, in sickness and—"

A strange buzzing filled Paige's ears, drowning out the minister's voice and ramping up the panic constricting her chest. The hand holding her bouquet shook, making the imported orchids tremble. Her mother's antique pearl choker strangled her.

No, no, no, she wanted to scream. *I don't love Brent. I don't want to spend my life with him.*

"—as long as you both shall live?" The minister raised an expectant gaze to her, cuing her to respond.

"I do," she rasped. Her answer seemed to come from the bottom of a deep well, a hollow, disembodied voice with its own will.

Brent squeezed her free hand and gave her a smile, which she dutifully mirrored, despite the legion of butterflies battering her stomach and the doubts shouting in her head.

She cast a quick glance to the front row where her mother

joyfully dabbed her eyes and her father beamed at her triumphantly. Her parents' happiness bolstered her courage.

"I'm so proud of you," Neil Bancroft had whispered to Paige as he escorted her down the aisle moments ago. "Brent is your perfect match."

She'd swallowed the bitter uncertainties that rose in her throat, wanting to reply, "No, he's *your* perfect match. Don't make me do this!" Instead, she'd forced a grin and nodded.

Marrying Brent was her destiny, her obligation. Marrying the man who would soon be the CEO of Bancroft Industries meant control of the family business would stay within the family. More important, she was making her father happy. Her father doted on Brent as if he were the son he never had.

Paige had long ago come to terms with the fact that her marriage was more a business merger than a love match. As the oldest daughter in the family, she knew her father expected her to put family obligations first. When Brent had proposed to her, with her father sitting across the table from them, she'd seen how the prospect of her marriage to his protégé had thrilled her father. Her engagement had earned her unprecedented praise and acceptance from her hard-to-please father.

A tug on her hand called her attention back to her groom, who was slipping an extravagant ring on her finger. "With this ring, I thee wed."

Her heart tap-danced as she turned to hand her bouquet to her sister Holly and receive from her Brent's ring.

Holly gave her a curious look, whispering discreetly, "You okay?"

Another fake smile and a tiny nod. "Of course."

Paige shoved down the twinge of envy for her sister's loving and happy marriage to a handsome doctor. Holly and Matt's Christmas wedding last winter had been a small affair but bursting with heartfelt affection and joy.

Paige drew a deep, steadying breath as she faced her groom with his wedding band in hand and prepared to recite her vows. She could make this marriage work if she kept the right attitude and put aside her childish dreams of a fairy-tale prince to sweep her off her feet. The kind of romantic dreams her youngest sister, Zoey, was chasing.

"I can't pretend I'm happy to see you marrying someone you don't love," Zoey had declared in the same phone call in which she explained her reasons for skipping Paige's wedding. Not having Zoey at her wedding broke Paige's heart, but her temperamental youngest sister had always been stubborn, opinionated and unpredictable. And so Zoey was God-knows-where with her latest loser boyfriend, protesting Paige's practical decision by boycotting the wedding ceremony.

Brent might not be her dream love match, but he had his good qualities. He was thoughtful, intelligent, generous, polite and ambitious. He tried hard to make her happy—and he tried even harder to make her father happy. He was comfortable, like her favorite old pair of slippers.

With a mental kick in the pants, Paige shook off the doubt demons plaguing her and firmed her resolve. Zoey was wrong. Marrying Brent Scofield was the right thing to do. She'd be fine, and she'd learn to love him. She'd make her marriage work.

With shaking hands, she lifted the gold band to Brent's finger. "With this ring, I—"

Slam!

The door at the back of the sanctuary crashed open, and Paige jerked her head toward the source of the distracting noise.

A man in a long trench coat strode down the center aisle toward the altar. "Sorry I'm late. But I didn't want to show up too soon and give the groom a chance to escape."

Brent snatched his hand from Paige's and stiffened as he faced the intruder. "Who are you, and what do you want?"

"Who I am doesn't matter. And you know what we want, Scofield."

Jake McCall surreptitiously reached for the sidearm hidden at his hip under his tuxedo coat and stepped smoothly between the intruder and the groom. He'd been so caught up in deciphering the odd reluctance and anxiety in the bride's expression that he'd allowed his vigilance over the groom's safety to lapse for valuable seconds. He shoved down the self-recriminations that would only serve as further distractions and shifted into battle mode.

Even as Jake drew his SIG Sauer P226 and moved into a more offensive position, Brent shifted out from behind him, addressing the man in the trench coat. "And if I refuse?"

As if on cue, several more men, all armed with rifles, appeared in the balcony and stepped through the side and back doors of the sanctuary.

A murmur of distress whispered through the congregation, and the bridesmaids huddled together behind the altar rail.

Jake's grip on his pistol tightened. Quickly, he began recalculating his best strategy to protect his client and avoid getting anyone else shot in the process. He sent a quick glance around the sanctuary, monitoring the other gunmen, then returned his attention to the ringleader. The man's trench coat, out of place on a rain-free summer day, bothered Jake. Not knowing what might be under that long coat bothered him more.

Trench Coat sent Brent a gloating smirk and jerked a nod toward Jake. "I see you were expecting us." Turning, he narrowed a menacing glare on Jake. "Drop it. Or my men will drop you and anyone else in the line of fire."

Jake hesitated only a moment before setting his pistol on the floor and kicking it toward Trench Coat. Ordinarily, he'd keep his weapon at all costs, but being outnumbered and outgunned with so many civilians at risk changed everything.

"Now…" Trench Coat faced the groom once more. "If you give us what we want, nobody has to get hurt."

"Brent? What is he talking about?" the bride asked, her expression stunned, terrified.

Matt Randall, who'd been introduced to Jake as the bride's brother-in-law, rose from the front pew and eased up behind Trench Coat.

Jake tensed. Clearly, Matt had some form of well-intended, but ill-advised heroics in mind. He tried to make eye contact with Matt to warn him off, but Matt's focus was on the man threatening the wedding party.

Just before Matt reached his target, Trench Coat jerked his head around and whipped open his coat to reveal the explosives he wore on his chest. He pulled his hand from his large coat pocket, his thumb hovering over the switch of a detonator. "I wouldn't try anything if I were you, pal."

The bridesmaids issued a collective gasp.

Brent raised both hands in a conciliatory gesture. "Take it easy. Your business is with me. Leave everyone else out of it. Let everyone else go, and I—I'll cooperate."

Trench Coat cocked his head and twisted his mouth in an eerie smirk. "Good to know. Hand over the bead, and we'll be on our way."

Brent cut a desperate glance to Jake. "I, uh, don't have it."

Trench Coat's face hardened. "You're lying. You knew we were after it, and you wouldn't leave it unprotected. It's here somewhere, and I'm getting tired of asking nicely." He glanced to one of his cohorts. "Scofield needs a little encouragement to cooperate."

The gunman gave a tight nod. Raised his rifle.

And shot the man at the end of the pew closest to him.

Screams rose from the congregation. Terrified people scrambled from their seats to run for the door. More shots were fired toward the escaping crowd as the gunmen moved in to block the door.

"Sit down!" Trench Coat roared.

A terrified hush fell over the church, and Trench Coat turned so everyone could see the bomb strapped to him. "I have enough C4 taped to me to blow this church to hell and back."

A prickle of intuition chased up Jake's spine. He'd worked with C4 during his navy SEAL training. The claylike material Trench Coat wore wasn't C4.

And these men weren't religious or political extremists on suicide duty. They were mercenaries after something Scofield had. Blowing themselves up would serve no purpose. The bomb was likely a fake, a scare tactic to win cooperation from the congregation and deter would-be heroes like Matt.

But the rounds in the goons' rifles were real enough, as they'd demonstrated.

With the hand not holding the fake detonator, Trench Coat pulled a .38 revolver from a coat pocket and leveled the gun at Brent. "The bead, Scofield. Now!"

Jake rocked to the balls of his feet, prepared to launch himself in front of a bullet or knock Trench Coat to the floor in an instant. "Brent, give him what he wants," he hissed through clenched teeth.

How could Scofield play his game of chicken with these terrorists when so many lives were at risk?

Brent sent him a stunned glance. "No!"

Trench Coat's aim shifted twenty degrees. Toward the bride. The .38 clicked as he cocked the hammer.

"No!" Brent threw himself on his bride, knocking her down just as Trench Coat fired.

In one rapid move, Jake dived for his pistol, rolled to his back and dropped Trench Coat with one shot to the head.

Bedlam erupted as the congregation ducked for cover or ran for the door. The other terrorists fired at will, trying to regain control of the frightened crowd.

Jake scrambled forward and seized the .38. The fake detonator lay beside the dead terrorist, forgotten.

Over the gunfire and screams, Jake heard the bride shout, "Brent! Someone help me!"

As he rushed toward the bridal couple, lying together on the floor, Jake spotted the blood spreading at Scofield's tuxedo collar.

He reached his client at the same time as Matt. The other man muscled him out of the way. "I'm a doctor! Let me help him!"

Jake yielded to the doctor but assisted in ripping open

Brent's ascot and tux collar. He balled his own cravat to stanch the flow of blood from the wound at Brent's jugular vein.

The bride huddled beside Brent, crying and clutching her groom's hand. "Hang on, Brent. Stay with us. Matt will help you."

Brent's fading gaze found his bride's, then shifted to Jake's as he rasped, "McCall…"

Guilt kicked Jake hard in the gut. He gritted his teeth in frustration and self-reproach. "I know. You hired me to protect you, and I didn't."

"Listen to me!" Scofield grabbed Jake's wrist with a grip that was surprisingly strong considering how much blood he'd lost.

Jake hesitated when he met the determined fire in his client's eyes.

"New…assignment. Paige has…what they want. Get her… out of here. Hide her." Brent struggled for a breath, the life light in his eyes dimming. "Keep…the bead safe… at all costs. National security…."

Jake frowned, straining to hear over the continued tumult in the sanctuary. "What bead?"

"Homeland compromised. No police—"

"What bead?" Jake demanded. "Where is it?"

"In…her…" Scofield paused, gasped, gurgled on the blood in his throat. Brent's gaze darted to something behind Jake. "Go!"

Jake whipped a glance over his shoulder in time to see one of the riflemen approach the altar, then pause to take aim on them.

Hooking an arm around the bride's waist, he hauled her to her feet and shoved her behind the pulpit. He took cover with her, shielding her with his body as the bullets whizzed past, missing them by inches. Peering around the side of the pulpit, Jake fired back at the rifleman. Hit him in the chest. The man slumped to the floor.

Burying his mouth in the bride's hair, he shouted directly

into her ear. "We're going out that side door to the limo. Move fast and keep your head down."

She shook her head, her eyes wide with terror. "But Brent—"

"Just do as I say! We run on three. One, two, three!"

Numb with shock and fear, Paige stumbled as Brent's hulking best man tugged her arm, propelling them toward the sanctuary's side exit. Her foot caught the hem of her Vera Wang gown, and she immediately tumbled to her knees. She bit her tongue as she landed with a jarring thud.

Jake sent her a dark scowl of impatience, as if she'd tripped on purpose, as if running in high heels with yards of satin and lace draped around her legs should have been easy.

Shaking from head to toe, she fumbled to untangle herself, fighting the billows of her skirt out of her way. In a daze of disbelief, she watched Jake knock away the muzzle of the rifle that a thug by the side door had swung toward them. Lobbing a fist to the thug's chin, Jake sent the guy sprawling on the floor, then turned to her. His square jaw was taut, and a lethal intensity blazed in his dark eyes.

Without warning, Jake planted his shoulder in her stomach. Wrapping his arm around her legs, he tossed her over his shoulder in a fireman's hold. The air whooshed from her lungs, and her world turned upside down. Dangling over his shoulder, she scrabbled for something to hold as he charged out the door. Paige fisted his tuxedo coat, but as Jake raced down the steps and across the churchyard, the heavy stomping of his feet bounced her like a rag doll. She groped frantically for a more secure hold, wrapping her arms around the expanse of his wide back.

Jake's shoulder gouged her belly. His fingers dug into her thighs. His feet and the ground filled her line of sight with a dizzying blur of motion. The bright sunshine and thick humidity of the Louisiana summer day beat down on them as he ran toward the front driveway.

A beautiful day for my wedding, she'd thought that morning when she arrived at the church. *The perfect day for my perfect wedding.*

Now bile and adrenaline soured her stomach and threatened to come up as she clung to Jake for dear life. The surreal screams from her friends and family, under assault in the sanctuary she'd been dragged away from, faded as they made their escape.

But the deafening gunfire followed them. A series of blasts thundered through the air. Paige winced as bits of concrete flew up at her when bullets peppered the ground. Bullets aimed at her and at Jake.

"Start the engine! Go, go, go!" Jake shouted to someone. He staggered to a stop, but before she could catch her breath or regain her bearings, he dumped her, unceremoniously, onto the backseat of the bridal limo.

"Let's move!" Jake yelled.

She battled away the curtain of ivory satin that had her tangled in an awkward knot, obscuring her vision. As she scooted across the seat, righting herself and restoring air to her jostled lungs, Jake lunged onto the seat beside her. He swung a handgun out the open car door and fired a couple of earsplitting shots. The limo driver hit the gas, and they rocketed down the church driveway, even before Jake had closed the limo door.

As the limo hurtled down the streets of Lagniappe, weaving through traffic and taking turns at a high speed, Paige was tossed about like a sock in the dryer. Her mind spun as well, reeling from the macabre turn of events. Her wedding had become a bloodbath. Brent had been shot. And her groom's high school friend, a man she'd met only four days ago, had bodily carried her out of harm's way like some tuxedoed superhero.

Dear God, was her sister hurt? Her parents? Her friends? And poor Mr. Diggle had been murdered in cold blood!

She must be dreaming. *If this is some anxiety-induced nightmare, please let me wake up now!*

For the first time, Paige said a prayer of thanks that her

youngest sister hadn't been at the wedding after all. At least Paige knew Zoey was safe.

The limo's back window shattered. Startled by the loud crash and rain of broken glass, Paige screamed.

"Get down!" Jake palmed her head and shoved her to the floor, covering her with his massive body. His weight pressed her back into the plush carpeting and biting shards of the window while his rock-hard chest and wide shoulders ground against the galloping beat of her heart. The heat of his exertion and the faint scent of sandalwood surrounded her. Despite the hell breaking loose around her, the solid wall of his body created a warm cocoon where, for a few moments, she felt marginally protected, fractionally less frightened.

She squeezed her eyes closed, only to see haunting images of Brent's blood, spraying bullets and crushed flowers. Chaos, death and destruction. At her wedding.

She shuddered.

You know what we want, Scofield.

Keep the bead safe at all costs.

Why had Jake brought a gun to the wedding? Had he expected trouble?

Who were those armed men, and what was Brent's link to them?

None of it made sense.

"Hit the highway out of town and don't stop until you're sure you've lost them!" Jake shouted to the driver.

Time kaleidoscoped, and Paige couldn't be sure if she'd huddled beneath Jake's protective cover for one minute or twenty. When the assault of gunfire stopped, he rolled off of her and sat back to take off his tux jacket and rip open the shirt at his throat. Her gaze gravitated to the pulse throbbing on his thick neck. A muscle in his jaw jumped as he gritted his teeth and eased forward to peer over the backseat.

She rubbed the spot at her temple where her head pounded.

"I think we lost them." Jake expelled a deep breath of relief as he pushed up to the seat at the back of the limo. He raked a hand through his short, inky-black hair and lifted a penetrating gaze to her. "Are you all right?"

Paige could only stare back at him, too stunned, too shaken, too confused by the violent attack at her wedding to know what to do or say. This kind of thing was only supposed to happen in the movies, not in real life. Not in her staid, well-planned, organized, boring life.

Jake extended a large hand to her. She studied the crimson smears on his fingers, and her stomach roiled. "You have blood on your hand. Brent's blood," she said stupidly, still too shell-shocked to edit her thoughts for statements of the obvious.

But Jake didn't laugh off or dismiss her banal comment. Instead, his expression darkened, and his jaw tightened. "I did what I thought was best, considering I was outnumbered, outgunned and had the lives of three hundred of your friends and relatives to factor in to my response to those thugs," he said bitterly. He massaged his knee and winced. "I know I screwed up. I know your fiancé is likely dead because of my screwup."

Paige's breath hitched, and a sharp ache sliced through her. *Brent could be dead.*

Jake jerked his gaze to the side window and huffed. His nostrils flared, and pain flooded his face for a moment before he schooled his expression and turned back to her. "I'm sorry."

She blinked, saying nothing for long seconds, realizing he'd taken her comment as condemnation and accusation. His tortured expression, his guilty confession twisted in her chest.

"I—I only meant…you have blood—" She pointed to his hands, then stopped when she saw the blood on her own fingers. She gaped at the red stains, her stomach seesawing as she discovered the smears on her dress, as well—the garish reminder of the violence she'd witnessed, of her futile attempts to help Brent when he'd been shot, of the unknown carnage she'd left at the church. It was *her* wedding. Didn't that make it her responsibility to see to the safety of her guests? How could she flee like a coward and leave everyone else to die?

And what choice in the matter had Jake given her, hauling her away like a duffel bag over his shoulder?

"Are you hurt?" Jake repeated, his tone demanding.

Paige drew a slow breath, forcing air into lungs paralyzed by shock, terror and grief. "I—I don't know." She looked up at Jake, needing answers. "What just happened? How… Why…?"

He leaned forward and put a hand under her elbow, helping her off the limo floor and onto the long seat ninety degrees from where he sat. "Good question. The sooner we get those answers, the better I'll be able to protect you and the bead."

"Protect me?"

Jake gave her a tight nod. "Those are my orders. That's what Brent asked just before we made our big exit."

"Your orders?" She hated sounding like some parrot, repeating everything Jake said, but her brain was still struggling to comprehend the horror of the past half hour and make sense of the insanity. "Who the hell are you *really?* And why did you think you had to bring a gun to my wedding?"

Jake flexed and balled his hand restlessly. "I really am an old friend of Brent's. But not his best friend—just the one with the most military training. He hired me a couple weeks ago to protect him until after the wedding. My being his best man was my cover. So you wouldn't ask questions."

Paige shook her head, more confused than ever. "Then… why are you here instead of protecting him?"

"Didn't you hear what he said before we made our exit? He told me to hide you and keep the bead safe at all costs." He narrowed a sharp gaze on her and extended his hand. "In fact, you should give me the bead for safekeeping."

Her head throbbed, and she swallowed the urge to scream her frustration with the endless riddles. "What *bead?*"

Jake's jaw tightened, and his dark eyes reflected his own frustration and impatience with the situation. "The one the terrorists who crashed your party were after, of course! The one you're protecting for Brent. Give it to me." He wiggled his fingers, urging her compliance. "Come on, Paige. Brent asked me to guard it. He said something about national security."

Paige barked a humorless laugh. "What does some bead have to do with national security? And what makes you think I have this…this *bead?*"

Squeezing his eyes shut, Jake massaged his right knee again and exhaled an irritated huff.

"Brent said you have what those guys who shot him were after," he said quietly, clearly struggling to keep his tone calm, though tension vibrated from him in palpable waves. "That's why I got you out of the church so fast. According to Brent, you have what the terrorists want, and it is my job to keep this *bead*—whatever it is—safe."

His wording smacked her between the eyes, and she flopped back on the seat, her chest aching, as if from a physical blow. "That's what he said? Keep the bead safe? That's why you hustled me out of there so fast? Why you risked your life to save me?"

Protect the bead. Not her. She was merely a pawn in Brent's dangerous secret agenda.

Jake rolled his eyes and groaned. "Isn't that what I just said? This conversation is getting old, Paige. Just give me the bead, okay?"

Something inside her snapped. Her patience, her composure, her illusions of her safe, orderly world shattered, and she grabbed her head, fisting her hands in her hair, further destroying the salon styling she'd received that morning. "I don't have any bead! I don't know what Brent thinks I have or why he told you I have it!" She hated her shrill tone, her loss of control. But getting shot at, learning the safety of some bead was more important to your fiancé than your safety, having your entire world thrown into chaos did that to a girl.

"I don't know why armed men attacked my wedding! And I don't know why my fiancé thinks he has something to do with national security! None of this makes sense to me!"

Jake's head snapped up, his attention drawn to something out the back window.

"What—"

Before she could finish her question, he grabbed her arm and yanked her back toward the floor. Paige gritted her teeth. She was getting tired of his manhandling.

"Stay down!" he shouted as he lowered the side window and leveled his handgun at some threat outside.

She heard the roar of an engine, too loud and high-pitched to be a car. It sounded more like a motorcycle. Then a hail of bullets hammered the limo, shattering more windows and pocking the far wall of the back compartment.

"I thought you said we'd lost them!"

Jake spared her only a brief glance. "Clearly, they found us again."

He pitched backward as the limo veered suddenly and bumped along the shoulder. His eyes widened, and he bit out a curse. Lunging forward, he climbed over her and shouted, "Hold on to something! Our driver's been hit."

Jake turned on the seat and rocked backward. With a hard kick, he knocked out the Plexiglas window partition between them and the front seat.

Paige scrambled across the floor, groping for a handhold as the vehicle swerved and bumped. She grabbed the pit of a wet-bar cup holder over her head and braced her feet on the long side seat on the opposite side of the compartment. Jake slid headfirst through the opening he'd created, dragging the driver—oh, God, was he dead?—off the steering wheel and into the passenger seat.

Paige bit down hard on her bottom lip, praying for a miracle, praying she and Jake weren't about to be shot or killed in a car crash. Praying she'd wake up from this far-too-realistic nightmare.

Bile rose in her throat, and tears burned her eyes as two truths clarified in her mind.

Brent was involved in something terrible and clandestine.

And her fiancé's dangerous secret might cost her her life.

Chapter 2

Jake fought the limo back under control and steered onto the highway. Checking the mirrors for any more surprise assailants, he took the first exit and headed in the opposite direction from the way the motorcyclist departed.

At his earliest opportunity, Jake pulled the limo off the road and stopped long enough to check the driver for signs of life. He pressed his fingers to the man's carotid artery, despite the glaring hole in his head that screamed proof that the driver was dead.

Paige appeared at the windowless gap between the front and back seats. "Why'd we stop? Is the driver—?"

"Don't look," he barked, harsher than he needed to, but tension had him wound tight. Tact was not at the top of his priorities at the moment. "Get down and stay there. You don't need this image in your head, and I don't know when we may get attacked again."

The rustle of satin and lace told him she'd complied.

"So what do we do now? Where are we going?" The tremble of fear in her voice sucker punched his gut.

"This is a work in progress, darlin'. I'll tell you when I know. First thing we have to do is get rid of this limo. It's conspicuous as hell." He whipped a quick glance over his shoulder to the backseat. Paige's wide green eyes made her look vulnerable, yet he also saw keen intelligence and stubborn determination in her expression that told him she was no frail flower that would wilt at any moment. Good. If this situation was half as dangerous as the past thirty minutes purported, she'd need a little starch in her to survive the coming days.

"First thing *you* need to do is lose the dress."

"*Excuse* me?" she said, her tone rife with offense.

He dismissed her misunderstanding with a twist of his mouth and a short sigh. "You do have other clothes, don't you? Like in a suitcase in the trunk? Packed for your honeymoon?"

"Oh…right."

He heard her embarrassment in her voice, and though he kept his eyes on the road, he imagined her ivory cheeks, flushed red as they had been the night before at the rehearsal dinner when she was the butt of her friends' and family's good-natured ribbing. Her modesty and discomfiture had struck him as unusual for a woman with so much going for her—beauty, brains, wealth, ambition and family and friends who clearly adored her. Most women he knew with so much going for them seemed to feel they were entitled to their privileged lives.

For someone who'd scraped and fought for everything he had, such arrogance was a huge turnoff to Jake.

He cleared his throat. "Not only is the dress conspicuous when we need to blend, it's hardly made for speed if we have to make a break for it on foot again." He searched the side of the road for a place where he could hide the limo.

"Do you think we will…have to flee on foot, I mean?"

He met her gaze in the rearview mirror. "I don't know what we may be up against. But we need to be ready for anything, and we can't call attention to ourselves. They'll be looking for us. So we've got to go to ground until we either figure out what they want," he said thinking aloud, "or know for certain they're not hot on our asses anymore."

"We should just call the police and let them handle it."

"Can't. Scofield said Homeland was compromised. I assume he means Homeland Security, which is exactly who the police will call if they think national security is at stake." He shook his head. "For now, at least, we do this alone."

Jake spotted a vacant gas station and parked the limo behind it, out of sight of the road. Hauling himself out of the front seat, he clenched his teeth in pain as his bum knee, the reason the navy had kicked him out of the SEALs, throbbed a protest. Sprinting for the limo with an extra hundred or so pounds over his shoulder hadn't been kind to his old injury. Refusing to let his pain get in the way of his duty, he tried not to limp as he retrieved a floral-print suitcase from the trunk.

When he yanked open the back door of the limo, she gasped.

"I assume this one's yours."

Paige pressed a hand to her chest and sucked in several deep, restorative breaths that drew attention to the low neckline of her dress and the gentle swell of cleavage the dress had clearly been designed to maximize.

A hot stab of lust jabbed him in the gills, and he gritted his teeth. Now was hardly the time to get distracted by Paige's assets.

"Yeah, that's mine." She reached for the luggage, and he batted her hand away before setting the suitcase flat on the seat.

"Pick something practical that you don't mind getting dirty. Something you can run in, even sleep in if necessary. That includes shoes. No high heels."

"What about you? Your tux doesn't say *blend in* or *ready for action* to me."

"Well, a tux isn't my first choice of attire for this debacle either. But since I'm a good six inches taller and fifty pounds heavier than Scofield, I doubt anything he had packed will fit me, so I'll have to make do for now."

She glanced away and worried her bottom lip with her teeth.

He cocked an eyebrow. "What's that look for?"

"I…need to call someone—my dad or my sister Holly—to see how Brent is. To see what happened after we left, to make sure everyone else is all right, to—" Her words caught on a sob, and her face crumpled. "Oh, God. Mr. Diggle was murdered! At my wedding! I—I can't even stand to think of anyone else being hurt…or *worse*. And B-Brent—"

She dissolved into tears, and Jake's gut pitched. He could handle blood and bullets. But tears left him floundering like a plebe on his first day of training.

Not that he couldn't understand her concern. She had every right to be upset about her family's safety, about her fiancé's condition. He rubbed his suddenly sweaty palms on his tux pants and slid onto the seat beside her. Taking her by the arm, he pulled her onto his lap and gave her back an awkward pat.

There, there, sprang to mind, and he clenched his teeth, refusing to mutter any such asinine mumbo jumbo.

But somehow *shake it off* or *suck it up, soldier* didn't seem appropriate, either. Comforting Damsels In Distress 101 hadn't been part of his SEALs training. And while he was as compassionate as the next guy, expressing his feelings and dealing with other people's softer emotions were as foreign to him as some of the locales where he'd served before a well-placed bullet left him with a career-ending knee injury.

Paige's fingers curled into his tux shirt, and she nestled her head in the curve of his throat, collapsing against him and indulging her crying jag. He plucked a few shards of the broken window from her hair, noticing the tiny cuts the shattered glass had caused on her neck and hands. His hands, too, for that matter.

They were damn lucky broken glass was all that hit them. The driver hadn't been as fortunate.

The fragrant white flowers woven into her hair tickled his nose, and he turned his head so that his cheek rested against the top of her head. Tightening his hold on her, he savored the crush of her curves and soft skin against him. He stroked her back, her bare arms, the soft tumble of hair that escaped carefully placed bobby pins.

When she trembled, he absorbed the tremor, feeling an answering quake reverberate at his core. Jake closed his eyes and inhaled deeply, clearing his mind, focusing on the problem at hand. What the hell was he supposed to do with Paige? Where would they go? Considering he'd been lusting after her since Scofield had introduced his bride earlier that week, how could he survive the next few days with his sanity intact?

Adrenaline had his nerves jumping. But the press of her body against his spiked his blood pressure and had heat flashing over his skin. He'd barely had a chance to catch his breath since Trench Coat and his merry band of thugs had opened fire, and comforting Paige wasn't helping him focus.

As he fought down the desire that wound him tight, his thoughts jumped back to the scene at the church, and a shudder racked him. Jake had been part of a convoy in Iraq that was ambushed. The gun- and mortar fire had been deafening, the casualties high and the resulting chaos devastating to morale. But today's attack, with so many civilian lives at stake, had shaken Jake far worse. Against such lopsided odds, Jake had felt overwhelmed…and useless. An unsettling sensation for a man trained by the navy to be among the most deadly, the most effective, the most skilled.

When Paige's tears subsided to sniffles, she backed from his embrace and sent him a chagrined glance. "I'm sorry. I just…it's all so—"

He shook his head and twitched his lips in an dismissive grin. "Forget it." He rubbed the back of his neck and blew a deep breath from puffed cheeks. "I'll…give you a minute to change and pull yourself together. Then we need to make tracks."

She nodded, and he climbed out of the backseat, scanning the surrounding area for anything suspicious, anything helpful. A moment later, she opened the back door and stepped out, wearing a pair of formfitting blue jeans and a New Orleans Saints T-shirt. Sports-team apparel had never looked so good. Paige had taken the rest of the bobby pins from her hair, and raven ringlets hung around her shoulders. Finger-combing her hair back from her face, she gave him a quick nod. "I'm ready."

Before they left, Jake searched the dead driver, found the man's cell phone and dialed 911. He told the operator where to find the body, and when asked for his name, Jake set the phone on the front seat, line still open, and signaled for Paige to follow him.

She hoisted her suitcase, which he immediately took from her, and as they started toward the road, she gave the bullet-riddled, ribbon-and-paint-decorated honeymoon getaway car one last sad look before falling in step next to him.

For an instant, sympathy plucked at him. No one deserved to have their wedding day ruined, and Paige's disappointment was palpable.

Then the bigger picture reared its head, and he shook off the silly sentimental lapse.

National security. Well-armed terrorists. His client shot and bleeding.

What was a spoiled wedding compared to the life-and-death stakes they faced? He had no business letting emotion interfere with his duty to his job.

Keep the bead safe at all cost.

Jake hesitated.

Paige has what they want.

"Wait." He turned back to the limo. "Get the dress. Bring it with us."

Paige tipped her head, her gaze querying. "Don't you think it's a bit cumbersome to carry? Not to mention still as conspicuous in our arms as on me."

He frowned. "I'm not looking forward to dragging it with

us, but Brent said protect the *bead*. Your dress is covered in beading." He scowled. "I don't see how the beads on the dress could be what he wants protected, but after getting shot at because of this *bead* already, I'm not willing to take the chance that it's not one of the embellishments on your gown. How about you?"

Her shoulders slumped. "I see your point."

He grabbed the dress and slung it over his arm, bunching up the yards of flowing satin to keep from tripping over it as they headed toward the street.

She sent him a side glance that asked, "Now what?"

Good question. When he'd signed on to be Scofield's bodyguard, he'd imagined the job would be a cushy assignment, indulging an old friend's belief that he was being followed, that he needed protection. All Brent had told him was that a business deal had gone sour, and he suspected the other party might try to hurt him. Jake hadn't asked questions, dismissing Scofield's concern as paranoia. His first mistake.

And he'd never bargained for extended duty, guarding his client's bride, a woman whose guileless green eyes and body built for sin were distractions he didn't need if he wanted to keep them alive.

"We'll thumb a ride back to town," he said, answering her unspoken question and trying not to grimace when pain from his knee shot fiery bolts through his leg. "From there, we'll rent a car to get…wherever."

"Look, I…I have two tickets to Jamaica in my purse. The plane leaves in three hours. Why don't we use the tickets to get out of the country and—"

"No." Jake imagined Paige in a bikini on a white-sand beach with a fruity island drink in her hand, and another blast of heat slammed him in the gut. "Do you think those thugs don't know where you were headed on your honeymoon?"

She raised her chin, blinked, then frowned her consternation. "But that's—"

"I guarantee they also know where you live, what you drive, where you eat lunch with your girlfriends, where you buy your four-dollar coffee and what route you use to get to the office."

Her troubled look grew stormier, an edge of panic creeping into her gaze. Slowing her pace, Paige pressed a hand to her chest and wheezed, her breathing shallow.

"Hey, don't do that. You'll hyperventilate." Jake seized her arms and drilled her with a hard look. "I need you to keep it together for me, all right?"

She closed her eyes and nodded. Sucking in a few deep breaths, she flexed and balled her hands at her sides, and when she met his gaze again, she seemed in better control.

"I won't… I'm not going to fall apart on you. I promise. This is just all so overwhelming, so out of the blue. I don't understand any of it, and—" She cut herself off with another deep inhalation. "I'll be fine. Really."

The rumble of a car engine called his attention to the road, where a late-model sedan rolled past. He stepped toward the traffic lane and waved the car down.

"Are you sure hitching's the best idea? How do we know we can trust them?" she asked.

Jake nodded toward the elderly occupants of the car. "Look at them. What's not to trust? Besides, if grandma and grandpa do give us trouble, I can take them both down before they know what hit 'em."

The elderly driver slowed to a stop and rolled down his window. "You kids all right?"

"We could use a ride into town. We had a bit of car trouble a little ways back." He hitched his thumb down the road, and when the older man's gaze drifted to the wedding dress, the blood on Jake's shirt and the tear tracks on Paige's cheeks, Jake added, "Our honeymoon's not off to a very good start. I got a nosebleed and ruined my shirt, then the car broke down." He glanced at Paige, sending her a silent signal with his eyes, asking for her cooperation. "And my wife is convinced we're going to miss our flight to Jamaica."

The older man turned to Paige. "Don't cry, sweetheart.

We'll take you back to town, and if you call the airline, I bet they could reschedule you for a later flight."

Paige forced a smile. "I hope so. Everything else has gone wrong today. I'd hate to think we'll miss our plane."

Jake opened the back door for Paige, and she climbed into the car. Once they were settled in the sedan, Paige and Jake listened to the older couple regale them with stories of the mishaps from their wedding fifty-two years ago and many of the disagreements since.

As they approached town, their elderly driver turned from the main road onto a side street that led into a residential area.

"Henry, where are you going? This isn't the right way!" the woman fussed.

"It's a shortcut."

Henry's wife harrumphed. "Shortcut, my fanny. Shortcut is your term for lost. Turn around and go back to the highway."

Paige sent Jake a worried side glance, and he lifted a corner of his mouth in amusement before returning his attention to the middle-class houses they passed.

"I'm not lost. Stop worrying," Henry returned.

"That's what you always say. I'm telling you—"

"Wait a minute," Jake interrupted, spotting a for-sale sign in one of the front yards. "Stop here."

Henry stomped the brakes, and the sedan stopped with a lurch. "Something wrong?"

Paige gave Jake a curious look.

"I just remembered that a friend of mine lives on this street." He opened the car door and tugged on Paige's hand. "We'll go to his house, use his phone to call the airline, arrange for a tow truck and so forth." He tugged harder on his "bride's" hand, encouraging her compliance. "We appreciate the ride, folks."

"I can—" their driver started, then fumbled, as Jake hauled Paige's suitcase from the backseat. "Well, all right. Good luck, kids."

Jake gave the couple a friendly wave as they drove away, then faced Paige's confused scowl. "You don't have a friend in this neighborhood at all. Do you?"

"No."

"Then why did we get out?"

"Because I found a place for us to lay low until we can regroup and plan our next move." Jake lifted her suitcase and headed across the street to the small Acadian-style house with the Realtor's sign in the front yard.

Paige grabbed his arm. "Hang on a minute. Where are—?" Her gaze darted to the for-sale sign then back to him. He could see the wheels turning in her mind. "Whoa! You are not thinking about breaking into this house, are you?"

"That's exactly what I'm thinking. There are newspapers in the driveway, the grass hasn't been mowed. It's obvious the house is vacant."

He jogged to the backyard, and Paige stumbled to keep up. "I don't care if it's vacant! It's still breaking and entering. I won't do it!"

Pulling a small army knife from his pocket, Jake got to work jimmying the lock on the back door. "I don't think you're in a position to be picky about your accommodations, princess."

She grabbed his wrist as he worked, and he met her fiery glare. "Who died and made you boss of me?"

His jaw clenched. "Scofield."

Paige drew back with a gasp as if slapped. The wounded look in her eyes burrowed to his marrow.

"I'm sorry." He ducked his head and rubbed the back of his neck. "That was uncalled for." Jake squeezed her shoulder and drilled her with a stare that brooked no resistance. "I don't like the idea of breaking the law any more than you do, but this house is the safest cover we have right now. We're not here to rob it or deface it. In fact, we'll leave it better than we found it. We'll clean up the yard before we go, so it doesn't scream 'vacant' anymore."

With a last wiggle of his blade, the lock popped, and the door swung open. "After you."

Paige hesitated, glaring at him with righteous indignation. "This isn't right. We could go to a hotel."

Jake struggled to keep his cool. "Nothing about this situation is *right*. But we can't fix anything if we're dead and, for now, this house is our best chance to stay alive. By now, those thugs have every hotel within a hundred miles under surveillance or on their radar in some way. I'm not willing to risk being spotted at a hotel." He planted a hand at the small of her back and nudged her inside. "Now get in before the neighbors see us and call the cops."

Pressing her lips in a tight line of discontent, Paige stamped into the house. When she reached for the light switch, he caught her hand.

"A vacant house wouldn't have lights on. We can't give any indication we're here."

Beneath his fingers, her pulse fluttered at her wrist. Her gaze clashed with his, and he felt an answering kick of adrenaline in his veins. The anger sparking in her eyes and flushing her cheeks made her even more beautiful. He suppressed the urge to plow his fingers through the thick tresses of raven hair swirling around her shoulders.

"So we're just supposed to sit here in the dark?" She turned her attention to the empty room, then back to him. "There isn't even any furniture."

"Sorry, princess. Five-star accommodations aren't always possible when you're on the run."

"Stop calling me *princess* like that," she said through gritted teeth.

He arched an eyebrow, more amused by her temper than put off by it. "Like what?"

"Like you think I'm some pampered diva."

"Aren't you?"

She growled and snatched her wrist from his grip. "Can I at least use my cell phone to call my family and make sure they're safe? Let them know I'm all right?"

Jake rolled the tension from his shoulders, knowing how his answer wouldn't be received. "No. Cell phones can be tracked. In fact…give me your phone. We have to get rid of it."

Paige sputtered, her eyes wide. "Get rid— But all my contacts are on—"

He seized her shoulders and gave her a gentle shake. "Listen to me, and listen good. You saw what those men were capable of. This is no game. I can keep you alive and help you figure out what is going on, what you have that they want, but you have to trust me. You have to do what I tell you without question. All right?"

She opened her mouth, but immediately snapped it shut again. Fear and defeat crossed her face, and her muscles slackened beneath his hands. When she nodded her understanding, instead of feeling he'd won her cooperation, he felt a sense of loss.

"Where's your phone?"

She pointed to the floral suitcase. "In my purse. I packed it for safekeeping during the ceremony and reception."

He lay the suitcase flat on the floor and opened it. He handed her the handbag that had been tucked in one corner, and Paige fished her cell phone out. With an irritated huff, she handed the phone to him. He tucked the phone in his pocket and strode to the empty living room. After glancing out the front window, he lowered the blinds. "I'm going back out to get us a few things for tonight. Clothes for me. Food. Cash for later. I'll pick up a prepaid phone while I'm out, and you can use it to call your family. Okay?"

"Aren't you afraid you'll be seen?"

He scoffed. "Give me some credit. I'm a SEAL. I know how to avoid being spotted."

Paige wrapped her arms around herself and rubbed her bare elbows, despite the stuffy heat inside the house. "What am I supposed to do?"

"Stay out of sight. And try to think what you have, what Scofield might have given you or hidden in your suitcase that terrorists would want. Make a list of everything he's given you in the last few months. We have to figure out what the hell this *bead* is."

Paige stared at him, looking dazed, overwhelmed.

He crossed the room to her and cradled her chin in his palm. "Hey. You all right?"

"Guess I have to be. Don't have much choice." Ducking her head, she muttered, "As usual."

Jake frowned. "What's that supposed to mean?"

She shook her head. "Never mind. You go do what you have to."

He lingered another moment, debating whether he should press the issue, deciding whether he should insist she go with him. In the end, he decided he could move faster and more discreetly without her in tow. She'd be safer here, stashed in the vacant house until he got back. But, just in case, he pulled his pistol out from under his shirt at the small of his back and wrapped her hand around it. "Keep this with you. Only put your finger on the trigger if you intend to fire."

The color drained from her face. "I can't... I've never—"

"Just aim, two hands, and squeeze the trigger." He tweaked her chin and lifted a corner of his mouth in a grin intended to calm her. "Just be sure before you fire that it's not me coming back from my supply run. Got it?"

She gaped at the pistol as if it were a venomous snake and hurriedly set it on the kitchen counter.

He headed out the back door they'd come in through, brushing aside the small curtain on a side window to look out first and check for neighbors who might see him leaving.

"Jake?" she called, stopping him.

He faced her. "Yeah?"

She hesitated, her expression puzzled and her gaze fixed on the ring on her left hand. "Never mind. It will keep."

"What is it, Paige? Tell me."

She sighed. "Well, I was just wondering... Am I married... or not?"

Chapter 3

Paige thumbed the elaborate ring Brent had insisted she have, and nausea swirled in her belly. "I mean, we said our vows, but I never finished giving Brent his ring, and the minister never declared us man and wife."

She glanced up at Jake, who frowned, rolled his shoulders and shifted his weight. He'd been undaunted when they'd been under fire, running for their lives. So why did her simple question make him uncomfortable?

Then another, more ominous thought occurred to her. "I don't even know if Brent survived the attack. How do I know I'm not a widow?"

Jake jutted out his chin. "Don't borrow trouble or get hung up on worst-case scenarios. Until we know otherwise we're going to assume Brent is alive and will be fine. Got it?"

He jammed his restless hands in his pockets and narrowed his eyes. "Did you sign the marriage license?"

Her pulse tripped. A weight seemed to lift from her chest, and the tension screwing her muscles in knots loosened. "No.

We were supposed to do that after the ceremony, before the reception."

"Then I'd say, in the eyes of the law, you're not married."

He had a point. She nodded her agreement and exhaled silently, determined not to show him her relief.

"Why?"

She jerked her head up to meet his querying gaze. "What do you mean, *why?* Wouldn't you want to know if you were married or not?"

He shrugged. "Depends on if I really wanted to be married in the first place. Otherwise, the technical question of whether I'm married or not is moot." His incisive dark eyes scrutinized her. "Even without the legalities in place, your intentions to wed are still valid, your love for your fiancé is unchanged, the commitment you've made to each other is unbroken. Signing the license is a mere formality, in my view." He lifted an eyebrow and angled his head. "Right?"

Paige grabbed the edge of the counter behind her as her knees wobbled. "O-of course."

"But…" Jake stepped toward her as his knowing gaze homed in on her. "If, by some chance, you were having second thoughts about getting married, if you weren't as committed to your intended as you let everyone believe…"

Paige squared her shoulders and raised her chin. "Just what are you implying?"

He lifted a dismissive hand. "I'm not *implying* anything. I'm saying I saw your expression before Trench Coat busted in. I saw the doubt in your face. I saw your reluctance."

Nervous energy shot through Paige, and she suppressed a tremble. "Don't be ridiculous." When she heard the lack of conviction in her tone, she cleared her throat and added, "You saw nothing more than typical jitters over being in front of a crowd. Or a…a moment of…*reflection* as I considered the… importance of the day and—"

"Bull."

She gasped and shot him an affronted look.

"You can tell yourself that if you want, but I know what I

saw." His steady, keen gaze rattled her. "The SEALs trained me to read people, read body language, read subtle clues in facial expressions."

Paige swallowed hard and pressed a hand over the riot of acid in her gut. "You're wrong. I had every intention of marrying Brent before…" She flicked her hand, knowing he could fill in the blank.

He held her gaze for several unnerving seconds. The heat in his mahogany eyes turned her bones to dust and stirred a flutter in her belly. Just his proximity had her acutely aware of his height, his unflinching power and his ex-navy SEAL brawn. When they'd fled the church, he'd carried her to safety and still had the strength to run for the waiting limo. Even now, without him touching her, her skin flashed hot and tingled when she thought of his large hands in intimate places as he lifted her, shielded her, *saved her life*.

"I…I don't think I've thanked you yet…for what you did. Without you, I don't know if I'd have gotten out of the church alive."

The muscles in his square jaw twitched. "I did what I was trained to do. What I was hired to do. Besides…your fiancé is the one who knocked you out of the way when Trench Coat would have shot you. The one who took a bullet for you."

Paige's breath snagged in her lungs. She blinked back the sting of tears and choked down the bile that his reminder of Brent's sacrifice brought to her throat. Brent was dying, might even be dead, because he'd saved her from an assassin's gun.

"On the other hand," Jake continued, "your life would have never been at risk if not for the infamous *bead* Scofield had that Trench Coat wanted. We wouldn't be in danger now if not for him giving you the bead to protect. If he knew something about a threat to national security, how could he knowingly draw the woman he claims to love into the crosshairs of such dangerous men?"

Paige's leg wobbled, and she sank to the floor. The truth

behind Jake's assessment crushed her with a suffocating weight. "M-maybe Brent didn't realize the danger—"

"He knew. That's why he hired me to be his bodyguard."

She raised her bleary gaze to Jake. "Why didn't he want me to know? If he was in danger…"

How could Brent have hidden something so vital from her? She shook her head, unable to make sense of the bizarre twists the day had taken.

Jake squatted beside her and brushed her hair back from her cheek, tucking it behind her ear. "I don't know why he didn't tell you what was going on. I know for damn sure, though, if I were in love with a woman like you, I'd move heaven and earth to keep her safe. I'd never put her life in jeopardy the way Scofield did yours. It's not right."

A jab of loyalty to Brent compelled her to defend him, despite her misgivings about the strange situation. "I'm sure he had a good reason why—"

"No! There's *never* a good reason to put someone you love at risk." Jake's fingers curled into fists, and he clenched his jaw. Shoving to his feet, he stalked back to the door. "I have to go now. Keep this door locked and the gun within reach. I'll be back before dark."

"But what am I—?"

Before she could finish her question, Jake was gone. The silence in the vacant house was deafening. The stillness filled her with a terrifying sense of isolation.

Alone with her thoughts, Paige replayed the horrifying events of the afternoon, searching for some explanation for her frightening and senseless circumstances.

Her fiancé valued a bead over her life.

Brent was involved in something with national security repercussions.

She'd never signed the marriage license.

Paige bent her legs and, propping her arms on her knees, buried her face in her folded arms. Not knowing if Brent survived the attack or if her family was safe was maddening, terrifying. Fatigue, fear and confusion pounded inside her skull, but she refused to give in to the tears that threatened. She'd cried enough today.

We're going to assume Brent is alive.

The time had come to take back the control she'd lost over her life that afternoon. While Jake was gone, she had to figure out what Brent had given her that the terrorists wanted. She had to make a plan of action for getting out of this predicament, and she had to start rebuilding her shattered life—a life *without* Brent Scofield.

A mix of trepidation, guilt and relief for her decision spiraled through her, tangling around her heart. She didn't love Brent. Never really had. And today proved she didn't know him as well as she thought she had. Reason enough to reconsider her engagement. But as Jake pointed out, Brent had willingly put her in danger, set her up to be the target of terrorists. *Terrorists,* for crying out loud! Bitter anger blasted through her.

Until she thought of the way Brent had leaped in front of a bullet for her.

A leaden grief weighted her heart, made it hard to breathe. How could she ever sort this mess out?

An image of Jake wavered behind her closed eyes, and an odd reassurance settled over her like a warm blanket. When all hell had broken loose at the church, he'd saved her. When she'd been paralyzed by fear, he'd taken action. When she'd had her emotional meltdown in the limo, he'd been there with a warm embrace—and spared her empty platitudes.

Jake didn't waste time indulging her wishful thinking or misleading her with what she wanted to hear. He respected her enough to give her the hard-boiled truth. He gave orders and expected results. And he'd proven himself more than capable of protecting her from the threat Trench Coat—as Jake had called the lead terrorist—posed her.

Lifting her head to look around the empty house, Paige took a deep, centering breath. She owed Jake so much already. The least she could do before he returned was come up with something concrete they could work from. Organizing, analyzing and reasoning were what she did best. She'd been useless to Jake earlier because the unexpected, unexplainable chaos of this afternoon had left her completely out of her element.

Now, with a determination to put some order back in her life, Paige began dissecting the events of the past several days, searching for some clue to what the *bead* could be. As she fell into her familiar patterns of problem solving and rational thinking, a soothing balm flowed through her. She'd be fine—as soon as she solved the riddles she'd been presented by this afternoon's events.

After two hours alone, frantically searching her memories for answers, Paige was no closer to a solution when Jake returned with a few supplies and a rental car.

He set the new cell phones, a bag of fast food and other miscellany on the floor beside her and returned his gun to the waist of the new jeans he wore. His tux was nowhere in sight. "Any trouble while I was gone?"

"No. Nothing." Eager to hear from her family, Paige snatched up one of the phones. "Are these working? Have they been activated?"

"Yeah. But keep your call brief." He drilled her with a hard look that echoed the gravity in his tone. "And don't tell anyone anything about where we are. Someone could be listening on the other end."

Paige shivered, despite the stuffy house, and dialed her father's phone. After several rings, the call went to voice mail, and her stomach sank with disappointment and concern. What if her father had been hurt?

"Hi, Dad. It's Paige," she told his voice mail. "I'm safe. Shaken by what happened today but unhurt. I love you, and—" her voice cracked, and she paused to clear the emotion from her throat "—I'll call again when I can. Bye." She disconnected and immediately dialed her sister Holly's cell phone.

Holly answered on the first ring. "Hello?"

The stress and worry in her sister's voice sent fresh waves of panic and anxiety rippling through Paige. "It's me, Hol."

"Paige! Are you okay? Where are you? Oh, God, we've been so worried about you!"

"I'm fine. I'm with Jake McCall. How…how is Brent? Is he—?"

"He's alive, but he's critical."

Paige received the news with mixed feelings. Relief that he was alive, and grief for the severity of his condition. She clutched the phone like a lifeline to her family, and tears blossomed in her eyes.

"He lost a lot of blood, Paige. He's unresponsive, and I'm afraid it's still touch and go whether he'll make it through the night. We're at St. Mary's with him. How soon can you get here?"

"I—I don't think I can come." She glanced up at Jake for confirmation.

He shook his head. "Too dangerous."

She pulled the phone away from her mouth. "He's dying. I need to be there!"

"So you can die, too? Those men were willing to kill to get the bead. They saw me hustle you out of there, so I guarantee they know you have whatever it is they're looking for. You're their new target."

"Paige? Paige, are you sure you're all right? What do you mean you're not coming? Brent is your husband. He may not make it through the night."

"Technically, I don't think he *is* my husband. We never signed the marriage license." Paige frowned, hearing herself. Brent was dying, and she was arguing with Holly about the legality of her marriage? What was wrong with her?

Holly was conspicuously quiet, and guilt rolled through Paige. But Holly had a storybook marriage with her husband, Matt, and her stepchildren. How could she understand Paige's complicated feelings toward Brent? *She* didn't even understand her mixed emotions.

Paige raked the hair back from her face with her fingers

and sighed. "What about everybody else? Are Mom and Dad all right? Matt and the kids?"

"We're all shaken but not physically hurt. I think Mr. Garcia was shot in the leg, and I heard something about Fran Coulter being taken to the hospital. Lots of folks were treated at the scene for minor injuries and shock." Holly paused. "Mr. Diggle is dead, though."

"I know. I—"

Jake circled his finger in the air, signaling her to wrap up her call.

"Holly, I have to go. Tell everyone I love them. I'll try to call again when I can."

"Wait! Where are you? When are you coming home?"

"I don't know when I'll be home. Soon, I hope." She rubbed her eyes when moisture blurred her vision. "Jake thinks I'm still in danger. He thinks those men are still after me. Brent said I have something they want. He told Jake to hide me, protect me until—"

Jake yanked the phone from her. "She'll call later. Don't try to find us. Don't call the police. I'll keep her safe, but it's important that we lay low for a while. Goodbye."

With that, he snapped the phone closed and handed it back to her.

Paige glared at him. "What are you d—?"

"I said keep it short, and don't tell them too much. Her phone was probably bugged."

A tremor crawled up Paige's spine. "Bugged? I—" A new possibility occurred to her, and her breath snagged. "Do you think they'd go after my family to get to me? That they'd hurt them to bring me out of hiding?"

Jake gave her a blank, unreadable look. "It's possible. You should keep your contact with them to a minimum. Just in case."

Paige hugged herself, bending at the waist as fear for her family's safety knotted in her chest.

Jake placed a warm hand at the nape of her neck and gently rubbed her tense muscles. "The sooner we figure out what those men want and what we're supposed to do with it, the better—for everyone." He nudged the greasy sack of fast food toward her. "Eat something."

He toed off the tennis shoes that had replaced his wing tips since his trip out, and he settled beside her with his long legs stretched in front of him. "Did you make a list of the things that Brent has given you in the last several weeks?"

"Yes. But I'm no closer to figuring out what those men wanted." Twisting her mouth in frustration, she peered into the sack of burgers and fries he'd brought back with him, and her stomach growled. She hadn't eaten all day, having been too nervous for breakfast or lunch and worried about getting her dress to zip. But with the interrupted wedding behind her, what did it matter if she ate fried potatoes and red meat? Tonight she wanted comfort food.

"You can't think of *anything* he's given you, anything you packed for the honeymoon that might not be what it seemed?"

She pulled out a burger and handed it to him, then plucked a French fry from the sack and munched as she shook her head. "Nothing. At Christmas, he gave me tickets to the ballet in Chicago, and we flew up there for a weekend. The trip and a set of Waterford red-wine goblets were my Christmas presents." She ate another fry, then unwrapped a burger. "For Valentine's, he sent me two dozen roses—now dead and tossed out." She accounted for the items with her fingers as she listed them for Jake. "We bought an antique desk together that is at a dealer's being refurbished. He gave me a folder with life, car and home owner's insurance information to file a couple of weeks ago."

Jake's head came up. "Did you read the file? Are you sure that's what was in it?"

She nodded. "Read it and added the information to the spreadsheet I'd started for our finances. There was nothing unusual there."

Jake grunted, then, waving the hand with his burger, motioned for her to continue. "What else did he give you?"

She held up her hand, fingering the elaborate wedding band. "Well, my ring, obviously."

He arched an eyebrow as he glanced at the ring, then held out his hand. "Can I have a closer look?"

She slid the ring off and passed it to him.

He narrowed his gaze on the setting and whistled. "Wow. This is…" His expression said he was searching for a tactful term.

Paige sighed. "Gaudy? I know. I tried to tell him it was over-the-top, that all I wanted was a simple band to match my engagement ring, but he wouldn't hear of getting me something as mundane as a plain gold band." She felt a twinge of disloyalty for her complaint, but something compelled her to rationalize the showy ring to Jake. "I think he felt he needed to give me an expensive ring to prove he was worthy of me."

Jake raised an eyebrow as he tossed an amused side glance at her. "Think pretty highly of yourself, do you?"

She scowled and grunted. "That's not what I mean. Brent's the one who was intimidated by our family's money. He came from a family that had nothing. Through a lot of sacrifice and ambition, he worked his way up the ladder in Bancroft Industries in record time and was making good money. But I think he always felt like, with me, he was marrying up and had to prove to someone that he could compete with my family's wealth. He didn't need to, of course. But buying me an expensive wedding ring seemed so important to him, I didn't argue."

Jake turned the domed and jewel-encrusted band over, examining it from every angle. "Your wedding ring is a rather personal and significant item to compromise on. Do you make a habit of letting Brent bully you to get his way?"

Paige hiked her chin up and squared her shoulders defiantly. But her gut swirled, and her heart tapped an anxious rhythm. She refused to let Jake, a man who'd likely never compromised his wishes in his life, see how close to the truth he was. "My ring is just a *thing*. When you grow up surrounded by *things*, you learn how little *real* value and significance they have. Preserving Brent's pride was more important to me than what kind of ring I had." She snatched the ring back and jammed it on her finger. "If I can make someone happy by compromising on something trivial like a ring, then…so be it!"

She swallowed hard, hoping she hadn't overreacted and given herself away with her vehemence.

Jake only stared at her with his enigmatic dark eyes. She felt naked under his knowing scrutiny.

The SEALs trained me to read people, read body language, read subtle clues in facial expressions, Jake's words echoed in her mind.

She plucked another French fry from the bag and angled her body away from him. Nibbling on the cold fry, she forced her breathing to stay even, despite the flutter of nerves his scrutiny caused.

She heard the fast-food bag rattle as he dug into it. "Well, we can't rule out the ring, but keep thinking. What about computer files? Something he asked you to pack in your suitcase or hold in your purse?"

She fidgeted with her earring, then gasped and spun back toward Jake.

"His grandmother's earrings! He wanted me to wear them for the wedding—"

Jake's face lit up. "The ones you're wearing?"

Nodding, she put a hand behind her right earlobe and tipped her head to show him.

Leaning closer, Jake brushed her hair out of the way for a better view. When his fingertips skimmed her cheek, a tingle raced over her skin. She tensed, hyperalert to his nearness as he examined the simple gold dangling earrings. She held her breath, all too aware of the fact that in her entire relationship with Brent, her fiancé's caresses had never elicited half the electricity in her that Jake's accidental touch had. Her heartbeat kicked into overdrive when his mahogany eyes met hers at close range. "May I take it off?"

The deep, husky timbre of his voice stroked her, and she had to swallow hard before she could speak. "Sure."

She scrunched her eyes shut and gritted her teeth, certain she'd come out of her skin as he fumbled to remove the jewelry from her lobe, his warm fingers teasing the erogenous zone behind her ear. When he leaned back, his attention narrowed on the delicate earring, she drew a shaky breath, puzzled by her schoolgirl reaction to him.

He saved your life today. This giddy, blood-pumping response to him must be some form of emotional transference or hero worship. An adrenaline-based response to your brush with danger.

Appeased by her explanation, Paige turned her attention back to her hamburger but found she no longer had an appetite. She lifted her gaze to Jake, whose brows were furrowed in concentration.

"There are no gems on them," she offered, taking off the other earring to hand to him. "Nothing that could be called a bead. They're just hammered gold and a wire hook. They're not even all that pretty. But they're family heirlooms, and he asked me to wear them for the wedding." When he held out his hand for the second earring, she dropped it into his hand, careful not to touch him.

Chicken.

He shook his head and curled his fingers around the jewelry. "Damn. I thought we had something, but you're right. There's nothing to these things, nothing I see as suspicious. Nothing that'd make terrorists want 'em or threaten national security." He puffed out a frustrated breath and took another large bite of his sandwich. "What else?" he asked as he chewed.

She fingered the hem of her shirt and shrugged. "He had me keep the plane tickets for Jamaica in my purse. And… well, he gave me a corsage to wear at the rehearsal dinner last night. He gave—"

"Where's the corsage?" His eyes were bright with interest again.

"At my house, in the refrigerator. I was hoping it would stay fresh until I got back from the honeymoon." She sat straighter. "I don't remember anything beadlike added as embellishment. But I suppose—"

"It's not the corsage." Jake's jaw tightened. "The bead is important. Something he wanted protected, guarded. He wouldn't have put it in something you'd leave in your refrigerator while the two of you jetted off to the islands." He pressed his mouth in a thin line of consternation. "There has to be something else. Think!"

"I'm trying!" Her inability to decipher this puzzle grated on her logical, analytical nature. Jake's dissatisfaction with her help challenged her innate need to please, to prove herself, to excel. "We're assuming the term *bead* is literal. We don't know that what he gave me is *bead*like at all. What if *bead* is an acronym or a code name?"

"You're right. We shouldn't think so narrowly."

He shoved to his feet and grabbed her wedding dress from floor. "Have you gone over this to see if he hid something in the beading?"

"I didn't see anything unusual. Besides, Brent didn't give me the dress. He hadn't even seen it until today."

He continued probing the decorated folds of satin with a wrinkle in his brow. "Maybe he hid something in your suitcase without telling you. Have you searched it?"

"Yes. I didn't find anything I hadn't packed myself."

The house was rapidly growing dark as the sun set outside. Without the use of lights, which would call attention to their presence in the vacant house, they'd soon be left in an all-encompassing darkness. Paige shuddered at the thought, remembering the terrifying blast of gunfire and Trench Coat's menacing smirk.

She had something terrorists wanted. Something they'd happily kill her to retrieve.

The pressure to come up with an answer bore down on her. She curled her fingers into her hair, pressing her temples with the heels of her hands. "I don't know! I have no idea what those men were after or why Brent thinks I have it!" Her voice cracked, thick with defeat and fear. "I've gone over the last few weeks again and again, and I just can't—"

Jake captured her head between his hands, startling her. She hadn't noticed his approach, and his calmly commanding grasp stole her breath.

"It's all right, Paige." As soon as he had her attention, his hands gentled to a soothing stroke that settled at the base of her skull. His fingers tangled in her hair, and his gaze held hers. "Don't worry about it. We'll figure this out another way."

In the wake of all he'd sacrificed this afternoon to save her, her failure gnawed at her belly. "I'm sorry. I don't know what—"

"Shh." His thumbs caressed her jaw, and she saw a warmth and understanding that she'd never seen before in his chiseled face and military-hardened attitude. Her pulse stumbled, and heat flooded her cheeks where his thumbs grazed her skin. "Maybe we're going about this all wrong. Maybe a better plan would be to get a fix on what this bead is and why it is a national security risk."

With Jake's hands in her hair, his muscled body so close, her voice fled, but she managed a small nod.

His touch made her dizzy, and a heady thrill tripped through her veins. She indulged in a leisurely study of his full lips, his slightly crooked nose and his angular cheeks, where the first hints of evening stubble had grown.

Jake McCall, with his navy SEAL body, military bearing and ruggedly handsome face, exuded a masculinity that shook Paige to the core. He was nothing like the soft-in-the-middle, somewhat geeky, scientist-type men she'd dated. Nothing like the man she'd almost married.

Guilt bit hard on her conscience when she thought of Brent. How could she swoon like this over Jake's tantalizing touch and bedroom eyes while her fiancé was in the hospital dying?

No. Not her fiancé. She couldn't marry Brent now, not after he'd lied to her, put her in danger, proven how little she knew about him. Her chest tightened as she thought about how disappointed her father would be. He'd introduced her to Brent, encouraged the marriage, been so proud of her...

But she'd never had more than friendly affection for the man her father wanted her to marry. She'd believed the love would grow over the years, had believed passion was a fleeting thing only the fortunate few ever really had. Because marrying Brent made her father happy, because she knew how important Brent's role in Bancroft Industries was, Paige had been willing to enter a marriage based on platonic feelings and good business. She'd thought it would be enough for her.

Now, the extent of her relief that she'd not legally married Brent today told her just how wrong the marriage was. But how could she let her father down? How could she jeopardize her family's position at Bancroft Industries?

"Paige?" Jake's deep voice called her from her troubled thoughts and refocused her attention on their more immediate problem.

"H-how..." she croaked, then paused to clear her throat and lick her dry lips. "How are we supposed to find out what the bead is?"

Jake's gaze darted to her mouth, his pupils dilating, and she felt his grip tighten subtly.

"My sister said Brent's unresponsive, so we can't ask him about it."

When she mentioned Brent, Jake's expression shifted, hardened, and he withdrew his hands from her face. His movements stiff, he rose to his feet again and stalked across the floor.

"What about your father? Maybe he'd know something."

Paige blinked and shook her head, unsure she'd heard him correctly. "My father? Why would he know anything?"

"He's the head of the company, about to pass over the reins to Scofield. If this has anything to do with Bancroft Industries, there's a good chance he knows something."

"Who said Bancroft Industries was involved?"

"Brent said a business deal had gone sour. As a medical

research and development company, Bancroft Industries has the means to engineer something that could pose a national security risk." He shrugged. "Can you think of any other way Brent could have gotten involved with terrorists? He have any questionable hobbies, travel to exotic places?"

Paige's shoulders slumped. "No. The company is his life."

The idea that her father's business, a company her grandfather had built from the ground up, could have been infiltrated by terrorists made Paige nauseated.

Jake faced her, his body taut and poised for action. "In that case, our focus should be on Scofield's role at Bancroft Industries. Can you get me inside? I need to search Scofield's office, take a look at his computer."

"I…guess so. In the morning, I can—"

"No. Tonight." Jake stepped over to her and, with a hand under her elbow, hoisted her to her feet. "If national security is at risk, then the clock is ticking. We have to move on this. *Now.*"

Chapter 4

Aₛ they drove to Bancroft Industries in the nondescript
Taurus Jake had rented on his last trip out, he briefed Paige
on his search plan. "Remember, the place is likely being
watched. We need to be as discreet and as quick as possible.
Get in, get the files and get out. Stay close to me and follow
my directions. Got it?"

Page sent him a worried look. "If those men are watching
the office, how do you expect to get in without being
seen?"

A buzz of energy flowed through Jake. After two years out
of action, it felt good to be back in his element. "Trust me,
okay? I once got a team of SEALs past thirty insurgents and
inside an embassy building in Iraq without being noticed. I'm
trained for this kind of thing."

He gave his aching knee a quick rub and tried to block out
the reminder of his last mission, the ambush, his failure. He'd
lost good men, most of his right kneecap and his career with
the SEALs.

As he drove past the driveway to Bancroft Industries,

Paige cut a sharp glance across the front seat. "That was your turn."

"Not until we do a little surveillance of our own. Study the grounds carefully, and tell me if anything seems out of place, no matter how minor."

He cruised past the parking lot without slowing, giving her little time to study the grounds.

She grunted and cast him a withering look. "How am I supposed to tell anything if you don't slow down and give me a chance to look?"

"What would you think if you saw a car slow down as it drove past your house?"

She leaned back against the seat and sighed her resignation. "I'd think they were casing the property with ill intent. I'd find it suspicious."

"Did you get anything on that pass? Picture the scene in your head and analyze it."

Paige chewed her bottom lip and closed her eyes. "The parking lot was emptier than usual for this time of night, but that's probably because we let so many employees have today off for the wedding. There would only be a skeleton crew working." She scrunched her nose and, angling her head, met his gaze across the dark front seat. "And there were more security cars than usual. Two at the front gate instead of one, and I think I saw another near the main entrance. Why would—?" Her expression said she'd answered her own question.

"Apparently after what happened today at church, your dad saw the connection to Bancroft Industries, as well, and decided to beef up security."

A deep V creased her brow. "I should be with my family. This mess affects them and the business as much as me. Maybe my dad could help us figure out what the *bead* is. Even though he's not involved with whatever Brent has done, my dad knows Bancroft Industries inside out. He could—"

"How do you know he's not involved?"

"My father is not involved with terrorists!" Paige's jade eyes flashed with anger.

"Twenty-four hours ago you'd have said the same about Scofield."

"That's different. I know my father, and he's not—"

"All right." Jake raised a hand in concession. Now was not the time to argue that point. He just prayed they didn't find evidence in Scofield's files that implicated the senior Bancroft. He'd hate to see Paige disillusioned, heartbroken if her father had a hand in something illegal, even traitorous. "What else did you notice?"

She shook her head. "I didn't have time to see much else. Can you drive by again?"

"This car may be bland, but if we make another pass, we'll be noticed."

She frowned. "So that's it? One quick drive-by is your idea of reconnaissance?"

He quirked an eyebrow and gave her a smug grin. "If you're good, once is enough. And I'm very good," he said, his voice dipping.

He hadn't intended the seductive timbre, but the cant of her head and spark of intrigue that simmered in her gaze told him clearly that she'd heard the unspoken message in his tone.

"Let's hope so," she replied smoothly.

Jake shoved down the kick of libido that tightened his muscles. Sexual banter with the woman he was supposed to be guarding was just the kind of distraction that could get them killed. Gripping the steering wheel harder, he refocused the surge of energy toward finding a place to leave the car where they could make a quick getaway if needed.

Ten minutes later, they approached the Bancroft Industries property on foot, skirting the parking lot and staying hidden in the woods that bordered three sides of the facility. Jake did a quick scan of the area, noting the location of security cameras, parked cars and shadowed corners where someone could be hiding.

He took Paige's hand in his, then nodded toward the car nearest them in the parking lot. "That's our first stop. Stay low and keep up. Ready?"

"Is all this cloak-and-dagger stuff really necessary?" she whispered. "This is my family's company. I've worked here since I was an intern the summer after my high school graduation. I should be able to walk in the front door, without the spy games, and without anyone questioning me."

"Except that it's your wedding night, your fiancé is in the hospital and the same gunmen who opened fire at your ceremony would like nothing better than to see you walk through the front door so they can grab you and torture you until you tell them where the bead is."

Her eyes filled with fear. "I only meant—"

"We run on three." They didn't have time for her to lament what should have been. They could have already been spotted at the edge of the woods. He hiked onto his shoulder the empty backpack he'd brought to carry out their booty. "One. Two. Three."

Jake sprinted for the sedan at the corner of the lot, hauling Paige along behind him and ignoring the ache in his knee. He had a job to do and no time to waste on his bum knee.

When they reached the cover of the car, she crouched beside him, barely winded.

"You have your security card to get us inside?"

She gave a jerky nod and held up the electronic key pass. "The door on the back side of the building is closest to Brent's office, but it has more security cameras on it. I suggest we head to the second side entrance…there—" She pointed across the parking lot to a door near tall flowering shrubs. "The bushes will help give us cover until we can get inside."

Impressed with her reasoning, Jake nodded. "What's inside that door? We won't come in at a guard station or high-traffic restroom, will we?"

She gave him a how-stupid-do-I-look look. "That's the research hall. Mostly laboratories that should be empty tonight. We'll go down a short hall and take the first left.

There's a supply closet, first door on the right, where we can stop to regroup if we need to."

Jake lifted a corner of his mouth. "For someone who was complaining about the cloak-and-dagger approach earlier, you're pretty good at this."

"I just know we need a plan. You need to know where we are going, what we're up against, and we needed a contingency place to hide…just in case. I like to be prepared."

His grin tugged broader. "Prepared is good, but I'm used to playing things as they come."

"If we're downloading Brent's computer files, then we'll need a way to open the files later. Right?"

Jake arched an eyebrow. He'd already thought through this problem, but he was interested to hear her solution. "Go on."

"Well, my office is at the near end of the hall where we'll go in. Third door on the left. I have an old laptop stashed in the bottom of my desk that I haven't used since the company's last computer upgrade. It's a dinosaur, but it works."

Snagging her laptop while they were inside was a better idea than what he'd planned. "Perfect. We'll get it first, then head to Scofield's office. Good thinking, Paige."

She twitched her cheek in a grin.

"Ready to go?"

Paige jerked a nod. "On three?"

He winked. Counted. And they ran.

By the time they'd retrieved her laptop and reached Brent's office, Paige's heart rate was in the stratosphere. Shaking to her core, she plastered herself to the corridor wall, waiting for Jake to pick the lock on Brent's office door.

Her sister Zoey would have been far better suited to this kind of high-stakes errand. But Zoey was still who-knows-where with her loser boyfriend traveling from poker tournament to poker tournament and running headlong for a major heartache.

Paige's breath snagged. Her youngest sister had seen the

truth all along. Marrying Brent had been a misguided attempt to please her father. But Zoey lived her life to the fullest, chose what made her happy and pursued her dreams without fear.

Meanwhile, Paige's perfect wedding had become a perfect nightmare, and she'd never been more frightened and uncertain of her future in her life.

She heard the snick of the door lock, and Jake pushed the door open, swept the beam of his flashlight around the office and motioned her inside. After quietly closing the door behind them, he whispered, "I'll search the file cabinet. You get us into his computer records."

Paige wiped her sweaty palms on her jeans and dropped into Brent's chair. The faint aroma of Brent's aftershave hung in the room. The familiar scent had never been her favorite, but now it seemed cloying and made her stomach turn.

She powered on his PC and immediately encountered a password-protected sign in. She bit her thumbnail, unmindful of the salon manicure she'd had yesterday for the wedding. Tonight, in light of the day's turbulent events, her French manicure was of little importance. Paige closed her eyes, wondering if her life would ever resemble "normal" again.

She knew she had only three tries to get Brent's password correct or the office system would lock her out until the IT guys could reset his account.

Sucking in a deep breath, she typed *PAIGE*. Hit Enter.

The computer beeped and flashed an error message.

Jake flipped quickly through stacks of paperwork, making split-second assessments of whether various documents or folders might have vital information. Without pausing from his work, he whispered, "Keep trying. Sometimes passwords are the most obvious things, nothing secure at all."

She tried Brent's birth date.

Error.

She had one more guess. Pressing her hands to her cheeks, she leaned back in the chair and closed her eyes again. Searched her memory. What was important to Brent? What would he use as his private security code?

The company was the focus of all his time and energy. His upcoming promotion.

Hands shaking, Paige typed in *BICEO*.

Bancroft Industries Chief Executive Officer.

The screen blinked, then the hard drive purred to life.

She was in. Paige waited impatiently for the start-up procedure to finish, glancing across the room where Jake was shoving folders of documents into a backpack.

Her stomach whirled. She was helping a stranger steal company property. If her father knew…

Paige laced her fingers and pressed her thumbs together, trying to calm her jitters. She was doing all this to protect her father and the company. To help stop terrorists. To save herself and her family from the men who'd opened fire at the church today. But breaking and entering, stealing files, hiding like a fugitive rankled her safe, law-abiding and orderly instincts.

Once she was at Brent's desktop screen, she searched the icons for one that might guide her to the list of his most recent work files. Jake finished ransacking the file cabinets, stuffing the materials in his backpack, and stepped closer to hover over her shoulder.

She found another password-secured program and tried the code that had worked before.

BICEO.

Error.

Growling her frustration and impatience, she tried again, typing *PAIGE* and holding her breath.

Error.

Jake said nothing, but his presence unnerved her. He was counting on her to work fast, find what they needed and not let simple passwords stop her from getting results.

He swiped a hand down his jaw. "Want me to try?"

"I can do this. I know him better than you do."

"Try *VERONICA*."

Paige twisted on the chair to meet Jake's gaze. "What? Why?"

"Veronica Salley was the love of his life in high school.

I heard they got engaged in college. Don't know why they broke up, but I'm betting it wasn't his idea. He was crazy about her."

"He wouldn't—"

"Try it."

"But I only have one guess left. If you're wrong, the system will shut down."

"Try it."

Huffing out her disagreement, Paige pounded out *VERONICA*. Hit Enter.

The computer flashed to a list of saved documents.

Jealousy bit hard, and Paige gritted her teeth. Why she should care about an old girlfriend of a man she'd decided she didn't love and couldn't marry, she couldn't say.

Jake handed her a tiny USB flash drive. "Save them all to this. Hurry."

After plugging the device the size of a pack of gum into the computer, she hit a few keys to start the download.

A green bar popped onto the screen to track the progress of the files transfer. Ten-percent complete. Fifteen percent...

She angled her head toward Jake. "Is there anything else we should—"

A series of loud pops sounded down the hall.

Startled, Paige yelped, and Jake grabbed her arm, tugging her down from Brent's chair and behind the mammoth wooden desk. She recognized the noise far too quickly, had heard it too often already today.

Gunfire.

Jake reached behind him for the gun tucked in his jeans. "Listen to me. I'll hold them off as long as I can. Watch that download, and the second it is finished, pull the flash drive and stash it somewhere safe, somewhere you won't lose it if we have to run."

Paige's answering laugh was half irony, half panic. "*If* we have to run?"

With his free hand, Jake cupped her face and drilled a hard, yet oddly comforting gaze on her. He was calm, assured, in control of the situation. "I know this looks bad. I know you've been through a lot today, and this is frightening. But you have to keep it together for me. Just stay calm, do what I tell you, and we'll get through this."

More gunfire echoed in the corridor. Closer. Louder.

The download read sixty-five-percent complete.

Paige's pulse hiked higher. "But they have us cornered in here! How are we supposed to get out of this office?"

His grip on her face tightened slightly. "I'll find us another way out."

Jake's steady mahogany gaze penetrated the shroud of fear surrounding her. His confidence and skill bolstered her wavering courage. She trusted Jake. He'd already saved her, come through for her so many times today.

She gave a jerky nod of cooperation.

Jake smacked a quick kiss on her forehead and shoved to his feet. Dragging a chair below the air vent, he used a knife blade to quickly loosen the screws holding the cover in place.

Download seventy-eight-percent complete.

More gunfire.

Paige snapped her gaze to the door. Three men clad in dark clothes and wielding large guns burst into the office.

Jake dropped and rolled back behind the desk with her as a spray of bullets pelted the wall behind her.

She swallowed her scream, too terrified to muster the breath needed.

Download ninety-two-percent complete.

Snatching up his gun, Jake aimed his weapon at the intruders and dropped two of them with deadly accuracy. The third man swung back into the hall for cover, shouting, "They're in here!"

Jake grabbed her wrist and shoved the gun into her hand. "Cover me."

She gaped at him. "Wh-what?"

"Aim at the door and squeeze the trigger. Hold them off. I gotta get that vent open." With that, he scuttled back to the chair where he stood to pry the air duct cover from the vent.

The man at the door swung around from the hall and fired at Jake.

"Paige!"

Her heart leaped to her throat. Hands shaking, she pushed to her knees, propped her elbows on the desk and fired off two rounds at the man in the door. The man screamed and grabbed his arm.

Download ninety-nine-percent complete.

Jake popped the vent cover free and shoved the backpack stuffed with paper files inside the duct. "Paige, let's go!"

"C'mon, c'mon!" she begged the computer.

The gunman fumbled for his weapon with his left hand, his firing arm hanging loose at his side. Raising his gun, he aimed now at Paige. She gasped and ducked, just as two bullets whizzed past her head. The wood paneling behind her splintered.

"Paige!" Jake rushed back behind the desk with her and nudged her toward the vent. "Move it!"

Download complete. Thank heavens!

She snatched the portable storage device from the USB port and shoved it in her jeans pocket.

Taking the gun from her, Jake finished off the guy at the door, just as his backup arrived.

Holding her breath, Paige ran for the chair under the vent and scrambled to find a handhold. A large hand planted on her bottom, shoving her up and into the narrow vent. She wiggled and squeezed, hurrying to clear the way for Jake as a fresh round of gunfire blazed.

Darkness swallowed her inside the vent. The tight passage reminded her of a tomb, and she fought off a cloying claustrophobia. Breathing raggedly, her arms trembling, she felt her way hand over hand, inching forward. Her hand bumped the large backpack full of files Jake had salvaged, and she pushed it deeper into the air return. When she found a side outlet, she pulled herself around the right angle. The side vent was large enough for her to sit up and turn around. Dim light from the open end of the vent illuminated the path she'd just come through.

Jake wasn't behind her. Panic roiled in her gut, filling her mouth with bitter fear. "Jake!"

From the office, she heard muffled grunts, loud thumps and breaking glass.

Her heart in her throat, she crawled back toward the office. "Jake!"

"Don't wait for me! Go!"

Relief swamped her knowing he was alive, yet she hesitated. Go without Jake?

A face appeared at the vent opening. Glowering. Bleeding.

Not Jake's.

She saw the flash of metal as the man raised a gun to the vent opening. Then a spray of red as a bullet hit his head.

Gasping, Paige scuttled back awkwardly, bumping her head and jamming her elbow. Her pulse thundered wildly in her ears, a harsh counterpoint to the sounds of violence echoing through the metal cave.

Twisting around, she crawled back into the side vent, feeling for a means of escape. But the side tunnel led to a large fan, blocked off with a sturdy steel screen. A dead end.

Struggling to keep her breathing even and not give in to the clamoring fear squeezing her chest, Paige turned around and crawled back the way she had come.

Still no Jake. More thumps. More gunfire. More grunts of pain.

Acid sawed in her stomach. If anything happened to Jake…

Paige closed her eyes and sucked in slow, deep breaths. She had to fight the panic, had to keep it together if she wanted to be any use to Jake. If she wanted to survive this nightmare.

Brent's fault. She was in all this danger because of Brent, because of the bead.

Anger slashed through her. How could he have claimed to

love her, then put her in this position? How could she have ever believed she loved Brent?

She rolled to her belly as she went back into the first, smaller duct. Shimmying forward on her hands and stomach, she scrunched along the tight tunnel, pushing the backpack in front of her, only to find that the duct narrowed as she crawled farther back. There was no way Jake, with his broad shoulders, would fit in this restricted space. And Paige wasn't too keen on the idea of trying to squeeze through herself and risk getting stuck. The air-return tunnel wasn't going to provide an escape.

Swallowing her disappointment and a fresh wave of fear, she backed up. The hard floor of the metal duct bit into her knees and elbows as she wiggled toward the side outlet, where there was space to turn around. If they couldn't get out through the HVAC ducts, how—?

"Paige?" Jake's deep voice was sweet music to her ears. No other noises came from the office. The silence was chilling.

"J-Jake?" A hand grabbed her ankle, and she gasped, flinched.

"Easy. It's me."

"We can't get through that way. One duct is too small, and the other is blocked."

"Forget it. I handled the problem. I'll help you down." Jake positioned her foot on his shoulder. "Bring the backpack."

As she found her footing, he skimmed his hand up her leg to her waist to help her balance as she crawled backward out of the vent. "What happened to—?"

Her breath caught when she saw the carnage in Brent's office. No less than six men—all clearly dead—broken furniture, scattered files, shattered glass. And blood.

On the floor. On the walls. On Jake.

Icy horror swept through her, and she clutched the backpack to her chest as if it could shield her from the grisly scene. "Oh, my God! Are you all right? How… What—?"

"I'll be fine." He wiped his bloody lip on his shoulder then stooped to take a large gun from the hands of one of the dead men. Pulling the backpack from her hands, he shoved the assault rifle toward her. "Take this. We're not in the clear yet."

She stifled the question that sprang to her mind—how had he overpowered all those men? Judging by the noises she'd heard, the odd angle of some of their necks and Jake's obvious injuries, she didn't *want* to know what SEAL-trained techniques he'd employed. Paige shuddered and stared down at the assault weapon in her hands. "M-maybe we should… call in the police now. This is all too—"

"No." Jake threaded his arms through the straps of the backpack and edged toward the door. "Brent was very clear. He said Homeland Security had been compromised. If we call the local police about this, they'll be obligated to call in the Feds. Until we know who and what we are dealing with, who we can trust, we do this alone." He peered around the door frame and hitched his head. "Come on. We need to hurry."

Paige stepped over a burly man whose dark eyes stared sightlessly at her. The urge to cry, to curl up and fall apart was strong, but digging deep and gritting her teeth, she crushed the temptation to give in to her weakness. Jake needed her to be strong, think clearly, be ready to follow his directions.

He took her hand and led her down the hall at a jog. Jake was limping, favoring his right leg. They paused at the intersection, where there was another corridor, long enough for Jake to peek around the corner. When he gave her the all-clear nod, they set off again. At the end of the hall, the night guard's body lay sprawled in a pool of blood. Her stomach rebelled at the sight. She remembered hearing gunfire before the terrorists had arrived at Brent's office. Now she knew why. Jake's grip on her hand was tight to the point of being painful, but Paige didn't dare pull away. She was keenly aware how dependent she was on him to get out of the building—and this entire macabre situation—alive.

Chapter 5

When they reached the rental car, Paige dropped onto the passenger seat and closed her eyes. A shudder raced through her, and she mumbled a prayer of thanks that they'd made it out of the building in one piece. Most of Bancroft Industry's security force hadn't been as lucky, thanks to the terrorists. Whoever these people were, they played hardball and would ruthlessly kill anyone who stood in their way.

Jake climbed in the driver's side and cranked the engine, giving the area a searching glance before he pulled the car from the cover of the bushes where they'd parked. "Show me the flash drive."

Paige fished in her pocket and pulled out the tiny device. Jake nodded. They drove in silence for several blocks before he spoke again. "Hey, you did a good job in there."

She cast a blank stare at him as he pulled to a stop at a red light.

"How can you say that? I crawled into the vent and hid. You single-handedly took out six men!"

"Not all at once. And you slowed that one guy with a good shot to the arm."

She shrugged, not wanting to think about having to shoot at the man who was trying to kill Jake. "But you knew the password to Brent's files would be his ex-girlfriend's name." She huffed with disgust. "That stung. How silly of me to think he'd use *my* name as a password. I'm only his fiancée."

He turned his palm up from the steering wheel. "Well, maybe that's why he didn't use it. Maybe he thought it was too obvious, not safe enough. They tell you to avoid things like birthdays and children's names, because they're too easily guessed."

"Maybe." Paige rubbed her hands over her arms, still shivering in a post-adrenaline crash. "But his password was still another woman's name. I think that speaks volumes. Don't you?"

He hesitated, casting a hooded side glance to her. "Yeah. I think it says he's still in love with Veronica, and you were justified in your doubts about marrying him."

She opened her mouth to deny again that she'd been having second thoughts at the wedding, then snapped her mouth closed. His eyes were too incisive, and arguing seemed pointless. He was right, and the pretense she'd been living had blown up in her face.

With a sigh she leaned back against the headrest. "Guess it also says he was using me to impress my dad and get the inside track on the CEO job when Dad retires this fall."

"Brent was always ambitious."

She grunted and turned to stare out the side window. "Very. I just didn't realize I was nothing more than a rung in his climb up the ladder."

"He cares about you."

Her shoulders drooped. "Don't patronize me."

"I'm not. I saw it in his face when he talked about you at the rehearsal. It may not have been love, but he cared. He cared enough to step in front of a bullet for you."

She whipped her head around to face him. "A bullet that

would never have been aimed at me if not for his secret life as a spy or a terrorist or whatever the hell he's mixed up in!"

Jake drew a deep breath and scrubbed a hand over his face. "Yes, he *did* drag you into this firestorm…which leads us back to my original point. Considering how this was dumped on you and all you've been through today, you did a good job tonight."

He parked the car along a residential curb and cut the engine. She recognized the vacant house where they'd hidden earlier several houses down the street. Apparently the empty home was their base of operation for the time being.

"You've a right to be proud of yourself," he continued. "It might have been messy, but we got what we went in for. We got his files, so…mission accomplished. Good work, partner."

Lifting a corner of his mouth, he held his fist out to her.

She blinked. Frowned.

After a moment, Jake reached for her hand, curled her fingers into a ball and tapped his knuckles against hers. The awkward fist bump shouldn't have meant so much to her. But the simple congratulatory gesture, coupled with his praise, spun a frisson of warmth through her that burrowed beneath the chill of her fear, her disappointment, her disillusionment.

Knowing she'd done something, *anything,* worthy of Jake's approval pleased her. Brought a small grin to her lips. "Thanks. You deserve the credit, though. I didn't—"

He pressed a finger to her lips, cutting her off. His touch sizzled through her, backed up her breath in her lungs.

"You sell yourself short. You showed courage, intelligence, forethought… I was proud of you."

When he added a quick, lopsided grin to his compliment, her pulse scampered. Jake turned to climb out of the car, giving her time to collect herself and shove down her body's reaction to him. The last thing she needed was a telltale shiver or something in her expression giving away her schoolgirl attraction to him.

Jake ushered her to the back door of the vacant house and had her wait on the stoop until he'd swept through each room to be sure no one was lying in wait for them. Once inside, she dropped wearily to the floor of the living room, glad now for the cover of the darkness. Jake's skill in reading her thoughts and interpreting her body language unnerved her. Now that they were out of harm's way, she wasn't sure how much longer she could keep her emotions at bay.

She hugged herself as she watched Jake's shadowy movements. She recognized the sounds when he took his gun out and reloaded it—the rattle of the bullets in his hand, the click when he locked the magazine into place.

The rustle of the curtains when he brushed them back to check the yard. The crinkle of paper when he pulled a cold hamburger from the fast-food sack and peeled the wrapper back.

"Want half this burger?"

She shook her head, then, realizing he'd likely not seen the gesture in the dark, whispered, "No, thanks. I'm not hungry."

Folding her arm under her cheek, she lay down on her side and stared into the inky blackness. Fatigue sank to the bone, but images of the day's horrors paraded through her mind, keeping her from falling asleep. After several minutes, she sighed and tried to find a more comfortable position on the hard floor.

"Don't think about it," Jake said.

"About what?"

"Whatever's keeping you awake. Probably the violence you witnessed today."

She didn't bother asking how he knew. Even without his skills in reading people, the cause of her restlessness was pretty obvious. "It's kinda hard not to think about it."

"I know, but try to focus on something good, maybe a favorite memory. Like…the last time you had lunch with your sister Holly."

She sighed.

"We were at Brundle's Deli…planning my wedding." The happy memory made her voice crack.

If only she could go back to that day last week, before…

"Come here." Jake moved to lie at her side. He nudged her closer, cradling her in the crook of his arm and pulling her head down to his shoulder. "Try to sleep."

Paige turned on her side and rested her hand on his chest. His heart bumped a steady cadence under her palm, and the slow, sure beat soothed her ragged nerves.

When Jake strummed his fingers up and down her spine, the hypnotic stroking made her whole body tingle. A feral, musky scent clung to him and teased her senses. In his arms, she felt both serenely safe and on the precipice of some unknown but exhilarating danger. For tonight, she didn't want to examine the contradiction. Instead, she curled her fingers into the soft material of his T-shirt. Closing her eyes, she indulged the urge to snuggle closer to him and feel the raw strength of his hard body pressed along the length of hers.

She shouldn't be so wildly attracted to another man on the same day she'd been about to marry Brent. But she hadn't planned to be so drawn to Jake, and Brent had never evoked the sensual response from her that Jake did. Brent had deceived her and put her at risk. And today, she'd admitted to herself that she didn't love Brent, didn't want to marry him.

"I know what you saw today was frightening for you." His deep voice rumbled gently like distant thunder in the dark room. "But Brent asked me to keep you safe, and that is what I'm going to do."

Paige scoffed. "Correction, he told you to keep the *bead* safe. I was just a by-the-way. The unfortunate one who had the damnable bead when everything hit the fan." She didn't try to mask the resentment in her tone. "Clearly, my safety wasn't his greatest concern or he'd never have put me in this position."

Jake raked his fingers through her hair, capturing the base of her skull and angling her head so that she looked up at him. "Brent may not have considered you the priority, but I do. I'm making it my job to see that you get through this safe and sound. You have my word, Paige."

A sliver of light from a street lamp sliced through the window blinds and illuminated his face. The pale glow highlighted the rugged angles in his cheeks, the square cut of his jaw—and reflected the determination in his dark eyes.

She held his gaze, mesmerized by the intensity that vibrated from him. In a moment, his attention shifted to her mouth, and Paige felt his muscles tense. Her pulse quickened, and her gaze gravitated to Jake's lips.

The air between them charged, grew thick with palpable heat and tension.

She read Jake's internal battle in his twitching cheek as he gritted his teeth, the flaring of his nose as he sucked in a slow breath. His fight for restraint buzzed through the taut muscles of his arms and the increasing tempo of his heartbeat under her hand.

After a mind-numbing day of having danger thrown in her face, her life thrust in the line of fire, Paige had little patience for the careful thought and reason she typically relied on. In that moment, she wanted only to savor the tempting sensations Jake stirred in her. She wanted to flout caution, ignore the voice that warned her to go slowly.

Without analyzing the impulse, she tunneled her fingers into his hair, closed the distance between them and brushed her lips against his. With their bodies aligned, she absorbed the shudder that raced through Jake. A groan hummed from his throat as he anchored her head between his hands and deepened the kiss. Tingling sparks shot through her blood, taunting her, thrilling her.

He was endearingly tentative at first, as if asking permission to be bolder. Paige settled the question for him by sweeping her tongue along the seam of his lips and sliding her leg over his. Her thigh bumped the hard ridge under his fly, and knowing that she'd aroused him filled her with a confidence—and recklessness—she'd never experienced. A surge of crackling energy coursed through her, urging her to sate the growing hunger, gnawing deep inside.

Jake's tongue parried with hers, and his fingers kneaded

her bottom. He lifted her hips and scooted beneath her so that she lay intimately draped atop him. His hands mussed her hair as their kiss escalated, as their bodies heated and the rest of the world fell away.

Paige hooked her legs around Jake's, and her caresses roamed restlessly over his wide shoulders, rock-hard arms and muscled chest. And still she wanted more. She craved the escape, the sweet oblivion his body offered. She ground her hips against his, and her hands pulled impatiently at his T-shirt. She wanted to feel his skin on hers, wanted to draw him closer, wanted to blot out everything except the mind-numbing sensations he awoke in her.

When she reached for the button on his jeans, he caught her hand and broke their kiss.

"Jake…" she rasped, moving her mouth to nibble the line of his jaw.

"Paige, stop." He captured her face between his hands and angled her chin up so he could meet her gaze. "We have to stop."

"Why? We both want it," she whispered breathlessly, her head still muzzy and unfocused. "And heaven knows, after today we've earned the right to a little pleasure…"

He pulled her head down to his shoulder with one hand and hugged her close with his other arm. "First, because we don't have protection."

She jolted, her pulse kicking with the sobering reminder of how she'd lost her usually pragmatic senses.

"And second, because…I can't take advantage of you. We both want this for the wrong reasons." When she stiffened, he tightened his grip on her. "You're vulnerable tonight. Frightened. Confused. You don't want to complicate those feelings with sex you may regret in the morning."

The cold splash of reality doused the sizzle in her veins and, feeling suddenly awkward and embarrassed, Paige shoved away from Jake. The one time she'd tossed caution aside, she'd made a fool of herself, throwing herself at Jake.

"I'm sorry. I shouldn't have—"

"Wait." He refused to release her when she struggled. "I'm not saying I don't want you. I'd think it was pretty obvious how much I *do* want you."

"Jake, you don't have to—"

Without warning, he rolled over so that she was pinned beneath him. "Paige, listen. You are an extremely desirable woman. And yes, I want you. But I can't forget the danger we're in. I can't afford to be distracted."

She shivered, despite the heat of his body pressed against her.

Jake smoothed a hand along her cheek. "And I can't ignore the fact that this morning you were engaged to a man I'd been hired to guard. A man I failed to protect when he needed me most. Making love to you would feel like…a betrayal."

Paige caught her breath. Jake was right to stop them, but hearing him enumerate the many ways she'd abandoned her good judgment rubbed salt in the wounds she'd suffered today. She squeezed her eyes closed, fighting back the burn of tears and chastising herself for her lapse, for her recklessness. "You're right. And…it won't happen again. I'm sorry."

"Don't apologize." Jake rested his forehead lightly against hers and sighed. "You did nothing wrong."

Despite the reminders why indulging her attraction to Jake was a mistake, the gentle caress of his breath on her cheeks still stirred a flutter in her belly, still created a warmth and intimacy that wrapped comfortably around her heart.

His knuckles brushed her cheek, and he pressed a kiss to her temple. "Now get some sleep."

She nestled down, closer to him. How she'd fall asleep with the distraction of his body pressed to hers she didn't know.

But somehow she did, because the next thing she knew, bright yellow sun streamed through the gaps in the window blinds and roused her from sensuous dreams of Jake.

Squinting against the beam of buttery light that hit her face, she sat up and glanced about, finding herself alone on the living room floor. She rubbed her eyes and raked her hair away from her face, knowing she had to look a wreck. She prayed the hot water was still on in the house. She needed a reviving shower in the worst way. "Jake?"

"Mornin'."

She twisted at the waist and found Jake behind the kitchen counter with a stack of papers in his hands. Shoving to her feet, she ambled into the kitchen, yawning and casting a curious glance at the clutter of paperwork on the counter. "Brent's files?"

He nodded, then hitched his head toward the far end of the counter. "Breakfast. The coffee's probably pretty cold by now, but it's caffeine, if you're as addicted as I am."

Smiling her thanks, she popped the plastic lid off the insulated cup waiting for her. She wasn't a big coffee drinker, but his thoughtfulness touched her.

"Sugar and creamer are in the bag with the doughnuts. I wasn't sure how you took your coffee, so…" He let his sentence trail off as he turned his attention back to the scattered papers spread before him.

She sipped the coffee and raised her gaze to study her raven-haired protector.

He rubbed his chin as he read the open file, and the scratch of his morning beard against his fingers sent a rush of heat skittering through her.

Last night she'd been prepared to have sex with this man who knew so little about her, he didn't even know how she liked her coffee. No matter how sexy Jake was or how scared she'd been, there was no excuse for letting herself be so… emotional and rash.

Zoey was the impulsive sister—and look where it had gotten her. Traveling the country with a gambler, supporting his addiction and living hand to mouth off *Zoey's* life savings.

But, Paige, she's happy. She loves this guy. Who are we to judge how she lives her life if she's doing what feels right to her, what makes her happy? Holly had said, the last time Paige complained about Zoey's poor choices. Holly—the peacemaker, the nurturer, the blissfully-wedded idealist. She saw only the good in Zoey. In everyone.

Jake grunted, pulling her out of her drifting thoughts.

She stepped toward him to glance over his shoulder. "What? Did you find something?"

He waved a hand toward the file he was reading. "There's a lot in here about new drugs and vaccines Bancroft was developing."

"Makes sense. Research and Development is the largest and most profitable branch of the company. Besides, that's where Brent got his start. He's a research junkie at heart, though he set his sights on leading the company when Dad announced his retirement plans a couple years ago."

Jake glanced over his shoulder to her. "Any one project in particular that he talked about more than others? Something big in production that he was excited about?"

Paige sipped her coffee as she tried to recall what Brent had mentioned working on recently. "Nothing that stands out. He talked about meetings he had, contracts he'd signed. Mostly daily agenda stuff. To be honest, I was so preoccupied the last several months with wedding stuff, those plans were what we talked about most often."

"Did he mention trouble with any project, holdups or delays?"

"Every project has its delays and red tape. Backlogs for approval at the FDA, requests for new studies, data that has to be reanalyzed. Problems are common."

He grunted again as he turned his attention back to the file.

Paige plucked a doughnut from the sack and shook off the extra powdered sugar before taking a large bite and savoring the sweet treat. "What can I do to help?"

Jake glanced up and rubbed the back of his neck. "You could set up your laptop and take a look at the files on the USB. I was waiting for you to get up before I turned on your computer." He shrugged. "Felt like an invasion of your privacy to get on your computer without you."

She chuckled and shook her head. "Like breaking into

Brent's office and stealing his files wasn't an invasion of privacy?"

"Way I see it, Brent gave up the right to privacy when he put national security in jeopardy."

The sweet pastry in her mouth soured. *National security.* What on earth had Brent gotten her involved in?

After brushing sugar from her fingers, she retrieved the laptop from Jake's backpack and opened the top. She plugged in the power cord and took a seat on the floor while the computer started up.

"This is interesting." Jake picked up the file he'd been studying and moved to sit beside her, spreading the folder of papers on his lap. "I found a receipt stuck in here with all the paperwork on this project he called Superbug."

Paige cast him a curious glance. "A receipt for what?"

"Your wedding ring." He handed her the itemized jewelry-store printout. "Why would that be in the files of the company's research projects?"

"Are you kidding? Did you see his office when we were there? Clutter everywhere. Brent was brilliant, but he was disorganized. Messy." She glanced at the receipt then handed it back to Jake. "It was probably just misfiled."

He hummed an acknowledgment but continued to stare at the paper. "He had your ring specially designed. Built from scratch according to a design he gave the jeweler."

Statements, not questions. Yet Jake's expression said he felt an explanation was in order.

"Yeah. I told you that last night. Remember?" She slipped the wedding ring off and handed it to Jake. Why was she even still wearing it? "He wanted to give me a ring he called *unique* and *special.* I always took that to mean exorbitant and showy."

Her laptop finished loading programs, and she plugged the flash drive into a side port. While Jake turned the ring over, examining it again, she tapped her keyboard and began opening files uploaded from the flash drive. She found Brent's schedule spreadsheet with his appointments, meetings, names and phone numbers.

Holding her breath, Paige scanned the calendar, looking for anything that seemed out of place, unusual. Maybe a contact she'd never heard him mention.

"What if the receipt wasn't misfiled?"

She raised her gaze to Jake when he spoke. "Meaning?"

"What if this ring, the design he ordered, was relevant to the research outlined in these files?" He tossed the ring up and caught it. "Why would he be so determined to design the ring himself?"

She lifted a shoulder. "I always thought that was romantic, even if I didn't like his design. The thought that he wanted to create something especially for me was sweet."

Jake curled his fingers around the ring, and a thoughtful hum rumbled from his throat.

"You think there's more to it than that. You think the ring has the bead in it. Don't you?"

"It's the most likely scenario at this point." He extended the ring to her, and she hesitantly took it from him.

"What should I do with it? If this bead thing is dangerous, I don't want to wear it."

"I doubt it's dangerous as is. And wearing it is the best way to keep up with it."

Paige scowled and stared at the gaudy jewelry. She had the ring halfway on her left ring finger before she stopped, choosing to slide it onto her right hand instead. When she glanced up at Jake, he arched an eyebrow and sent her a knowing look.

Self-conscious heat crept up her neck as she returned her attention to her computer screen. "I found Brent's date book. Maybe something—"

"Shh!" Jake warned, jerking to attention and waving her silent. He cocked his head as if straining to hear something, then crept to the window. Pressing his back to the wall, he peered through the tiny gap between the blinds and the windowsill. And grumbled a scorching expletive.

"We have company. Clear out—fast!"

Chapter 6

Staying low, Jake hurried back to the counter and raked the scattered papers into a folder.

Paige's pulse skyrocketed, terror spiking in her with a full-body shudder. "Is it the terrorists?"

Visions of more gunfire, more blood, more death made her head swim. Trembling, she closed her laptop and jammed it in Jake's backpack.

He scooped up messy piles of paper, shoved the files in the pack with her computer and snatched the doughnut bag from the counter. "No. The Realtor is here with buyers. She's showing them the yard, the landscaping now. We'll go out the back."

Some of the tension in her chest loosened, but Jake's haste and concern still frazzled her.

"Get everything." He aimed a finger across the room where her suitcase and wedding dress lay on the floor. "We can't let anyone know we were here—unless you want B and E charges on your police record."

B and E. *Breaking and entering.*

Her breath stuttered. She'd almost forgotten they were trespassing.

Paige grabbed the dress, tossed it to Jake. With her coffee in one hand and her suitcase in the other, she followed Jake to the back door. Heart thundering, she waited while he checked the yard through the side window.

When the lock on the front door rattled, he opened the back door and rushed her out.

Paige gave the empty house a brief encompassing glance, double-checking that they'd gotten everything. On the living room floor next to the spot where they'd slept, she spotted Jake's gun.

She gasped. Pointed. "Jake!"

He turned to look and gritted out another curse.

"I'll get it. You go!" Dumping her wedding dress over her arm, he shoved her outside, directing her with a quick hand gesture. "Cut through that neighbor's driveway. Meet me on the next street."

Trying not to trip over the draping folds of her gown, Paige scurried down the back steps. Her suitcase bumped against her legs. She tried to be discreet, tried not to attract attention, but dragging a suitcase and wedding dress, she was hardly low profile.

Hurry, Jake!

When she reached the next residential street, she spotted a large recreational vehicle in a driveway and made a beeline for it. She crouched behind the behemoth, watching and waiting for Jake. Her thudding heartbeat counted the precious passing seconds. After two full minutes, more than enough time for him to nab the gun and meet her, Jake still hadn't shown.

What would she do if Jake had been seen? Detained? Arrested? She chewed her bottom lip, her anxiety growing as she considered what could be keeping him. A sheen of perspiration beaded on her forehead, and Paige began planning her next move. If Jake never came…

She had the ring. Her dress. Her suitcase. Which meant she probably still had the bead. Jake had said going to the police or FBI was risky, that Brent had indicated they couldn't be trusted for some reason.

Brent was in the hospital, weak, possibly dying.

Her father would help her. So would her sisters. But how could she draw any more danger back to her family? She swallowed against the knot forming in her throat.

Without Jake, she was alone. Despite the steamy Louisiana temperatures, a chill slithered through her. Where was Jake? What was keeping him?

Jake pressed himself against the back wall of the closet where he'd taken refuge and gritted his teeth in frustration. Rather than starting the home tour with the kitchen, just off the entry hall, the Realtor had brought the buyers straight back to the living room to enjoy the view of the backyard. He'd only had time to dash for the utility closet and prayed no one explored the storage options—yet. Getting caught didn't worry him. If discovered, he'd have no problem getting past the Realtor and her clients and getting away—but getting away unseen would be far better.

He hoped Paige had made tracks and cleared the backyard before the buyers reached the windows to admire the yard's amenities. For five full minutes, the Realtor gushed about the landscaping, the safe neighborhood, the wonderful school district and the underground sprinkler system.

"And wait until you see the oversize tub and walk-in closets in the master bathroom!" the Realtor cooed. Finally the thump of footsteps and drone of voices moved down the hall.

Jake cracked open the closet door and peered out, scanning the living room. All clear.

With the pantherlike stealth the SEALs had taught him, he crossed the floor and slid out the back door. He kept out of sight, using fences and shrubbery for cover as he made his way through the neighbor's yard and out to the next street. He scanned the road for Paige, and in the gap under a large motor home, he glimpsed a red suitcase, a white gown and two feet.

He made a point of scuffling his feet as he approached so that he didn't startle her. He didn't need her yelping and drawing more attention to them than their strange collection of cargo already did.

"Paige?" he called quietly, and she darted from behind the RV and threw herself into his arms.

"Jake, thank heavens! What took you so long?"

The distress in her wide green eyes made her look all the more vulnerable, fragile. Beautiful. A frisson of heat burrowed into him.

Earlier, when she'd strolled into the kitchen, rumpled from sleep, he'd almost jumped out of his skin. He'd had to draw on all his reserves not to let on how just the sight of her, tousled and free of makeup, roused carnal images. By keeping his eyes off her and his attention focused on Scofield's files, he'd brought his body's instant reaction to her under control. Barely.

He rubbed her back briefly and stepped away before the press of her curves fired a libido he'd had only a fingernail grip on since last night. "Just detained for a minute. No problem."

"No problem? What if you'd been caught?" Her voice quivered, and her eyes rounded.

He couldn't remember the last time he'd had someone who cared enough about him to worry for his well-being. That she cared enough to be concerned did strange things to his heart. Then again, she could have just been anxious for her own safety, not his.

"I might have been seen, but I wouldn't have been caught." He gave her a smug grin to cover the jumpy sensation her concern stirred in his chest. Their hasty getaway was a walk in the park for him, but he found the idea that Paige had worried about him unsettling. Foreign. Intoxicating.

"So now what do we do?" She sagged against the RV, and her shoulders slumped.

He rolled the strange tension from his shoulders and glanced around. "We find a new place to stay."

"No more vacant houses!" Passion and conviction fired her gaze. "I hate the idea of trespassing, of breaking into someone else's home. Even if it is vacant and for sale."

He nodded. Now that he'd had a little more time to plan their next move, he agreed that they needed to go another route this time.

"Can't we just go to a hotel?" Paige's eyes pleaded with him, and compunction tugged at him. "We could drive somewhere out of town, even out of state."

"How would we pay for it without leaving a paper trail? Do you have hundreds in cash with you?"

"Well, no, but I have enough for a couple nights, anyway."

Jake rubbed his cheek, turning the situation over in his head. Where could they stay that was out of the way, but still provided shelter and—

His gaze darted up to the RV Paige leaned against. He stepped closer and ran his hand down the side wall, kicked the tires. "That's it. An RV."

Paige jerked her head up, her eyes wide. "No, Jake. No way! You are *not* stealing this RV! I won't allow it! No more breaking the law. There has to be a way to do this without—"

He caught her chin in his hand and dropped a quick kiss on her mouth. "Not this one. I'm not a thief."

Paige stared at him, looking poleaxed. With her pupils wide and her bowed lips parted in surprise, she raised a hand to her mouth and drew a shaky breath. Jake had to call on every bit of his willpower to keep from kissing her again.

He cleared his throat and said, "We'll rent a camper."

Paige curled her lips in and closed her eyes. When she looked up at him again, her dubious expression spoke for her reluctance. "We're going to *camp?* Where?"

"A campground, of course." He paused. "Wait. Are you telling me you've never been camping?"

She flashed him a weak grin. "Does cheerleading camp count?"

"Did you stay in tents or cabins?"

"More like the dorms at the host college."

He snorted his dismissal and shook his head. "Darlin', you are overdue. You're going to love roughing it."

"Roughing it? Can't we get one of the RVs with the bathroom and kitchen and regular bed?"

He tugged up his cheek and winked at her. "We'll play it by ear, see what's for rent and how far our cash goes." He looped the backpack over his shoulder and picked up her suitcase. Nodding toward the wedding dress, he frowned. "Since Brent didn't give you the dress, I think we can safely assume that the bead isn't one of the sequins on your gown. Can we ditch the dress now?"

"Ditch it? Like leave it here?"

"You really want to keep hauling it around with us?"

"Jake, it's a Vera Wang! Do you know what it is worth?"

He gave her a disgruntled frown, then hesitated. "Do you know where there's a consignment shop or secondhand store where we can sell it? The extra cash would help us out a lot."

She pulled her shoulders back, sending him an appalled look that finally melted to resignation. "You're right. I don't need it anymore. If selling it will help us, then that's what we should do."

"It's from Vera Wang's spring collection. Only worn once, although..." Paige cringed and rearranged the folds of satin to show the consignment shop owner the dress's new flaw. Blood stains. "I'm afraid it's far from like-new quality."

She cast a side glance to Jake, who looked decidedly uncomfortable in the feminine shop, standing among the frilly prom dresses and lacy wedding gowns.

The older lady slid her reading glasses down her nose to examine the stain. "Is this red wine?"

Paige swallowed. "Um, no, ma'am. It's...blood."

The woman hummed a noncommittal response and eyed

the stains more closely. "Should I ask how you got blood on your wedding gown?"

"No," Jake said flatly.

The woman gave Jake a curious look, then held the dress up. "Well, it is an exquisite gown. And since most of the blood is on the skirt, not the bodice, I think with a little creative tailoring, I can salvage the dress." She rummaged under the counter and pulled out a slim catalog. "Vera Wang, you say?"

Paige nodded and pointed in the catalog to the listing for her dress. "There it is."

Jake leaned closer, glancing at the listing. His eyes widened, and, making a funny choking sound, he sent Paige a stunned look. "Eight thousand dollars?" he mouthed.

The shop owner whistled. "I can't give you anywhere near retail, you understand. I'll have to deduct for the work I'll have to invest, plus a standard markdown since it is used."

Paige nodded. "I understand."

Five minutes later, they returned to the rental car with a hefty sum in Paige's purse.

"You know..." she said, giving her hand a considering scrutiny, "we could sell or pawn my engagement ring, too."

Jake settled in the driver's seat and cranked the engine. "You'd be willing to part with it? What about its sentimental value?"

Paige only leveled a stare at him.

When he caught her gaze, he grunted. "Okay, we can hock it if you're willing."

She shrugged. "I am. Its greatest value to me now is in how it can get us through the next several days. Heaven only knows what kind of expenses we'll run into, and if we can't use our credit cards, since the charges could help the wedding-crashing terrorists track us down, we're gonna need cash."

He narrowed his eyes. "You're sure?"

"Brent got us into this." She held up her hand and thumbed the diamond solitaire. "His ring is going to help get us out."

Jake backed out of the parking space, his expression deeply

thoughtful. "What if the bead he says you have is the diamond in your engagement ring? I'm not sure we should part with it until we know more about what we're dealing with."

"Yes, but I've had this ring for over two years. Why would the terrorists think Brent had the bead now if he gave me my engagement ring two years ago? Haven't we decided the bead has to have been hidden in something he's given me just in the last few weeks?"

Jake twisted his mouth as he drove. "I see your point. Brent told me the threat he'd needed protection from was due to a recent turn of events, a recent deal that went bad. So maybe we can eliminate the engagement ring." He scratched the two-day stubble on his chin and grunted. "Okay, we'll find a pawnshop first, then a camping store where we can get our new digs. I don't like being out like this where we can be spotted. Once we're settled at a campsite, we'll dive back into the rest of those files. Finding the bead is our priority. It's the key to this whole nightmare."

"It is important to park the camper on a level surface and secure the wheel braces before raising the top," Jake read from the manual that came with the pop-up tent-camper they'd rented at a sporting goods megastore with the money they got by selling her dress and engagement ring.

Paige stood beside him at the Shady Acres campground and shook her head in disbelief. "I don't get it. How are we supposed to camp in that little box?"

"Hang tight. It's not set up yet." He lowered his gaze to the manual again and continued setting up the pop-up camper, following the step-by-step instructions. "The top raises, and the sides slide out to make the beds. Believe it or not, there's even a stove, a table and seats in there." He scowled at the manual. "When I figure this out," he mumbled under his breath.

"But I—"

He raised his gaze to her again when she stopped abruptly. "But what?"

She squared her shoulders and gave him a forced smile. "Never mind. I trust you. I just have a steep learning curve here, seeing as how I've never—" She glanced around at the other wooded campsites where children played tag and their parents chatted amiably with neighboring campers from folding chairs. "—done this before."

Jake grinned. "Honey, this is four-star accommodations compared to some of the places I've slept while on missions in the Middle East."

But for Paige, who'd clearly led a rather pampered lifestyle, the canvas-walled, crank-top tent-camper was roughing it. Jake studied the skeptical shadows in her eyes. Although she'd kept her concerns to herself for the most part, he'd caught her nibbling her bottom lip several times since they hitched the trailer to the rental car that afternoon. Now, when she caught him studying her, she straightened her posture and flashed a tenuous smile.

Obviously, being outside of her comfort zone, not knowing what to expect, rankled her need for order and control. Her highly organized mind and impulse to analyze spun their wheels in the unknown territory she found herself in. He admired her for the grace she'd shown so far. She had to have a number of gripes with his choice to camp—the mosquitoes munching on them, the heat, the lack of private bathroom facilities—yet she'd not complained.

"Need some help?"

Jake glanced toward the balding man wearing a faded Atlanta Braves T-shirt who'd spoken. A woman with graying brown hair pulled back in a ponytail followed a step behind, smiling warmly.

"Uh, thanks, but I've—"

"Name's Pat Appelman. And this is my wife, Diane. We used to have a fold-down camper before we bought the monster over there." Pat hitched his thumb over his shoulder to the large RV parked in the next campsite.

Paige's face brightened politely, and she offered her hand to Pat and Diane. "Paige Ba—"

"Bailey," Jake interrupted, almost shouting the name.

Paige sent him a startled look, and he pasted on a grin as he divided a glance between Paige and the Appelmans.

"Paige and Jake *Bailey.* We're, uh…newlyweds, and she forgets to use her new married name sometimes." *Smooth, McCall. Real subtle.* Staying in character, he stepped up beside Paige and wrapped his arm around her waist, pulling her close to his side and kissing her temple. "Isn't that right, honey?"

"Um, right. Bailey…silly me." He felt the tremor that raced through her. Or was that his own shudder, a kick of lust for having her curves pressed close to him? A flash of memory teased him. Her body on his last night. Hot kisses. The spontaneous passion and heat…

Sweat beaded on his brow that had nothing to do with the Louisiana summer afternoon.

"So where are you folks from?" Diane asked, smiling pleasantly.

Paige looked up at him expectantly.

"Texas," he offered.

"Big state." Pat laughed. "Where about in Texas?"

"Amarillo." Paige sent him a smug grin, as if to say, *two can play this game.*

Diane nodded. "We're from Baton Rouge. We heard this part of the state had some nice camping, so we headed up here on a lark. We've made a lot of spontaneous trips since we became empty-nesters."

"Don't suppose you kids have any children yet, being newlyweds and all?" Pat asked.

Paige shook her head, smiling politely, but Jake felt the slight tensing of her muscles. The idea of having babies with Paige shot a surreal sensation, an odd longing through Jake that made his head buzz. Family was a concept he held at arm's length, a subject too intimate and raw to consider. Like staring into the sun, he had to look away quickly or risk the damaging effects.

"Listen, kids, later tonight we'll have a big campfire and

roast hot dogs and marshmallows." Diane motioned to them with a sweep of her arm. "Why don't you come over and join us? We have plenty!"

Jake groaned internally. Maybe camping had been a mistake. Clearly, slipping into the campground quietly and keeping a low profile was not an option. Not if all the neighbors were as outgoing and curious as the Appelmans.

A refusal was on the tip of his tongue when Paige piped in, "We don't have other plans for dinner, and that sounds like fun. Count us in. And thank you."

Pat glanced to the pop-up camper. "Sure you don't want a hand?"

Before Jake could answer, Pat was taking over. In minutes, their neighbor had the rented camper set up and was showing Jake all the features inside. The fold-down table, the slide-out beds, the tiny refrigerator and electricity hookup.

Finally their loquacious neighbors headed back to "the monster," leaving Jake and Paige to settle into the small camper.

Jake's gut tightened when he considered the coming days, sharing these cramped quarters with Paige. Twenty-four/seven contact. All-day and all-night exposure to her vulnerable green eyes and the sweet scent that clung to her.

Gritting his teeth, he focused on the job at hand. He only had to remind himself that national security was at risk to bring his libido under control. Almost.

He pulled out the stack of files from Scofield's office, eager to get to work after the day full of delays and distractions.

But Paige's restless movement around the tiny camper, her quiet sighs and nervous tongue clicks as she set up the laptop and logged on, kept him hyperaware of his roommate. He sat across from her at the tiny fold-up table. Doubling as the baseboard for one of the beds when folded down and laid between the two bench seats, the table barely had space for him to spread a file and for her to park the laptop. Beneath the table, her knees bumped his when she shifted, and Jake almost swallowed his tongue as an unexpected jolt of electricity crackled through him.

Curling his fingers into his palms, he struggled to focus on the dry reading in the files, but the deep breath he took to clear his mind was scented with Paige's shampoo, or her perfume, or whatever the source of the intoxicating floral aroma that swirled around her.

He cast a furtive glance in her direction. She studied the computer screen with rapt attention. If the brush of their knees had rattled her as much as it had him, she showed no sign of it. With one hand maneuvering the roller-ball mouse, Paige alternately chewed her manicured fingernail and tapped the polished nail on her teeth.

What did it say about him that he found her nervous habit endearing, mesmerizing?

Says you're way too easily distracted, pal. Get a grip!

"Hey, Jake, take a look at this." Paige waved a finger toward the computer screen, and her gaze shifted to meet his. "I'm looking through Brent's planning calendar, and the entry for tomorrow is kinda weird."

Jake turned the laptop to face him and read the entry.

June 13—Gates—3
18* 30' 0" N 77* 55' 0" W

"What do you suppose that means?" Paige waved a hand in query. "*Gates 3.* Is that like an airport gate number? Could the rest be an ID number or an account number or—?"

"No." Jake shook his head as he met her eyes. He knew the pattern of numbers well. "I'd say they're coordinates, GPS. Except it looks like he used an asterisk instead of the circle for degrees."

"Coordinates for what? For where?"

He lifted a shoulder, scratched his chin. "Ballpark guess would be somewhere in the Caribbean. Which, considering that's where you were honeymooning, makes sense, but doesn't help us out much. This could be the coordinates of an address where he had a meeting."

"Or of a restaurant he wanted to take me to, or of a land-mark tourist attraction he wanted me to see." Her tone was somewhat defensive, and like the many other times she'd tried to defend or justify Scofield's motives or actions, Jake had to suppress a twist of frustration and…what?

He tightened his jaw and tried to decipher the secondary emotion that left a sour burn in his throat and had his muscles tensing. Jealousy?

He had no reason to be envious of Brent Scofield. He could easily compete with his old friend in most any aspect—appearance, physical ability, worldly experience, money. So why did Paige's loyalty to Scofield rankle him so much?

Jake quickly squelched the thought before it could fully form. Loyalty was a luxury that he'd learned could easily be snatched away. He had no use for something so fickle.

"Without a way to check these coordinates, there's no point speculating about the location."

Paige leaned back on the bench seat and crossed her arms under her breasts. He tried not to stare at the enticing way the gesture plumped her cleavage. And failed.

A man had his limits.

"Can't we plug the coordinates into the internet and find out where they're for?"

He jerked his gaze to her face when she spoke. "Yeah, but we have no cell-phone reception out here in the boonies, much less a Wi-Fi connection. But next time we're in town, we'll stop by the library or a coffee shop where we can get on the internet." He spun the laptop back around for Paige. "Meantime, keep looking. Maybe something else in there will give us a clue."

"So what are you finding?" She waved a finger at the papers he'd spread on the tabletop.

Besides how easily you distract me?

Jake cleared his throat and riffled through the papers. "Most of this seems pretty routine. Memos and forms related to research projects. Marketing reports…" He lifted a meaningful glance to her. "Your handiwork, I take it?"

She twitched a quick grin. "If I was writing marketing reports on a product, then it was out of development and on the market. Doesn't seem likely anything widely available would be what the terrorists are after."

"Yeah. That's what I'm thinking." Jake closed a couple of folders and shuffled them to the bottom of his stack. Tapping the file now on top with his pen, Jake caught Paige's gaze. "This *PMB-611* file, the one he calls Superbug, looks like the most recent study."

She tipped her head and lifted a shoulder. "It may be the one he started most recently, but we have multiple research projects ongoing at any time. Can you tell from what's there what the project was researching? What kind of drug was in development?"

Jake flipped back through the papers to find a report he'd read earlier. "Um, it says…'part of a progressive study to manufacture a vaccine for drug-resistant flu.'" He looked up from the page. "Drug-resistant-flu vaccine? Isn't that an oxymoron?"

She smiled. "In a way, I guess. But the flu strains that are currently resistant to drug therapy are the very ones we need most to find a vaccine or treatment for. New flu viruses show up every year. Older viruses mutate and adapt to the current treatments so that the drugs are less effective." She sighed. "It's a never-ending battle."

"Fortunately…for Bancroft Industries and other drug developers' pockets."

She frowned, lines of discontent pleating her forehead. "Bancroft's products save thousands—*hundreds of thousands*—of lives every year! Do you know how many people die from just the regular seasonal flu every year?" She paused briefly and arched a delicate eyebrow. "Thousands. Globally, the number could be as many as half a million."

Jake cocked his head, stunned. "Really? That many? I knew the number was high, but…"

"Yeah. And with the recent emergence of avian and swine flu, researchers are scrambling to find new vaccines for the new variants of the virus. A pandemic, like the one in 1918 that infected about five hundred million people and killed fifty million worldwide, could develop any day and spread in a matter of weeks." Passion and gravity for her subject blazed in her eyes.

"Yeah, I watch the news. I heard all this when the bird and swine flus showed up."

"So…Bancroft Industries is just doing its part to try to stop diseases like that from decimating the population." She paused. "Among other worthy projects."

Jake drank in the flush in her cheeks, the green fire in her eyes and the husky, authoritative undertones in her voice as she made her point.

Damn, but she was sexy when she got riled…

"But they also stand to make millions of dollars if their product is approved to fight one of these diseases." He lifted a corner of his mouth when her eyes widened in dismay. "I mean, come on, you're in marketing. It's always about the bottom line."

She shoved to her feet, her expression reflecting hurt and disgust. "Yes, the company makes money. Business is business. But my grandfather and my father did not pour their lives' work into Bancroft Industries just to get rich off the illness of others! They wanted to help stop illness and needless deaths. They wanted to contribute to society in a positive way. It's not all about the money!"

Jake leaned back as far as he could on the narrow bench seat and stacked his hands behind his head. "A little touchy about your family's wealth, Paige?"

"You brought it up! And you made it sound like I should be ashamed that my father's company is successful. That all his hard work and his contributions to medical research were based in greed. That Bancroft—"

"Whoa!" Jake whipped a hand out to cut her off. "I didn't mean any offense. Really."

Paige glared at him, her expression dubious and her arms akimbo. After a moment, he took one of her hands between his, rubbing the back with calming strokes of his thumb. "I'm sorry if anything I said insulted you or your family." Her expression softened, and he added, "Or Bancroft Industries."

She drew a deep breath and exhaled slowly. "Okay."

Before he released her hand, he brought it to his lips and pressed a chaste kiss to the back of it. His eyes held hers, and he watched her pupils widen, her eyes darken to the color of a deep lake. He felt himself sinking in that deep green water, drowning in the desire he saw reflected in her eyes. Reluctantly, he dropped her hand and tore his gaze away.

He leaned forward, hovering over the files from Brent's office, but his attention was shot. All he could think about was how much he wanted to pull Paige close and taste her sweet lips as he had mere hours ago.

And what would she think if he *did* kiss her? She wasn't as vulnerable today. She wasn't shaking with the shock of the carnage and gunfire at Scofield's office or reeling from her disrupted wedding as she had been last night. She'd had some time to collect herself, to know if kissing him was what she really wanted or just a gut response to an oversupply of adrenaline and life-threatening circumstances. Yet even with the luxury of a day's perspective, Paige's eyes warmed when he touched her. Her lips trembled when he held her gaze, and the air between them crackled the way the summer sky produced heat lightning.

Jake ducked his head, clenching his teeth until his jaw ached. Getting involved with his client's fiancée—even his client's ex-fiancée—was asking for trouble. They had big enough problems dealing with terrorists chasing them, some undefined threat to national security hanging over their heads and no solid leads to tell them what the hell they were mixed up in. His duty to protect Paige started with protecting her from himself. He knew without asking that she was not the one-night-stand type.

Paige was society weddings and Vera Wang dresses. She needed commitment, security, love.

He was a loner, black ops in third-world countries and dusty military fatigues. And he had nothing to offer her but his pledge to get her out of this debacle alive. Knowing this shouldn't bother him. He was used to keeping people at arm's length. So why did the prospect of walking away from Paige at the end of this assignment leave him feeling so…empty?

Chapter 7

Later that afternoon, Paige unzipped the canvas that covered the camper window and peeked outside.

Instantly, Jake jerked to attention. "What's wrong? Did you hear something?"

"It's a campground, Jake. I hear plenty of noise. Nothing to worry about." She flashed him a wry grin. "Unless that kid who has been blaring his rap music plans to keep his speakers on very late tonight."

Jake pulled a face. "I think if that happens, I could be convinced to remove his speakers from him. Permanently."

He stretched his arms over his head, and his T-shirt pulled taut across his broad, muscled chest.

Paige's mouth went dry, and she shoved to her feet from the narrow bench seat. "Actually, I was checking to see if our neighbors had their fire going yet. I'm beginning to crave a roasted hot dog."

After several hours huddled around the small camper table, searching Brent's files, Paige needed a break. Trying to ignore Jake, or rather, her magnetic attraction to Jake, was a bit like trying to ignore a rattlesnake coiled on the floor. And like a rattlesnake, Paige feared the powerful temptation Jake posed could come back to bite her if she didn't keep her guard up.

She knew her interest in Jake was purely physical—he had an elite soldier's body, a movie star's face and dark bedroom eyes she could get lost in. She knew her reaction to him was emotional—he'd saved her life, comforted her when she was falling apart and shown her nothing but kindness. And she knew even considering a relationship with Jake was impractical and illogical—she couldn't see anything they had in common, and the timing couldn't be worse, days after her doomed wedding, while running from dangerous thugs.

The way Paige saw it, emotionalism and physical attraction were poor reasons to fall for a man, and the absence of the two ingredients she looked for, practicality and logic, cinched the deal. Falling for Jake would be a huge mistake.

But knowing he was all wrong for her wasn't enough, apparently, to keep her nerves from tingling every time their knees brushed under the small table or her pulse from scampering when he held her hand and looked into her eyes. She'd nearly melted into a puddle of goo when he held her hand to apologize for his comments about Bancroft Industries profiting from the products they designed to fight disease.

Or maybe the reason her heart was racing had more to do with the implication that she, as a Bancroft, was spoiled. That her wealth somehow put her in an untouchable class that he resented.

Heaven knows, Brent always felt he had to strive toward a higher mark to be "good enough" for her. And she'd hated it. She wanted to be loved and accepted for who she was, not what she had. And she wanted the man she loved to know her affection was not tied to monetary worth or status in society.

Jake closed the paper files and rubbed his eyes. "Dinner does sound good, and I wasn't looking forward to the canned and packaged stuff we bought today."

Paige peeled back the corner of the zipped window

cover. Diane Appelman spotted her and waved from behind a crackling campfire. "I think they're ready for us." She smoothed a hand over the wrinkles in her cotton khaki shorts, a wasted effort. The manners her mother had bred into her from birth plucked her conscience. "I feel bad going empty-handed. Grab that can of corn. Can that be heated over a campfire?" she asked as she stepped back to give Jake room to scoot out from the table.

How were they supposed to share such tight quarters without going nuts?

"Sure. I bet the Appelmans have any number of ways to cook over an open fire." He picked out two cans of corn and two of baked beans to contribute to dinner and, after putting the cans in a plastic sack, ushered her outside.

A swarm of annoying bugs flew in her face the minute they stepped outside, and she swatted at them, swallowing the groan of disgust that rose in her throat. As much as she hated bugs, she hated the idea of the terrorists finding them more. If Jake thought camping was their best bet for staying hidden, she would play along without complaint.

She shuddered. Even if that meant sharing her legs with a cloud of hungry mosquitoes. She gritted her teeth and slapped at the pesky menaces nipping her calves.

"Come over here by the fire, honey!" Diane called to her. "The bugs hate the smoke. And I have bug repellent you can use."

Paige accepted the can of spray the woman handed her as they approached the neighboring campsite. "Diane, you're my new best friend."

The older woman chuckled. "When you've been doing this as long as we have, you learn to be prepared. Don't worry. The bugs are worst now, at dusk. In a minute, Pat will get the citronella torches going, and you'd be surprised how few bugs you'll see then."

Paige turned to Jake. "Make a note for our next trip for supplies. Citronella and bug repellent."

He massaged the base of her neck with his free hand. "Roger that, sweetheart."

Dry warmth from the campfire baked her face, while another sort of heat blasted through her from his touch. The endearment he'd addressed her with had been for show, part of the role of newlyweds they played for their neighbors, but a flutter of sweet longing tap-danced in her chest. Brent had always been so formal, had never used a pet name for her, so Jake's use of such an intimacy caught her off guard.

Jake passed the plastic bag to Diane. "Our contribution to dinner."

Diane peeked in the sack. "Why, thank you, honey. I'll get a pan and start these heatin'."

As Paige settled in the lawn chair Pat set up for her, she caught a movement in the shadows of her peripheral vision. Jumpy from the past couple days of insanity, she jerked her head toward the movement, searching the fading daylight near their camper for whatever had caught her attention.

A small black cat crept out from under the trailer hitch and inched nearer the campfire. Paige pressed a hand over her stumbling heart and exhaled with relief. A cat. It was just a cat. Not terrorists or assassins with automatic weapons.

Still, as her pulse eased back to a normal speed, she scooted her lawn chair closer to Jake's.

Pat passed her and Jake each an extra-long-handled fork and nodded to a platter of hot dogs on top of a nearby cooler. "Help yourself. The roasting is as much fun as the eating."

With a rumble of her stomach, Paige followed Jake's lead, and soon the smoky scent of their supper filled the air. The aroma brought the black cat out from the shadows to skirt the edge of the campsite, as well. He sniffed the air and eyed the cooking hot dogs with interest.

"Is that your cat?" Paige asked Pat, pointing.

Pat glanced up from the campfire. "Naw. He's a stray. He's been around here before, begging for scraps. And since Diane, the soft-heart, feeds him, we're a regular stop on his evening rounds now. She calls him Nate and had some convoluted explanation of how she came up with the name. Something about the fact that he has no tail, and she thought he was a girl at first and…" Pat waved a hand of dismissal. "Whatever."

No tail? A sympathetic pang speared her heart, and Paige tore off the tip of her hot dog and tossed it toward the cat. "Here ya go, Nate. Come on, kitty."

Nate looked wistfully at the meat, then blinked warily at the three humans huddled around the fire. Finally he trotted forward, gulped down the bite of hot dog, then scurried back to the shadows under the trailer hitch. Paige's heart broke for the skinny, maimed stray.

"Okay, veggies are heating," Diane announced as she came back out of their RV.

"We met Nate," Paige said as Diane took a seat beside her.

The woman smiled. "He's a sweet cat, but rather skittish. Doesn't quite know what to make of people…or if he can trust people not to hurt him."

Jake elbowed her in the ribs. "Hey, stop staring at the cat and watch your dog. It's on fire."

Paige gasped and pulled her charred wiener from the flames. Jake helped her blow out the fire, and they all chuckled over her mishap.

"Rookie," Jake teased with a warmth in his eyes that washed over her like a pleasant summer breeze.

She and Jake passed an enjoyable evening, chatting with the Appelmans, making s'mores and drinking iced tea.

After a couple of hours in front of the glowing campfire, Paige could wait no longer to use the restroom. She stood and glanced around the dark, wooded campground, uncertain where the facilities were. "Diane, which direction is the restroom?"

"It's through the trees, that way." The older woman aimed a finger over her shoulder. "Tell you what, I'll go with you."

Jake stood, a troubled look on his face. "No, I'll take her."

Pat and Diane gave him curious, amused looks, and Paige

chuckled awkwardly. "Um...*sweetheart,* I think I can go to the bathroom by myself."

He cleared his throat and leveled a stern stare at her. "*Sweetie,* maybe I need to use the facilities, too."

The Appelmans grinned, and Paige gave Jake a teasingly haughty look. "In that case, you can come with."

They thanked the Appelmans for sharing their dinner, their fire and their conversation and said good-nights as they left. Once they were out of earshot, swallowed by the darkness of the night, Paige leaned closer to Jake and muttered, "Do you really have to go, or was that an excuse to get away from our hosts? 'Cause I thought they were nice. I had fun tonight... despite the bugs."

Jake draped an arm around her shoulders as they walked. The gesture spun a mix of pleasure and security through her. She hadn't anticipated how dark the walk through the trees to the community bathhouse would be, and foreign sounds— chirps, croaks and buzzing—filled the evening air.

"They seemed nice enough." Jake twitched a grin, visible only as a flash of white teeth in the thin moonlight that seeped through the trees. "Told ya you'd like camping."

She returned a mock scowl. "I said I had fun roasting hot dogs and chatting with the Appelmans. The jury is still out on camping."

He pulled on her shoulder, guiding her around a stump she hadn't seen until the last second. Clearly, his night vision was better than hers. Paige nestled closer, wrapping her arm around his waist. "Then why—"

"I came with you because it's my job to keep you safe."

His statement hung in the air for a moment as her heartbeat stumbled. She glanced around the black woods, wondering what threats—wild animals?—Jake knew about but wasn't telling her. "From what?"

"After the past two days, you have to ask?"

Despite the sultry summer temperature, a chill skittered down her spine. "You mean... But I thought we were camping out here, because it was a safe hideout! If you think—"

"Don't panic. I don't necessarily think there's a bogeyman waiting in the bathroom to grab you. But we have to be alert. They *could* track us here. I just want to be careful."

When she shivered, he rubbed his hand down her arm and gave her a quick squeeze.

"Look, we're probably safe here for now, but …" They passed under a security light as they neared the bathhouse, and he paused, turning to her. With a hand on each of her shoulders and his mahogany eyes drilling into her, he said, "I want you to promise me you won't go anywhere without me. Not to the bathhouse, not for walks with Diane, not anywhere. Got it?"

"You're going to come with me every time I have to pee? When I shower?"

His pupils grew slightly, and a muscle in his jaw ticked. The idea of him joining her in the shower sent a rush of heat to her belly, and the desire that had been growing between them coiled tighter.

His nostrils flared as he took a deep breath and cleared his throat. "I want to check things out before you go into a building blind. We just don't know when or where Trench Coat's cohorts might show up."

The gravity of his warning burrowed deep inside her, scaring her more than the wild beasts she'd imagined moments ago. She'd take an encounter with a raccoon or even a coyote over a gun-wielding terrorist any day.

When she remained silent, grappling with the knowledge that even in this remote campground they were vulnerable to attack, Jake shook her slightly. "Do you understand?"

"I…yes." Her voice cracked, and she swallowed hard to moisten her suddenly dry throat.

"Promise me."

She nodded stiffly. "I promise."

"Okay." He guided her closer to the door of the ladies' bathroom. "You wait here while I have a look inside."

"What if there are other women in there? This is a community bathhouse, after all."

He glanced toward the door. "I know how to be discreet."

She arched an eyebrow and leaned back against the cinder-block wall of the bathhouse to wait.

Jake stepped just inside the bathhouse door and cocked his head as if listening, then disappeared inside briefly.

While she waited, she scanned the dark woods. She'd never known how completely black it got at night outside the city, away from street lights and security lamps and car headlights. A stir of motion to her left sent her pulse scampering.

She pressed her back farther up against the rough concrete wall. Where was Jake, and why was it taking so long to check a few bathroom stalls?

Her mouth going a bit drier, she strained to see through the murky night. She heard a twig snap.

"Hello?"

No answer. Then the blur of motion separated from the dark woods, moving closer.

Nate, the black cat.

Paige exhaled sharply and shook her head at the cat. "Jeepers, Nate. You know how to scare a girl. That's twice tonight!"

He sat down several feet from her and blinked as if bored.

"Did you like your hot dog? Were you able to mooch more dinner off the other campers?"

"Who are you talking to?"

Paige jolted at the sound of Jake's voice behind her and whirled around. "Don't sneak up on me like that!"

He shrugged and tipped his head. "You should pay closer attention to your surroundings so no one can sneak up on you." He glanced past her and repeated, "Who were you talking to?"

She waved her hand toward the spot where Nate sat. "Uh, the cat from earlier was here. I guess you scared him off."

He hitched his head toward the bathroom. "All clear. You can go in."

Paige resisted the urge to roll her eyes. He had her best interests at heart, even if his measures seemed like overkill.

When they'd finished at the bathhouse, they picked their way back through the dark campground to the tent-camper.

When Jake flipped on the small light in the camper, Paige shook her head. "I never thought I took much for granted, but even having electricity in this glorified tent is...a blessing."

"Nothing but the best for my girl." Jake gave her an ironic smile, and a funny flutter stirred in her chest. She couldn't be sure if it was his "my girl" comment or the teasing edge to his voice that had her ruffled.

She was trying to be a good sport about camping, even though everything about the experience was foreign to her. Her family vacationed in luxury hotels in historic parts of Europe or exotic ports of call. But if Jake thought this camper, this campground, by virtue of its obscurity, was the safest place to hide until they figured out how to solve the mess they were in, then she'd cooperate fully, not complain.

She trusted Jake. But...

She paused, watching Jake climb onto one of the two beds situated on either side of the camper.

What if the terrorists did track them here? Then what would they do? The flimsy door lock and largely fabric walls of their rented home were far from secure if the bullets started flying and the wedding crashers wanted to get in and slit their throats in the middle of the night.

"Jake..."

Lying on his back with his hands stacked behind his head, he angled his face toward her. "Yeah?"

"What's our contingency plan?"

"What do you mean?"

"If we're found here. Then what?"

He sighed tiredly. "We...get the hell out of Dodge and do something else. I know this arrangement isn't your usual cup of tea, but I promise you we're safe here...for now."

"For now. But what happens when they do figure out where

we are? You said yourself these guys aren't just gonna go away."

He grunted. "If that happens, I'll figure something out. We've got a couple alternatives, but I prefer to keep things fluid. Play it by ear. Not get boxed in with a limited mind-set, but keep my options open."

Paige's gut clenched. "Play it by ear? Jake, our lives are at stake! And the security of our country, if Brent's to be believed. We need a concrete plan."

Jake scowled and turned to stare up at the tented ceiling over his berth. "Trust me, okay? This is my area of expertise. While you were earning your master's degree in marketing and helping the family business earn more millions, I was sleeping in foxholes and inserting my SEAL team behind enemy lines."

Paige tensed. He sounded…resentful. Judgmental.

"I'm not doubting your abilities, Jake. That's not my point. I just want to know we have a backup plan if—"

"I've got your back, Paige. I'm gonna keep you safe." His tone was calmer now. Warmer. "I promise."

His reassurances helped. Some. But she thrived on planning. Needed organization and structure to feel…safe. She blinked, pondering that realization.

She needed order, goals and a blueprint for action in order to feel secure. Why?

Her family had always loved and supported her. Her job had always fulfilled her professionally. She'd never wanted for anything in her life.

So why did she need structure and contingencies to feel secure?

She toed off her shoes and flipped the light off. After crawling under the sheet of her bed, a mirror image of the one across the camper where Jake slept, she closed her eyes and mulled that question.

She heard the rustle of cloth across the camper and heard a telltale swish and muted thump—the sound of jeans being stripped off and dumped on the camper floor.

She tried not to think about Jake, sleeping no more than ten feet away in his underwear.

Or in the buff. Was he naked?

An enticing sensation shimmered over her, coiling low in her belly. She fisted the sheet in her hands and gnawed her bottom lip. What was she going to do about her undeniable attraction to Jake? As if she needed any clearer message that he was all wrong for her and a sexual fling now would be reckless, his attitude toward her education, the family's money, the success of Bancroft Industries confirmed the differences between them.

That distance between where she stood and his opinion of her stung more than it should.

Paige stared into the complete blackness, listening to the lullaby of night sounds outside. But her mind was restless, and she couldn't sleep. She glanced toward Jake's bed, even though she could see nothing in the inky darkness. "Jake?"

"Hmm?" he rumbled groggily.

"You think I'm spoiled, don't you?"

He remained silent for so long, she thought he might have drifted off to sleep and wouldn't answer. Or his silence was an affirmation of her suspicion. Or—

"I've never said you were spoiled."

She sighed. "You didn't have to. I can tell."

"Well, you're wrong."

"Am I? When my family's money comes up, you tend to act so..." She searched for the right word.

"It's not the money," he said before she could finish her thought. "Well, maybe a little. I guess I'm wary of that kind of wealth. And maybe just a little jealous. But—"

His bed creaked as he stirred, and she waited for him to continue. When he didn't, she prodded, "I take it your family didn't have much money when you were growing up? Is that it?"

Another long silence followed, and then, "No, it was the family I didn't have. I, uh...grew up in foster homes. Six by the time I left high school to join the navy."

Paige's heart clenched. "Oh, Jake…"

"So when you talk about how close you are to your sisters, or how your parents must be worried about you, or—I guess I'm a little envious that you have so many people that care about you, people who'll stand by you no matter what. I've never really had that."

"What about the SEALs? I always heard the rigors of special-forces training and warfare bonded the members of special-forces teams like family."

He heaved a heavy sigh. "Yeah, that's what I used to think, too." Pause. "Until they kicked me out of the family."

"Kicked you out?"

"I messed up my knee real bad during a roadside bomb attack. You can't be a SEAL with a bum knee, so I got my walking papers."

"Just like that? Couldn't they reassign you to a desk job or noncombat—"

"I didn't want to be a desk jockey!"

The pain in his tone reverberated in the darkness, and the pressure in her chest twisted harder. "I'm sorry. I…"

"The SEALs had felt like a family to me. More than any foster family ever did. I always knew I was an outsider, taken into a foster home. Every home was temporary. I learned not to grow dependent on anyone in a foster home, because…I'd be moved on soon enough."

Paige heard clearly what Jake didn't say. It vibrated in the thick silence of the dark camper. He'd learned not to give his love or allow himself to form attachments to his foster families. He'd been hurt when he opened his heart, when he'd sought love and permanence. Pain clawed her, laying her heart open to the bitter wounds he'd suffered at such a young age.

"When I was a SEAL, I thought I'd found the place where I belonged. I trusted the other guys in my unit with my life, and they trusted me with theirs. We did have something like a family bond. But…" He huffed, sounding frustrated. "When the navy discharged me…"

Her throat was tight, clogged with emotion. "It felt like a betrayal?"

"Something like that."

"Don't you keep in touch with the guys form your SEAL team?"

Once again he stayed silent for long moments before answering. "I can't."

"Of course you can! Pick up the phone. Send an email. Write a let—"

"They're dead."

Paige gasped. Her stomach lurched.

"Most of my team was killed in that roadside bombing. Besides me, only two other guys lived. Tommy was killed a few weeks later in Baghdad, and Mark…" He hesitated. "He made it back stateside like I did, also booted from the navy because of his injuries."

Paige held her breath, fearing what would come next.

"He was killed by a drunk driver a few months ago."

Paige squeezed her eyes shut, aching for all of Jake's losses. "That's awful, Jake. I'm s—"

"*Hell,* why whitewash it? *He* was the drunk driver. He drowned himself in the bottle when he got home from Iraq and was wasted when he got behind the wheel. The freaking idiot!" Frustration and misery colored his tone. Jake bit out an expletive. "I don't know why I'm telling you all this. I've never—"

She swallowed hard, searching for her voice. "I'm glad you did. I think…maybe it was time you did tell someone. Keeping it cooped up inside—"

"Is what I should have done. Airing my dirty laundry serves no purpose, so don't hand me any psychoanalysis or some crap about 'sharing my feelings.'"

She winced and choked down the platitudes waiting on her tongue. Squeezing the sheet in her fist tighter, she angled her head to gaze blindly across the camper toward his bed. "Then why did you tell me?"

"You asked."

She chuckled softly. "I asked why you thought I was spoiled."

"And a bunch of other follow-up questions that…" He grunted. "Hell. I don't know."

He sounded charmingly embarrassed, and she grinned.

"It's dark in here," he said, and she heard his bed squeak again as he shifted his weight.

She pulled a face, knowing he couldn't see it. "Duh. So?"

"It's easier to be honest, to…spill your guts, when it's dark. When no one can look at you, and you don't have to see people's reactions. Or so I hear. Guess it must be true, since I—" A buzz of lips accompanied his exhaled breath. "Just forget I said anything, and go to sleep."

Paige rolled to her side, facing Jake in the darkness, and pillowed her hands under her cheek. She wouldn't push him. "Sure. Good night, Jake."

But she knew it would be a long time before she fell asleep. He'd given her far too much fodder for her restless thoughts and analytical mind.

Chapter 8

The next morning, Jake woke early after a restless night of little sleep. When he did manage to steal a few minutes of shut-eye, his dreams were vivid and disturbing—roadside bombings where he found Paige dead among the carnage, meetings with his child-services caseworker where she told him he had failed his duty as a SEAL, campfires where the flames leaped out to grab Paige while she cried, "Why didn't you plan for this?"

He woke in a sweat that had nothing to do with the humid June morning and the lack of air-conditioning in their camper. Keeping the sheet around his waist, he bent to collect his jeans from the floor. In the watery light of daybreak that seeped into the camper, Jake studied Paige's profile. She had her back to him, her curvy hip and trim waist draped by her sheet, and her long dark hair spread in a chocolate cascade against the white pillowcase.

Peaceful. Beautiful. Off-limits.

A fist of emotion blindsided him and squeezed his lungs.

Last night had been a mistake. Lulled into a false sense

of privacy and emotional security by the still, dark night and Paige's soft, reassuring voice, he'd told her things he'd never shared with anyone. He'd bared parts of his soul he rarely acknowledged even to himself. And what had he gotten for his honesty? An endless parade of nightmares and the prospect of her pitying looks today.

Hell. What had he been thinking?

He scrubbed his face and finger-combed his hair. If she mentioned his late-night ramblings, he could always downplay them, shrug them off as inconsequential.

He blew out a sleep-deprived sigh. Paige was smarter than that. He could only hope she'd respect his request to forget the conversation ever happened.

His stomach growled, and as quietly as he could, he rummaged through the bag of groceries they'd bought yesterday on the way to the campground. He selected a couple of granola bars and an apple, then set up the collapsible table to start working his way through Scofield's files again.

There had to be more clues to what the bead was, what Brent had gotten mixed up in, than what the research files he'd read yesterday indicated.

Flu vaccines. GPS coordinates in Brent's datebook. A jeweler's receipt. How did it all fit together? What was the bigger picture he was missing? Did Paige know something she didn't know she knew, something that might have seemed inconsequential to her when she first learned it?

He opted to take his turn reading through the files on Scofield's computer. Scofield likely thought his password-protected computer files were safe. He'd likely not kept a hard copy of anything truly incriminating.

He opened Paige's laptop and said a prayer that the battery lasted long enough for him to get something accomplished today. The low-wattage electric hookup the campsite provided wasn't sufficient to recharge the computer battery. Soon, he and Paige would have to go back into town and find an internet café where they could broaden their research and recharge the laptop.

But today, he wanted to lay low. Scour the files they had. Tap Paige's memory once more, now that she'd had time to look at her relationship with Brent from a fresh perspective.

The laptop beeped and chirped as it started up, and Paige stirred. She rolled to her back, then jerked her head to face him with a gasp. "Oh, it's you." She rubbed her eyes. "For a minute, I forgot where I was and—"

"Sorry I woke you. I was trying to be quiet." He held up a granola bar. "Breakfast?"

She laid her arm over her eyes and groaned groggily. "Later."

He turned his attention back to the computer, which awaited his next command. He logged in using Paige's password and started opening documents to read.

Sheets rustled, and Paige slid her feet to the floor and raked her tousled hair back from her face. He hazarded a glance at her.

Damn, but she was sexy in the morning, rumpled from sleep as if she'd just been thoroughly…

Jake dropped his gaze to the screen again and shoved the thought aside. For starters, Paige was not the sort to indulge in one-night stands or raucous sex. He knew that much about her after just a few days with her. She would *make love*. Emphasis on the emotion.

Which was all the reason he needed to keep his mind off Paige and any notion of sharing her bed.

He swallowed hard, fighting the temptation to peek up at her again as she smoothed out the sheets on her bed and managed, through some admirable contortions, to change shirts without ever being topless.

"Making love" doesn't preclude lusty, aerobic, thoroughly satisfying sex.

When the thought popped into his head, his hands shook so hard, he had to reenter a file name three times before he got it right.

She cleared her throat. "Um…Jake?"

Paige's voice sent a wave of heat over his skin, deep into

his belly. He clenched his teeth and kept his head bent over the computer. "Yeah?"

"I need to go to the bathhouse. I want to get a shower… among other things."

His eyes darted up to hers now. She had a towel over her arm, a bottle of shampoo in her hand, her bottom lip caught in her teeth.

Damn, he wished she wouldn't bite her mouth that way. It made him want to nibble that lip himself. And somehow the gesture made her green eyes look wider and more vulnerable.

"You said you wanted to go with me wherever I went. Even to the bathhouse."

He closed the computer and scooted it back. "Right." He slid out from the bench seat and jammed his feet in his shoes, praying his jeans didn't look as tight as they felt.

He'd been part of a lot of dangerous, top secret missions as a SEAL. But being Paige's bodyguard, sticking by her wherever she went, being near her 24/7, may well be the toughest assignment he'd ever undertaken.

Paige spent a hot, wearisome day cooped up in the tiny camper with Jake, going over Brent's files. Even after hours of tedious reading and note taking, they'd not learned more than what they knew yesterday. The bead was *probably* in her wedding ring. Brent's most recent project with R and D was for a new flu vaccine. To date, the vaccine was still in the works, nothing terrorists should be interested in.

Besides the strange GPS coordinates, Brent's datebook didn't mention any unexplained meetings or contacts that Paige didn't recognize. None of the older projects mentioned in his files could be construed as any threat to national security, including an attempt by Bancroft Industries to create a drug to treat erectile dysfunction.

When he discovered the notes on that development project, Jake sent her a hooded glance. "So maybe not all of your products are developed to save lives. Maybe this project was about cashing in?"

Paige sent him a patient glance. "Doesn't quality of life count for anything?"

"Mmm-hmm. Counts for $2.6 million in gross sales for the company, according to your market research."

She gave him a wry grin, then cocked her head. "Although I find your interest in the product…fascinating."

Jake's eyes widened, and color flushed his cheeks. "I don't—" he fumbled.

Paige chuckled, but her mind flashed back to that morning when Jake had stood from behind the table to escort her to the bathhouse. She'd seen for herself that Jake *didn't*. Not by a long shot…

Danger, her conscience screamed. Any consideration of Jake's virility was definitely a treacherous path for her. Working in such close proximity all day had been hard enough.

As the day passed, his wide shoulders seemed to fill more and more of the cramped space. When the heat of the day had led him to shed his shirt, she'd nearly swallowed her tongue. And the sexy, low rumble of his voice as they dissected Brent's reports, looking for useful information, had made her belly quiver on more than one occasion. His deep, throaty *mmm-hmms* as he reviewed new information reminded her of the gentle roll of thunder announcing a sultry summer storm. Or of a man savoring a good orgasm.

Now it was her turn to blush. She felt the sting of heat in her cheeks and covered her embarrassment by shoving to her feet and pacing to the other end of the camper—all of about six feet—to stretch the kinks from her back.

She hitched a thumb toward the door and stuttered, "I'm… gonna go—"

Jake started to slide out from the table, and she held up her hand.

"Down boy. I just want some fresh air. I won't leave our campsite."

He rolled his muscled shoulders and nodded once. "I'm gonna read the last few files we downloaded from Brent's computer before I call it quits for the day."

"Suit yourself."

"Later, if you'll help me gather up some wood, we'll have our own campfire tonight."

With a nod of agreement, she staggered out of the sweltering camper to the equally stifling outdoors. She sent an envious glance toward the Appelmans' RV, where a window air-conditioning unit purred quietly. That morning, the Appelmans had been pulling out of the campsite with fishing equipment loaded in the back of their truck when Jake and Paige had returned from the bathhouse.

She longed for just a couple minutes in front of the cool breeze of that window unit....

She glanced back toward their own rented camper and sighed. Maybe a cold shower would better suit her needs. Last week, if someone had told her she'd be so powerfully attracted to a man so ill-suited for her, she'd have laughed. But then, if that same someone had suggested Brent was involved in something nefarious and was wanted by terrorists, she'd have had a similar reaction. Preposterous!

But she was undeniably drawn to Jake. So she had to either figure out how to control her lusty urges or just have a fling with Jake and work the erotic longing out of her system. She dropped onto a large log that a previous enterprising camper had placed near their fire pit as a bench.

Have a sexual fling with Jake? Was she nuts?

Paige plowed her fingers into her sweat-dampened hair and groaned. Tempting as the notion was, that kind of recklessness was more Zoey's style. Paige couldn't commit to something so bold without considering the ramifications. For starters, although she was on the pill, using a condom, too, would provide additional protection. Before she slept with Jake, she'd have to buy—

Paige shook her head and scoffed. *Before she slept with Jake?* As if it were a done deal, an inevitability?

The heat was affecting her reasoning, her *sanity*. She and Jake were nothing alike. She wasn't even sure he liked her much. He seemed to resent the family's money.

It's not the money. Jake's whispered confession last night teased her memory, and her heart tripped. *I guess I'm a little envious that you have so many people that care about you.*

She squeezed her eyes shut, trying not to think about the pain that had filled Jake's voice last night when he'd told her about being bounced from one foster home to another and about the loss of his navy family. He'd been burned so many times.

Was there something she could do to prove to him that not everyone in his life would be so fickle?

Yet even as she had that thought, Brent's deception, the lies of their relationship ricocheted through her head. She'd faithfully kept her promises to Brent, even though she hadn't loved him, but her loyalty and commitment hadn't been enough to forge a meaningful, lasting relationship. Why was it her sisters, even flighty, irresponsible Zoey, could make relationships work, when she couldn't? What else did she need to do to prove herself? She wasn't above putting hard work into making a relationship work, but all her sacrifices with Brent had been for naught. What else—?

Jake stepped out of the camper, and Paige snapped her gaze up, losing her train of thought in an instant. Damn it, how did Jake do that? Around him, all rational thought fled, her concentration shattered and her hormones took control.

He met her inquiring gaze and shrugged. "So much for reading those last few files. The laptop died."

"We have an electric hookup. Can't we recharge the battery? Run it off the hookup?"

He shook his head. "Not enough juice here. We'll need to take it into town, find a low-profile place where we can hang out for a couple hours without attracting attention. Someplace with Wi-Fi would be good. I have a few questions I want to research on the net."

He strolled over and sat beside her on the log bench. His

slightly musky, somewhat woodsy, thoroughly sexy scent drifted to her on a stir of breeze. The masculine aroma danced along every nerve ending, firing all her senses. She'd never been so *aware* of a man in her life. The sound of his voice, the scent of his shampoo, the color of his eyes, the feel of his lips on hers…

Heat flashed through her, raising her already high body temperature. She lifted her face to the pitifully insufficient waft of humid air, looking for some shred of relief from the June heat wave.

"So three days in, and we really don't have much more to go on than when we started." She watched a boy toss a Frisbee to an energetic dog a few campsites away and sighed her frustration with their progress. "We still have no clue what the security threat is and what to do about it. Or how to get the gun-toting goons off our backs."

Chapter 9

The next day, after loading anything that could be relevant to their case in the rented Taurus, they headed back into Lagniappe to find an internet café. Near a large mall, they found a coffee shop that boasted Wi-Fi access that met their needs.

While Jake was occupied, she eased across the coffee shop, nearer to the order counter where she had a modicum of privacy. Using the prepaid cell phone Jake had bought her the first night they were in hiding, Paige punched in Holly's cell-phone number.

"Hello?" Holly sounded tired, uncertain, wary.

"It's me."

"Paige! How—?"

"I'm fine, but I don't have much time to talk. Are you still in Lagniappe? How are Mom and Dad? Have you heard anything from Zoey? Is Brent conscious yet?"

"Whoa. Slow down! And to answer your questions—yes, worried sick, no, and yes."

Paige performed a mental rewind to remember what

she'd asked and match the answers. When she reached the last answer, she blinked, gasped. "Brent's awake? He survived?"

Her heart hammered an expectant, hopeful rhythm. If she could get to St. Mary's hospital and talk to him...

"He woke up a couple hours ago, but he's weak," Holly replied. "The doctors are about to operate to fix some new complications that have come up. Something about damaged veins or arteries.... They say in his condition, it's risky surgery, but without the repair, the veins could tear at any time, and he'd die."

Brent was awake, but for how long? She bit down on her bottom lip and tried to squelch the trill of panic rising in her chest. She had to talk to him before he went into surgery. Brent had answers she and Jake needed. "Is he alert? Is he coherent?"

"Yes." Holly paused. "Paige, if you have...*things* you need to say to Brent, things to settle between you for your own peace of mind, you should come. You should be here when he goes into surgery and—"

Paige glanced across the coffee shop where Jake had his head down, his attention focused on the laptop. "I—I can't come, Hol. Those men are looking for us. It's too dangerous."

"Paige, Brent needs you! If the man I loved was dying, wild horses couldn't keep me away!"

Paige swallowed the bitter taste of guilt that rose in her throat. "Holly, I...I don't love Brent. I...never did." Silence screamed through the line, and Paige squeezed the phone tighter. "Holly?"

"I kinda wondered...before the wedding. I mean, you didn't seem happy. Not truly happy, like I am with Matt."

Not like I am with Jake.

The thought popped into her head unbidden, and Paige's pulse spiked.

Jake made her happy. Despite the mosquitoes, the fear of being found by Trench Coat's band of thugs, the total upheaval of the past several days, she was happy. She loved matching wits with Jake, loved his wry humor, loved his courage and sense of duty. She felt safe with him. She had an inner peace about Jake that she'd never known with Brent. An assurance that she was where she was meant to be.

I always knew I was an outsider.

The echo of Jake's words from the other night sent a sharp pain to her core. He still held himself apart, kept a distance between himself and others.

"Paige? Are you still there?"

"Yeah, I—" On the heels of the disappointment over Jake's isolationism, an impulse prodded Paige to act, to do something to show Jake they made a good team. She hadn't been much use to him so far, but she had a chance now to earn his respect, prove herself a valuable asset to the mission. "Holly, how long before Brent's surgery? Do I have time to come talk to him?"

"I thought you said it was too risky?"

She sighed, nibbling her bottom lip. "I'll have to disguise myself or something, but I need to talk to Brent. It's important."

Jake caught her gaze and scowled. He made a slashing motion across his throat.

She returned a nod and pressed the phone closer to her ear, as if she could be nearer her sister. "Hol, I have to go. If I talk too long, they might trace the call."

"Wait! What are you going to do? I'm worried about you."

"Bye, Hol. Love you." Folding the phone closed, she crossed the coffee shop and pulled her chair close to Jake's. She peered over his shoulder to the laptop screen.

"What did your sister say?" he said without looking up.

She didn't bother asking how he knew she was talking to her sister. It was a reasonable guess. "She said Brent was awake."

He didn't say anything, but his body tensed. The telltale muscle in his jaw twitched, giving away his consternation.

"Holly said the doctors have to operate. It's a risky procedure, and—"

"You can't go. They'll have men watching the hospital."

"Jake, if he can tell us—"

"No. Too dangerous. My first job is to keep you alive. Doing anything about this *bead* is ancillary to that objective."

Paige heaved a deep sigh, although she'd expected as much, even told Holly as much.

But even knowing the risk of visiting Brent in the hospital didn't ease the persistent drumbeat in her head that demanded answers.

Leaning closer to Jake, she studied the computer screen. "What did you find?"

"Well, I mapped out the GPS coordinates in Brent's planner, but they must be wrong. Or they relate to something other than an address. They're for a point ten miles off the coast of Jamaica."

Paige drew a slow breath, thinking. "Our honeymoon was supposed to be in Jamaica. Maybe he meant the coordinates to be someplace on the island. Like I said before, maybe he was planning a surprise for me on the island, like a special dinner or bike ride…"

"Why not use an address, then?" Jake drummed his fingers on the table, his brow creased as he thought. "Does Brent dive?"

"Dive?"

"Scuba dive. Maybe these are the coordinates of a shipwreck or coral reef he wanted to explore."

Paige shook her head. "He doesn't dive. At least, not that I know of." A memory tickled her mind. "Although…"

Jake turned an open expression to her, waiting.

"He talked about us going boating or deep-sea fishing one day while we were in Jamaica. I told him I get seasick even on small boats, but he was insistent. He told me I could stay back on the island and shop if I wanted, but he was hell-bent on going out fishing one day of our honeymoon."

Jake rocked his chair back on two legs. "Could mean something. Or it could just mean he really wanted to go fishing on his honeymoon. It was his vacation too, so—" He shrugged.

Paige leveled a flat stare on Jake. "We're talking about Brent. Brent doesn't fish. His idea of sport is a racquetball game on an air-conditioned court."

The more she thought about Brent's insistence on the fishing trip, the odder it seemed to her. Why was Brent so set on going? One more question she was itching to ask him.

If she could figure a way into the hospital to see him without being noticed.

Jake clicked a tab at the top of the screen to switch to another browser window he had open. "I also found an address for the jeweler who did the work on your ring. I plan on paying him a visit today and finding out what special instructions Brent may have given him." He clicked to open another web page. "And I found some interesting reading about flu vaccines and where research stands in stopping a pandemic. I'd like to find a place where I can print out this article and a few others to read more carefully later."

She tucked her hair behind her ear, mentally canvassing the neighborhood, trying to recall the local businesses. "There's a place a couple blocks over called Acme Copies. I think they have public-use printers."

"That's our next stop, then." Jake bookmarked the site, then closed the browser windows and shut down the laptop.

Donning the backpack, Paige followed Jake out to the Taurus. As she climbed into the car, she noticed a beauty shop across the street with a display of wigs in the front window. Blond wigs. Wigs the color of Holly's hair.

Holly could come and go from Brent's room without suspicion.

Maybe there was a way to visit Brent without being seen—if she could first get away from Jake.

* * *

If her plan was to work, she had to act fast. Jake wouldn't need long to print out the pages he'd bookmarked on the internet.

Paige slipped the ring off her finger and tucked it securely in a side pocket of Jake's backpack. If her plan didn't work and she was caught—she shuddered at the thought—at least the ring, the infamous bead, would be safe with Jake. Keeping her gaze on Jake, she moved quietly toward the door of the printing shop while he plugged the laptop to the printer and tapped the keys to bring up the web pages he wanted in hard copy. She backed farther from him, nearer the door. Opened the door quietly. And ran.

Clutching her purse to her chest, Paige darted down the block, back toward the beauty shop with the wigs. Under her breath she muttered a series of prayers. That Jake would forgive her. That her plan would work. That she wouldn't be too late to see Brent.

That she wouldn't be caught. Killed.

By the time she reached the beauty shop, she was out of breath and could barely talk. But she had no time to waste. She grabbed the blond wig she wanted from the display in the front window and jogged to the counter to pay for it.

One of the hairdressers stepped over to the register. "Can I help you?"

"Just need…to pay…for this," she gasped and slapped the wig on the counter, adding a pair of sunglasses and a silk scarf from a display by the register.

The hairdresser frowned. "Are you all right?"

Paige nodded. "Just out…of breath. I…ran here."

With a dubious look, the hairdresser rang up the wig. "Someone chasing you?"

"I—" Paige hesitated and considered telling the woman she was running from a violent and vindictive ex-boyfriend, but lying was anathema to her. She'd already skirted the line between right and wrong enough in recent days. "I'm just in a hurry."

After handing the woman enough cash to cover her purchase, and without waiting for change, Paige scurried to the door and contemplated how she was to get to the hospital. As disguises went, her wig-scarf-shades combo wasn't much cover, but under the circumstances and with her being in a hurry, she prayed it would suffice. She studied the street for a moment, wishing a taxi would drop out of the sky, when a city bus chugged by and stopped at the next corner. She wasn't sure where the bus was headed, but it was going in the general direction of the hospital. And away from Jake.

She'd just pushed open the beauty shop door and stepped onto the street when the roar of an engine eclipsed the noise of the other traffic. Her heart in her throat, Paige jerked her gaze down the block toward the print shop. Jake was rocketing up the street toward her.

In an instant, she darted back inside the beauty shop and hid behind a large plant near the door.

She watched Jake whiz by, his head swiveling back and forth as he scanned both sides of the street looking for her. Guilt plucked at her, and she fought the temptation to run out to the sidewalk and flag him down. She had to talk to Brent, had to know what made the bead a threat to national security, had to know how Brent had become involved with terrorists and how she could put an end to the danger they were all in.

Jake cruised past the beauty parlor again, slowing in front of the coffee shop to give the interior a longer look, then sped down the street.

The bus at the corner chugged, and the brake lights blinked off. Paige shoved through the front door of the beauty shop and raced to the bus as it began pulling away from the curb. She banged on the door and waved to the driver.

He scowled but stopped and opened the door for her.

"How near to St. Mary's hospital do you run?"

"Closest stop is at the corner of Eighth and Cherry, near the courthouse."

Paige did a mental calculation. The parish courthouse was about a half mile from the hospital. Walking distance.

With a nod, she took a seat and dug the prepaid phone out of her purse. She hit redial and waited for Holly to answer.

"I have a plan," she said without preamble when her sister picked up. "Can you meet me in the ladies' restroom by the information desk on the first floor of the hospital?"

"Trade clothes with me," Paige ordered Holly after exchanging hugs and tearful greetings.

Holly pulled a face. "Do what?"

Paige removed the sunglasses and silk scarf she'd worn over her hair. "I want to see Brent before his surgery, but I can't go up to his room as me. Jake is certain the terrorists, whoever they are, are watching Brent's room, expecting me to come by."

Holly shook her head and wrinkled her nose. "And?"

Paige took a deep breath, searching for patience. Her jitters weren't Holly's fault, and her sense of urgency would have to wait until Holly understood the risks. "And they think I have something they want. They'll grab me or kill me to get what they're after." Holly's face reflected a growing horror, but she let Paige finish. "So I have to go up to see Brent as you. You've already been there today, in those clothes, so that's how I have to look when I go upstairs."

Holly shook her head slowly. "How did you get involved in something like this?"

"That's what I intend to find out from Brent. This is something he did." At Holly's incredulous look, Paige sighed. "You should know, I'm not going to marry Brent. I never should have said yes when he proposed. I didn't love him. I thought I was doing the right thing for the family, for Bancroft Industries, and…for Dad. I knew our engagement made him so happy. But I—"

Holly caught her sister's shoulders. "You don't have to explain yourself. You did what you thought was right at the time. Now you know differently, and you have a chance to correct matters." She pulled her sister into a tight hug. "All I want for you is to be happy. Listen to your heart. Trust it. Don't let your head think you out of something wonderful because it doesn't look right on the surface. Sometimes life's greatest happiness is found in unexpected places."

Paige squeezed her eyes closed, and an image of Jake shimmered behind her eyelids.

Holly pulled away and started unbuttoning her blouse. "I'll trade clothes with you, but…I'm not sure we're the same size anymore."

Paige began undressing, as well. "But we've been the same size, traded clothes back and forth our whole lives."

Holly pulled her loose top back and curved a hand around a tiny bump at her belly. "That was before I got pregnant, though."

Paige paused, blinked. Squealed. "Oh, my gosh! Holly, really? Why didn't you say anything?"

"I was going to—when you got back from your honeymoon. I didn't want to steal your thunder. Your wedding had been in the works for almost two years, and I felt selfish stealing the spotlight."

Tears of joy prickled Paige's eyes. "I'm so happy for you. And Matt, of course. And…oh, wow! When are you due?"

"Around Christmas. Perfect, huh? I might get to share a birthday with my baby!"

Paige's mind spun in myriad directions. Anticipation of her niece or nephew's birth at the holidays. A fresh determination to keep her sisters safe from whatever threat Brent had entangled her in. Wondering whether she'd ever find someone to have children with.

What kind of father would Jake be? Protective, for sure. Thoughtful. But could he get past the hurts of his childhood and open his heart to a child of his own?

First he had to let down his guard long enough to let a woman close. Paige longed to be the one to find a way into Jake's heart, the one he trusted enough to let beyond his protective defenses.

"Paige? Yoo-hoo. Hello?" Holly waved a hand in front of her, snagging her attention back to the present. "Where'd you go just then?"

Paige blinked and shook off the daydream. "Just thinking."

Holly chuckled. "I figured as much with you. Thinking, dissecting...they are your hallmarks."

She knew Holly meant no ill will with her comment. She *had* always been the analytical sister. But lately she'd come to envy Zoey's free spirit, Holly's nurturing optimism. If she didn't think everything to death, could she find the kind of happiness and love her sisters had?

A buzzer of some sort sounded in the hall outside the restroom, prodding Paige to action. She didn't have the luxury of the time she wanted to spend planning with Holly for the birth of her sister's baby. Brent was heading to surgery soon. Jake would be looking for her. The terrorist were watching... waiting to strike. Time was critical.

She hastily peeled off the rest of her clothes and handed them to Holly, who gave her her clothes in return. Holly's clothes were loose but not enough to be noticed. Holly, on the other hand, couldn't snap Paige's jeans closed and just pulled her shirt down to cover the gap.

As Holly helped Paige tuck her long, dark hair under the blond wig, Paige met her sister's gaze in the mirror over the sink. "You'll have to wait here. We can't have two Hollys walking around the hospital."

Her sister nodded her understanding and gave her another hug for luck and safety. "Be careful."

After promising she'd take care, Paige slipped out of the bathroom and headed upstairs to Brent's room.

She kept a wary watch as she made her way through the busy hospital corridors, but had to admit to herself she had no idea what she was looking for. The terrorists would be smart enough to have their operative blend in. Whoever was watching Brent's room wouldn't be visibly toting a large gun, wearing suspicious black garb, or have a sign around their neck.

Keeping her head down and trying not to attract attention, Paige forced herself to walk, not run, to Brent's room. Stepping into the private room, she flinched when she saw the numerous tubes and wires hooked up to him, his paler than normal complexion, the dark shadows beneath his eyes.

Her gasp roused him, drew his gaze. A frown dented his forehead as he studied her. "Holly?"

Seeing for herself that he was alive, Paige sighed with relief. She stepped closer, brushing the bangs of the wig back from her eyes. "No. It's me. Paige."

Brent's nostrils flared around the nasal cannula feeding him oxygen, and he pressed his mouth in a firm line of discontent. "You shouldn't have come. It's too dangerous!" His voice was scratchy, little more than a whisper. "Jake's supposed to be protecting you! Why did he—"

"Jake doesn't know I'm here. He wouldn't approve, but—" Paige pulled a chair to the bedside and leaned close to Brent, keeping her voice low. "I had to see you, had to talk to you. You have to explain this to me. What happened at the church? Who are these people, and why—"

"I'm sorry, Paige. So sorry. I never meant—"

"To put my life in jeopardy by secretly giving me some… *thing* that puts our nation at risk? It's too late for sorry, Brent. Now you have to make things right. Help me understand what Jake and I are up against."

He sighed and lowered his eyes. "It was only for a few days. I was going to retrieve the bead once we were in Jamaica. Switch the rings." His gaze dropped to her hand, and his eyes rounded. "Where is it? Where's your wedding ring?"

Paige blew out a satisfied breath. "We figured the bead you were talking about had to be in the ring." She gritted her teeth and glared daggers at him. "So much for it being a token of your affection, huh?"

"Paige, I—" He glanced away, his expression guilty, before returning an urgent look to her. "Where is it?"

"With Jake. Now you answer a few questions. First, *what* is the *bead?* Why is it a threat to national security? Why do those men want it?"

"That's three questions." Brent lifted his cheek weakly in a feeble grin.

Paige's returned stare held no humor. "Answer me, Brent. You owe me the truth."

He nodded, then winced and brought a hand to his neck. "You're right."

She noted the heavy white bandage on his throat, remembering the bone-chilling minutes when Brent had been shot and blood had seeped from his wound. Paige averted her eyes, steeling herself for what she knew would be difficult to hear.

Brent closed his eyes and curled his fingers into the hospital blanket covering him. "The bead is a nano-size capsule, a nanotube, that contains a sample of a virus we created to aid in our research and development of a super-flu vaccine."

"Nano-size," Paige repeated, dredging up her college science to put the term in context.

"Yeah. Meaning it is in the scale of a nanometer. One billionth of a meter."

"Billionth? With a *b?* It's hard to imagine something so small." She shook her head and tried to wrap her brain around the concept.

Brent filled in the blank for her. "A human hair is typically about one hundred thousand nanometers wide. A typical virus is about one thousand nanometers. You need an atomic force microscope to see something that small, but nanotechnology is the future of science and medicine. There are tremendous strides being made every day to find new treatments for disease, new compounds to improve quality of life..."

When he paused for a breath, she interrupted. "I've read about the science and the aspirations to apply nanotech to many areas of life and research. I just didn't know Bancroft was conducting any nanotechnological research."

He met her eyes, but hesitated. "We...purposely kept it on the down low."

"Who is 'we'? Did my dad know?"

"Not in depth. He only knew we were doing sensitive, landmark research. He trusted me to handle the details until we had something...viable."

"Meaning?" Paige leaned closer, her stomach bunching in dread.

Brent visibly swallowed, then licked his cracked lips. "We were trying to develop a potent, deadly strain of flu—strictly in the laboratory—so we'd have a way to test the viability of the vaccine we were working on. The recent scares with swine flu and avian flu brought home to the public what medical researchers have known for years. We need an effective way to stop a super-virus. The company that developed and sold the vaccine that could prevent a pandemic stood to make a fortune."

"You created a super-virus? The very kind of disease that could cause said pandemic?"

He nodded. "Except...my super-virus is even more deadly that the Spanish flu that caused the 1918 pandemic."

She goggled at the idea. While she understood the concept in theory, the idea of creating what you hope to destroy seemed...sickly ironic. "What if this super-virus were to get out of the laboratory somehow? What if you started a pandemic with the disease you created before you found the vaccine you wanted?"

"Come on, Paige. You know medical research well enough to know how carefully laboratory materials and specimens are handled. Extreme precautions are taken to avoid accidentally releasing bio-threats. Our man-made virus was perfectly safe in the lab. We needed it for our research."

Paige's spine tingled as she keyed in on his choice of words. "*Was* safe? Past tense."

Brent stiffened and cut his gaze away again. The passion that had lit his face as he explained and defended the volatile research drained from his face, leaving him wan and pasty-looking. "Word of our man-made virus leaked out, and...I started getting calls."

"Go on." Icy fingers closed around Paige's throat.

"Other companies wanted to buy our virus for similar research. We were sitting on a gold mine of potential revenue. I scrambled to file for the patent. Meanwhile, the offers I was getting...began to change. The sums grew. The buyers..." He sent a desperate, frantic look to her. "Foreign governments, leaders of private militia...the offers were staggering. But I knew these people didn't want PMB-611 for medical research. They wanted to use it as a weapon. They wanted it for bioterrorism."

Paige was letting Brent's revelation take hold when the initials he'd used snagged her attention. "PMB-611. That's what you named the virus?"

A telltale flush tinted Brent's cheeks. "I—" He sighed. "Yeah."

"My initials are *PMB*."

"Yeah."

"And 611?"

"Our wedding date. June 11."

Paige's laugh held no humor. "You named your deadly super-virus after *me* and our *wedding date?*"

He raised a hand. "I meant it as an homage to you, not an insult. I thought the virus would help Bancroft Industries become a leader in medical research, help us develop a vaccine that would save the world from a lethal pandemic. I thought it would earn the company more money than you'd ever dreamed. More money than your father ever imagined."

Paige sat back. She struggled to draw air into her suddenly leaden lungs. Brent used an ex-girlfriend's name as a password on his computer. But her initials, her wedding date...she was immortalized with the name of a deadly germ that could start a catastrophic plague. Now she knew how Typhoid Mary felt.

She forced enough moisture into her mouth so she could

swallow. She lifted a scowl to Brent. "You sure know how to sweep a girl off her feet."

"Paige, you don't understand. The vaccine we were working on—"

"Forget it." She gentled her tone. Stressing him more than this conversation already would couldn't be good for his condition. "My feelings about the way you named your super-virus don't matter in the grand scheme. Tell me about the bead. The nanotube."

Jake pulled the Taurus into a parking space near the print shop and killed the engine. Where the hell was Paige?

His gut clenched. He feared the worst. Had the wedding crashers managed to grab her while he had his back turned? He found it hard to imagine they'd been able to walk in, nab Paige and get out of the store without him hearing or sensing anything.

His hands tightened on the steering wheel as the only other logical scenario repeated in his head. She'd ditched him. He was loath to examine why that truth left such a hollow, achy feeling in his chest, why her abandonment felt like a betrayal, why Paige had the power to elicit such a strong gut reaction from him in the first place. Protecting her was a job like any other he'd been assigned. Why couldn't he do his job without complicating things, letting things get personal?

Exhaling sharply, he tried to focus on the problem at hand. He'd failed again. He'd let his guard down for seconds, and Paige had disappeared.

Where would she have gone, alone, without transportation, without money?

Without cover or protection. Damn it!

The obvious answer left him in a cold sweat.

The hospital. To see Scofield. Double damn it!

Didn't she know how vulnerable and exposed she was there? The thugs who'd busted up her wedding would be crawling all over the hospital, waiting for her. Even if the police or Paige's family had added guards at Scofield's door, they could have already gotten to Brent by now.

He slammed a hand through his wind-mussed hair and muttered a blazing curse under his breath. After shouldering open the car door, he stormed back into the print shop to pick up the hard copies of the pages he'd ordered. He paid cash for the copies and jammed them into his backpack with the laptop. Striding back to the sidewalk, he scanned the street, hoping, praying Paige would scurry up to him with a smile and a story about how she'd just gotten hungry and stepped into the bakery next door for a bran muffin.

But she was nowhere in sight. He gritted his teeth so hard they hurt. Mad at himself for letting her give him the slip, furious with Paige for putting herself at risk and terrified that her disappearance meant she'd been kidnapped, Jake debated his options.

The hospital remained the best place to start. He needed to find a way to get to Scofield's room and get Paige out without being noticed. A clandestine insertion was a cakewalk for him. He'd entered heavily guarded buildings and extracted persons of interest more times than he could count. But those missions had been well-planned, timed to the second. He could hear his commanding officer's voice berating him, telling him that going in half-cocked could get him killed. Jake's fly-by-the-seat-of-his-pants approach had given his CO more than one reason to ream him out.

And while going into the hospital unprepared was dangerous, Paige had left him no option. He had to get her out… and pray he wasn't too late.

Chapter 10

"Like I said, the nanotube has a viable sample of PMB-611. Enough to infect several hundred people, say a room full of people at a concert or on a subway or airplane. The disease progresses fairly quickly and is contagious within hours of exposure."

"Long enough for the unknowing victims to start the global spread of the disease if dispersed on a key international flight." Paige gnawed her lip. "Is…is the nanotube safe? C-can it break and infect me and Jake?"

Brent shook his head. "Not as long as it is embedded in the ring. I had it encapsulated in the faux diamond."

She arched an eyebrow. "Faux diamond? The hunk of rock isn't real?"

Another slight head shake. "It's a special cut glass. An expert could tell the difference quite easily, but I only needed to disguise the nanotube, hide it in the fake ring for a few days. I had planned to—" He paused and swallowed hard.

"Please continue," she said with a hard glare. "What had you planned?"

"I was meeting someone. Passing the nanotube off to them while we were in the Caribbean."

"A terrorist?" She couldn't hide the scathing tone of accusation.

He blanched. "No. I had a contact within CDC. After I swapped the decoy ring with your real ring, we picked a safe location to meet, to transfer the decoy, with the nanotube and sample to him, and—"

"This location... Was it at sea? Were you meeting by boat?"

He blinked as if stunned she knew. "How did you—?"

"I saw the GPS coordinates in your planner." If he was curious how she'd gotten his planner, he didn't show it. "And I remembered you'd been insistent about deep-sea fishing on our honeymoon."

Brent turned up a palm, his expression pleading for understanding. "I knew how dangerous the situation had become, and I wanted the sample in safe hands in case..."

She shuddered. "In case certain terrorists caught up to you and demanded the bead?"

She interpreted his guilty look as a *yes*. "Who are they, Brent? How did they know about the bead and that you'd have it at the wedding?"

"I don't know what terror group they are with. Only that they are dangerous and well-funded, and they mean business."

Paige leaned closer, hardly believing her ears. "Why in the world would you get involved with people like that, Brent? What were you thinking!"

"I didn't know they were terrorists at first! I...I'd arranged to sell them the virus before I smelled a rat. When I started getting cold feet and questioning them, the arrangements turned ugly fast. They threatened me, ransacked my house, started following me. They...grabbed me once. Late at night. I'd been at the office working, and..." He shivered visibly and closed his eyes. "Let's just say, they demonstrated their lethal potential."

"Why didn't you tell me? How could all this have happened to you without me knowing?" she asked.

Opening his eyes, he found her gaze. "I made sure you didn't find out. To protect you and…because I was ashamed. I—I lied to you, covered my tracks and…planning the wedding kept you busy, distracted."

Paige rubbed her temple. "So how did they first contact you?"

"They had posed as buyers for the Department of Defense, for our government, the military. I thought it was my civic duty to cooperate with the DOD. And I thought about how the money would set us up for life. They offered a hell of a lot of money for the sample, and…I saw a chance to—"

"Get rich quick?" she offered when he let his words trail off.

A muscle in his jaw twitched, and he sent her a scornful glance. "What if I did want to make a fast buck? A lot of bucks? I was doing it for you!"

Paige shot up from her chair, her hands fisted at her sides. "For me? Don't you dare try to lay this at my feet! I don't care about money. I wasn't marrying you for your bank account. You know that!"

"No, you were marrying me to make Daddy happy, weren't you?"

She gasped. "I—"

"Don't try to deny it, Paige," he said softly. "I know it wasn't because you loved me. I could see that much in your eyes."

She opened her mouth to deny his claim, but no sound came out. It was the truth, after all. But she hated the pain in his face.

"Tell me something. If those men hadn't arrived and interrupted the service—" His expression was bleak. "Would you have gone through with it? Would you have married me?"

"Of course! I'd made a commitment to you. I—"

"I saw your reluctance. Heard the hesitation in your voice."
He sighed. "The truth, Paige. What would you have done?"

She blinked back the burn of tears. "I...don't know."

"And now?" he asked in little more than a whisper. "What
are you going to do now? What happens to us?"

Her chest twisted at the forlorn look in his eyes, the dim
hope that flickered across his face. Could he really have had
feelings for her? Did he still?

"There is no *us,* Brent. Not now. Not after all that's hap-
pened." She swiped at the moisture that dampened her cheek.
"I'm sorry. I should never have promised to marry you when
I knew deep in my heart it was a mis—"

When she hesitated, looking for a word that wouldn't hurt
his feelings, he said, "Mistake?"

"A...misrepresentation of my feelings for you. I misled you
to believe—"

He laughed without humor. "Come off it, Paige. I'm smarter
than that. I knew you didn't love me. You aren't that good
of an actress. I knew what we had was an arrangement of
convenience."

"And that was enough for you? Don't you want more for
yourself?" She thought about the arguments she'd had in the
past with Zoey on this subject, the happiness she saw between
Holly and Matt. The confusing feelings Jake evoked in her
and the temptations she'd faced around him the past few days.
"What about passion and romance and the real, deep-down joy
of being with a person who makes you feel alive and whole
and..."

Paige dropped heavily back into her seat, realizing what
she was saying. Jake made her feel...feminine, alive. For the
first time in years, she woke with an excited contentment about
what the day to come might hold. She was falling in love with
Jake.

"Paige?" Brent's voice jerked her attention back to the
hospital room. "What is it? You look upset."

She shook her head, as if doing so would clear away her
tangled feelings toward Jake. Her issues with Jake could wait.

Right now, she needed answers. Needed to get out of the hospital and back to the campground before someone saw her and recognized her.

"Never mind what I was thinking. What's important now—besides you getting well, getting back on your feet—is that you tell me everything I need to know about your contact at the CDC and what Jake and I are supposed to do with the nanotube. How do we get these terrorists off our backs?"

Ten minutes later, much longer than Paige had felt it was safe to spend with Brent, she had detailed information about Brent's CDC contact, what little information he knew about the terrorists who'd contacted him and a general plan in mind to bring this whole nightmare to an end.

Holly had been waiting for her in the women's restroom for almost thirty minutes now, and Paige was anxious to trade clothes again, don the scarf and sunglasses and slip out a back door of the hospital. She glanced nervously down the corridor outside Brent's room before she headed toward the elevator. She made it halfway to the nurses' station, saw nothing suspicious.

Then a strong arm seized her from behind….

Covering her mouth with a wide hand, her captor pulled her into a supply closet.

Icy terror balled in her stomach. A scream formed in her throat, but the smothering hand kept her from drawing the air she needed to voice it.

"Be quiet, and don't panic," a low, familiar voice rumbled in her ear. "I'm not going to hurt you, Holly."

When his grip loosened, Paige spun around, landing a punch on Jake's arm. "That's for scaring ten years off my life!" She raised her chin and glared at him. "And it's not Holly. It's me."

Jake did a double take, lifting a wisp of the wig for closer examination. He wore hospital scrubs a size too small for him and a surgical mask, which he jerked down to talk. "Paige?" Then hotly, "How about the scare you gave me?" He returned a dark glare and lowered his volume again. "Jeez, Paige, I thought you'd been kidnapped by those goons! I've been going crazy for the last hour!"

She held up a hand to cut him off. "Save the lecture. I know you said you thought it was too dangerous, but I've been careful." She poked him in the chest. "Even you thought I was Holly."

He scowled. "Because I only saw you from the back." He gave her clothes and wig a more thorough scrutiny. "Not bad though. Those her clothes?"

"Yes. And she's waiting for me in the downstairs restroom as we speak, so…can this argument wait until we get back to the campground?"

A muscle jumped in his jaw, giving away his continued frustration with her. She had a lot to make up to him for worrying him. But the information she'd gotten from Brent should go a long way toward that end.

He gave a tight nod. "Let's go. I've got the car in the rear parking lot." He started for the closet door, then sent a guarded look over his shoulder to her. "You go first. We shouldn't be seen together. But I'll be right behind you. In case of trouble."

Her heart still thumping double-time thanks to Jake's grab, Paige eased back out into the hall and walked quickly, but not so fast that she drew attention, to the elevator. The car arrived and just before the door closed, scrubs-clad Jake slipped in with her.

"Was Brent awake? Did you learn anything?" he asked.

"Yes and yes. It's worse than we thought. We were right that the bead is in my wedding ring. The bead has a nanotube inside that contains a deadly virus."

Without looking at her, he shushed her under his breath. "Not here."

"You asked!"

"A yes or no question. We'll get into the details later where it's safe."

The elevator dinged as they reached the bottom floor. With

a huff of frustration, Paige stepped off, glanced around the lobby, then headed for the ladies' room where Holly waited.

Her sister rushed over when she entered. "About time! How did it go?"

"We alone?" Paige asked, glancing toward the empty stalls.

"Yeah."

Paige started unbuttoning the blouse to return to Holly. "Jake's waiting for me outside. I have to go back into hiding with him until…until this mess gets resolved. Tell Mom and Dad that I'm safe. I'm with Jake, and…this should all be over soon."

"I hate this, Paige! We're worried sick about you! It's bad enough that Zoey's flitting around the country, incommunicado."

Paige handed the blouse and stretchy pants back to Holly. "I'm sorry. I don't really have a choice. Please, be safe. These men could try to hurt you to get to me."

Holly's brow furrowed. "Dad's hired extra security since the wedding. Both at Bancroft and at the house."

Paige nodded as she pulled on the last of her own clothes and the scarf-and-shades combo to hide her face. "Good." She pulled her sister into a hug. "I love you. Take care of my new niece." She laid a gentle hand on her sister's abdomen.

"Or nephew…"

Paige smiled, tears filling her eyes. "No. It's a girl. Another Bancroft woman to carry on our tradition."

Holly wiped a tear from her own face. "Be safe. I love you, too."

Paige emerged from the bathroom in her own clothes. Jake hustled her down the hospital corridor, his gaze sweeping the length of the hall, keeping a vigilant watch for suspicious activity. Heat blasted them as they stepped outside and crossed the blacktop parking lot to the rental car.

He unlocked and opened the door for Paige, who gave him a satisfied look as she settled in the passenger seat.

He cocked an eyebrow. "What?"

"I did it. I got in to see Brent, questioned him about the bead and we got out without anyone seeing us or shooting at us."

He pressed his lips in a thin line. "Don't get cocky. We're not in the clear yet." Jake closed her door and scanned the parking area as he circled to the driver's side of the Taurus. The interior of the car had become an oven in the summer sun, and sweat popped out on his face within seconds of climbing inside. He cranked the engine and shot Paige a glance as he checked over his shoulder to back out.

She yanked the silk scarf from her head and tousled her thick dark hair. "Jeez, this thing is hot." She returned Jake's stare with a wide-eyed expression. "I have so much to tell you. I know what the security threat is and what our next move has to be."

Jake's gut tightened. As much as he wanted to know everything right then, he knew their higher priority was getting out of sight. "Save it. We'll go over everything back at the campground."

As he pulled out of the parking lot and merged into the downtown traffic, Paige turned the air-conditioning on full power, high fan.

"I learned something else today, too. About my sister." A broad smile lit her face, and she sighed contentedly. "I'm going to be an aunt! Holly is pregnant with her first child!"

Jake gave Paige the requisite grin, although the idea of children stirred uneasily in his gut. Family, kids, a white picket fence were all foreign concepts for him. Seeing how happy Paige was for her sister told him all he had to know about Paige's own wish for that kind of domestic bliss. The uneasy roil in his gut became a hollow ache.

Knowing he couldn't give Paige what she wanted, couldn't be the man she needed, hurt more than he cared to admit. When had he started thinking beyond the end of this mission? His job was to keep Paige safe and protect the bead to contain the national security threat. So why was he thinking in terms of any future for them past that?

He mulled that point fruitlessly, the empty pit in his chest growing deeper, until they reached the edge of town and headed for the highway back to the campground. To distract himself from that unsettling line of thought, he rolled his shoulders and sent her a puzzled look. "How is this Holly's first baby? I thought she and her husband had two kids."

As he returned his attention to the road, he glimpsed a blue sedan gaining on them quickly. *Two sedans,* he amended when the second car pulled forward into view.

"They do. They're Matt's kids from his first marriage. She's adopting them, but this is her first biological baby. The first Bancroft grandbaby by blood."

"Mm," he hummed in acknowledgment, but his focus was on the identical sedans. A prickle of alarm nipped his neck.

Jake sped up, looking for an exit. The sedans caught up to them but didn't pass. Grinding his back teeth, Jake took the next exit. Checked his mirrors.

The blue sedans followed.

He muttered an earthy curse word and squeezed the steering wheel.

"What?" Paiged asked, sending him a worried look.

"We have company. Hang on."

Paige twisted toward the back window as Jake took the first right turn he got to, then a left. The two blue cars stayed on their tail. He sped up, and the sedans matched his speed.

"They're still there!" Paige cried.

"Not only are they still there, they're not trying to hide the fact they're there." Acid churned in his gut. "Get my gun out of the glove compartment."

She did, and passed it to him. For several more blocks, Jake tried in vain to lose their pursuers.

Finally, the first sedan seemed to tire of the chase and raced ahead of them.

"Are they leaving?" Paige's voice held surprise and hope.

Jake knew better, and his body tensed even tighter. He

didn't have a chance to answer her wishful thinking before
the first sedan jerked to a stop at an angle mere feet in front
of them.

Jake braked hard to avoid hitting them, then slammed the
rental car into Reverse. But the second car pulled up to the
back bumper of their rental, boxing them in.

The doors of the first car flew open, and two armed men
climbed out.

"Lock your door," he told her, knowing how little the move
would mean if the goons wanted to get inside. If they started
shooting…

"Get down. On the floor. Stay there until I tell you otherwise." He wrapped his fingers around his SIG Sauer, and
with his free hand, he cut the wheels sharply. He backed up,
crashing into the second car, then shifted back into Drive. He'd
intended to drive off the shoulder, cross-country if needed,
to get away. But one of the armed men was already at Paige's
door.

He smashed her window with the butt of his gun. She
screamed. Glass rained down on her.

Jake leveled his weapon on the barrel-chested goon at the
passenger door. "Stand back!"

The driver's window shattered, and the cold kiss of steel
touched his temple.

"Drop your weapon, or I'll drop you," a high-pitched male
voice grated behind him.

"Do it!" the goon at Paige's door echoed.

Jake hesitated. His gun was all he had to defend Paige. If
he put it down…

A sharp blow slammed into his skull, and the edges of his
vision dimmed.

"Paige," he rasped, reaching for her.

And then…nothing.

Chapter 11

"Jake!" Paige screamed as his eyes rolled back and he slumped on the seat. She scrambled to reach him, tears filling her eyes. Instantly, the passenger door was yanked open, and a burly man grabbed her upper arm.

"No!" She flailed and fought, but against his brawn she stood no chance. He hauled her out of the car and shoved her toward the waiting blue sedan.

If you get in the car you're as good as dead. She remembered a self-defense video that she'd watched with Zoey a couple years ago that instructed women to fight with all they had for release.

And she fought. She clawed, she struggled, she jerked.

Until the beefy guy with his paw clamped on her arm and stuck a gun in her face. Icy, instinctive fear washed through her. Froze her.

"Get in the car."

She tried to scream again, but even her throat seemed paralyzed.

Jake! Jake! Help! her brain screamed.

The goon shoved her roughly into the backseat, and before the door closed, she cut a glance toward the rental car.

Jake hadn't moved.

Bile surged into her throat. Oh, God! Was he dead? What had they done to him?

"Get the boyfriend. Bring him, too," the driver shouted.

The beefy guy took two steps back toward the rental car then stopped. "We got company. Forget the guy. Let's move!" He climbed in next to her and gave her a leering grin. "We got what we need."

The second man, who'd hurt Jake, joined them on the backseat, frowning.

With a thud, the back door closed, and the sedan screeched away.

If you get in the car, you're as good as dead.

Paige's chest squeezed, and tears burned her eyes. She was dead.

Jake blinked. Black spots swam before his eyes, and nausea roiled in his gut. When he raised his head, lightning shot through his skull.

Squinting against the pain, he peered through the windshield in time to see Paige shoved into the blue sedan. A big ape of a man followed her in and slammed the door.

No! Alarms blared in his head. *No!*

He glanced desperately around the front seat, searching for his gun.

The squeal of tires cut his search for his SIG Sauer short. He glanced up just as the blue sedan pedaled away. The second car followed.

Jake's heart clenched, and a sinking sense of failure settled over him like a boulder in his chest.

His head throbbing, Jake blinked the world into focus. A fresh shot of adrenaline cleared the last remnants of haze from his brain.

He hadn't lost her yet. As long as he kept the blue sedan in sight, he had a chance to rescue Paige.

Jamming the car into gear and battling the headache from hell, he tore after the sedan.

Paige scuttled across the backseat, moving as far away from the beefy man as she could. She shook to her core, terrified of what they might do to her and worried sick about Jake.

Please, God, let Jake be all right!

"Wh-who are you? What do you want?" she demanded, although she knew what they wanted. She rubbed her fingers, almost involuntarily, and only then remembered she wasn't wearing the ring. She'd put it in Jake's backpack for safekeeping.

"We'll ask the questions. If you cooperate, we may even let you live." The beefy man snaked a hand out to stroke her cheek, and she flinched. "The world needs pretty women like you."

His leering expression made her stomach turn. The gun he held loosely in his hand sent a shiver to her bones. She didn't doubt for a minute that these men would shoot her if she didn't give them what they wanted.

But she didn't have what they wanted.

Jake did.

A fresh wave of icy fear washed through her. Not only could she not turn over the ring to save her life, telling the men where the ring was would put Jake's life in grave danger. Again.

Because Jake would surely resist, and these men would have no qualms about killing him. Acid puddled in her stomach, and her lunch seesawed and rebelled.

"Where is the bead with Scofield's nanotube?" the second man in the backseat growled, getting in her face. She recognized him now as one of the men who'd crashed her wedding with Trench Coat. Apparently, this man was now the ringleader.

"I—" she started, her voice cracking. "I don't—"

"And before you tell us you don't know what we're talking about, know this. We know you were at the hospital. We know you talked to Scofield. We know Scofield claims to have passed the bead to you at some point. Considering that you and your new boyfriend were in Scofield's office the other night, we know you are working with Scofield to keep us from getting the nanotube with the virus." He waved his gun in front of her. "So answer very carefully."

Paige's mouth grew dry, knowing her answers could put people she cared about in grave danger. If she gave up the location of the nanotube to these goons, they could use the virus in a weapon and start a terrible flu epidemic, costing thousands, even millions of people their lives.

She shuddered. But if she didn't give these men something, she'd be killed, pretty or not.

Think, Paige, think!

Ringleader had only said he knew that she'd been at the hospital, not that he'd heard any of her conversation with Brent.

Paige curled her fingers into a fist, digging her fingernails into her palm. And reasoning out her options. She had to tread lightly. If she lied, and they caught her in the lie, because they had been listening in Brent's hospital room...

"I—I only learned the truth about the bead and the virus in it today...when I saw Brent at the hospital."

That much was true.

"Go on." Ringleader gestured with the gun for her to proceed.

Their driver took a corner at a high speed, and Paige was thrown against the beefy thug who'd grabbed her. The sour smell that clung to him made her stomach roil harder.

Where they going? It would behoove her to pay attention to where they were. In case she got free and had to tell someone—Jake, the cops, her father—where she was.

She craned her neck to see out the window, and Ringleader jabbed her in the ribs with his weapon.

"Stop stalling! What did Scofield say? Where is the damn bead!"

Paige shivered as her captor's voice elevated, sounding

more taut and angry with every word. She had to give him something to earn his trust, had to let him think she was cooperating, even if…

"He said he put the bead in…m-my ring." Her heart clenched as the words spilled out, but a heartbeat later, inspiration struck, and her hopes soared. "In my engagement ring."

Ringleader narrowed his eyes on her as if debating whether to believe her, then shot his cohort an inquiring glance.

"Could be done. He coulda hid that nanotube in about anything."

"He had a special glass bead made to look like a diamond. He…switched rings on me one night when I had my engagement ring off washing dishes. I never suspected anything." The lies rolled off her tongue, and she prayed she could be convincing and also not paint herself into a box that would trap her.

Ringleader arched a dark eyebrow, and his gaze darted to her left hand. With a rough grab, he jerked her hand up to study her fingers.

"Where is it? Where's the ring?"

"Well, see…here's the thing…I didn't know what he'd done. I didn't know about the nanotube, and—" The dark glare Ringleader narrowed on her almost tripped her up.

She swallowed hard as bile clambered up her throat. Once she'd calmed the sick roll in her gut, she offered them another tiny truth that would buy her and Jake more time. "I pawned it. For the cash. I sold it, a—" Her heart stumbled as she made a split-second decision. "And my wedding ring." Her pulse kicked higher as she prattled on, hoping to convince them of her story. "I was mad at Brent, knew I wasn't going to marry him after he'd betrayed me like this, and the money was—"

"Bull." Turning to his cohort, he barked, "She's got it somewhere. Search her."

Paige gasped, and her stomach roiled as she was subjected

to a rough, thorough and intimate search. "Stop it! I pawned it," she cried, battling Beefy Guy's hands. "I swear! I sold—"

"Where?" Ringleader cut her off. "What pawnshop?"

"I…don't remember the name of the shop."

Beefy Guy cocked his gun and angled it toward her. "Try harder."

Paige gasped and divided a frantic look between the scowling men. "I…think it had initials… like ABC Pawn or AAA Pawn or EZ Pawn. I know it was on the south side of town near the airport."

Along with dozens of other pawnshops. Maybe the sheer volume of pawnshops on the south side of town would keep these goons searching for a day or two.

She and Jake needed just twenty-four to forty-eight hours to find Brent's contact in the CDC, arrange to meet him and pass over the nanotube. She wished they could just go to the FBI or police, but Brent had repeated his warning not to. He had reason to believe the terrorists had help from someone within Homeland Security.

Ringleader still looked unconvinced, but he leaned forward and barked to the driver, "Head south. Call Bern and tell him to work up a list of every pawnshop in the city, listing the ones in the southern part of the city first." He glanced back to Paige with a suspicious scowl. "We're going shopping."

Jake kept the blue sedans in his sights but, by keeping several cars between him and his target, stayed far enough back not to be spotted.

Though pain pounded in his head, guilt hammered harder. He'd blown it again. He'd asked Paige to trust him to keep her safe, and he'd let her down.

He'd let her get snatched from the seat beside him. *Hell.*

Whatever it took, he would get Paige back. He would save her before those slime bags had a chance to—

A sharp ache reverberated in his skull. He could have a concussion. The pain made his eyes tear, and he clenched his teeth, fighting to stay conscious. When he touched his fingers to the goose egg on his head, he found a small bleeding cut.

Didn't matter. All that mattered was getting to Paige, getting her away from the terrorists before they could hurt her.

Ahead of him, the first blue sedan jerked a hard right-hand turn. The second sedan didn't.

Jake blinked as his vision swam, making sure he'd seen correctly. The blue sedans were splitting up?

A chill prickled Jake's nape. If he were two men, he'd follow the second car to see where it went. Maybe he'd find out more about who was behind the terrorist group and what they were after.

But he was only one man, and his priority, his only *real* goal, was Paige's safety.

Gripping the steering wheel so tightly his skin blanched, Jake shook off another wave of nearly blinding pain.

I'm sorry, Paige. I'm so sorry. Hang on. I'm coming.

When he reached the side street where the first car had turned, Jake followed.

"Tabor and Henchcliff can take the first half of the list, and we'll do the second half." Ringleader had gotten on his cell phone as soon as Paige told him about the pawnshop, and in short order, he had his minions scouring the city for her ring.

Her heart sank. She'd hoped the tidbit she'd given him would keep him busy for days, buying her time. Apparently, Ringleader had enough guys on his payroll to start a miniature dragnet combing the city's southside shops.

"The ring is an emerald-cut diamond solitaire set in white gold. It would have been brought in in the last three days by a pretty brunette." He sent her another side glance that made her stomach do serious flip-flops. "If anyone asks, it's an heirloom and the poor jilted darling hadn't known the family history. Got it?"

Ringleader snapped the cell phone closed and jammed it

in his shirt pocket. On his lap, his hand flexed and closed around his handgun.

Paige took a deep breath for courage. "Look, I told you what you wanted to know. Can't you let me go now?"

A muscle jumped in Ringleader's jaw, and his icy blue eyes narrowed on her. "Not until we have the ring and confirm that the nanotube is in it and intact." He leaned closer, and a fresh jolt of fear spilled more acid into her stomach. "If you and your new boyfriend have done anything to damage the bead…" His glare darkened. "It won't go well for you."

Trembling to her core, Paige squeezed her eyes shut and tried to slow her ragged breathing. Instead, behind closed eyes, she saw Jake slumping forward after he was smacked in the head. She heard Brent saying, "The super-virus is even more deadly than the Spanish flu that caused the 1918 pandemic." She smelled the blood that had splattered the walls the night she and Jake had been cornered in Brent's office. And a familiar, unsettling feeling crept over her…

When Paige was fourteen years old, her family had visited a theme park, and she'd gamely climbed on the biggest roller coaster. If ten-year-old Zoey could ride the Green Monster, so could she. But when the ride had crested the top of the first hill, a paralyzing fear had washed through Paige. Not because of the speed of the train or the height of the hill, but because she'd felt completely helpless. She'd known she had absolutely no control over the roller coaster and had been terrified. Since that day at the theme park, whenever she'd felt a complete loss of control over her life, Paige did the same thing she'd done on the Green Monster.

She threw up.

Now, scrunched between two armed men, hurtling down the highway, with the responsibility of keeping her country safe from the deadly virus her ex-fiancé created, control over her circumstances once again dangled beyond her reach. Her gut surged with the same nausea and panic she'd known when she'd seen the steep and undulating track that lay ahead for the roller coaster.

"Um…" She paused to swallow the bitter taste already climbing her throat. "We need to pull over."

"What?" Ringleader snarled.

"I think I'm…gonna be sick."

Her captor glowered at her, his expression pure suspicion. "Like hell."

"I don't know, Steward." Beefy Guy angled his head to study her, leaned closer. "She don't look so good. Kinda pale and—"

The sour smell surrounding Beefy Guy was the last straw. Paige's lunch rose in her throat in a violent wave. In the last seconds of coherent thought, before she gave herself over to abject misery and humiliation, she knew she could use her moment of weakness as a weapon. A tool.

Or else her split-second decision would backfire in the worse possible way.

Turning her head and throwing her shoulders forward, she aimed for Ringleader's lap, his hand. His gun.

"What the hell?" Ringleader bellowed, his face twisting in disgust. "Oh, my God! You bitch!" He shoved her away with a none-too-gentle thrust and yelled to their driver. "Pull over! Now!" After taking one look at his soiled gun, he flung his weapon on the floor of the car and wiped the mess from his hand on the backseat.

As the car jerked to the side of the road, Paige was tossed against Beefy Guy, who shrank away from her as if she carried the plague.

A second wave of nausea built to a roiling crescendo in her gut, and she pressed one hand to her mouth while gesturing wildly with the other.

Beefy Guy frantically fumbled to open the door.

She scrambled to climb over him and get out of the car. Again, she took advantage of her opportunity and purposely drove her knee into Beefy Guy's groin as she clambered across his lap to the shoulder of the road.

He hollered in pain and doubled over.

Despite the heat, despite the sick pitching in her stomach,

despite the odds against success, Paige knew she might never get a chance like this again. While Ringleader and Beefy Guy reeled from her unpleasant surprise attack, Paige ran.

Chapter 12

Jake tensed when the blue sedan abruptly stopped at the side of the road. This part of Lagniappe had few buildings, mostly offices for blue-collar businesses—plumbers, pest control a mom-and-pop grocery—spread out along a two-lane road amid numerous empty lots and weed-infested fields. Had he been spotted? Did the Wedding Crashers know he'd followed them?

Jake gritted his teeth and did what he did best—think on his feet, make snap decisions in high-stakes moments. Rather than pull over and wait the situation out, Jake saw what may be his only chance to act, to overtake the blue sedan and get Paige back.

He was outmanned and unarmed now—unless…

Jake fumbled on the floor under the driver's seat. His fingers closed around the familiar grip of his P226. *Thank God!*

He snatched the pistol off the floor, where he'd dropped it when he'd been knocked out, and sped forward. As he approached the blue sedan, the passenger-side back door flew open, and Paige stumbled out.

Jake's heart missed a beat. She was alive, appeared unharmed.

He didn't question, only reacted.

As Paige ran from the sedan, Jake wheeled the rental car in front of her and slammed on the brakes. With a scream, she came up short and sent a frightened, disoriented look through the windshield.

"Get in!" he yelled to her, making his head throb in protest.

"Jake!" She hesitated one startled second before sprinting to the passenger door and quickly climbing in. "How did you—I thought—"

He stomped the gas pedal before she could finish, before she even had the door closed. She fought to hang on and shut her door as they peeled away.

When they passed the blue sedan, Jake aimed his SIG Sauer at the rear tire, fired and hit his mark. "Buckle in. This could get dicey."

"Get dicey?" She barked a humorless laugh, then clamped a hand over her mouth. "Oh, man. I'm gonna be sick again."

As he rocketed down the narrow two-lane street, thankful the traffic was sparse, he shot her a glance. "Sick?"

She nodded and leaned her head back. "That's how I got away. I…threw up on Ringleader."

Jake chortled. "Oh, that's rich! Brilliant!"

"I tend to do that when I get really upset, really stressed out." She glared at him, apparently not seeing the humor in the situation that he did. "They pulled over so I could finish my business on the side of the road, and I saw my chance—"

Jake slapped the steering wheel and tamed his laughter to a broad grin. "Darling, that is a prime example of the kind of in-the-moment, tactical strategizing that would have made my CO in the SEALs proud. You worked with what you had and used it to your advantage. Simply brilliant!"

She gaped at him as if he'd lost his mind. "I didn't plan to get sick! I couldn't help it! That's how I respond to having my life threatened!"

"My point exactly. You can't plan for the unexpected. You have to know how to go with your gut…" He cut a sly glance and a wry grin toward her. "No pun intended."

She returned a sour smile.

He checked his rearview mirror and saw no sign of the blue sedan behind him. The grip of anxiety squeezing his chest loosened, and the drumbeat of pain in his head eased. But he knew better than to assume they were in the clear.

Rather than head straight back to the campground and risk an unseen tail following them, Jake headed toward the city limits, out to the countryside where long stretches of flat farmland allowed a clear view of the traffic behind him for many miles. Only when he was certain they had no one tailing them would he head back to the opposite side of town and their campsite.

Paige fell silent, and she rode with her eyes shut, her complexion pale, her breathing deep. He gave her the time she needed to calm her ragged nerves and work past the stress-induced nausea.

Pride swelled in his chest for her quick thinking, whether she could see the significance of her actions or not. For someone who claimed to be all about planning and organization and contingencies, she'd shown she could handle herself under fire.

He set the rental car's cruise control and settled back, rolling the tension from his shoulders and realizing the sharp throb in his skull had subsided to a dull ache. Progress.

With a lingering side glance, Jake drank in the image of Paige beside him. With her tangled hair, rumpled shirt and makeup-free face, she reminded him more of a wild adventuress than the pressed-and-pleated society bride he'd met last week. He liked this Paige. She had a raw sensuality about her that she kept hidden with her buttoned-down shirts and stiff formalities.

"Jake?" she said without opening her eyes, and he wondered briefly if she had felt his scrutinizing gaze.

"Yeah?"

She had more color in her cheeks now, and he took that as a good sign. Her breathing had steadied, but new worry lines creased her forehead.

"I told them…that the bead was hidden in my engagement ring." She opened her eyes now and angled her head toward him. Her troubled green gaze arrowed through him.

"I had to tell them something, and…"

"Your *engagement* ring, not the wedding ring?"

She nodded. "But when they saw I wasn't wearing it, I told them we'd also pawned the engagement ring. That's probably where they're headed now. They were making a list of all the pawnshops in town to start searching."

"You didn't tell them which shop we used?"

"I couldn't remember which shop we used. I was flustered and trying to give them something to appease them without selling out my country or putting you at risk."

"Me?"

She winced and nodded. "I put the wedding ring in your backpack before I left for the hospital. For safekeeping…in case I—" She didn't finish the thought, only sighed and turned her face away. "I told them we pawned my wedding ring, too. At the time it seemed like the right move. If I'd been mad enough at Brent to pawn my engagement ring for the cash, it seemed logical to me that I'd have also hocked the wedding ring. I figured they'd see that logic, too, so…"

"Makes sense. What's the problem?"

"Well, think about it. What happens when they find the right pawnshop and get my engagement ring?"

"Nothing. You said in the elevator at the hospital that Scofield confirmed the bead was in your *wedding* ring."

"But they're bound to ask for the wedding ring, too. To cover their bases. They'd be stupid not to. And these thugs may be vicious, but I doubt they're stupid."

He connected the dots and sighed. "And when the pawnshop

tells them you *didn't* pawn another ring, they'll know you lied about the wedding ring and put two and two together…"

"And get four." She held up four fingers. "Four words. *Bead in wedding ring.* And they'll be right back on our trail, except now they'll know what they're after."

Jake clenched his teeth, and immediately regretted it when another bolt of pain streaked through his skull. He pinched the bridge of his nose, wishing he had a couple of ibuprofen tablets for his headache. "You did what you thought you had to. Don't get worked up about it."

"I all but told them where the nanotube is hidden!"

He winced when she raised her voice. "But—" He raised his palm, signaling her to hold her volume down. "First they have to find us. We've shaken their tail, and we'll go back to the campground and lay low until we figure out our next move."

Her face brightened, and she pivoted on the seat to face him. "I know our next move. Brent gave me a name. He had a guy in the Centers for Disease Control with whom he'd arranged a clandestine meeting. He was going to give this guy the nanotube, ensuring the virus would be safe within the strict regulations and security measures of the CDC."

Jake frowned. "How do we know we can trust this guy?"

"Brent trusted him. He said he'd vetted him and knew his reputation."

Jake lifted a palm in agreement. "Works for me."

"He told me how to get in touch with this William Gates and give him the wedding ring. Gates would know how to extract the nanotube and recover the virus safely for future testing."

"And the rest of the virus has been destroyed? You know, all of this is for nothing if the Wedding Crashers can get the virus some other way."

"Steward."

Jake pulled a face. "Excuse me?"

"I think the ringleader's name is Steward. I heard Beefy Guy call him that once."

Jake nodded and filed that tidbit of information away.

"And, yes, the rest of the virus is gone. He told me today that one night at the Bancroft laboratory, when he'd known the terrorists were closing in on him, he'd incinerated everything except what was put in the nanotube." She pulled her bottom lip into her teeth, and her shoulders slumped. "But what's in that nanotube is still enough to start a global pandemic if it were properly weaponized."

Jake's chest tightened. He'd seen the effects of biowarfare both in the flesh and in training films. "So this is no ordinary flu we're talking about, I take it."

"Worse than the Spanish flu of 1918."

"That killed fifty million people."

"Yeah."

Jake squeezed the steering wheel harder and muttered a curse.

Behind them, the sun sank low over the horizon, and power poles cast long shadows across the endless rows of farmers' crops they drove past. Time to head back to the campground.

He sent Paige a hard look and braced himself. "Okay, tell me everything Scofield said about getting the ring to this Gates guy."

As they drove back to the campground, Jake listened silently while Paige relayed everything she'd learned from Brent, everything they'd discussed. Everything. His expression remained stony as she revealed how Brent had gotten caught up in the lure of money, how he'd only belatedly realized the buyers posing as federal officials weren't who they'd said. She repeated Brent's instructions on how to contact William Gates, his contact within the CDC.

Whether Jake was simply overwhelmed by the information, as she had been, or if he was mentally dissecting the news and making strategic plans as she now was, she couldn't be certain. His inscrutable face remained hard, his eyes distant.

Was he even listening? How could he hear they were in

possession of a monumentally deadly, incredibly tiny virus sample that terrorists wanted to weaponize and show no outward emotion or reaction at all?

Or maybe he was just as tired from the day's events, as stunned by the ramifications of Brent's research, as boggled by their responsibility to protect the virus as she was. She sighed and leaned back against the headrest.

"I also told Brent it was over, that I didn't love him and couldn't marry him."

Now Jake's head whipped toward her, his face registering intrigue. "You did? How did he take it?"

"He wasn't surprised. He seemed to be expecting it."

Jake said nothing, but he fixed a penetrating gaze on her for several seconds before returning his attention to the road.

"Sad, huh?" She studied his profile in the warm light of the setting sun. "Until a couple days ago, everyone knew I didn't love Brent, that our marriage was a mistake, except me. And my dad. He was so happy to see me marrying Brent. I let my dad's enthusiasm blind me."

"Why, do you think?"

She chortled in disbelief. "Why did I want my dad to approve of my choice of husband? Why did I want my dad to be happy?" She shook her head as if the answer should be obvious. "He's my dad, Jake. I love him."

"So that means his happiness is more important than your own?"

"No! I didn't say that."

"But that's what you were doing, isn't it? Putting your dad's wishes, his needs and happiness, before your own?"

She bristled defensively. "Of course not. I liked Brent well enough. Marrying him seemed logical and practical. We were well matched, and he was the heir apparent to take over the company from my dad, and—"

"Do you hear yourself?" Jake interrupted. His tone vibrated with an edge of anger or frustration that startled Paige.

She blinked at Jake, unsure how to respond.

He dragged a hand over his face and shot her a side glance

that teemed with energy and emotion. The contrast to his earlier stoicism left her breathless.

"You *liked* Brent *well enough?* Marrying him was *practical?*" He snorted in derision. "Paige, you buy a car or a computer because it's *practical*. And saying you liked Brent *well enough* reeks of settling for less than you deserve."

She gaped at him. "I—"

"You don't pick your husband according to your *dad's* choice to run the company. The man you marry should be—"

"Someone who makes *me* happy." She sighed and rolled her eyes. "Yeah, yeah. I've gotten this speech before from Zoey."

"Well, Zoey was right. But I was gonna say he should be someone who gets you hot and bothered, who makes you—"

"Horny? Is that the word you're looking for?" She scoffed, but even discussing sex with Jake made her skin feel too tight, hot and prickly. "'Cause there's a lot more to a marriage than sex, Jake."

He shot her a scowl. "I know that. And, yeah, *horny* works for me. That's part of what I'm saying, but not everything."

Her nerves jangling, Paige let her gaze roam over his hard, square jaw, his large hands gripping the steering wheel, his taut muscles that seemed as tightly wound as hers. Looking at Jake, she remembered her high-school physics class, and the term "potential energy" sprang to mind. He was pure strength, raw power and high-octane fuel ready to ignite. For days she'd felt the sizzle of attraction sparking between them. He'd have to have been dead to have missed it.

Her mouth dried. What would it be like to have all of his energy and intensity focused on her during sex? The thought lit a sensation like firecrackers in her blood.

Jake turned dark, hooded eyes toward her as if he'd read her thoughts. He opened his mouth, then closed it again and frowned before returning his gaze to the road. "The man you marry should be someone who loves you. You deserve that,

Paige. You deserve love and devotion and all that happily-ever-after stuff. The house with the picket fence."

Another pause. "And respect. And friendship. And, yeah… passion. Not just in sex, but…for life. You say you and Brent were the same, but sometimes *same* equals boring. As smart as you are, you should have someone who challenges you, someone you can fight with, someone who'll keep you on your toes and make your life interesting."

She harrumphed. "Maybe I don't want to fight with my husband. Maybe I like boring. Sometimes boring equals security and order. Maybe those things are more important to me than whether I have a great sex life." She gritted her teeth, wondering how they'd gotten on such a personal subject. Wondering why she was so uncomfortable defending her position to Jake.

Wondering if maybe she was getting a glimpse of Jake's deepest yearnings cleverly disguised as a dissection of *her* life.

Paige drew her bottom lip between her teeth, mulling that possibility. "And maybe that's what *you're* looking for in a wife. Someone passionate and interesting and spontaneous." All things she wasn't. With that realization, her heart sank. They might have sparks between them, but she and Jake had vast differences that made any future together impossible.

"I'm not marriage material, so that's a moot point."

He was shutting her out again, and after the intimate examination of her choices, his retreat raised her temper. "What does that mean, not marriage material? You think because you didn't have a traditional family growing up, because the navy released you from combat duty, that somehow you're unwanted or unworthy of a family?"

"Leave it alone, Paige." He pinched the bridge of his nose and squeezed his eyes shut as if in pain.

She remembered his head injury, and her irritation fled, replaced with concern. "Is your head okay? Should we take you to the E.R.?"

He gave his head a small shake. "Naw, I'll be fine. I've got a goose egg, maybe a cut, but it doesn't hurt that bad. If I start showing symptoms of a concussion, I'll let you know."

She stared at him skeptically. "Promise? You're not just being the tough guy, playing through the pain?"

He sent her a quick, stiff grin. "I'm fine. And we have more important matters to discuss than my reasons for not marrying. Like how to get that nanotube to Gates."

He narrowed his eyes and firmed his mouth. "Walking into the CDC offices and just handing it to him is not an option. Security at the CDC offices, the terrorists on our tail, the history of this case make that pretty obvious. I mean, Scofield had a rendezvous off the Jamaican coast set up for the transfer. And we don't have the luxury of time to make the kind of intricate arrangements Scofield was planning." Jake shifted restlessly on the front seat as he drove, and a tingle of apprehension nipped Paige's spine.

"But we can't go off half-cocked either. We have to make a workable plan. Including contingencies." The urgency she'd hoped to put in her tone sounded tremulous, more like fear. Yet she couldn't deny Jake's fly-by-the-seat-of-your-pants approach was more than a little worrisome to her.

Jake sent her a side glance. "Ever hear the expression, 'Man plans, God laughs'? As you discovered today for yourself, you can't plan for every possible twist of fate. It's better to play it by ear." He squared his shoulders, and a muscle in his jaw twitched. "I know I failed Brent at the wedding. I know I failed you today when those goons grabbed you. But if you'll trust me with this, I promise I will do whatever it takes to protect the nanotube from the terrorists. And I would die before I let them hurt you."

A chill slithered down her back. "I believe you."

But Jake dying in the course of this mission was exactly what she feared.

Chapter 13

That evening, Paige and Jake built their own campfire and shared a meal of tuna sandwiches and potato chips from the nonperishable supply of food Jake had bought earlier. As meals went, tuna was hardly gourmet, chips not exactly healthy, but Paige savored every bite of her dinner. Being kidnapped, facing death and losing her lunch had left her starving and more appreciative of simple things.

Eating beside the glowing campfire with Jake made the food feel special, romantic.

Until she thought of his declaration that afternoon. *I'm not marriage material*.

She'd known as much about Jake, yet the reminder plucked at her, left her off balance and feeling empty. She shifted on the hard log-bench, but her discomfort had more to do with her conversation with Jake about the qualifications of her husband-to-be.

"We should get a new rental car. The Wedding Crashers have seen this one—" Jake hitched his head toward the Taurus. "—and will be looking for it."

His comment snapped her out of her musings and back to the more pressing issue that faced them. For all his talk of playing things by ear, Jake was clearly in strategy mode. He sat on the ground with his legs crossed and his back propped against the fat log where she sat. His gaze was distant, meditative, as he stared into the fire.

"Wouldn't it be faster to fly to Atlanta? We still have some cash from the engagement ring for airline tickets." She glanced at him then poked idly at the fire with a stick she'd found and intended to use to roast marshmallows later.

"Airport's probably being watched. Atlanta is only a day's drive, and this way we have our own transportation, more control over our situation."

Paige nodded her agreement. The more control they had over the transfer of the ring, the nanotube, the virus, the better.

A movement in her peripheral vision startled Paige, made her heart jump. She jerked her head toward the edge of their campsite and spotted Nate, the stray black cat.

Paige took a cleansing breath. She'd been jumpy ever since they got back. Though Jake had assured her they hadn't been followed, she didn't feel as safe tonight as she had previous nights at the campground.

She watched Nate creep forward, sniffing the air. His gaze zeroed in on her tuna sandwich, and he meowed plaintively.

"Hey, Nate, ole boy. You want some of this tuna, don't you?" she cooed softly.

Jake snorted. "Is the Pope Catholic?"

Paige shoved to her feet, went inside the camper to retrieve a paper plate and another can of tuna. After opening the can and dumping the contents on the plate, she carried her offering to Nate outside.

The cat scurried back a few steps when she approached, although his nose twitched and his eyes were bright with anticipation.

Paige set the plate down and stepped back. Nate blinked at her, then cautiously crept forward to eat. She backed away quietly, careful not to spook their dinner guest, and rejoined Jake by the fire. "The poor thing is starved."

Jake glanced toward the cat, who wolfed down the canned tuna. "I'm sure he finds plenty of scraps around here in the trash. And a wild cat like that is bound to be a good hunter."

"Maybe. I still feel sorry for him."

"Because you have a soft heart." Jake wrapped his hand around hers and stroked her wrist with his thumb. The delicate caress stirred her pulse and sent heady sensations humming through her.

The crackling of the fire, the chirping of the summer frogs and the sough of a light breeze in the leaves sang a lulling harmony. If she didn't know better, she could almost believe that nothing existed outside the bubble of light created by their campfire. Almost.

She watched Nate gobbling his dinner and savored the quiet moment. After wolfing down most of the food, the cat sat up, licking his lips, and regarded her with a satisfied look on his face.

"He seems like such a sweet cat. He'd have made someone a good pet if he hadn't been abandoned out here."

Jake's only response was a grunt of acknowledgment, and when she turned to study his profile in the flickering light from the fire, she realized how much Nate and Jake had in common.

Alone in the world. No family. No real home. Clearly needing the affection she had to offer but too scarred by their pasts to risk letting her get close. So much potential for love lost to a greater fear of getting hurt.

"Heartbreaking…" she murmured.

"He'll be fine." Jake dropped her hand to pick up a stick and poke at the glowing coals. "He'll have a tougher life than a pampered house cat, but he'll be okay."

Paige swallowed hard to clear the lump from her throat. "Will he?"

Leaning back against the log-bench and stacking his

hands behind his head, Jake met her gaze. "Sure he will. 'Cause there'll always be another softy like you through the campground who'll feed him and look out for him, even if they can't turn him into a pet."

Paige felt her eyes water, and she jerked her gaze away.

Nate stood and stretched his lithe body before giving a soft meow and trotting off into the night. *There'll always be another softy.*

But, *damn it,* what if she didn't want him drifting from one soft heart to the next, rambling through life? Rootless. Searching. Never giving real love a chance.

Maybe she wanted to be the one to tame him, give him a home, give him her heart.

Paige bit her bottom lip and watched the cat disappear into the black shadows, realizing the one she wanted so desperately to share her love with...wasn't Nate.

It was Jake.

Jake woke abruptly in the wee hours of the night with a pervading sense that something was not right. He strained to listen, thinking that maybe a suspicious sound had roused him.

The crickets chirped. The frogs sang. A mosquito buzzed near his ear. All else was quiet. Still.

Too quiet.

And he knew what had woken him. Not a new sound, but the absence of Paige's quiet snoring.

He sat up and strained to peer through the dark camper to Paige's bed. He perked his ears, listening for the light rasp of her breathing. Nothing.

His pulse hammered, and he swung his legs off the bed and crept across the shadowed camper. "Paige?" he whispered harshly.

No answer. Her bed was empty.

Paige was gone.

Every muscle in his body tensed. The panic that had consumed him earlier in the day when he'd seen Paige grabbed and thrown into the blue car swamped him again. Except a sharper fear sliced through him. This afternoon, he'd seen who took Paige, had been able to follow the car, had known he'd get Paige back somehow…whatever it took. Now, he had no leads. He'd slept through her disappearance. He'd failed her when she needed him.

Pain ripped through his chest. Guilt and recriminations gnawed his gut. Fisting his hands, he began pacing the tiny floor of the camper. He had to do something, had to find her, had to—

Jake paused and dropped his chin to his chest. *Slow down. Think. Don't let your emotions run away and blind you.*

Damn it, that was the problem. Where Paige was concerned, he'd been letting his emotions get in the way, distract him from the job he had to do. He swallowed hard, clearing his mind and gritting his teeth. She'd promised not to go anywhere without him, but…maybe she'd just stepped outside for a minute. Maybe she'd just gone to the bathroom, or…

He flipped his wrist and checked his watch. Three o'clock.

Would Paige have really gone anywhere in the dark woods in the middle of the night alone? Not likely, but he had to check.

Wasting no time, he grabbed a flashlight and his gun and bolted from the camper.

"Paige?" he called, not caring who he woke. He swept the beam of light around the dark campground as he hurried toward the bathhouse. His head throbbed, his bad knee ached, but he ignored the pain. Rocks and sticks jabbed the soles of his bare feet, but he wouldn't take the time shoes required. Those seconds could be the difference between finding Paige in time or…not.

"Paige?" He startled a deer grazing at the edge of the camping area. His own pulse staggered, and he quickened his step. "Paige!"

As he neared the bathhouse, he heard two unmistakable noises. Water running…a shower.

And a low moaning.

Heart in his throat, Jake burst into the women's bathhouse, following the noises. "Paige!"

A gasp. "Jake?"

He darted toward the shower stalls, gun up, ready.

With a sweep of his hand, he shoved back the curtain of the first stall.

Nothing. The second. Empty.

The third.

Paige screamed. Her eyes flew to the gun.

"Do you mind?" she grated, her eyes flashing angrily.

She was alone. Unharmed. Safe.

Relief flowed through him so hard and fast it left his knees weak. He braced a hand on the tile wall, catching his breath. He set the gun and flashlight on the bench in the dressing area of the shower stall and tried to hide the tremble in his hands.

Then anger flooded him as the fear receded.

"Of all the stupid…" He aimed a finger at her, his rage tightening his muscles and making his head throb.

"Jake, get out!"

"I told you not to go anywhere without me! After today, I'd have thought the reason why would be painfully clear!"

Her gaze returned the daggers he shot her. "Jake! Get. Out!"

"Hell, Paige, do you have any idea what I thought when I woke up and you were gone?" He jammed a hand through his hair, while the mix of postpanic adrenaline and gut-grinding frustration seesawed sickly in his stomach.

"I'm sorry I worried you," she grated through clenched teeth, not sounding the slightest bit repentant. "Now, get the hell out of my shower!"

He drew a breath to fling another accusing assault at her, but stopped. Like a dousing with icy water, her shouted command finally penetrated the red haze of anger and fear that had tied him in knots since he woke up minutes ago. He stiffened. Took a step back.

And looked at her. Really looked at her.

Her eyes were red and puffy from crying—the moaning sound he'd heard. He absorbed the misery in her eyes like a kick in the chest. What had made her cry? Why—?

"Please, Jake…" She glared at him, but her pink-cheeked expression held something else…

And then he dared to let his gaze drift from her face.

Like a stunned child stating the obvious, his brain registered what he should have recognized sooner. If he hadn't been so wrapped up in his fear and subsequent fury.

She was showering. She was…naked.

Paige had her arms crossed over her chest and her lower body turned ninety degrees, giving him a profile view. A sultry, curvy, mouth-drying view.

His entire body tensed, and he stood paralyzed, mesmerized. Thrumming.

He followed the rivulets of water that coursed from her wet hair, slicked to her scalp and hanging in thick ropes around her shoulders. The hot shower spray pounded her pale skin, the heat leaving her ivory complexion tinted with a rosy hue. Billows of steam swirled around her, creating a dreamlike quality to the erotic image she cast.

Pounding desire stirred in his belly and spread fiery tongues through his blood.

An alarm screamed in his head, warning him away, but his feet were rooted, his attention locked on the vision straight out of his sexiest fantasies.

"Jake?"

The trembling, quizzical quality of Paige's voice, more than the sound of his name, brought his gaze back to hers.

A puzzled frown knit the bridge of her nose, and her jade eyes searched his.

Worried. Curious. Wanting…

As he studied her face, trying to decipher the myriad emotions swirling in her eyes, her gaze gave him the same slow, measured scrutiny he'd given her. His bare feet, bare chest, boxer briefs that did little to hide his state of arousal.

Damn. In his panic, in his rush to find her, he'd not so much as pulled on his jeans before bolting from the camper into the night. He was as good as naked himself. In a steamy shower. With a woman whose vulnerable green eyes and sensual lips had been tempting him for days.

Double damn.

"You've been crying," he said inanely, his voice thick. *Again with the childlike stating of the obvious. Good job, McCall. Brilliant.*

"I...kept thinking about...today when...well, I c-couldn't sleep and...I didn't want to wake you." Her chin trembled slightly before she bit her bottom lip to stop it.

Her eyes teared up again, and his heart squeezed until he couldn't breathe.

"I'm sorry, Jake." He could barely hear her whisper over the whoosh of the water. "I d-didn't mean to scare you."

He couldn't answer. His mouth was too dry, his throat too tight.

Her eyes flickered down his body again. Her pupils grew to large, dark pools, and desire glowed in their fathomless depths.

Where before he couldn't make his feet move, now he couldn't stop himself from closing the distance between them. The shower spray soaked him as he slid a hand to the nape of her neck and drew her to him. He dipped his head and captured her lips.

And he was lost.

The touch of Jake's lips sent the third shock in as many minutes to her overtaxed nerves—his sudden armed appearance in her shower, the realization that he, too, was virtually naked...and highly aroused. And now the electrifying jolt as his lips seized hers. The surge of energy, the crackling sensation that swamped her, short-circuited any semblance of reason or clear thinking. They must have. Why else would she be wrapping her arms around his neck and pressing the full length of her body against the hot, hard length of his?

She curled her fingers into his hair, angling her head to deepen the kiss. Shimmering sparks shot through her and coalesced low in her belly. Her hips canted forward, straining toward his as the hot, pulsing need in her grew.

A pleasured moan rumbled from her throat, and Jake answered in kind. She met the thrust of his tongue with an eager parry. A muddle of lust left her light-headed and blissfully muzzy. When her legs trembled, he folded her into his embrace, one hand sliding over her bottom to anchor her, the other splayed on her thigh.

And still they weren't close enough for her. She clambered to rise on her toes, to hook her leg around his hip. Sinking his fingers into her bottom, Jake scooted her against the tile wall and lifted her so that her hips were in perfect alignment with his. She rode the thick ridge of his arousal and gasped as powerful shock waves ripped through her.

They were in a public shower. But instead of deterring her, knowing they could be caught was exciting, enticing…slightly scandalous. Highly erotic.

They had terrorists after them. But instead of sobering her, the element of danger, the fear she'd already survived heightened her senses, made the moment sharper, clearer, more intense.

Jake was the wrong man for her in so many ways…though at the moment her overwhelmed brain couldn't conjure one. All Paige knew was the flood of fiery sensation flowing through her.

Need clawed her. Desire sizzled through her blood. Reason was tossed aside as the chaotic frenzy in her body shouted down rational thought.

She tightened the grip her legs had around his hips and, secure in the solid strength of his arms, she leaned back, giving him access to her breasts. Jake's hungry mouth descended on one tautly budded nipple while the warm shower spray lashed the other. The gentle tug of his lips, light scrape of his teeth and erotic flick of his tongue battered her with tingling heat. The urgency pounding inside her ramped to the edge of control.

"Jake," she rasped, arching her throat. Feeling the first quiver of climax.

But she didn't want to shatter yet. She wanted him with her. Inside her. "Please…"

She raked her fingers down his back to grab the wet fabric of his briefs. Awkwardly, she tugged them down, fighting them past the grip of her legs, the bulge of his erection. Finally, with a quick swipe of his hand, Jake shoved the briefs down his thighs.

Admiring the masculine beauty of him, Paige stroked her fingers along the length and heat of him. Jake bucked and tensed, making a strangled sounding moan.

"Oh, Paige…that. Feels. So. Good." He shuddered as if barely containing himself, and the pure pleasure on his face infused her with a sense of empowerment and joy, a carnal freedom that sweetened what was already shockingly satisfying.

His gaze locked with hers. Hot. Dark. Penetrating.

And dismayed. His jaw tightened.

"We don't have protection," he rasped, his voice deep and full of frustration.

She blinked, nodded. "I'm on the pill."

The relief that washed over his face would have been comical had she not been so tightly wound, so ready to come apart. Impatient for the climax hovering just beyond her grasp, Paige wrapped her arms around his neck and pulled herself up. And sank onto him.

He filled her, stretched her, stroked her in just the right way. A feeling of completion that had nothing to do with the mind-numbing physical sensations zinging through her body settled in her heart. She felt whole in a way she never had before. The joining of their bodies felt cosmically ordained.

And intensely stimulating.

As Jake thrust deeper, the tidal wave of sensations stole her breath. He pistoned his hips, driving deeper and pushing her closer to the edge. She arched her neck, and he pressed hot, openmouthed kisses along the curve of her throat. A low growl vibrated in his chest, swelling to a roar of satisfaction as his body shuddered and his grip tightened. His lusty groan sent her crashing into her own sweet oblivion. The powerful throb of her body matched the thundering beat in her chest.

She held Jake tightly, resting her face against his shoulder and mentally staggering under the assault of emotions she'd never known before. With her logical mind turned off, her heart screamed what she'd tried to deny before now.

She loved Jake.

She never wanted to be without him. Would do anything to make him happy. Wanted to give herself over to him, not only physically but spiritually, emotionally…completely. That was the wholeness she'd experienced when they'd joined their bodies, the sense that she'd found her soul mate.

This was the fulfilling joy and deep affection that had assured Holly that Matt was her future. The kind of passion and devotion that led Zoey to leave home and follow her boyfriend around the country.

The kind of happiness and ardor she'd never felt for Brent. When stripped of her defenses and the protests of her analytical brain, the depth of her feelings for Jake couldn't be ignored.

Recognizing her feelings for what they were should have given her a sense of peace. Instead, her gut clenched, and her strategic mind whispered, *"So you love him. What are you going to do about it?"*

For that question, she had no answer.

Jake wore the beach towel Paige had taken to the shower around his waist as they hurried back through the dark grounds to their camper. Once safely ensconced inside, he ripped the towel off and drew her back into his arms.

"Just so you know, before I left the hospital after the bombing in Iraq, I was tested for just about everything you can imagine. There's been no one since then. You're safe with me." She hadn't asked, had trusted him at the bathhouse, but he wanted her to know, to be certain.

Paige blinked at him, then let her gaze skim down his naked body, her eyes darkening with desire again. "No one? In...how long ago did you leave the SEALs?"

"Couple years now." He smoothed a hand along her cheek, dropped a kiss on her forehead. "Let's just say...I had other priorities in recent months. And the idea of one-night stands left me cold."

She tipped her head, opened her mouth as if she wanted to comment on his confession, but she snapped her mouth closed again, and her brow furrowed thoughtfully. "Mm. And I've only been with Brent. So you're safe with me, too."

He stiffened when she mentioned Scofield's name but tried to hide his guilty reaction. Scofield had hired Jake to protect him, then given him the charge of keeping Paige safe. Jake gritted his teeth. He'd done neither.

What he *had* done was ravish his client's fiancée mere days after taking over her protection. *Ex-fiancée,* a voice in his head corrected. Although what difference did it make, really? She was off-limits.

Some bodyguard he made. He couldn't even protect Paige from himself.

Sobering, he stepped back from her and balled his hands at his sides. "I'm sorry about... I shouldn't have..." He huffed his frustration. Who was he kidding? He wasn't a bit sorry. Making love to Paige had been pure nirvana, an experience he'd cherish in the lonely days and months to come.

Paige lifted a delicate eyebrow and stepped closer. "Did I complain?" She trailed a finger down his chest, and his nerve endings fired like live wires. "We both wanted it."

He drew a deep breath, trying to steel himself to the effect of her skin brushing his as she shed her bathrobe and pressed herself more fully against him. "That doesn't make it any less of a mistake."

She frowned and lifted wounded eyes to his. "Why is it a mistake?"

He gripped her arms to push her away but couldn't bring himself to move her back. She felt too good, fit too perfectly against him. Holding her felt too…right.

He shook his head to clear his thoughts. "Sex muddies the picture. Blurs the lines between us. And I…I can't give you the commitment you need."

She tilted her head back, a wrinkle at the bridge of her nose. "Did I ask for a commitment? I'm willing to wait for you, to give you time…"

He sighed. "I don't want to hurt you, Paige."

"Then don't." She rose on her toes to press a kiss to his lips. A rush of heat swept through him.

Rallying his defenses, he tightened his grip on her arms and met her gaze with a hard stare. "Paige, look at me and tell me that you're not, even as we speak, forming emotional attachments to me, telling yourself how your feelings for me have deepened because of what just happened. Tell me you're not thinking that things are different between us now."

Her eyes glistened with tears. "Things *are* different now, Jake."

He shook his head. "No. Nothing's changed. We're still the same people we were two hours ago—with different paths, different lives, different needs. Don't convince yourself you're falling in love. Believing you have feelings for me will only lead to heartache, Paige."

She pressed her mouth in a firm line and stepped back. "Earlier today, you told me different was good. That it would keep me on my toes and make my life interesting. That I needed someone with passion in order to be happy."

"I know, but I meant—"

"You make me happy, Jake." She reached for him again and raked cool fingers through his damp hair. "You can't deny we have passion together…in spades. We just proved that. And if you give me a chance, I'll prove to you how much I *do* love you."

His gut clenched, and a viselike pressure squeezed his heart. "Paige, don't…"

Her arms circled his neck, and she trailed butterfly kisses along his jaw, stealing his breath. "Don't shut me out, Jake. I know you've been hurt but, please…let me love you."

Gritting his teeth, he fought down the swell of pain in his chest. He'd heard similar requests before. From foster mothers asking him to trust. Only to betray him and send him away when he reached out.

By SEAL officers demanding his best, his commitment. Only to cut him loose after he'd sacrificed everything for his country.

How could he justify risking his heart with Paige? If he let himself love her, then lost her—

He didn't finish the thought. Just the suggestion revived the horror and sickening panic that had seized him when she'd been grabbed this afternoon. When he'd failed to keep her safe. What if—

With shattering clarity, the truth raked through him. What if he took the risk of loving Paige and failed her in some way? If he couldn't make her happy, if he couldn't keep her safe, if he couldn't give her the kind of life she deserved.

If she left him…

He shuddered, and Paige hugged him tighter. "Give me a chance to prove to you how much I care," she said, her voice cracking.

Jake buried his face in her hair, inhaling the sweet scent of her shampoo. He wanted to memorize her scent, the way she felt in his arms, the way her breath caressed his skin.

"Make love to me again, Jake," she whispered and tugged him toward her bed.

The air caught in his lungs. He wanted her so much it hurt, but how could he make love to her and not lose another piece of himself to her?

"Please, Jake. Trust me…." She nibbled the sensitive spot on his throat, and blood whooshed past his ears, left his head buzzing.

Maybe he couldn't give her a future, but he had the chance

tonight to show her what she meant to him. He could give her one night.

And he'd store up the memories of their passion for the cold and empty days to come.

Chapter 14

The jostling of the camper bed woke Paige early the next morning, and she rubbed bleary eyes to bring the day into focus. A sweet ache in her muscles revived memories of hours spent last night, her body twined with Jake's. Her heart swelled until she thought it might burst.

She touched a tender spot on her neck where Jake's unshaven chin had gently abraded her, and she smiled. Last night, Jake had been tender, and patient, and thorough.

Then demanding, and thrilling, and intense.

They'd probably woken their neighbors with their noise, but she didn't care. Making love to Jake had been better each time. Beyond her wildest dreams.

She propped on her elbow, letting the sheet slide low on her breasts, and watched Jake move around the tiny camper.

"Good morning, hot stuff." She gave him a coy grin to match her singsong tone.

He turned from shoving his spare clothes into his backpack and regarded her with a serious expression. Too serious.

"Morning," he mumbled. And turned away to continue stuffing the backpack.

She shoved down the niggling concern over his behavior and folded back the corner of the sheet. "Wanna come back to bed for a while?"

When he glanced over his shoulder, she waggled her eyebrows suggestively.

Jake's jaw tensed, and a muscle twitched in his cheek. "Can't. We gotta go. We're leaving as soon as we can get packed up."

More than the finality of his announcement, his brusque tone sent a shiver to her marrow. Where was the man whose deep, lulling voice had whispered sweet nothings as he'd joined their bodies just hours ago? Where was the warmth and affection that had been in every touch, every look, every kiss?

"Why the rush? Has something happened?"

"Nothing new. I just want to get on the road. Atlanta is at least eight hours away, and the sooner we get near a cell tower so we can call Gates, the better," he said without looking at her.

Paige tugged the sheet back up, clutching it under her chin, feeling self-conscious in the wake of Jake's cool attitude this morning. She gnawed her bottom lip, reviewing everything that had been said last night. What had caused his withdrawal?

He'd tried to distance himself after they'd made love in the shower, but she'd thought they'd moved beyond his fears and doubts when they'd spent the rest of the night in each other's arms. Was he having second thoughts? Regrets? A relapse of his commitment fears?

A heavy, cold ball of dread settled in her stomach. Hadn't last night shown him how much she cared? What else did she need to do to prove her feelings to him?

Paige knew they had more pressing issues facing them today, matters of national security, desperate terrorists on their tail, a deadly virus to keep safe. But how could she face

Jake, face her future, if she didn't find a way to work things out between them?

"Jake, about last night—"

"You better get dressed. It shouldn't take more than a half hour or so to get the camper folded down and hitched up to the Taurus. We can eat breakfast on the road."

Paige clenched her teeth when he interrupted. Clearly he thought last night was a closed subject. He was wrong.

Wrapping the sheet around her, she swung her feet over the side of the bed and nailed him with a hard stare. "What's wrong with you? Why are you being so abrupt and distant this morning?"

"Nothing's wrong. I just want to trade out the rental car for one the terrorists haven't seen and get on the road. The sooner we get the ring to Gates, the sooner we put this nightmare behind us."

"And then what?"

He paused and sent her a confused look. "What do you mean?"

"What happens to us after we give the ring to Gates?"

Jake shrugged. "Well, the Wedding Crashers will have no real reason to come after us. We won't have the virus anymore." He paused and frowned, adding, "Except that we can identify them to the authorities…hell. Well, we'll cross that bridge later."

A chill slithered down Paige's back. Even when this was over, it might not be *over* over. Would the terrorists come after them to silence them? Paige shook her head and shoved that frightening thought aside. One problem at a time.

"No, I mean what about *us?* What happens to you and me, our relationship? Last night was—"

"Great." He forced a smile. "Is that what you want to hear? Last night was fantastic. The best. But like I told you, there is no *us.* Not now, not when this is over."

Paige squeezed the sheet in her hand until her knuckles were bloodless. Her head reeled dizzily. "But last night—"

"See? This is why I said it was a mistake. You're reading

more into what happened than there was. It's distracting you from the bigger picture of getting that nanotube to Scofield's guy at the CDC. That is our one and only job. Got it?"

So that's how he wanted it, huh? The heat of anger and frustration swirled through her, mixing with the weight of hurt crushing her chest. She yanked the sheet back and stomped to her suitcase to find something clean to wear. With her jaw taut and her motions jerky, Paige dressed silently, occasionally shooting a dark look toward Jake. Though she resented being treated so coldly, especially after the deep intimacy they'd shared last night, she knew better than to push the issue of their future with him. He was preoccupied with delivering the ring to Brent's CDC contact. Surely, once the virus was safely transferred to the CDC, she'd get the chance to prove her love to Jake, and they'd get past his commitment issues. Wouldn't they?

Last night, she'd been certain they could. She'd tasted the kind of happiness Holly had with Matt, and Paige had seen the life she wanted with Jake.

But in light of Jake's withdrawal this morning, a tremor of uncertainty and a cold frisson of fear clouded her bright outlook.

As she threw her dirty clothes into her suitcase and zipped it closed, her lungs tightened until she could barely breathe. All her life she'd dealt with trouble by analyzing and problem solving. But her relationship with Jake wasn't an issue that could be critically dissected and solved through logic and elbow grease. This was a matter of the heart, of her soul, of her emotions. She was out of her league, didn't know if she could find the resolution and the happy ending she wanted so desperately. This emotional minefield scared her more than the Wedding Crashers or deadly viruses.

Because she could lose Jake.

Jake turned on his prepaid cell phone and checked the reception as soon as they hit the main highway into town. Service was still questionable, and since he didn't want to risk the call being dropped, he decided to wait a few minutes before trying to call William Gates. He handed the phone to Paige. "Keep an eye on the reception. When we have all the bars, I'll call Gates."

"*I* can call Gates."

Her tone was churlish, but he couldn't blame her. His behavior this morning had to have hurt her. But he couldn't let her see what last night had meant to him. He needed to make a clean break from her, and any mixed messages from him would only make their inevitable separation harder for her.

He rubbed a hot spot on his chest, but the ache, the gnawing pain wasn't a surface injury. The hurt was deep. Internal. Agonizing.

Because his heart was breaking.

He hadn't wanted to get involved with Paige, hating the idea of hurting her. But he'd never considered how much an ill-advised tryst with Paige would wound him. He'd let his emotions get in the way of what he knew was right and distract him from his assignment.

Protect the nanotube. And protect Paige.

The best way to accomplish the first goal was to shove down the nagging heartache that consumed him when he thought of leaving Paige. Focus on getting to Atlanta undetected and transferring Paige's wedding ring to William Gates.

The second goal…

His brain rebelled. He hated even considering what Paige's best interest meant for him. But Paige needed a man who could give her stability, family, long-term happiness. His life, to date, had been anything but stable. He knew nothing about building a family. And he had serious doubts about keeping a well-bred, wealthy career woman like Paige happy—outside the bedroom, that is—when he knew nothing of the lifestyle she was accustomed to. Hell, she hadn't even been *camping* before this week with him. They had almost nothing in common.

You told me different was good. That it would keep me on my toes and make my life interesting. Paige's accusation from last night haunted him. He'd believed what he'd told her when he said it. But he'd never imagined he could be the one to shake up Paige's staid, regimented life, challenge her, help her see that her own happiness wasn't based on pleasing others.

Paige's prepaid cell phone rang, jarring Jake from his thoughts. He sent her a quizzical look. "Did you give your number to anyone?"

"Not...exactly. But..." She checked the phone's screen. "Holly apparently got the number from her caller ID when I talked to her earlier."

Jake sighed. "Make it quick. Don't tell her where we're going...in case someone is listening."

Paige's green eyes still held shades of anger and hurt, and now, as she punched the button to answer her sister's call, wary concern darkened her gaze. She spoke briefly with her sister, assuring her she was safe, listening with increasing consternation to whatever report Holly gave, then hung up and turned to him. "Brent came through his surgery fine. They kept him sedated the rest of the evening, but when he woke up this morning, he asked to see my dad. Holly says Brent and Dad talked for over an hour, and when Dad came out, all he would say is, 'Call Paige and check on her. I have arrangements to handle.' She wanted to know if I knew what kind of arrangements Dad could have meant." She pressed her fingers to her eyes and drew a shaky breath. "You don't think Brent would have told my dad what is going on, do you? He'd been so secretive about the nanotube and the virus before..." She dropped her hands to her lap and sent him a wide-eyed look shimmering with fear. "Jake, what if Brent has involved my dad in this mess? If he put my dad in danger, put him on the terrorists' radar with some errand or sensitive information, I'll...I'll kill him myself!"

Jake bit down so hard on his back teeth his jaw ached. Having Neil Bancroft involved with this assignment could throw a monkey wrench into things. God only knew what Brent had told Bancroft to do, and Jake hated surprises. But he wouldn't put it past Scofield to panic, call in reserves, whether those reserves were qualified to handle the situation or not. And in Bancroft's case, most likely not.

"If the terrorists go after my family to manipulate me—" Paige's voice trembled, choked with tears.

He stretched a hand toward Paige to soothe her agitation, but quickly thought better of touching her. Sitting this close to her, smelling her shampoo and hearing her quaking sighs made it hard enough to keep his mind off her and the way they'd passed the late hours of the night. He snatched his hand back and squeezed the steering wheel. "Let's not borrow trouble. Your dad is a smart man. He knows something dangerous is happening. He saw what happened at the church. By now he's heard about the break-in and bodies in Brent's office. I guarantee he's hired extra protection for the family, alerted the police, done everything in his power to lock down the company."

Paige nodded. "Holly mentioned something about that when we talked yesterday." She frowned. "But I didn't see anyone guarding her at the hospital."

"They were there. I saw them."

"You did?"

"I've learned to spot so-called undercover protection. It's possible Holly didn't even know she was being watched. These guys were good, but I recognized them for what they were."

"How do you know they weren't with the terrorists?"

He sighed. "I just knew. I have enough training, enough hands-on experience to just...*know*. There were telltale signs. For instance, after I found you, while you traded back clothes with Holly, there was a guy near the restroom with a bulge under his scrubs who lingered too long writing in a chart. He checked his cell a couple times, glanced at me and clearly recognized me, but did nothing. Meaning he was on our side."

"Why didn't you tell me any of this earlier?"

He shrugged. "Maybe I should have, but if you'll remember, not long after that you were grabbed, and later..."

"And later?"

He scowled. "Why can't you trust me? Trust that I'm doing what I have to to keep you and the nanotube safe? If I don't explain every step, every detail to you, it's because I don't see where it is important for you to know."

"It's not important for me to know my family is being protected?" Exasperation and sarcasm saturated her tone.

"I didn't say that, and…could we not argue the point?"

"Oh, but I need someone to fight with." She crossed her arms over her chest. "Or don't you remember that element of your perfect man for me?"

Jake squeezed the steering wheel tighter. "Paige, I'm not—"

"Yeah, you've made that point perfectly clear." She huffed angrily. "Just…forget it."

When he glanced at her, her chin was trembling, but she quickly firmed her mouth and turned toward the passenger window. Her rigid silence sliced deep into his heart.

And Jake knew the pain might never go away.

Several times over the next six hours, Jake tried to call William Gates to set up a meeting, but Brent's CDC contact didn't answer either of the phone numbers Brent had given her. Paige could tell the inability to reach Gates was wearing on Jake as much as it frayed her own jittery nerves.

Still, she gave Jake the silent treatment for the majority of the trip to Atlanta. Not because she didn't have plenty she wanted tell him, but because every time she tried to bring up issues she felt were unresolved between them, her throat would clog with emotion. She didn't want Jake to know how deeply he'd hurt her, or how concerned she was about meeting with Gates.

With each passing mile, she grew more restless. She was desperate to work out a backup plan, in case they couldn't reach Gates. The one time she'd broached the subject of calling the Atlanta police to escort them to the meeting, to provide security for the exchange, Jake flatly turned the idea down.

"The cops will want to know where we got the virus, will have to call in Homeland Security—which Scofield said to avoid—will have a boatload of red tape and questions that will delay us…" He vigorously shook his head. "No. No way. The idea is to keep this as simple and low-key as possible. Go in, hand off the ring and get out. Period. Clean, surgical, fast. Bringing in the cops is the opposite of low-key, Paige."

"Okay! I get it. I just wish we had some kind of contingency, some fallback plan in case—"

"In case I screw up?"

Paige balled her hands, growling her frustration with Jake. "No! Just in case something goes wrong."

He took a deep breath and blew it out slowly. "Look, I know the plan's not perfect, but I can think on my feet. It's what I do, Paige. This kind of assignment is what I'm trained for."

"I know, but…planning and problem solving are who *I* am."

Jake drummed the steering wheel with his thumbs, his mouth pulled in a grim line. "Scofield trusted me to see this through. Why can't you?"

Paige's lungs contracted. She did trust Jake, didn't she? So why was it so hard to let go of the restless need to call in outside help? They'd come this far alone. The transfer of the ring was a simple enough process.

Go in, hand off the ring and get out. They could do that alone. Right?

After a moment, when she still hadn't answered him, Jake turned to meet her gaze. His dark eyes held a penetrating seriousness that matched their grave situation. But something more as well…

A question. A plea. A *need*.

Her answer, her *trust* meant a great deal to him, though he'd never say as much. Seeing this yearning, this…*vulnerability* in her hero warrior rocked her to her core. For all his posturing and protests, despite his emotional distance and barriers, Jake cared. Enough to need her trust. Not just on some strategic level, but on a deeply personal level.

For a man who'd felt betrayed and rejected so many times in his life, trust was not only hard to give, but also as much of a need as oxygen or water. Or love.

She tried to swallow past the lump in her throat, tell him that she did trust him, that he could trust her—with his heart…

But his cell rang.

The moment was lost. The spell broken. The gossamer connection severed.

Jake snatched the phone up from the console between the seats and checked the caller ID. His eyes widened. "It's Gates."

Jake thumbed the answer button and raised the phone to his ear. "Hello?"

"This is Will Gates. I see by my caller ID that you've called here several times today. Is there something I can do for you?"

"Yes, sir. Thank you for calling back. My name is Jake McCall, and I'm a friend of Brent Scofield's."

He paused briefly to see how Gates reacted to the name.

Silence. Then, warily, "Go on."

Pulling in a deep breath, Jake launched into an explanation, starting from the day Scofield had hired him as a bodyguard and finishing with their request to meet him and release the nanotube into the care and keeping of the CDC. "We could meet you at your office if you'd like, but I thought it might be better if we—"

"No! Not my office. That'd be tricky on many levels. Security protocols, the attention you'd attract. I—" Gates hesitated, and Jake heard him sigh, the sound full of the man's indecision and reluctance to get involved. "Are you sure there's no other way? Homeland Security—"

"Is not an option, according to Scofield. He believes there are individuals within relevant agencies with ties to the terrorists. But as soon as you get the virus locked up at CDC, you do whatever you feel you must."

"I don't know. Are you sure the nanotube is safe? I can't expose my family to a deadly virus."

Jake spent the next five minutes convincing Gates to cooperate and getting detailed directions to the man's house. "Remember, this has to stay under the radar, so no police. We give you the ring, and you take it to the CDC labs for safekeeping and further testing. No fuss, no muss."

I just wish we had some kind of contingency, some fallback plan in case—

In case I screw up?

His earlier exchange with Paige resounded in his head like a gong. He'd come dangerously close to showing his hand to her, to letting her see his selfish reason for wanting to finish this mission without outside help.

She might not blame him for his earlier failures in this assignment, but he couldn't let them rest. He needed to redeem himself, he needed to finish this on his own terms. He needed to prove to her, to *himself,* that he wasn't the failure his earlier screwups indicated. How could he even *think* about tackling commitment, a future relationship, if he couldn't even get this simple assignment right? How could he justify asking Paige to depend on him for her future safety and happiness if he couldn't even protect her and the ring through this simple transfer?

Pride goeth before destruction....

The phrase one of his foster mothers used to quote buzzed through his head, incriminating him. Acid pooled in his gut. Now was not the time for vacillation and indecision. It was time for action. Determination. Purpose.

Jake had suggested meeting at a neutral location but Gates insisted his house was safe.

"I'll send my wife and kids to the movies. When can you be here?" Gates's voice brought him out of his turbulent thoughts.

Firming his resolve, Jake answered, "Two hours, max."

* * *

Ninety minutes later, Jake and Paige stopped near the Atlanta city limits for gasoline and to use the restroom. Gates's house was a matter of minutes from the quickie mart where they refueled and refreshed, and the closer they got to their destination, the more Paige's nerves jangled, the more her nervous nausea grew. She still believed they needed a backup plan. The lack of a contingency plan tied her in knots, screamed for attention.

Standing at the sink in the ladies' room, Paige splashed cool water on her face and took deep breaths, fighting the urge to throw up.

Scofield trusted me to see this through. Why can't you? The pain in Jake's voice when he'd asked for her cooperation reverberated in her thoughts, battling with the voice of reason. She did trust Jake, she told herself. Making alternate plans didn't detract from her faith in his skills. It simply made good sense. Right? Or did her desire for extra security, for a fallback plan, undermine the trust she was trying to build with Jake, the trust he needed from her?

Paige braced her arms on the sink and stared at a face she barely recognized. She was a mess. Her hair was loose and tousled. She wore no makeup. The creases and dark circles around her eyes spoke of the lack of sleep she'd had last night.

Her heart gave a painful thump. She couldn't regret last night, despite Jake's change of heart this morning. Giving herself to Jake was a decision she'd made for herself, for her heart, because it was right for *her*.

She'd followed Jake's judgment throughout this nightmare scenario, but she needed to feel she had some control over the outcome of the exchange. She was on the Green Monster again, in the backseat with Ringleader and Beefy Guy. Her gut roiled, and she made up her mind. Jake needed her trust, but she needed security, control. Backup.

With a trembling hand, she pulled the prepaid cell from her purse and dialed.

Chapter 15

Standing beside Jake on William Gates's stoop, Paige pressed a hand to her swirling stomach and waited for Brent's contact to answer the door. The CDC researcher lived in an upscale neighborhood, his house a virtual carbon copy of the other McMansions lining the street. When they got no response to their doorbell summons, Paige wondered briefly if they had the wrong house.

Jake cast her a worried side glance. "You okay?"

She took a calming breath and nodded. "Just ready for this to be over."

"Amen to that."

They waited another few seconds, then Jake tried the doorbell again and added a knock. Finally, after what seemed an awfully long delay for someone who should have been expecting them, Gates opened his front door. He looked just like the picture they'd found of him on the internet when they stopped for lunch at a fast-food joint with Wi-Fi. Except...

His expression was wan, nervous. Terrified.

Warning bells clanged in Paige's head. Beside her, Jake tensed.

"William Gates?" Jake asked, offering his hand. "I'm the one who called—"

"I'm sorry, but I'm terribly busy and expecting company—" Gates said in a rush, closing the door as he spoke.

Jake shot an arm out to brace the door. "*We're* the ones who called. We—"

"Yes," came a voice behind Gates. "Come in."

The door opened, revealing a man with a gun behind the CDC researcher.

Ringleader, aka Steward.

"We've been expecting you." A gloating smile tugged the corner of Steward's mouth.

Before she could blink, Jake yanked her behind him and whipped his gun from his waistband. Under his breath, he growled, "Get out of here, Paige. Run!"

Icy terror washed through Paige, rooting her.

"Not so fast," Steward said smoothly, angling his weapon toward Gates's head. "Put the gun down, or I'll waste him." Flicking a glance over Jake's shoulder, he shouted, "Get them in here, and let's get this over with."

"Go!" Jake shoved her, took the first step down from the stoop. She stumbled with him but came up short as four men rounded the sides of the house and closed in on them. They weren't brash enough to flash their weapons on the residential street, but Paige didn't doubt they were armed.

Jake swung his gun up, but one of Steward's men was already on top of him, tackling him. Jake swung at his captor, struggled to get free. And received a hard blow to the jaw for his efforts.

"Jake!" Greasy fear balled in her gut.

Jake's lip was swollen and bleeding, and he looked dazed as the thug jerked him to his feet. Took Jake's gun.

Paige's gut pitched.

They were trapped. Surrounded. Outnumbered.

With hasty steps, the other men closed in and hustled them back to the stoop. Inside.

The thud of the closing door echoed with a finality that sent chills to Paige's bones.

Gates's throat convulsed as he swallowed. "Please, *no*. I swear I don't have what you want. I don't know anything about—"

"Shut up!" Steward snapped, jabbing harder with his gun. To his men, he said, "Take them all to the back room."

As the goons herded them roughly to the back of the house, Jake shot a lethal glare at Steward. "Let Paige and Gates go. You don't need them."

Steward stuck his face in Jake's. "I'm calling the shots now, hero." He turned his gaze toward Paige, her hand. The ring. "Besides, Ms. Bancroft has what we need."

Paige tucked her hand behind her back. Too little. Too late.

Dear God, she couldn't let these men get the virus. Brent had been clear about the devastation the virus would wreak if terrorists released it on the public. Her gaze flew to Jake's.

He was working on a plan, wasn't he? Mr. I'm-trained-to-think-on-my-feet. His expression revealed nothing.

Paige scrambled. Stalled. Maybe if she bought him time…

As they were led into a windowless back room, she faced Steward, squaring her shoulders and faking a courage she didn't feel. "How did you know we were coming here?"

He turned up a palm dismissively. "Same way we've monitored you for days. We bugged your sister's phone."

Fresh fear writhed in Paige, thinking of these men eavesdropping on Holly's calls. "H-how?"

Steward shrugged, his expression bored. "We followed her to the emergency room when they took Scofield in from the church. Let's just say that during the commotion, she… wasn't especially vigilant over her purse. I planted the bug in seconds, and she was never the wiser."

Paige's stomach seesawed. "Don't you dare hurt my sister!"

Steward scoffed. "I have no interest in harming your sister. She was a tool to find you."

Just as Jake had warned.

Guilt swirled through her. She'd defied Jake more than once to call Holly. If she'd listened to him…

Scofield trusted me to see this through. Why can't you?

"That still doesn't explain how you knew we'd be here," Jake said. "Paige never mentioned Gates's name or where we were headed when she talked to Holly this morning." He sent her a glance, as if to confirm he was right.

A prickle skittered down her spine. She *hadn't* said anything to Holly about their plan for today! So how—?

"I didn't say she did." Steward smirked. "Holly heard it from their father."

Paige jolted. "My dad? But—"

Holly had said their father had talked to Brent.

Call Paige and check on her. I have arrangements to handle.

Her dad knew she was here? What else had Brent confided to her father?

Her heart thundered, anxiety building. What arrangements was her father making?

"Now, are you going to give us the ring with the nanotube—" Steward stepped toward her, his hand extended "—or do we have to cut off your finger to get it?"

She gasped and shrank back, only to bump into the thick chest of one of the other henchmen.

"She doesn't have the virus. I do."

All heads swiveled to face Jake. His face was stony, unflinching. He sounded so sincere, she almost believed him. The staccato beat of her pulse kicked faster.

Steward's expression darkened. "She told us the nanotube was encased in a glass bead that Scofield built into her ring."

Paige swallowed hard, working to steady her voice. "I lied."

Steward swung his glare back toward her. If she could just stall a little longer, maybe...

"I also told you the bead was in my engagement ring, didn't I? I guess by now you've discovered that was a lie. And I told you I'd hocked my wedding ring. Also a lie."

Steward's hands balled at his sides, and a muscle in his cheek twitched. His gaze narrowed on her as if he was trying to decide what to believe.

"Hell, Steward, just off them both, and we'll search 'em when they're dead," the goon behind her grumbled. "You know they have it here somewhere. This is taking too effing long."

A car door slammed outside. Voices drifted in. Young voices. Female voices.

Gates tensed. Gasped. His eyes grew wild and desperate.

"Will? We're home!" a woman called. "The movie was sold out."

In that moment of distraction, Jake launched an elbow into the gut of the ape behind him. Spun. Sliced a stiff hand into the goon's throat. One down. Four left.

Following Jake's lead, Paige stomped hard on the instep of the man behind her. He howled in pain but grabbed her arm, wrenching it behind her. Lashing out with her free hand, she gouged at her captor's eyes. Kneed him in the groin. He sank to the floor, clutching his stomach, but still had the presence of mind to swipe at her legs. With a hard blow to the back of her knees, he brought her to the floor. Paige used the adrenaline coursing through her to fuel her fight. She kicked at the thug, battering him with her feet.

From the corner of her eye, she saw Jake battling two men at once.

A door squeaked. "Will, what—?"

A gun fired.

"Elaine!"

Children screamed. Gates lunged for the door. Another pop of gunfire.

Steward shouted to his men. In the chaos, Piage glanced toward Jake. He was bleeding but still fighting. She had to help him. Swing the odds in their favor…

Her ears ringing, Paige searched the floor. Surely her thug had dropped his weapon. Or she could steal it. Or—

Bingo! She saw a silver gun on the carpet…just a few feet away…

She stretched toward it, reaching—

And a hard shoe came down on her wrist, crushing her arm. Pain shot to her shoulder.

"Nice try, Ms. Bancroft." Steward crouched over her pinned hand.

And wrenched the gaudy wedding ring from her finger.

Horror sliced through her. She couldn't let him take the nanotube!

Brent's desperate plea rasped in her head. *Keep the bead safe…at all costs. National security…*

"Jake!" she screamed. "He has the ring!"

Jake tensed, a sinking sensation settling in his gut.

For a few moments, they'd had Steward and his men off guard, had been gaining ground. But with her panicked cry, Paige had given Steward exactly what he needed. Solid evidence that the nanotube was in the ring.

And with the ring in Steward's possession, he and his men had no reason left to keep any of them alive.

The tumult and confusion he'd capitalized on when Gates's family arrived unexpectedly was already fading to a tense standoff.

Gates lay on the floor, blood seeping from his arm. His wife cowered beside him.

Another of Steward's men shuffled back into the room, dragging two preteen girls, both deathly pale and sobbing, in by the arm. Three more innocents caught up in this hellish situation. More lives at stake, more ways Jake could mess up and get civilians killed.

The man who'd been holding Paige rose slowly from the floor, murder in his eyes as he seized her arm again. The man Jake had incapacitated was still unconscious, but another ape, the one who'd fired on Gates, still held his weapon to Jake's temple.

The advantage they'd gained briefly had swung decidedly back into Steward's favor.

"Please," Gates rasped, "don't hurt my family. They have nothing to do with any of this!"

Jake met Paige's gaze briefly. Her eyes pleaded with him to do something. His chest constricted. He'd rather take a knife in his gut than let Paige down. But what choice did he have now?

Knowing how little he could do with Gates and his family at risk, with a gun at his head, with the ring in Steward's possession, Jake was short on options.

"Finally," Steward crowed, examining the ring. "Hmm, damn ugly thing." He arched an imperious eyebrow at Paige. "You let Scofield give you *this* as a token of his affection? Where's your pride?"

Paige stiffened, and rage roiled in Jake's gut.

"Watch your mouth, Steward," he growled.

With a dismissive sneer toward Jake, Steward turned to the thug holding Gates's daughters. "Thurman, have a look."

Thurman released the girls, who rushed to huddle with their parents, and stepped over to take the ring from Steward. Pulling an elaborate-looking jeweler's loupe from his pocket, Thurman walked to a floor lamp for better light. A hush settled over the room.

Jake's mind spun, thinking in fast forward.

After examining the ring for several seconds, Thurman lowered the loupe and faced Steward. "Without an atomic microscope, I can't be sure what it is, but there's definitely something in there. And that is definitely cut glass, not a diamond. I'd say we've got a hit."

Thurman crossed the floor. Held the ring out to Steward.

And Jake threw his head back as hard as he could, bashing the nose of the goon behind him. The next instant, while the man cradled his broken nose, Jake wrenched free and lunged. Tackled Thurman. Pried the ring from his hand. Rolled toward Paige.

Gasps and startled screams from Gates's girls peppered the air.

Shaken from his smug sense of victory, Steward grabbed for his gun. As Steward and Thurman surged toward him, Jake scrambled mentally. He had to protect the ring, take it out of play, eliminate possession as a factor…

Steward's pistol swung up.

And Jake popped the ring in his mouth. Forced enough spit on his tongue to swallow.

"Jake?" Paige gasped.

Steward's eyes widened in disbelief. "You ass!"

Thurman and Steward exchanged now-what looks.

Jake eased closer to Paige.

"Don't. Move." Steward angled his gun toward Paige. "Or your girlfriend is dead."

"Are you insane?" she hissed.

"Trust me."

She shook her head. "I don't see how—"

The man holding Paige's arm yanked hard, silencing her.

Finally, Steward narrowed a menacing glare on Jake and stepped close. "Don't think you've won. While I'd like to keep Ms. Bancroft alive until we verify the nanotube is in the ring, I'm not above killing some of the other deadweight we've acquired, if it will ensure your cooperation." Twisting to look over his shoulder, Steward looked to the man holding Paige. "Do you have your knife?"

Releasing Paige, the goon stooped to pull a smooth-edged blade from under his pant leg.

Cold dread spun through Jake. Damn. He knew what was coming.

Steward motioned to the other men. "Hold him."

Thurman and the two other thugs moved forward, surrounding Jake. He swung at the first man to reach him, battled the second man's grip when he grabbed his arm, resisted, but within minutes, they had him subdued and spread-eagled on the floor.

To Knife, Steward said, "Cut him. I want that ring back."

"No!" Paige rushed forward, and Steward caught her with an arm around her waist. She struggled, crying. "Please, stop! Don't touch him!"

"Paige, no!" Jake shouted. "Don't give him a reason to hurt you!"

When Knife dropped to one knee beside him, brandishing his blade, Jake shifted his attention to that very real threat, the imminent pain, the likely death awaiting him.

An earthy obscenity filtered through his thoughts. *This is gonna suck.*

Jake gritted his teeth and tensed his stomach muscles.

Knife raised his weapon and plunged it into Jake's gut.

Lightning-hot pain streaked through him. Paige and the female Gateses screamed.

Suddenly, with a blinding flash and deafening boom, all hell broke loose.

Chapter 16

Stunned by the bright light and earsplitting noise, Paige froze. What was happening?

An instant later, men in flak jackets, helmets and gas masks swarmed the room, shouting, "Police! Everyone down! Drop your weapons!"

By the looks of it, the entire Atlanta SWAT department now buzzed through the Gateses' home, armed with assault weapons and riot gear. Steward was knocked to the ground, disarmed. Then Knife. And Thurman.

Relief so sweet it brought tears to her eyes flooded through Paige. Help had arrived. Just in time.

Or almost in time. *Jake!*

Despite the police orders to lie on the floor, hands out, Paige crawled toward Jake in a rush. A large gash on his stomach poured blood on the carpet. Panic surged through her, and she whipped her shirt over her head to stanch the flow. "Help him! Please, he's been stabbed!"

"Get down! Hands out!" She was shoved unceremoniously to the ground beside Jake, and her hands yanked behind her.

With her cheek pressed to the floor, Paige fought the swell of desperation clamoring inside her. Jake angled his head to meet her gaze. Evidence of the pain he suffered radiated from his dark eyes, tightened his mouth and lined his forehead. His skin was growing frighteningly pale. "Paige…"

Brusque hands frisked her. She squirmed, trying to catch the eye of the officer pinning her to the ground. "No! Please, he needs help!"

"Hold still, ma'am."

"But I'm the one who called the police!"

Jake rasped a sharp, strangled sound, drawing Paige's attention.

A new pain and disappointment filled his eyes. "*You…* called them?"

Guilt sliced her to the core. She'd doubted Jake, defied him. Wounded him.

"I'm sorry," she whispered. But he turned his face away.

"Just cooperate, ma'am, and let us get this sorted out," the SWAT officer on her back said. "We actually had more than one call. Earlier today, we had two reports of a biohazard being delivered to this residence."

"Two calls?" Paige's thoughts spun. Around her she heard the grumbles and grunts of Steward's men being subdued and cuffed. The Gates girls crying. More police officers arriving.

The SWAT member finished patting her down and helped her to her feet. "First call came in early today from Louisiana. A man. Said his daughter was in danger."

Her heart tripped. "My dad called you, too?"

The officer gave her an appraising look. "Are you Paige Bancroft?"

"Yes!" Now they were getting somewhere.

The officer nodded. "En route, we received reports of gunfire called in by neighbors, then heard screams as we arrived. We had to consider everyone suspect until we knew we had the situation under our control. Just be patient, and we'll sort this out."

Frustration and fear for Jake gnawed her stomach. "We don't have time for patience! Jake's been stabbed! He's dying!"

The policeman jerked his head toward the floor where Jake lay bleeding. "We're doing all we can. An ambulance is en route."

Paige dropped her gaze to find two men huddled over Jake. One patted him down for weapons while another worked to stop the bleeding from his abdomen. His eyes were closed, and he remained eerily still. Terror climbed her throat. Squeezed her chest. "Jake!"

Jake opened his eyes to slits. The commotion around him was a blur. Except for Paige. He focused on her, even as the edges of his vision dimmed. Pain burned his gut, but the sharpest ache centered near his heart. The only relief he had was in knowing Paige was safe.

It was over. The cops would pick up where he'd dropped the ball.

A dry thickening in his throat made it hard to speak, but as he held Paige's gaze he mumbled, "Failed."

Then darkness swallowed him.

"Paige?"

Paige jerked her head up from her contemplation of the emergency-room floor. When she spotted the tall, silver-haired man striding briskly toward her, tears rushed to her eyes. "Daddy!"

She threw herself into her father's arms and sobbed on his shoulder.

"Thank God you're all right!" Neil Bancroft held Paige in a breath-stealing embrace. "When Brent told me what he'd asked you to do—"

She felt the shudder race through her father that finished his sentence for him. For long, silent minutes, they simply held each other, and Paige fought to regain her composure. Now was not the time to fall apart. She'd already given her full statement to the police and repeated it for the FBI. But the nightmare wasn't over.

Jake was still in surgery, fighting for his life.

As long as the doctors had to stitch up his belly anyway, they had decided, with encouragement from law enforcement, to surgically remove the ring from Jake's stomach.

The last word Paige had from William Gates, whose arm had been treated for a surface gunshot wound, was that the ring was in safekeeping with the Atlanta police. Arrangements were being made to transfer the nanotube to Gates's lab at the Centers for Disease Control once a pile of paperwork and red tape was cleared up.

She should have been ecstatic. The virus was safe. Her responsibility to protect PMB-611 was finished.

But Jake was not out of the woods yet. Even now, surgeons were scrambling to repair the damage done by Knife's blade. The hurt, accusing look he'd sent her before he blacked out haunted her.

You...called them?

Swiping at her runny nose and damp eyes, Paige backed out of her father's arms. "Jake was stabbed, Daddy. He lost a lot of blood, and—" Her voice broke, and her eyes filled with tears again. "I hurt him. He asked me to have faith in him, to trust him, but I...I was scared, and—"

When she broke down in tears again, Neil Bancroft escorted her to a chair at the edge of the waiting room. "Ah, Paige, darling, tell me everything. Start at the beginning."

And she did. From Brent's whispered orders to hide the "bead" after he'd been shot to the SWAT team's storming of the Gates residence, Paige left nothing out.

Except her feelings for Jake and the way they'd passed last night.

Her father listened carefully, interrupting only twice to ask questions. When she was done, her father explained how Brent, consumed with guilt and worry for Paige, had summoned Neil to his hospital room and finally confessed to the senior Bancroft his culpability in the unfolding events. Learning the truth from Brent, Neil had immediately called the authorities in Atlanta to arrange police support for the exchange at Gates's house and the company's private plane to bring him to Georgia to find Paige.

Paige shook her head. "But Brent knew Jake was with me. He'd asked Jake to hide the ring and protect me."

Neil leaned back in the formed-plastic chair and sighed. "True. But Brent wanted to be sure you were okay. Like you, he's big on contingencies." Her father paused and furrowed his brow. "Sounds like I owe Jake a great debt of gratitude for keeping you safe."

Her heart twisted. "And I repaid him by defying the one request he made of me. The one thing I knew mattered most to him. Proving my trust."

"Proving?" Neil frowned. "Honey, why should you have to prove—?"

"Paige Bancroft?" a nurse in green scrubs called to the waiting room, interrupting whatever her father had been prepared to say.

She hurried to meet the petite nurse, eager for news of Jake. "I'm Paige."

"Mr. McCall got out of surgery about an hour ago and is about to be moved to a private room. He's awake and asking to see you."

Relief made her knees tremble. "He's all right? They stopped all the bleeding? Repaired all the damage?"

"He'll have to take it easy for several weeks, but, yes. He'll be just fine."

Paige was so relieved to hear Jake was okay, she let the fact that no one had told her Jake had been out of surgery for an hour slide. A wide smile blossomed on her face. "Where is he?"

The nurse directed her down the corridor, and Paige ran down the hospital hall with her father at her heels. As they reached the recovery room, Jake was being wheeled out on a gurney on his way to a private room.

"Jake!" Paige shoved aside one of the nurses and wrapped her hand around Jake's. His color was vastly better than it had been when they rushed him into surgery, and his eyes had the fire and vital intensity back that she'd grown to love. "The nurse said you were asking for me. I would have come sooner, but I only just now heard you were out of surgery."

"I wanted to be sure you were okay." Jake's gaze traveled past her, over her shoulder. "Your father's here."

She nodded. "After Brent got out of his surgery yesterday— jeez, was it only yesterday?—he told Dad what was going on, where I was and how Bancroft Industries was involved. Dad arranged a corporate plane to fly over here this morning so he could find me."

Jake's gaze shifted back to Paige. "Good." He lowered his eyes and angled his head away from her. "Then my work is done. You can go home with him…get back to your family, your job."

Paige's stomach quickened. A hollow, defeated quality permeated Jake's tone. Squeezing his hand, she bent over him. "Not until you're well enough to come with us."

His dark eyes found hers, and the finality she read in their depths jolted her. Scared her.

"Our business together is finished, Paige. My doctor said he gave the ring to the cops. The bead is safe, and so are you. Go home."

"But…" Paige fumbled, crushed by Jake's rejection. "What if Steward has other operatives who come after me to exact revenge, or—"

"No. I just gave my statement to the FBI." His gaze darkened when he mentioned the police, and compunction kicked her in the chest. "According to the guys I gave my statement to, Ralph Thurman, one of the guys at Gates's, is rolling over to cut a deal. He's given up names and details on the terrorist organization. Including people inside the Department of Defense. Those not in custody now, will be soon."

"Who are these terrorists? Who funds them?" her father asked.

Jake shrugged. "The cop didn't know."

"I'll have my people look into it," her father said. "I'm sure we'll hear more, once they've had time to dig further into the investigation."

Neil extended his hand to Jake, and Jake slipped his fingers from Paige's grasp to shake her father's hand. "Son, thank you. You kept my girl safe, and I can never repay that."

"Forget it." Jake nodded to Neil but turned a penetrating gaze to Paige. "I was just doing the job I was hired to do."

His words hit her like ice. Cold. Hard. Final.

There is no us. Not now, not when this is over. He'd said as much this morning, but she'd dared to hope he'd change his mind once they'd delivered the ring. Once they were safe.

Framing his face with her hands, she leaned close, whispering fiercely, "Don't shut me out, Jake. I love you, and if you let me show you how much, I can—"

"Go home with your father, Paige." He wrenched her hands from his cheeks and met her pleas with a stony stare. "You belong with your family. Not here."

"But—"

"Goodbye, Paige."

The nurse she'd shoved aside earlier now pushed Paige back from Jake's side. "Excuse me. We need to take him upstairs now."

As the nurses rolled Jake's gurney toward the elevator, he wouldn't even look at her.

And Paige felt her heart shatter.

Chapter 17

"Want to talk about it?"

When her father spoke, Paige turned from the view of billowing clouds out the small jet window. She didn't pretend not to know what he meant. Her dad wasn't deaf or blind. He'd heard what she told Jake before Jake dismissed her so abruptly, and he'd seen the leak of tears she couldn't contain as they'd left for the airport in a taxi.

She squared her shoulders and struggled to present a brave face. "I really don't know what to say. So much has happened to me, so much has changed in a matter of days. I'm kind of... shell-shocked."

Neil laid a warm hand on her knee. "I take it your feelings for Brent have changed. He told me you'd ended it with him."

Paige sucked in a deep breath for courage. "Actually, my feelings for Brent are the same." She paused, and her father arched an eyebrow in query. "The truth of the matter is, I never loved him."

Now Neil frowned and shifted in his seat to face her more

fully. "My goodness, Paige, what are you saying? You were about to marry him. I thought the two of you were ideal for each other."

She nibbled her bottom lip and scrunched her nose, feeling like a little girl again under her father's heavy stare. "That's... why I accepted his proposal. I saw how happy you were, and logically, we should have been perfect for each other. We have a lot in common. But..."

Same equals boring. Her heart fluttered restlessly when Jake's assessment flitted through her thoughts.

"I tried to love him, Dad, but he just didn't..." *make me burn the way Jake did.*

Her face grew hot, and she turned back to the window briefly to gather her composure and hide the telltale flush in her cheeks.

"He didn't make you happy."

She swallowed hard and screwed up the nerve to face her father's disappointment. "No. I'm sorry, Dad. I know you liked him, and—"

Neil snorted. "Why should my opinion matter?"

She turned her palm up. "Because you're my dad. I've always wanted to make you proud and have your approval."

His scowl deepened. "And you thought I'd approve of your tying yourself to a man you didn't love?"

"I...well, I thought I'd learn to love him. When I analyzed our relationship, I didn't see any reason why we shouldn't have a successful marriage. On paper, we were perfectly matched. And Brent was your choice to take over the company, so logically—"

"Paige Michelle, you have a gift for logic and analysis, but logic and analysis have no place in deciding matters of the heart."

"But—"

He raised a hand to cut her off. "Let's get one thing straight," he said in the deep timbre that had commanded boardrooms for forty years. "*I* am happy about your choice of spouse only if *you* are happy. Where did you get the idea that I would want you to settle for a husband you didn't love?"

She gaped like a fish, but she was speechless.

Zoey had said almost the same thing to her months ago, before she stormed out of the house the last time. Paige scrunched her nose.

"If you believe that, then explain to me why you were so angry with Zoey about her relationship with Derek."

Neil stiffened. "Angry? I was never angry with Zoey. I want Zoey to be happy, to be safe, same as I do you. She's the one who lost her temper when I tried to reason with her."

Paige rolled her eyes. She didn't want to argue semantics with her dad. Considering she shared her father's opinion of Derek, playing devil's advocate on Zoey's behalf felt odd enough. But her father's answer meant a great deal to Paige. "Zoey says she loves Derek. She says he makes her happy. So why can't you accept her choice of husband and be happy for her?"

Her father's expression darkened, his brow creasing with worry lines. "I believe she does love Derek, and that's what bothers me. Because he doesn't love her. I'd stake my life on that." He poked the armrest for emphasis. "He hasn't married her. Instead, he's dragged her around the country, spending her money to play poker wherever he can find a game." Neil's jaw tightened. "The guy's a con. He's using her for her money, and when he tires of her or once he's emptied her accounts, he'll dump her and break her heart. How can I support her in something I know is going to bring her trouble and heartache down the road?"

"I hope you're wrong about Derek, but…I'm afraid you're right." Paige's belly rolled with concern for her sister's well-being. She missed Zoey, missed her sister's bright smiles and exuberance. Her zest for life. Her friendship.

"Now…" Her father readjusted his suit coat, tugging at the sleeves, his nonverbal cue that he considered the matter closed and was moving on. "About this Jake McCall. You told him you love him. But does he make you truly happy, or are your feelings for him something you engineered through critical analysis and statistics based on your shared traits?"

Neil cut a side glance and lifted the corner of his mouth.

Paige blinked, startled to realize her father was teasing her. They hadn't teased each other in years. Not since she graduated college and joined the family business. She hadn't wanted anyone to think she had an inside track at the company because of her personal relationship with her dad. She had kept their relationship at Bancroft strictly professional, all business.

Looking back, she now saw how that formality had spilled over into their private relationship. The spontaneous jokes and hugs had dwindled, replaced with shop talk and professional politeness. Had that lack of familial warmth in recent years contributed to her feeling that she had to earn his approval by marrying Brent?

Setting that issue aside for the moment, she focused on his question. Did she love Jake?

She curled her fingers into the plush leather armrest. "My feelings for Jake are a moot point at best, considering he wants no part of a relationship with me."

"Are you sure about that?"

Paige jerked her gaze up to meet her father's. "He said as much. More than once." Leaning her head back, she angled her head toward the puffy clouds out her window. "The thing is…he grew up in foster homes and never felt he had a stable home or real love. Then he lost the family he adopted when he became a SEAL because he was forced off the team after an injury. And because several close SEAL friends died, both in the line of duty and once back home. He's been burned too often, had his trust betrayed—" Her heart throbbed painfully with guilt. "—and so he won't give his heart to a relationship again." She sighed and glanced back at her father. "I tried to show him how much I love him. Tried to prove to him that my love was real and wouldn't change, but—"

"Hold it right there, young lady." Her father aimed a finger at her, his tone stern.

Her heart pounded the way it did when she'd been scolded as a child.

"At the hospital, you said something about proving your trust as well, and I didn't get a chance to address it then. But I can't let it pass again." He took her hand in hers and squeezed, his green gaze softening. "Paige, love and trust and loyalty, all the building blocks of a solid relationship, aren't something you should have to prove or earn or work for. Either they are there, or they aren't. Love you have to earn isn't real love. Trust you have to prove isn't authentic. Love isn't meant to be analyzed or fit into a schedule. How do you explain the fact that in a matter of days you've lost your heart to a man so different from you?"

Her pulse slowed, and she held her breath. "I can't explain it. It's crazy. It just…happened."

"Love defies the odds. Love doesn't follow criteria." His eyes brightened with an intensity that speared to her core. "Paige, honey, real love is *unconditional*."

She blinked, stared at him as she processed what he was saying. Intellectually, she already knew everything he was saying, but a small voice inside her whispered that somewhere along the line, her brain and her heart had gotten their wires crossed.

"You didn't need to marry Brent to make me happy or earn my approval or my love, sweetie. You have it. Always. Forever. No matter what. No strings attached."

She gripped her father's hand with both of hers. "And you have mine, Daddy."

He squeezed her hands tighter, underlining his next point. "If you love Jake, you shouldn't have to prove it to him, either. He may have a hard time accepting it, letting it past his protective shields, but if your love is real, he'll know it, deep down. He'll feel it. Real love shines through every word, every action, every look and touch."

Paige chewed her bottom lip, mulling over her father's admonition.

"Sweetie, I know control is important to you, but you can't

make someone love you. Just like you have no control over who you fall in love with."

Paige's pulse scampered. *No control...*

Was that why her feelings for Jake scared her so much?

"Real love is deep, abiding...and has no qualifiers. Can you say that about your feelings for Jake?"

A sob rose in her chest, tears puddling in her eyes. "Yes. Absolutely."

Her father sat back and drew a deep, thoughtful breath. "And yet...you are here with me, instead of at his bedside."

The air whooshed from her lungs. "But..." She rasped and had to stop to find the breath to speak. "You heard him! He sent me away. He didn't want me there!"

"I also saw the look in his eyes when you turned and walked away. Paige, that man loves you. I'm betting he pushed you away because he didn't want to risk rejection. Or he believed he was sparing you some kind of pain or disappointment."

Her heart was a rock beneath her ribs. Cold, hard, heavy.

"And I played right into his fears of loss by leaving." Her gut pitched. What had she done?

"We're almost home now, and your mother and Holly are frantic to see you and assure themselves that you are safe. But whenever you're ready to return to Atlanta, I'll make sure you get priority on the flight schedule."

Tears spilled from her eyelashes as she threw her arms around her father's neck. "Thank you, Dad. I love you."

Jake tossed down his fork and shoved the plate of mystery meat aside. He wasn't hungry.

Throwing back the blanket on the hospital bed, he slid his legs to the floor. He wasn't tired, either. He was restless, sick of being cooped up in this hospital room.

Three days post-op, his pain was well under control, and he could walk without feeling his gut was going to split open. He should have been released yesterday, but because his blood pressure had been slightly elevated since his surgery, he'd been kept an extra night. For observation.

But Jake didn't need medical professionals to tell him why his blood pressure was up. He knew the reason.

He'd screwed up with Paige. Let her walk away. Lost the best thing that ever happened to him.

He'd had nothing but time to think as he lay in his bed and stared at the acoustic tile ceiling. Time to realize what he'd lost. Time to look at why he'd pushed her away. Time to recall his SEAL team CO grating, "Fear is inevitable in this job. You can either make fear your friend, use it to sharpen your senses and push you to achieve more. Or you can allow fear to be your enemy, let it lead you to failure.

He'd failed with Paige because his fear still stood sentinel over his heart. He knew why.

He squeezed the bedsheets in his fists and gritted his teeth. At first he'd been hurt that she hadn't believed in him, hadn't trusted him to handle the situation at Gates's and had called the authorities. Then he'd been disgusted with himself, ashamed that his arrogant pride and determination to finish the assignment without outside help had nearly gotten Paige and other innocent civilians killed. He admitted, belatedly, that she'd made the right call. The number of unexpected variables that cropped up, from Steward learning of the transfer at Gates's to Gates's wife and daughters returning early, had quickly spiraled the situation out of control. He'd needed a contingency plan after all. Thank God Paige had arranged one.

Finally, this morning, after a sleepless night of self-recrimination, he'd moved past his pointless should-haves and if-onlys and realized an important truth. It didn't matter who did what or how the crisis had ended.

It was over.

The virus sample was safe. Paige was safe. And according to the FBI agents who'd questioned him multiple times over the past several days, the men behind the raid on Paige's wedding and the attempts to steal the virus had been rounded up in a nationwide sweep. The homegrown terrorist cell had been on the Homeland Security radar for years. The men inside the

Department of Defense whom Brent had believed to be traitors were, in fact, investigating Brent's communications with the cell. All Jake had to do now was be available to testify at the terrorists' trial.

And figure out what to do about Paige, how to move past his debilitating fear of loss.

His doctor had promised he could be released today, but so far, no one had been by to sign the papers that would spring him. Pressing a hand to the stitches just below his ribs, Jake hobbled restlessly toward the small window to look out. The hazy Atlanta skyline sprawled across the horizon. He stared without really seeing until a knock at his door brought him around.

"Jake?"

He recognized Holly immediately, though her resemblance to Paige had his pulse thumping and his blood pressure, no doubt, spiking again. He hoped the nurse didn't come by now to check his vitals or he'd be stuck here another night.

"Holly, what are you doing here?" He glanced past her to the hall, hoping maybe she hadn't come alone.

"Paige isn't with me," she said, obviously reading the hope in his expression. "Matt, the kids and I were driving through Atlanta on our way back to our home in North Carolina, and I thought I should stop to see you."

"Oh." Jake mentally kicked himself for the idiotic mono-syllabic reply and the disappointment he couldn't keep from his tone. He shuffled stiffly back to the bed and sat down. "Going home, huh?"

"We'd already stayed in Lagniappe longer than we intended, but I couldn't leave until I knew Paige was home and safe."

Jake nodded awkwardly, staring at the floor. "Then she's okay?"

Holly moved farther into the room. "She's home and safe. But she's anything but okay."

Jake jerked his head up. "Wh-what's wrong with her?"

Crossing her arms over her chest, Holly stepped closer and

scowled. "She's heartbroken, dummy. She told you she loves you, and you sent her packing!"

Guilt sluiced through him, congealing in his gut as a cold lump of regret. "I never wanted to hurt her."

Holly's expression softened. "I know that. And I know how confusing and complicated relationships can be. Matt and I had our share of issues to work out before we married. What matters is that you don't give up. If you love my sister…and my dad thinks you do—"

Jake stiffened. "Your dad?"

"He was here, remember? He saw the little exchange between you two and read between the lines."

Feeling a bit queasy, he leaned back against the stacked pillows at the head of the bed and groaned.

"Yeah, kinda overwhelming sometimes, isn't it? The whole family knowing your business and adding their two cents?" Holly rested her hip on a corner of the bed and chuckled. "Well get used to it, Jake, because Paige comes with the whole Bancroft brood. Sisters, parents, brother-in-law and kids…"

Holly placed a hand on her belly in a protective gesture, and Jake lifted a corner of his mouth. "Congratulations, by the way. Paige told me you were expecting."

Holly beamed. "Thanks." Then her face sobered. "So this is why I'm here… From the minute Paige got back to Lagniappe with Dad, she's been chomping at the bit to fly back here to be with you. She says she loves you, and she belongs at your side."

Warmth seeped through the cold knot in his gut, buoying his hope.

"She told me about your hang-ups regarding commitment and family, too. Which is why I've spent the last three days finding ways to detain her."

Jake frowned. "Detain her?"

"Yeah. I've done everything I could think of to keep her in Lagniappe. Well, the police helped. They've had lots of questions for her. But I even faked premature labor, the lowest kind of deception, so that she wouldn't jet off to be with you."

Jake stared at Holly, stunned.

"Don't you want to know why?" she asked, flipping up a palm in query.

"Because I hurt her. Because you don't think I deserve her." Statements, not questions.

"Wrong! Because she deserves to know how you really feel. You pushed her away, so it is *your* obligation to be the one to fix this. *You* have to go to *her*."

Jake sat taller, squared his shoulders. "And say what?"

Holly rolled her eyes. "*I love you* would be a good place to start." She paused, angled her head. "Assuming you do."

His nostrils flared as he filled his lungs. "More than anything."

Holly flicked a hand. "Well, there you go. I took the liberty of arranging the Bancroft Industries jet for your convenience. It's waiting at an airstrip in Marietta for you." Holly hiked her purse strap on her shoulder and turned toward the door.

"Wait! I—"

She turned and gave him a patient look. "What?"

"Just because I love her doesn't mean I'm cut out for marriage and family and…and—"

Holly stepped to the edge of the bed and met Jake's gaze with eyes the same shade of jade as Paige's. "No one knows the future, Jake. Giving someone your heart is risky, yes. Scary, sure. It takes a blind leap of faith. But you're not going into this alone. That's the beauty of a marriage. You work at it together. You both give your best, and forgive each other's faults. You're a team. A team cemented by love." She paused and furrowed her brow. "Okay, that sounded corny, but you get the point, right? If you love Paige and can deal with the idea of me—" she struck a pose "—as your sister-in-law, then I suggest you get your ex-SEAL butt to Louisiana and tell my sister how you feel."

She finger waved as she sauntered out of the room. "Gotta run. Matt and the kids are waiting downstairs."

Jake stared at the empty door for long seconds after Holly left. Then laughed.

Paige loved him. Despite all the ways he'd messed up, let her down.

You're not going into this alone. You're a team.

He just hoped Paige would see it that way.

Paige hurriedly tossed the last of the clothes she'd laid out into her suitcase and zipped her luggage shut. If she rushed, she could catch the commercial flight from Lagniappe to Atlanta that left in just over an hour. After innumerable delays, from the FBI questioning her to Holly's false-alarm miscarriage, she was determined to get back to Atlanta, to *Jake,* today. *Now!* Enough delays!

But when she'd called the Bancroft hangar to arrange the company jet her father had promised, she'd learned the jet was out on some mysterious errand, not due to return until later today. Thus the commercial ticket. She was tired of waiting.

When her doorbell rang, she considered ignoring it. She didn't have even a few spare minutes to get rid of a salesman, another reporter or a busybody neighbor. But the ring was followed by an insistent pounding. The urgency of the loud knock gave her pause.

Lugging her suitcase with her, she trooped down to the front door, answered the increasingly insistent summons.

And caught her breath.

Jake's gaze drifted from her face to her suitcase and back. "Going somewhere?"

When she still couldn't find her voice amid her shock and the rush of emotion, she shook her head slowly.

He lifted a corner of his mouth. "Can I come in?"

Holding the edge of the door for support, she nodded and stumbled back to let him in. "A-are you all right? Your injury—"

"Is healing well. It's my heart that's hurting. That's why I'm here." He held her gaze but wiped his hands on his jeans, his jaw tight and tense.

"Wh-why *are* you here?" she finally managed to rasp.

"Because you are."

A desperate hope swelled painfully in her chest, and the sting of tears pricked her sinuses. "I—I was just on my way to Atlanta. To be with you."

"I know. I talked to Holly earlier today."

She blinked her surprise. "You did?"

"She stopped by to see me at the hospital on her way home."

Paige's breath backed up again. "And?"

"She helped me see a lot of things from a different perspective." He rubbed the generous stubble on his jaw, stubble that made him look ruggedly dangerous. An image completely contradicted by the wistful, vulnerable expression in his eyes. "I thought that we were too different to find any common ground for a future. But Holly helped me think in terms of what we could be as a *team*."

A tremble started in her chest and spread through her limbs. Moisture blurred her vision, and she swiped at her eyes. "A team?"

"With the SEALs, I learned that the best teams use the strengths of all the members to build a stronger whole...like at Gates's."

Her body tensed. Guilt for second-guessing Jake flowed through her like tar in her veins.

He shuffled his feet as if he was nervous. "When the situation started getting out of control, when my bag of in-the-moment tricks was running low, your contingency plan saved the day."

She frowned. "What? But I betrayed you. You asked me to trust you and I—"

"Did what I was too thickheaded and stubborn to do. You've been a valuable part of this team," he said, waving a hand between them, "all through this ordeal. Our differences balance each other. You made the right call at Gates's, Paige. I'm the one who failed *you*."

She stiffened her spine and narrowed a sharp look on him.

"Jake McCall, I'm about sick of hearing you talk about how you've failed me, failed Brent, failed…your aunt Petunia!" She stepped forward and poked him in the chest with her finger. "You saved my life on my wedding day. You were up against hugely lopsided odds, and you did what you had to do to protect the most lives. You gave one-hundred-and-ten percent to stop the people bent on weaponizing a deadly virus, and you kept your word to Brent by keeping me alive throughout this ordeal. You are a hero, not a failure. You're…" She paused to swallow hard when a lump clogged her throat. "You're *my* hero."

Jake stared at her, his eyes suspiciously damp. "I'd rather be…your husband."

Paige drew a sharp breath.

"If you can forgive me, for pushing you away. For letting my fear get in the way of telling you how much I love you when I had the chance. Because I do love you, Paige."

Tears flooded her eyes, joy filling her chest until she could barely speak. But her father's wisdom whispered to her. She squared her shoulders, lifted her chin. "Unconditionally?"

Jake wrinkled his brow in question and stepped back, staring at her with a puzzled frown.

Paige's heart cramped. If he didn't give his heart freely, without strings, than was it really love?

Finally, after what felt like a lifetime, but was in reality just a few nerve-racking seconds, Jake's confusion seemed to melt away. A knowing grin spread across his face, and he caught her hand to pull her close. "Completely. Deeply. And unconditionally. I want our marriage to be a partnership where we both are heard, both compromise, both share the best of ourselves…and the worst. Your opinion matters to me, Paige. In fact, I didn't bring you a ring today because I want you to pick the one you like."

She tugged a grin. "Any ring without a secret nanotube in it works for me…as long as it's from you."

Jake drew a deep breath, his eye brightening with expectation. "Does that mean yes? That you'll marry me?"

"Yes, yes, yes!" With a laugh that bubbled from an over-flowing heart, Paige launched herself into his arms.

"Ah, ow!" he rasped, bending at the waist and clutching his stomach. "I think you busted my stitches."

Paige jerked back with a gasp, horrified. "Oh no! Oh, Jake, I'm sorry! Do you need a doctor?"

He reached for her, flashing a bright smile, and drew her close again with a satisfied sigh. "No, sweetheart, I have all I need right here in my arms."

As Paige angled her head to accept Jake's kiss, her heart whispered its assurance that she was finally where she belonged.

* * * * *